A Jacobite Exile:
Being the
Adventures of a Young
Englishman
in the Service of Charles
the Twelfth of Sweden

G. A. Henty

Contents

A JACOBITE EXILE:

BEING THE ADVENTURES OF A YOUNG ENGLISHMAN IN THE SERVICE OF CHARLES THE TWELFTH OF SWEDEN

by

G. A. Henty

Preface.

My Dear Lads,

Had I attempted to write you an account of the whole of the adventurous career of Charles the Twelfth of Sweden, it would, in itself, have filled a bulky volume, to the exclusion of all other matter; and a youth, who fought at Narva, would have been a middle-aged man at the death of that warlike monarch, before the walls of Frederickshall. I have, therefore, been obliged to confine myself to the first three years of his reign, in which he crushed the army of Russia at Narva, and laid the then powerful republic of Poland prostrate at his feet. In this way, only, could I obtain space for the private adventures and doings of Charlie Carstairs, the hero of the story. The details of the wars of Charles the Twelfth were taken from the military history, written at his command by his chamberlain, Adlerfeld; from a similar narrative by a Scotch gentleman in his service; and from Voltaire's history. The latter is responsible for the statement that the trade of Poland was almost entirely in the hands of Scotch, French, and Jewish merchants, the Poles themselves being sharply divided into the two categories of nobles and peasants.

Yours sincerely,

G. A. Henty.

Chapter 1:
A Spy in the Household.

On the borders of Lancashire and Westmoreland, two centuries since, stood Lynnwood, a picturesque mansion, still retaining something of the character of a fortified house. It was ever a matter of regret to its owner, Sir Marmaduke Carstairs, that his grandfather had so modified its construction, by levelling one side of the quadrangle, and inserting large mullion windows in that portion inhabited by the family, that it was in no condition to stand a siege, in the time of the Civil War.

Sir Marmaduke was, at that time, only a child, but he still remembered how the Roundhead soldiers had lorded it there, when his father was away fighting with the army of the king; how they had seated themselves at the board, and had ordered his mother about as if she had been a scullion, jeering her with cruel words as to what would have been the fate of her husband, if they had caught him there, until, though but eight years old, he had smitten one of the troopers, as he sat, with all his force. What had happened after that, he did not recollect, for it was not until a week after the Roundheads had ridden away that he found himself in his bed, with his mother sitting beside him, and his head bandaged with cloths dipped in water. He always maintained that, had the house been fortified, it could have held out until help arrived, although, in later years, his father assured him that it was well it was not in a position to offer a defence.

"We were away down south, Marmaduke, and the Roundheads were masters of this district, at the time. They would have battered the place around your mother's ears, and, likely as not, have burnt it to the ground. As it was, I came back here to find it whole and safe, except that the crop-eared scoundrels had, from pure wantonness, destroyed the pictures and hacked most of the furniture to pieces. I took no part in the later risings, seeing that they were hopeless, and therefore preserved my property, when many others were ruined.

"No, Marmaduke, it is just as well that the house was not fortified. I believe in fighting, when there is some chance, even a slight one, of success, but I regard it as an act of folly, to throw away a life when no good can come of it."

Still, Sir Marmaduke never ceased to regret that Lynnwood was not one of the houses that had been defended, to the last, against the enemies of the king. At the Restoration he went, for the first time in his life, to London, to pay his respects to Charles the Second. He was well received, and although he tired, in a very short time, of the gaieties of the court, he returned to Lynnwood with his feelings of loyalty to the Stuarts as strong as ever. He rejoiced heartily when the news came of the defeat of Monmouth at Sedgemoor, and was filled with rage and indignation when James weakly fled, and left his throne to be occupied by Dutch William.

From that time, he became a strong Jacobite, and emptied his glass nightly "to the king over the water." In the north the Jacobites were numerous, and at their gatherings treason was freely talked, while arms were prepared, and hidden away for the time when the lawful king should return to claim his own. Sir Marmaduke was deeply concerned in the plot of 1696, when preparations had been made for a great Jacobite rising throughout the country. Nothing came of it, for the Duke of Berwick, who was to have led it, failed in getting the two parties who were concerned to come to an agreement. The Jacobites were ready to rise, directly a French army landed. The French king, on the other hand, would not send an army until the Jacobites had risen, and the matter therefore fell through, to Sir Marmaduke's indignation and grief. But he had no words strong enough to express his anger and disgust when he found that, side by side with the general scheme for a rising, a plot had been formed by Sir George Barclay, a Scottish refugee, to assassinate the king, on his return from hunting in Richmond Forest.

"It is enough to drive one to become a Whig," he exclaimed. "I am ready to fight Dutch William, for he occupies the place of my rightful sovereign, but I have no private feud with him, and, if I had, I would run any man through who ventured to propose to me a plot to assassinate him. Such scoundrels as Barclay would bring disgrace on the best cause in the world. Had I heard as much as a whisper of it, I would have buckled on my sword, and ridden to London to warn the Dutchman of his danger. However, as it seems that Barclay had but some forty men with him, most of them foreign desperadoes, the Dutchman must see that English gentlemen, however ready to fight against him fairly, would have no hand in so dastardly a plot as this.

"Look you, Charlie, keep always in mind that you bear the name of our martyred king, and be ready ever to draw your sword in the cause of the Stuarts, whether it be ten years hence, or forty, that their banner is hoisted again; but keep yourself free from all plots, except those that deal with fair and open warfare. Have no faith whatever in politicians, who are ever ready to use the country gentry as an instrument for gaining their own ends. Deal with your neighbours, but mistrust strangers, from whomsoever they may say they come."

Which advice Charlie, at that time thirteen years old, gravely promised to follow. He had naturally inherited his father's sentiments, and believed the Jacobite cause to be a sacred one. He had fought and vanquished Alured Dormay, his second cousin, and two years his senior, for speaking of King James' son as the Pretender, and was ready, at any time, to do battle with any boy of his own age, in the same cause. Alured's father, John Dormay, had ridden over to Lynnwood, to complain of the violence of which his son had been the victim, but he obtained no redress from Sir Marmaduke.

"The boy is a chip of the old block, cousin, and he did right. I myself struck a blow at the king's enemies, when I was but eight years old, and got my skull well-nigh cracked for my pains. It is well that the lads were not four years older, for then, instead of taking to fisticuffs, their swords would have been out, and as my boy has, for the last four years, been exercised daily in the use of his weapon, it might happen that, instead of Alured coming home with a black eye, and, as you say, a missing tooth, he might have been carried home with a sword thrust through his body.

"It was, to my mind, entirely the fault of your son. I should have blamed Charlie, had he called the king at Westminster Dutch William, for, although each man has a right to his own opinions, he has no right to offend those of others--besides, at present it is as well to keep a quiet tongue as to a matter that words cannot set right. In the same way, your son had no right to offend others by calling James Stuart the Pretender.

"Certainly, of the twelve boys who go over to learn what the Rector of Apsley can teach them, more than half are sons of gentlemen whose opinions are similar to my own.

"It would be much better, John Dormay, if, instead of complaining of my boy, you were to look somewhat to your own. I marked, the last time he came over here, that he was growing loutish in his manners, and that he bore himself with less respect to his elders than is seemly in a lad of that age. He needs curbing, and would carry himself all the better if, like Charlie, he had an hour a day at sword exercise. I speak for the boy's good. It is true that you yourself, being a bitter Whig, mix but little with your neighbours, who are for the most part the other way of thinking; but this may not go on for ever, and you would, I suppose, like Alured, when he grows up, to mix with others of his rank in the county; and it would be well, therefore, that he should have the accomplishments and manners of young men of his own age."

John Dormay did not reply hastily--it was his policy to keep on good terms with his wife's cousin, for the knight was a man of far higher consideration, in the county, than himself. His smile, however, was not a pleasant one, as he rose and said:

"My mission has hardly terminated as I expected, Sir Marmaduke. I came to complain, and I go away advised somewhat sharply."

"Tut, tut, man!" the knight said. "I speak only for the lad's good, and I am sure that you cannot but feel the truth of what I have said. What does Alured want to make enemies for? It may be that it was only my son who openly resented his ill-timed remarks, but you may be sure that others were equally displeased, and maybe their resentment will last much longer than that which was quenched in a fair stand-up fight. Certainly, there need be no malice between the boys. Alured's defeat may even do him good, for he cannot but feel that it is somewhat disgraceful to be beaten by one nearly a head shorter than he."

"There is, no doubt, something in what you say, Sir Marmaduke," John Dormay said blandly, "and I will make it my business that, should the boys meet again as antagonists, Alured shall be able to give a better account of himself."

"He is a disagreeable fellow," Sir Marmaduke said to himself, as he watched John Dormay ride slowly away through the park, "and, if it were not that he is husband to my cousin Celia, I would have nought to do with him. She is my only kins-woman, and, were aught to happen to Charlie, that lout, her son, would be the heir of Lynnwood. I should never rest quiet in my grave, were a Whig master here.

"I would much rather that he had spoken wrathfully, when I straightly gave him my opinion of the boy, who is growing up an ill-conditioned cub. It would have been more honest. I hate to see a man smile, when I know that he would fain swear. I like my cousin Celia, and I like her little daughter Ciceley, who takes after her, and not after John Dormay; but I would that the fellow lived on the other side of England. He is out of his place here, and, though men do not speak against him in my presence, knowing that he is a sort of kinsman, I have never heard one say a good word for him.

"It is not only because he is a Whig. There are other Whig gentry in the neigh-bourhood, against whom I bear no ill will, and can meet at a social board in friend-ship. It would be hard if politics were to stand between neighbours. It is Dormay's manner that is against him. If he were anyone but Celia's husband, I would say that he is a smooth-faced knave, though I altogether lack proof of my words, beyond that he has added half a dozen farms to his estate, and, in each case, there were complaints that, although there was nothing contrary to the law, it was by sharp practice that he obtained possession, lending money freely in order to build houses and fences and drains, and then, directly a pinch came, demanding the return of his advance.

"Such ways may pass in a London usurer, but they don't do for us country folk; and each farm that he has taken has closed the doors of a dozen good houses to John Dormay. I fear that Celia has a bad time with him, though she is not one to com-plain. I let Charlie go over to Rockley, much oftener than I otherwise should do, for her sake and Ciceley's, though I would rather, a hundred times, that they should come here. Not that the visits are pleasant, when they do come, for I can see that Celia is always in fear, lest I should ask her questions about her life at home; which is the last thing that I should think of doing, for no good ever comes of interference between man and wife, and, whatever I learned, I could not quarrel with John Dor-may without being altogether separated from Celia and the girl.

"I am heartily glad that Charlie has given Alured a sound thrashing. The boy is too modest. He only said a few words, last evening, about the affair, and I thought that only a blow or two had been exchanged. It was as much as I could do, not to rub my hands and chuckle, when his father told me all about it. However, I must speak gravely to Charlie. If he takes it up, every time a Whig speaks scornfully of the king, he will be always in hot water, and, were he a few years older, would become a marked man. We have got to bide our time, and, except among friends, it is best to keep a quiet tongue until that time comes."

To Sir Marmaduke's disappointment, three more years went on without the position changing in any Way. Messengers went and came between France and the English Jacobites, but no movement was made. The failure of the assassination plot had strengthened William's hold on the country, for Englishmen love fair play and hate assassination, so that many who had, hitherto, been opponents of William of Orange, now ranged themselves on his side, declaring they could no longer support a cause that used assassination as one of its weapons. More zealous Jacobites, although they regretted the assassination plot, and were as vehement of their denunciations of its authors as were the Whigs, remained staunch in their fidelity to "the king over the water," maintaining stoutly that his majesty knew nothing whatever of this foul plot, and that his cause was in no way affected by the misconduct of a few men, who happened to be among its adherents.

At Lynnwood things went on as usual. Charlie continued his studies, in a somewhat desultory way, having but small affection for books; kept up his fencing lesson diligently and learned to dance; quarrelled occasionally with his cousin Alured, spent a good deal of his time on horseback, and rode over, not unfrequently, to Rockley, choosing, as far as possible, the days and hours when he knew that Alured and his father were likely to be away. He went over partly for his own pleasure, but more in compliance with his father's wishes.

"My cousin seldom comes over, herself," the latter said. "I know, right well, that it is from no slackness of her own, but that her husband likes not her intimacy here. It is well, then, that you should go over and see them, for it is only when you bring her that I see Ciceley. I would she were your sister, lad, for she is a bright little maid, and would make the old house lively."

Therefore, once a week or so, Charlie rode over early too Rockley, which was some five miles distant, and brought back Ciceley, cantering on her pony by his side, escorting her home again before nightfall. Ciceley's mother wondered, sometimes, that her husband, who in most matters set his will in opposition to hers, never offered any objection to the girl's visits to Lynnwood. She thought that, perhaps, he was pleased that there should be an intimacy between some member, at least, of his family, and Sir Marmaduke's. There were so few houses at which he or his were welcome, it was pleasant to him to be able to refer to the close friendship of his daughter with their cousins at Lynnwood. Beyond this, Celia, who often, as she sat alone, turned the matter over in her mind, could see no reason he could have for permitting the intimacy. That he would permit it without some reason was, as her experience had taught her, out of the question.

Ciceley never troubled her head about the matter. Her visits to Lynnwood were very pleasant to her. She was two years younger than Charlie Carstairs; and although, when he had once brought her to the house, he considered that his duties were over until the hour arrived for her return, he was sometimes ready to play with her, escort her round the garden, or climb the trees for fruit or birds' eggs for her.

Such little courtesies she never received from Alured, who was four years her senior, and who never interested himself in the slightest degree in her. He was now past eighteen, and was beginning to regard himself as a man, and had, to Ciceley's satisfaction, gone a few weeks before, to London, to stay with an uncle who had a place at court, and was said to be much in the confidence of some of the Whig lords.

Sir Marmaduke was, about this time, more convinced than ever that, ere long, the heir of the Stuarts would come over from France, with men, arms, and money, and would rally round him the Jacobites of England and Scotland. Charlie saw but little of him, for he was frequently absent, from early morning until late at night, riding to visit friends in Westmoreland and Yorkshire, sometimes being away two or three days at a time. Of an evening, there were meetings at Lynnwood, and at these strangers, who arrived after nightfall, were often present. Charlie was not admitted to any of these gatherings.

"You will know all about it in time, lad," his father said. "You are too young to bother your head with politics, and you would lose patience in a very short time. I do myself, occasionally. Many who are the foremost in talk, when there is no prospect of doing anything, draw back when the time approaches for action, and it is sickening to listen to the timorous objections and paltry arguments that are brought forward. Here am I, a man of sixty, ready to risk life and fortune in the good cause, and there are many, not half my age, who speak with as much caution as if they were graybeards. Still, lad, I have no doubt that the matter will straighten itself out, and come right in the end. It is always the most trying time, for timorous hearts, before the first shot of a battle is fired. Once the engagement commences, there is no time for fear. The battle has to be fought out, and the best way to safety is to win a victory. I have not the least doubt that, as soon as it is known that the king has landed, there will be no more shilly-shallying or hesitation. Every loyal man will mount his horse, and call out his tenants, and, in a few days, England will be in a blaze from end to end."

Charlie troubled himself but little with what was going on. His father had promised him that, when the time did come, he should ride by his side, and with that promise he was content to wait, knowing that, at present, his strength would be of but little avail, and that every week added somewhat to his weight and sinew.

One day he was in the garden with Ciceley. The weather was hot, and the girl was sitting, in a swing, under a shady tree, occasionally starting herself by a push with her foot on the ground, and then swaying gently backward and forward, until the swing was again at rest. Charlie was seated on the ground, near her, pulling the ears of his favourite dog, and occasionally talking to her, when a servant came out, with a message that his father wanted to speak to him.

"I expect I shall be back in a few minutes, Ciceley, so don't you wander away till I come. It is too hot today to be hunting for you, all over the garden, as I did when you hid yourself last week."

It was indeed but a short time until he returned.

"My father only wanted to tell me that he is just starting for Bristowe's, and, as it is over twenty miles away, he may not return until tomorrow."

"I don't like that man's face who brought the message to you, Charlie."

"Don't you?" the boy said carelessly. "I have not noticed him much. He has not been many months with us.

"What are you thinking of?" he asked, a minute later, seeing that his cousin looked troubled.

"I don't know that I ought to tell you, Charlie. You know my father does not think the same way as yours about things."

"I should rather think he doesn't," Charlie laughed. "There is no secret about that, Ciceley; but they don't quarrel over it. Last time your father and mother came over here, I dined with them for the first time, and I noticed there was not a single word said about politics. They chatted over the crops, and the chances of a war in Europe, and of the quarrel between Holstein and Denmark, and whether the young king of Sweden would aid the duke, who seems to be threatened by Saxony as well as by Denmark. I did not know anything about it, and thought it was rather stupid; but my father and yours both seemed of one mind, and were as good friends as if they were in equal agreement on all other points. But what has that to do with Nicholson, for that is the man's name who came out just now?"

"It does not seem to have much to do with it," she said doubtfully, "and yet, perhaps it does. You know my mother is not quite of the same opinion as my father, although she never says so to him; but, when we are alone together, sometimes she shakes her head and says she fears that trouble is coming, and it makes her very unhappy. One day I was in the garden, and they were talking loudly in the dining room--at least, he was talking loudly. Well, he said--But I don't know whether I ought to tell you, Charlie."

"Certainly you ought not, Ciceley. If you heard what you were not meant to hear, you ought never to say a word about it to anyone."

"But it concerns you and Sir Marmaduke."

"I cannot help that," he said stoutly. "People often say things of each other, in private, especially if they are out of temper, that they don't quite mean, and it would make terrible mischief if such things were repeated. Whatever your father said, I do not want to hear it, and it would be very wrong of you to repeat it."

"I am not going to repeat it, Charlie. I only want to say that I do not think my father and yours are very friendly together, which is natural, when my father is all for King William, and your father for King James. He makes no secret of that, you know."

Charlie nodded.

"That is right enough, Ciceley, but still, I don't understand in the least what it has to do with the servant."

"It has to do with it," she said pettishly, starting the swing afresh, and then relapsing into silence until it again came to a standstill.

"I think you ought to know," she said suddenly. "You see, Charlie, Sir Marmaduke is very kind to me, and I love him dearly, and so I do you, and I think you ought to know, although it may be nothing at all."

"Well, fire away then, Ciceley. There is one thing you may be quite sure of, whatever you tell me, it is like telling a brother, and I shall never repeat it to anyone."

"Well, it is this. That man comes over sometimes to see my father. I have seen him pass my window, three or four times, and go in by the garden door into father's study. I did not know who he was, but it did seem funny his entering by that door, as if he did not want to be seen by anyone in the house. I did not think anything more about it, till I saw him just now, then I knew him directly. If I had seen him before, I should have told you at once, but I don't think I have."

"I daresay not, Ciceley. He does not wait at table, but is under the steward, and helps clean the silver. He waits when we have several friends to dinner. At other times he does not often come into the room.

"What you tell me is certainly curious. What can he have to say to your father?"

"I don't know, Charlie. I don't know anything about it. I do think you ought to know."

"Yes, I think it is a good thing that I should know," Charlie agreed thoughtfully. "I daresay it is all right, but, at any rate, I am glad you told me."

"You won't tell your father?" she asked eagerly. "Because, if you were to speak of it--"

"I shall not tell him. You need not be afraid that what you have told me will come out. It is curious, and that is all, and I will look after the fellow a bit. Don't think anything more about it. It is just the sort of thing it is well to know, but I expect there is no harm in it, one way or the other. Of course, he must have known your father before he came to us, and may have business of some sort with him. He may have a brother, or some other relation, who wants to take one of your father's farms. Indeed, there are a hundred things he might want to see him about. But still, I am glad you have told me."

In his own mind, Charlie thought much more seriously of it than he pretended.

He knew that, at present, his father was engaged heart and soul in a projected Jacobite rising. He knew that John Dormay was a bitter Whig. He believed that he had a grudge against his father, and the general opinion of him was that he was wholly unscrupulous.

That he should, then, be in secret communication with a servant at Lynnwood, struck him as a very serious matter, indeed. Charlie was not yet sixteen, but his close companionship with his father had rendered him older than most lads of his age. He was as warm a Jacobite as his father, but the manner in which William, with his Dutch troops, had crushed the great Jacobite rebellion in Ireland, seemed to him a lesson that the prospects of success, in England, were much less certain than his father believed them to be.

John Dormay, as an adherent of William, would be interested in thwarting the proposed movement, with the satisfaction of, at the same time, bringing Sir Marmaduke into disgrace. Charlie could hardly believe that his cousin would be guilty of setting a spy to watch his father, but it was certainly possible, and as he thought the matter over, as he rode back after escorting Ciceley to her home, he resolved to keep a sharp watch over the doings of this man Nicholson.

"It would never do to tell my father what Ciceley said. He would bundle the fellow out, neck and crop, and perhaps break some of his bones, and then it would be traced to her. She has not a happy home, as it is, and it would be far worse if her father knew that it was she who had put us on our guard. I must find out something myself, and then we can turn him out, without there being the least suspicion that Ciceley is mixed up in it."

The next evening several Jacobite gentlemen rode in, and, as usual, had a long talk with Sir Marmaduke after supper.

"If this fellow is a spy," Charlie said to himself, "he will be wanting to hear what is said, and to do so he must either hide himself in the room, or listen at the door, or at one of the windows. It is not likely that he will get into the room, for to do that he must have hidden himself before supper began. I don't think he would dare to listen at the door, for anyone passing through the hall would catch him at it. It must be at one of the windows."

The room was at an angle of the house. Three windows looked out on to the lawn in front; that at the side into a large shrubbery, where the bushes grew up close to it; and Charlie decided that here, if anywhere, the man would take up his post. As soon, then, as he knew that the servants were clearing away the supper, he took a heavy cudgel and went out. He walked straight away from the house, and then, when he knew that his figure could no longer be seen in the twilight, he made a circuit, and, entering the shrubbery, crept along close to the wall of the Muse, until within two or three yards of the window. Having made sure that at present, at any rate, no one was near, he moved out a step or two to look at the window.

His suspicions were at once confirmed. The inside curtains were drawn, but the casement was open two or three inches. Charlie again took up his post, behind a bush, and waited.

In five minutes he heard a twig snap, and then a figure came along, noiselessly, and placed itself at the window. Charlie gave him but a moment to listen, then he sprang forward, and, with his whole strength, brought his cudgel down upon the man's head. He fell like a stone. Charlie threw open the window, and, as he did so, the curtain was torn back by his father, the sound of the blow and the fall having reached the ears of those within.

Sir Marmaduke had drawn his sword, and was about to leap through the window, when Charlie exclaimed:

"It is I, father. I have caught a fellow listening at the window, and have just knocked him down."

"Well done, my boy!

"Bring lights, please, gentlemen. Let us see what villain we have got here."

But, as he spoke, Charlie's head suddenly disappeared, and a sharp exclamation broke from him, as he felt his ankles grasped and his feet pulled from under him. He came down with such a crash that, for a moment, he was unable to rise. He heard a rustling in the bushes, and then his father leapt down beside him.

"Where are you, my boy? Has the scoundrel hurt you?"

"He has given me a shake," Charlie said as he sat up; "and, what is worse, I am afraid he has got away."

"Follow me, gentlemen, and scatter through the gardens," Sir Marmaduke roared. "The villain has escaped!"

For a few minutes, there was a hot pursuit through the shrubbery and gardens, but nothing was discovered. Charlie had been so shaken that he was unable to join the pursuit, but, having got on to his feet, remained leaning against the wall until his father came back.

"He has got away, Charlie. Have you any idea who he was?"

"It was Nicholson, father. At least, I am almost certain that it was him. It was too dark to see his face. I could see the outline of his head against the window, and he had on a cap with a cock's feather which I had noticed the man wore."

"But how came you here, Charlie?"

"I will tell you that afterwards, father. Don't ask me now."

For, at this moment, some of the others were coming up. Several of them had torches, and, as they approached, Sir Marmaduke saw something lying on the ground under the window. He picked it up.

"Here is the fellow's cap," he said. "You must have hit him a shrewd blow, Charlie, for here is a clean cut through the cloth, and a patch of fresh blood on the white lining. How did he get you down, lad?"

"He fell so suddenly, when I hit him, that I thought I had either killed or stunned him; but of course I had not, for it was but a moment after, when I was speaking to you, that I felt my ankles seized, and I went down with a crash. I heard him make off through the bushes; but I was, for the moment, almost dazed, and could do nothing to stop him."

"Was the window open when he came?"

"Yes, sir, two or three inches."

"Then it was evidently a planned thing.

"Well, gentlemen, we may as well go indoors. The fellow is well out of our reach now, and we may be pretty sure he will never again show his face here. Fortunately he heard nothing, for the serving men had but just left the room, and we had not yet begun to talk."

"That is true enough, Sir Marmaduke," one of the others said. "The question is: how long has this been going on?"

Sir Marmaduke looked at Charlie.

"I know nothing about it, sir. Till now, I have not had the slightest suspicion of this man. It occurred to me, this afternoon, that it might be possible for anyone to hear what was said inside the room, by listening at the windows; and that this shrubbery would form a very good shelter for an eavesdropper. So I thought, this evening I would take up my place here, to assure myself that there was no traitor in the household. I had been here but five minutes when the fellow stole quietly up, and placed his ear at the opening of the casement, and you may be sure that I gave him no time to listen to what was being said."

"Well, we had better go in," Sir Marmaduke said. "There is no fear of our being overheard this evening.

"Charlie, do you take old Banks aside, and tell him what has happened, and then go with him to the room where that fellow slept, and make a thorough search of any clothes he may have left behind, and of the room itself. Should you find any papers or documents, you will, of course, bring them down to me."

But the closest search, by Charlie and the old butler, produced no results. Not a scrap of paper of any kind was found, and Banks said that he knew the man could neither read nor write.

The party below soon broke up, considerable uneasiness being felt, by all, at the incident of the evening. When the last of them had left, Charlie was sent for.

"Now, then, Charlie, let me hear how all this came about. I know that all you said about what took place at the window is perfectly true; but, even had you not said so, I should have felt there was something else. What was it brought you to that window? Your story was straight-forward enough, but it was certainly singular your happening to be there, and I fancy some of our friends thought that you had gone round to listen, yourself. One hinted as much; but I said that was absurd, for you were completely in my confidence, and that, whatever peril and danger there might be in the enterprise, you would share them with me."

"It is not pleasant that they should have thought so, father, but that is better than that the truth should be known. This is how it happened;" and he repeated what Ciceley had told him in the garden.

"So the worthy Master John Dormay has set a spy upon me," Sir Marmaduke said, bitterly. "I knew the man was a knave--that is public property--but I did not think that he was capable of this. Well, I am glad that, at any rate, no suspicion can fall upon Ciceley in the matter; but it is serious, lad, very serious. We do not know how long this fellow has been prying and listening, or how much he may have learnt. I don't think it can be much. We talked it over, and my friends all agreed with me that they do not remember those curtains having been drawn before. To begin with, the evenings are shortening fast, and, at our meeting last week, we finished our supper by daylight; and, had the curtains been drawn, it would have been noticed, for we had need of light before we finished. Two of the gentlemen, who were sitting facing the window, declared that they remembered distinctly that it was open. Mr. Jervoise says that he thought to himself that, if it was his place, he would have the trees cut away there, for they shut out the light.

"Therefore, although it is uncomfortable to think that there has been a spy in the house, for some months, we have every reason to hope that our councils have not been overheard. Were it otherwise, I should lose no time in making for the coast, and taking ship to France, to wait quietly there until the king comes over."

"You have no documents, father, that the man could have found?"

"None, Charlie. We have doubtless made lists of those who could be relied upon, and of the number of men they could bring with them, but these have always been burned before we separated. Such letters as I have had from France, I have always destroyed as soon as I have read them. Perilous stuff of that sort should never be left about. No; they may ransack the place from top to bottom, and nothing will be found that could not be read aloud, without harm, in the marketplace of Lancaster.

"So now, to bed, Charlie. It is long past your usual hour."

Chapter 2: Denounced.

C harlie," Sir Marmaduke said on the following morning, at breakfast, "it is quite possible that that villain who acted as spy, and that other villain who employed him--I need not mention names--may swear an information against me, and I may be arrested, on the charge of being concerned in a plot. I am not much afraid of it, if they do. The most they could say is that I was prepared to take up arms, if his majesty crossed from France; but, as there are thousands and thousands of men ready to do the same, they may fine me, perhaps, but I should say that is all. However, what I want to say to you is, keep out of the way, if they come. I shall make light of the affair, while you, being pretty hot tempered, might say things that would irritate them, while they could be of no assistance to me. Therefore, I would rather that you were kept out of it, altogether. I shall want you here. In my absence, there must be somebody to look after things.

"Mind that rascal John Dormay does not put his foot inside the house, while I am away. That fellow is playing some deep game, though I don't quite know what it is. I suppose he wants to win the goodwill of the authorities, by showing his activity and zeal; and, of course, he will imagine that no one has any idea that he has been in communication with this spy. We have got a hold over him, and, when I come back, I will have it out with him. He is not popular now, and, if it were known that he had been working against me, his wife's kinsman, behind my back, my friends about here would make the country too hot to hold him."

"Yes, father; but please do not let him guess that we have learnt it from Ciceley. You see, that is the only way we know about it."

"Yes, you are right there. I will be careful that he shall not know the little maid has anything to do with it. But we will think of that, afterwards; maybe nothing will come of it, after all. But, if anything does, mind, my orders are that you keep away from the house, while they are in it. When you come back, Banks will tell you what has happened.

"You had better take your horse, and go for a ride now. Not over there, Charlie. I know, if you happened to meet that fellow, he would read in your face that you knew the part he had been playing, and, should nothing come of the business, I don't want him to know that, at present. The fellow can henceforth do us no harm, for we shall be on our guard against eavesdroppers; and, for the sake of cousin Celia and the child, I do not want an open breach. I do not see the man often, myself, and I will take good care I don't put myself in the way of meeting him, for the present, at any rate. Don't ride over there today."

"Very well, father. I will ride over and see Harry Jervoise. I promised him that I would come over one day this week."

It was a ten-mile ride, and, as he entered the courtyard of Mr. Jervoise's fine old mansion, he leapt off his horse, and threw the reins over a post. A servant came out.

"The master wishes to speak to you, Master Carstairs."

"No ill news, I hope, Charlie?" Mr. Jervoise asked anxiously, as the lad was shown into the room, where his host was standing beside the carved chimney piece.

"No, sir, there is nothing new. My father thought that I had better be away today, in case any trouble should arise out of what took place yesterday, so I rode over to see Harry. I promised to do so, one day this week."

"That is right. Does Sir Marmaduke think, then, that he will be arrested?"

"I don't know that he expects it, sir, but he says that it is possible."

"I do not see that they have anything to go upon, Charlie. As we agreed last night, that spy never had any opportunity of overhearing us before, and, certainly, he can have heard nothing yesterday. The fellow can only say what many people know, or could know, if they liked; that half a dozen of Sir Marmaduke's friends rode over to take supper with him. They can make nothing out of that."

"No, sir; and my father said that, at the worst, it could be but the matter of a fine."

"Quite so, lad; but I don't even see how it could amount to that. You will find Harry somewhere about the house. He has said nothing to me about going out."

Harry Jervoise was just the same age as Charlie, and was his greatest friend.

They were both enthusiastic in the cause of the Stuarts, equally vehement in their expressions of contempt for the Dutch king, equally anxious for the coming of him whom they regarded as their lawful monarch. They spent the morning together, as usual; went first to the stables and patted and talked to their horses; then they played at bowls on the lawn; after which, they had a bout of sword play; and, having thus let off some of their animal spirits, sat down and talked of the glorious times to come, when the king was to have his own again.

Late in the afternoon, Charlie mounted his horse and rode for home. When within half a mile of the house, a man stepped out into the road in front of him.

"Hullo, Banks, what is it? No bad news, I hope?"

And he leapt from his horse, alarmed at the pallor of the old butler's face.

"Yes, Master Charles, I have some very bad news, and have been waiting for the last two hours here, so as to stop you going to the house."

"Why shouldn't I go to the house?"

"Because there are a dozen soldiers, and three or four constables there."

"And my father?"

"They have taken him away."

"This is bad news, Banks; but I know that he thought that it might be so. But it will not be very serious; it is only a question of a fine," he said.

The butler shook his head, sadly.

"It is worse than that, Master Charles. It is worse than you think."

"Well, tell me all about it, Banks," Charlie said, feeling much alarmed at the old man's manner.

"Well, sir, at three this afternoon, two magistrates, John Cockshaw and William Peters--"

("Both bitter Whigs," Charlie put in.)

"--Rode up to the door. They had with them six constables, and twenty troopers."

"There were enough of them, then," Charlie said. "Did they think my father was going to arm you all, and defend the place?"

"I don't know, sir, but that is the number that came. The magistrates, and the constables, and four of the soldiers came into the house. Sir Marmaduke met them in the hall.

"'To what do I owe the honour of this visit?' he said, quite cold and haughty.

"'We have come, Sir Marmaduke Carstairs, to arrest you, on the charge of being concerned in a treasonable plot against the king's life.'

"Sir Marmaduke laughed out loud.

"'I have no design on the life of William of Orange, or of any other man,' he said. 'I do not pretend to love him; in that matter there are thousands in this realm with me; but, as for a design against his life, I should say, gentlemen, there are few who know me, even among men like yourselves, whose politics are opposed to mine, who would for a moment credit such a foul insinuation.'

"'We have nothing to do with that matter, Sir Marmaduke,' John Cockshaw said. 'We are acting upon a sworn information to that effect.'

"Sir Marmaduke was angry, now.

"'I can guess the name of the dog who signed it,' he said, 'and, kinsman though he is by marriage, I will force the lie down his throat.'

"Then he cooled down again.

"'Well, gentlemen, you have to do your duty. What do you desire next?'

"'Our duty is, next, to search the house, for any treasonable documents that may be concealed here.'

"'Search away, gentlemen,' Sir Marmaduke said, seating himself in one of the settles. 'The house is open to you. My butler, James Banks, will go round with you, and will open for you any cupboard or chest that may be locked.'

"The magistrates nodded to the four soldiers. Two of them took their post near the chair, one at the outside door, and one at the other end of the room. Sir Marmaduke said nothing, but shrugged his shoulders, and then began to play with the ears of the little spaniel, Fido, that had jumped up on his knees.

"'We will first go into the study,' John Cockshaw said; and I led them there.

"They went straight to the cabinet with the pull-down desk, where Sir Marmaduke writes when he does write, which is not often. It was locked, and I went to Sir Marmaduke for the key.

"'You will find it in that French vase on the mantel,' he said. 'I don't open the desk once in three months, and should lose the key, if I carried it with me.'

"I went to the mantel, turned the vase over, and the key dropped out.

"'Sir Marmaduke has nothing to hide, gentlemen,' I said, 'so, you see, he keeps the key here.'

"I went to the cabinet, and put the key in. As I did so I said:

"'Look, gentlemen, someone has opened, or tried to open, this desk. Here is a mark, as if a knife had been thrust in to shoot the bolt.'

"They looked where I pointed, and William Peters said to Cockshaw, 'It is as the man says. Someone has been trying to force the lock--one of the varlets, probably, who thought the knight might keep his money here.'

"'It can be of no importance, one way or the other,' Cockshaw said roughly.

"'Probably not, Mr. Cockshaw, but, at the same time I will make a note of it.'

"I turned the key, and pulled down the door that makes a desk. They seemed to know all about it, for, without looking at the papers in the pigeonholes, they pulled open the lower drawer, and took two foreign-looking letters out from it. I will do them the justice to say that they both looked sorry, as they opened them, and looked at the writing.

"'It is too true,' Peters said. 'Here is enough to hang a dozen men.'

"They tumbled all the other papers into a sack, that one of the constables had brought with him. Then they searched all the other furniture, but they evidently did not expect to find anything. Then they went back into the hall.

"'Well, gentlemen,' Sir Marmaduke said, 'have you found anything of a terrible kind?'

"'We have found, I regret to say,' John Cockshaw said, 'the letters of which we were in search, in your private cabinet--letters that prove, beyond all doubt, that you are concerned in a plot similar to that discovered three years ago, to assassinate his majesty the king.'

"Sir Marmaduke sprang to his feet.

"'You have found letters of that kind in my cabinet?' he said, in a dazed sort of way.

"The magistrate bowed, but did not speak.

"'Then, sir,' Sir Marmaduke exclaimed, 'you have found letters that I have never seen. You have found letters that must have been placed there by some scoundrel, who plotted my ruin. I assert to you, on the honour of a gentleman, that no such letters have ever met my eye, and that, if such a proposition had been made to me, I care not by whom, I would have struck to the ground the man who offered me such an insult.'

"'We are sorry, Sir Marmaduke Carstairs,' Mr. Peters said, 'most sorry, both of us, that it should have fallen to our duty to take so painful a proceeding against a neighbour; but, you see, the matter is beyond us. We have received a sworn information that you are engaged in such a plot. We are told that you are in the habit of locking up papers of importance in a certain cabinet, and there we find papers of a most damnatory kind. We most sincerely trust that you may be able to prove your innocence in the matter, but we have nothing to do but to take you with us, as a prisoner, to Lancaster.'

"Sir Marmaduke unbuckled his sword, and laid it by. He was quieter than I thought he could be, in such a strait, for he has always been by nature, as you know, choleric.

"'I am ready, gentlemen,' he said.

"Peters whispered in Cockshaw's ear.

"'Ah yes,' the other said, 'I had well-nigh forgotten,' and he turned to me. 'Where is Master Charles Carstairs?'

"'He is not in the house,' I said. 'He rode away this morning, and did not tell me where he was going.'

"'When do you expect him back?'

"'I do not expect him at all,' I said. 'When Master Charles rides out to visit his friends, he sometimes stays away for a day or two.'

"'Is it supposed,' Sir Marmaduke asked coldly, 'that my son is also mixed up in this precious scheme?'

"'It is sworn that he was privy to it,' John Cockshaw said, 'and is, therefore, included in the orders for arrest.'

"Sir Marmaduke did not speak, but he shut his lips tight, and his hand went to where the hilt of his sword would have been. Two of the constables went out and questioned the grooms, and found that you had, as I said, ridden off. When they came back, there was some talk between the magistrates, and then, as I said, four constables and some soldiers were left in the house. Sir Marmaduke's horse was brought round, and he rode away, with the magistrates and the other soldiers."

"I am quite sure, Banks, that my father could have known nothing of those letters, or of any plot against William's life. I have heard him speak so often of the assassination plot, and how disgraceful it was, and how, apart from its wickedness, it had damaged the cause, that I am certain he would not have listened to a word about another such business."

"I am sure of that, too," the old butler said; "but that is not the question, Master Charles. There are the papers. We know that Sir Marmaduke did not put them there, and that he did not know that they were there. But how is it to be proved, sir? Everyone knows that Sir Marmaduke is a Jacobite, and is regarded as the head of the party in this part of the country. He has enemies, and one of them, no doubt, has played this evil trick upon him, and the putting of your name in shows what the motive is."

"But it is ridiculous, Banks. Who could believe that such a matter as this would be confided to a lad of my age?"

"They might not believe it in their hearts, but people often believe what suits their interest. This accusation touches Sir Marmaduke's life; and his estate, even if his life were spared, would be confiscated. In such a case, it might be granted to anyone, and possibly even to the son of him they would call the traitor. But the accusation that the son was concerned, or was, at any rate, privy to the crime intended by the father, would set all against him, and public opinion would approve of the estates passing away from him altogether.

"But now, sir, what do you think you had best do?"

"Of course I shall go on, Banks, and let them take me to join my father in Lancaster jail. Do you think I would run away?"

"No, sir, I don't think you would run away. I am sure you would not run away from fear, but I would not let them lay hands on me, until I had thought the matter well over. You might be able to do more good to Sir Marmaduke were you free, than you could do if you were caged up with him. He has enemies, we know, who are doing their best to ruin him, and, as you see, they are anxious that you, too, should be shut up within four walls."

"You are right, Banks. At any rate, I will ride back and consult Mr. Jervoise. Besides, he ought to be warned, for he, too, may be arrested on the same charge. How did you get away without being noticed?"

"I said that I felt ill--and I was not speaking falsely--at Sir Marmaduke's arrest, and would lie down. They are keeping a sharp lookout at the stables, and have a soldier at each door, to see that no one leaves the house, but I went out by that old passage that comes out among the ruins of the monastery."

"I know, Banks. My father showed it to me, three years ago."

"I shall go back that way again, sir, and no one will know that I have left the house. You know the trick of the sliding panel, Master Charles?"

"Yes, I know it, and if I should want to come into the house again, I will come that way, Banks."

"Here is a purse," the butler said. "You may want money, sir. Should you want more, there is a store hidden away, in the hiding place under the floor of the Priest's Chamber, at the other end of the passage. Do you know that?"

"I know the Priest's Chamber of course, because you go through that to get to the long passage, but I don't know of any special hiding place there."

"Doubtless, Sir Marmaduke did not think it necessary to show it you then, sir, but he would have done it later on, so I do not consider that I am breaking my oath of secrecy in telling you. You know the little narrow loophole in the corner?"

"Yes, of course. There is no other that gives light to the room. It is hidden from view outside by the ivy."

"Well, sir, you count four bricks below that, and you press hard on the next, that is the fifth, then you will hear a click, then you press hard with your heel at the corner, in the angle of the flag below, and you will find the other corner rise. Then you get hold of it and lift it up, and below there is a stone chamber, two feet long and about eighteen inches wide and deep. It was made to conceal papers in the old days, and I believe food was always kept there, in case the chamber had to be used in haste.

"Sir Marmaduke uses it as a store place for his money. He has laid by a good deal every year, knowing that money would be wanted when troops had to be raised. I was with him about three weeks ago, when he put in there half the rents that had been paid in. So, if you want money for any purpose, you will know where to find it."

"Thank you, Banks. It may be very useful to have such a store, now."

"Where shall I send to you, sir, if I have any news that it is urgent you should know of?"

"Send to Mr. Jervoise, Banks. If I am not there, he will know where I am to be found."

"I will send Will Ticehurst, Master Charles. He is a stout lad, and a shrewd one, and I know there is nothing that he would not do for you. But you had best stop no longer. Should they find out that I am not in the house, they will guess that I have come to warn you, and may send out a party to search."

Charlie at once mounted, and rode back to Mr. Jervoise's.

"I expected you back," that gentleman said, as he entered. "Bad news travels apace, and, an hour since, a man brought in the news that Sir Marmaduke had been seen riding, evidently a prisoner, surrounded by soldiers, on the road towards Lancaster. So that villain we chased last night must have learnt something. I suppose they will be here tomorrow, but I do not see what serious charge they can have against us. We have neither collected arms, nor taken any steps towards a rising. We have talked over what we might do, if there were a landing made from France, but, as there may be no landing, that is a very vague charge."

"Unfortunately, that is not the charge against my father. It is a much more serious business."

And Charlie repeated the substance of what Banks had told him, interrupted occasionally by indignant ejaculations from Mr. Jervoise.

"It is an infamous plot," he said, when the lad had concluded his story. "Infamous! There was never a word said of such a scheme, and no one who knows your father would believe it for an instant."

"Yes, sir, but the judges, who do not know him, may believe it. No doubt those who put those papers there, will bring forward evidence to back it up."

"I am afraid that will be the case. It is serious for us all," Mr. Jervoise said thoughtfully. "That man will be prepared to swear that he heard the plot discussed by us all. They seized your father, today, as being the principal and most important of those concerned in it, but we may all find ourselves in the same case tomorrow. I must think it over.

"It is well that your man warned you. You had best not stay here tonight, for the house may be surrounded at daybreak. Harry shall go over, with you, to one of my tenants, and you can both sleep there. It will not be necessary for you to leave for another two or three hours. You had better go to him now; supper will be served in half an hour. I will talk with you again, afterwards."

Harry was waiting outside the door, having also heard the news of Sir Marmaduke's arrest.

"It is villainous!" he exclaimed, when he heard the whole story. "No doubt you are right, and that John Dormay is at the bottom of it all. The villain ought to be slain."

"He deserves it, Harry; and, if I thought it would do good, I would gladly fight him, but I fear that it would do harm. Such a scoundrel must needs be a coward, and he might call for aid, and I might be dragged off to Lancaster. Moreover, he is Ciceley's father, and my cousin Celia's husband, and, were I to kill him, it would separate me altogether from them. However, I shall in all things be guided by your father. He will know what best ought to be done.

"It is likely that he, too, may be arrested. This is evidently a deep plot, and your father thinks that, although the papers alone may not be sufficient to convict my father, the spy we had in our house will be ready to swear that he heard your father, and mine, and the others, making arrangements for the murder of William of Orange; and their own word to the contrary would count but little against such evidence, backed by those papers."

They talked together for half an hour, and were then summoned to supper. Nothing was said, upon the subject, until the servitors had retired, and the meal was cleared away. Mr. Jervoise was, like Sir Marmaduke, a widower.

"I have been thinking it all over," he said, when they were alone. "I have determined to ride, at once, to consult some of my friends, and to warn them of what has taken place. That is clearly my duty. I shall not return until I learn whether warrants are out for my apprehension. Of course, the evidence is not so strong against me as it is against Sir Marmaduke; still, the spy's evidence would tell as much against me as against him.

"You will go up, Harry, with your friend, to Pincot's farm. It lies so far in the hills that it would probably be one of the last to be searched, and, if a very sharp lookout is kept there, a body of men riding up the valley would be seen over a mile away, and there would be plenty of time to take to the hills. There Charlie had better remain, until he hears from me.

"You can return here, Harry, in the morning, for there is no probability whatever of your being included in any warrant of arrest. It could only relate to us, who were in the habit of meeting at Sir Marmaduke's. You will ride over to the farm each day, and tell Charlie any news you may have learnt, or take any message I may send you for him.

"We must do nothing hastily. The first thing to learn, if possible, is whether any of us are included in the charge of being concerned in a plot against William's life. In the next place, who are the witnesses, and what evidence they intend to give. No doubt the most important is the man who was placed as a spy at Sir Marmaduke's."

"As I know his face, sir," Charlie said eagerly, "could I not find him, and either force him to acknowledge that it is all false, or else kill him? I should be in my right in doing that, surely, since he is trying to swear away my father's life by false evidence."

"I should say nothing against that, lad. If ever a fellow deserved killing he does; that is, next to his rascally employer. But his death would harm rather than benefit us. It would be assumed, of course, that we had removed him to prevent his giving evidence against us. No doubt his depositions have been taken down, and they would then be assumed to be true, and we should be worse off than if he could be confronted with us, face to face, in the court. We must let the matter rest, at present."

"Would it be possible to get my father out of prison, sir? I am sure I can get a dozen men, from among the tenants and grooms, who would gladly risk their lives for him."

"Lancaster jail is a very strong place," Mr. Jervoise said, "and I fear there is no possibility of rescuing him from it. Of course, at present we cannot say where the trial will take place. A commission may be sent down, to hold a special assizes at Lancaster, or the trial may take place in London. At any rate, nothing whatever can be done, until we know more. I have means of learning what takes place at Lancaster, for we have friends there, as well as at most other places. When I hear from them the exact nature of the charge, the evidence that will be given, and the names of those accused of being mixed up in this pretended plot, I shall be better able to say what is to be done.

"Now, I must mount and ride without further delay. I have to visit all our friends who met at Lynnwood, and it will take me until tomorrow morning to see and confer with them."

A few minutes after Mr. Jervoise had ridden off, his son and Charlie also mounted. A man went with them, with a supply of torches, for, although Harry knew the road--which was little better than a sheep track--well enough during the day, his father thought he might find it difficult, if not impossible, to follow it on a dark night.

They congratulated themselves upon the precaution taken, before they had gone very far, for there was no moon, the sky was overcast, and a drizzling rain had begun to come down. They could hardly see their horses' heads, and had proceeded but a short distance, when it became necessary for their guide to light a torch. It took them, therefore, over two hours to reach the mountain farm.

They were expected, otherwise the household would have been asleep. Mr. Jervoise had, as soon as he determined upon their going there, sent off a man on horseback, who, riding fast, had arrived before night set in. There was, therefore, a great turf fire glowing on the hearth when they arrived, and a hearty welcome awaiting them from the farmer, his wife, and daughters. Harry had, by his father's advice, brought two changes of clothes in a valise, but they were so completely soaked to the skin that they decided they would, after drinking a horn of hot-spiced ale that had been prepared for them, go at once to bed, where, in spite of the stirring events of the day, both went off to sleep, as soon as their heads touched the pillows.

The sun was shining brightly, when they woke. The mists had cleared off, although they still hung round the head of Ingleborough, six miles away, and on some of the other hilltops. The change of weather had an inspiriting effect, and they went down to breakfast in a brighter and more hopeful frame of mind. As soon as the meal was over, Harry started for home.

"I hope it won't be long before I can see you again, Harry," Charlie said, as he stood by the horse.

"I hope not, indeed; but there is no saying. My father's orders are that I am to stay at home, if people come and take possession, and send a man off to you with the news privately, but that, if no one comes, I may myself bring you over any news there is; so I may be back here this afternoon."

"I shall be looking out for you, Harry. Remember, it will be horribly dull for me up here, wondering and fretting as to what is going on."

"I know, Charlie; and you shall hear, as soon as I get the smallest scrap of news. If I were you, I would go for a good walk among the hills. It will be much better for you than moping here. At any rate, you are not likely to get any news for some hours to come."

Charlie took the advice, and started among the hills, not returning until the midday meal was ready. Before he had finished his dinner there was a tap at the door, and then a young fellow, whom he knew to be employed in Mr. Jervoise's stables, looked in. Charlie sprang to his feet.

"What's the news?" he asked.

"Master Harry bade me tell you, sir, that a magistrate, and four constables, and ten soldier men came today, at nine o'clock. He had returned but a half-hour when they rode up. They had an order for the arrest of Mr. Jervoise, and have been searching the house, high and low, for papers. No one is allowed to leave the place, but Master Harry came out to the stables and gave me his orders, and I did not find much difficulty in slipping out without their noticing me. Mr. Harry said that he had no news of Mr. Jervoise, nor any other news, save what I have told you. He bade me return at once as, later on, he may want to send me again. I was to be most careful that no one should see me when I got back, and, if I was caught, I was on no account to say where I had been to."

The farmer insisted upon the young fellow sitting down at the table, and taking some food, before he started to go back. He required no pressing, but, as soon as his hunger was satisfied, he started again at a brisk run, which he kept up as long as Charlie's eye could follow him down the valley.

Although the boy by no means wished Mr. Jervoise to be involved in his father's trouble, Charlie could not help feeling a certain amount of pleasure at the news. He thought it certain that, if his father escaped, he would have to leave the country, and that he would, in that case, take him as companion in his flight. If Mr. Jervoise and Harry also left the country, it would be vastly more pleasant for both his father and himself. Where they would go to, or what they would do, he had no idea, but it seemed to him that exile among strangers would be bearable, if he had his friend with him. It would not last many years, for surely the often talked-of landing could not be very much longer delayed; then they would return, share in the triumph of the Stuart cause, and resume their life at Lynnwood, and reckon with those who had brought this foul charge against them.

That the Jacobite cause could fail to triumph was a contingency to which Charlie did not give even a thought. He had been taught that it was a just and holy cause. All his school friends, as well as the gentlemen who visited his father, were firm adherents of it, and he believed that the same sentiments must everywhere prevail. There was, then, nothing but the troops of William to reckon with, and these could hardly oppose a rising of the English people, backed by aid from France.

It was not until after dark that the messenger returned.

"Master Harry bade me tell you, sir, that a gipsy boy he had never seen before has brought him a little note from his father. He will not return at present, but, if Mr. Harry can manage to slip away unnoticed in the afternoon, tomorrow, he is to come here. He is not to come direct, but to make a circuit, lest he should be watched and followed, and it may be that the master will meet him here."

Charlie was very glad to hear this. Harry could, of course, give him little news of what was going on outside the house, but Mr. Jervoise might be able to tell him something about his father, especially as he had said he had means of learning what went on in Lancaster jail.

He was longing to be doing something. It seemed intolerable to him that he should be wandering aimlessly among the hills, while his father was lying in Lancaster, with a charge affecting his life hanging over him. What he could do he knew not, but anything would be better than doing nothing. Mr. Jervoise had seemed to think that it was out of the question to attempt a rescue from Lancaster; but surely, if he could get together forty or fifty determined fellows, a sudden assault upon the place might be successful.

Then he set to work reckoning up the grooms, the younger tenants, and the sons of the older ones, and jotted down the names of twenty-seven who he thought might join in the attempt.

"If Harry could get twenty-three from his people, that would make it up to the number," he said. "Of course, I don't know what the difficulties to be encountered may be. I have ridden there with my father, and I know that the castle is a strong one, but I did not notice it very particularly. The first thing to do will be to go and examine it closely. No doubt ladders will be required, but we could make rope ladders, and take them into the town in a cart, hidden under faggots, or something of that sort.

"I do hope Mr. Jervoise will come tomorrow. It is horrible waiting here in suspense."

The next morning, the hours seemed endless. Half a dozen times he went restlessly in and out, walking a little distance up the hill rising from the valley, and returning again, with the vain idea that Mr. Jervoise might have arrived.

Still more slowly did the time appear to go, after dinner. He was getting into a fever of impatience and anxiety, when, about five o'clock, he saw a figure coming down the hillside from the right. It was too far away to recognize with certainty, but, by the rapid pace at which he descended the hill, he had little doubt that it was Harry, and he at once started, at the top of his speed, to meet him.

The doubt was soon changed into a certainty. When, a few hundred yards up the hill, he met his friend, both were almost breathless. Harry was the first to gasp out:

"Has my father arrived?"

"Not yet."

Harry threw himself down on the short grass, with an exclamation of thankfulness.

"I have run nearly every foot of the way," he said, as soon as he got his breath a little. "I had awful difficulty in getting out. One of the constables kept in the same room with me, and followed me wherever I went. They evidently thought I might hear from my father, or try to send him a message. At last, I got desperate, and ran upstairs to that room next mine, and closed and locked the door after me. You know the ivy grows high up the wall there, and directly I got in, I threw open the casement and climbed down by it. It gave way two or three times, and I thought I was gone, but I stuck to it, and managed each time to get a fresh hold. The moment I was down, I ran along by the foot of the wall until I got round behind, made a dash into that clump of fir trees, crawled along in a ditch till I thought I was safe, and then made a run for it. I was so afraid of being followed that I have been at least three miles round, but I don't mind, now that my father hasn't arrived. I was in such a fright that he might come and go before I got here."

Chapter 3: A Rescue.

The two lads walked slowly down the hill together. Harry had heard no more than Charlie had done, of what was going on. The messenger from his father was a young fellow, of seventeen or eighteen, with a gipsy face and appearance. How he had managed to elude the vigilance of the men on watch, Harry did not know. He, himself, had only learnt his presence when, as he passed some bushes in the garden, a sharp whisper made him stop, and a moment later a hand was thrust through the foliage. He took the little note held out, and caught sight of the lad's face, through the leaves, as he leant forward and said:

"Go on, sir, without stopping. They may be watching you."

Harry had thrust the note into his pocket, and sauntered on for some time. He then returned to the house, and there read the letter, with whose contents Charlie was already acquainted. Eagerly, they talked over what each had been thinking of since they had parted, early on the previous day; and discussed Charlie's idea of an attack on Lancaster jail.

"I don't know whether I could get as many men as you say, Charlie. I don't think I could. If my father were in prison, as well as yours, I am sure that most of the young fellows on the estate would gladly help to rescue him, but it would be a different thing when it came to risking their lives for anyone else. Of course I don't know, but it does not seem to me that fifty men would be of any use, at all, towards taking Lancaster Castle. It always seemed to me a tremendously strong place."

"Yes, it does look so, Harry; but perhaps, on examining it closely, one would find that it is not so strong as it looks, by a long way. It seems to me there must be some way or other of getting father out, and, if there seems even the least bit of a chance, I shall try it."

"And you may be sure I will stand by you, Charlie, whatever it is," Harry said heartily. "We have been just like brothers, and, of course, brothers ought to stick to each other like anything. If they don't, what is the use of being brothers? I daresay we shall know more, when we hear what my father has to say; and then we may see our way better."

"Thank you, Harry. I knew you would stick by me. Of course, I don't want to do any mad sort of thing. There is no hurry, anyhow, and, as you say, when we know more about it, we may be able to hit upon some sort of plan."

It was not until eight o'clock that Mr. Jervoise arrived. He looked grievously tired and worn out, but he spoke cheerfully as he came in.

"I have had a busy two days of it, boys, as you may guess. I have no particularly good news to tell you, but, on the other hand, I have no bad news. I was in time to warn all our friends, and when the soldiers came for them in the morning, it was only to find that their nests were empty.

"They have been searching the houses of all Sir Marmaduke's tenants, Charlie, and questioning man, woman, and child as to whether they have seen you.

"Ah! Here is supper, and I am nearly famished. However, I can go on talking while I eat. I should have been here sooner, but I have been waiting for the return of the messenger I sent to Lancaster.

"Yesterday morning there was an examination of your father, Charlie, or rather, an examination of the testimony against him. First the two letters that were discovered were put in. Without having got them word for word, my informer was able to give me the substance of them. Both were unsigned, and professed to have been written in France. The first is dated three months back. It alludes to a conversation that somebody is supposed to have had with Sir Marmaduke, and states that the agent who had visited him, and who is spoken of as Mr. H, had assured them that your father was perfectly ready to join, in any well-conceived design for putting a stop to the sufferings that afflicted the country, through the wars into which the foreign intruder had plunged it, even though the plan entailed the removal of the usurper. The writer assured Sir Marmaduke of the satisfaction that such an agreement on his part had caused at Saint Germains, and had heightened the high esteem in which Sir Marmaduke was held, for his long fidelity to the cause of his majesty. It then went on to state that a plan had been already formed, and that several gentlemen in the south were deeply pledged to carry it out, but that it was thought specially advisable that some from the north should also take part in it, as, from their persons being unknown near the court, they could act with more surety and safety. They would, therefore, be glad if he would take counsel, with the friends he had mentioned, as to what might seem to them the best course of proceeding. There was no occasion for any great haste and, indeed, some weeks must elapse before the blow was struck, in order that preparations should be made, in France, for taking instant advantage of it.

"The rest of the letter was to the same purpose, but was really a repetition of it. The second letter was dated some time later, and was, as before, an answer to one the knight was supposed to have written. It highly approved of the suggestions therein made; that Sir Marmaduke and his friends should travel, separately and at a few days' interval, to London, and should take lodgings there in different parts of the town, and await the signal to assemble, near Richmond, when it was known that the king would go hunting there. It said that special note had been made of the offer of Sir Marmaduke's son, to mingle among the king's attendants and to fire the first shot, as, in the confusion, he would be able to escape and, being but a boy, as he said, none would be able to recognize him afterwards.

"In the event, of course, of the first shot failing, the rest of the party, gathered in a body, would rush forward, despatch the usurper, cut their way, sword in hand, through any who barred their path to the point where their horses were concealed, and then at once scatter in various directions. For this great service, his majesty would not fail to evince the deepest gratitude, upon his restoration to his rightful throne, and pledged his royal word that each of the party should receive rank and dignity, together with ample estates, from the lands of which the chief supporters of the usurper would be deprived.

"So you see, Charlie, you were to have the honour of playing the chief part in this tragedy."

"Honour indeed!" Charlie exclaimed passionately. "Dishonour, sir. Was there ever so infamous a plot!"

"It is a well-laid plot, Charlie, and does credit to the scoundrel who planned it. You see, he made certain that Sir Marmaduke would be attainted, and his estates forfeited, but there existed just a possibility that, as you are but a boy, though a good big one, it might be thought that, as you were innocent of the business, a portion at least of the estate might be handed to you. To prevent this, it was necessary that you also should be mixed up in the affair."

"Has John Dormay appeared in the matter so far, Mr. Jervoise?"

"Not openly, Charlie. My informant knows that there have been two or three meetings of Whig magistrates, with closed doors, and that at these he has been present, and he has no doubt, whatever, that it is he who has set the ball rolling. Still, there is no proof of this, and he did not appear yesterday. The man who did appear was the rascal who tried to overhear us the other night. He stated that he had been instigated by a gentleman of great loyalty--here one of the magistrates broke in, and said no name must be mentioned--to enter the household of Sir Marmaduke, a gentleman who, as he believed, was trafficking with the king's enemies. He had agreed to do this, in spite of the danger of such employment, moved thereto not so much by the hope of a reward as from his great loyalty to his majesty, and a desire to avert from him his great danger from popish plots. Having succeeded in entering Sir Marmaduke's service, he soon discovered that six gentlemen, to wit, myself and five friends, were in the habit of meeting at Lynnwood, where they had long and secret talks. Knowing the deep enmity and hostility these men bore towards his gracious majesty, he determined to run any hazard, even to the loss of his life, to learn the purport of such gatherings, and did, therefore, conceal himself, on one occasion behind the hangings of a window, and on another listened at an open casement, and did hear much conversation regarding the best manner in which the taking of the king's life could be accomplished. This, it was agreed, should be done in the forest at Richmond, where all should lie in wait, the said Sir Marmaduke Carstairs undertaking that he and his son would, in the first place, fire with pistol or musquetoon, and that, only if they should fail, the rest should charge forward on horse, overthrow the king's companions, and despatch him, Mr. William Jervoise undertaking the management of this part of the enterprise. No date was settled for this wicked business, it being, however, agreed that all should journey separately to London, and take up their lodging there under feigned names; lying hid until they heard from a friend at court, whose name was not mentioned, a day on which the king would hunt at Richmond. He further testified that, making another attempt to overhear the conspirators in order that he might gather fuller details as to the manner of the plot, he was seen by Master Charles Carstairs, who, taking him by surprise, grievously assaulted him, and that he and the others would have slain him, had he not overthrown Master Carstairs and effected his escape before the others, rushing out sword in hand, had time to assail him.

"During his stay at Lynnwood he had, several times, watched at the window of the room where Sir Marmaduke Carstairs sits when alone, and where he writes his letters and transacts business, and that he observed him, more than once, peruse attentively papers that seemed to be of importance, for, after reading them, he would lay them down and walk, as if disturbed or doubtful in mind, up and down the room; and these papers he placed, when he had done with them, in the bottom drawer of a desk in his cabinet, the said desk being always carefully locked by him.

"That is all that I learnt from Lancaster, save that instructions have been given that no pains should be spared to secure the persons of those engaged in the plot, and that a special watch was to be set at the northern ports, lest they should, finding their guilt discovered, try to escape from the kingdom. So you see that your good father, Sir Marmaduke, is in a state of sore peril, and that the rest of us, including yourself, will be in a like strait if they can lay hands on us."

"But it is all false!" Charlie exclaimed. "It is a lie from beginning to end."

"That is so, but we cannot prove it. The matter is so cunningly laid, I see no way to pick a hole in it. We are Jacobites, and as such long regarded as objects of suspicion by the Whig magistrates and others. There have been other plots against William's life, in which men of seeming reputation have been concerned. This man's story will be confirmed by the man who set him on, and by other hidden papers, if necessary. As to the discovery of the documents, we may know well enough that the fellow himself put them there, but we have no manner of proof of it. It is evident that there is nothing for us but to leave the country, and to await the time when the king shall have his own again. My other friends, who were with me this afternoon when the news came from Lancaster, all agreed that it would be throwing away our lives to stay here. We all have money by us, for each has, for years, laid by something for the time when money will be required to aid the king on his arrival.

"Having agreed to take this course, we drew up a document, which we all signed, and which will be sent in when we have got clear away. In it we declare that being informed that accusations of being concerned in a plot against the life of William of Orange have been brought against us, we declare solemnly before God that we, and also Sir Marmaduke Carstairs and his son, are wholly innocent of the charge, and that, although we do not hesitate to declare that we consider the title of the said William to be king of this realm to be wholly unfounded and without reason, and should therefore take up arms openly against it on behalf of our sovereign did occasion offer, yet that we hold assassination in abhorrence, and that the crime with which we are charged is as hateful in our sight as in that of any Whig gentleman. As, however, we are charged, as we learn, by evilly disposed and wicked persons, of this design, and have no means of proving our innocence, we are forced to leave the realm until such time shall arrive when we can rely on a fair trial, when our reputation and honour will weigh against the word of suborned perjurers and knaves.

"We were not forgetful of your father's case, and we debated long as to whether our remaining here could do him service. We even discussed the possibility of raising a force, and attacking Lancaster Castle. We agreed, however, that this would be nothing short of madness. The country is wholly unprepared at present. The Whigs are on the alert, and such an attempt would cost the lives of most of those concerned in it. Besides, we are all sure that Sir Marmaduke would be the first to object to numbers of persons risking their lives in an attempt which, even if, for the moment, successful, must bring ruin upon all concerned in it. Nor do we see that, were we to remain and to stand in the dock beside him, it would aid him. Our word would count for no more than would this protest and denial that we have signed together. A prisoner's plea of not guilty has but a feather's weight against sworn evidence.

"At the same time, Charlie, I do not intend to leave the country until I am sure that nothing can be done. As force is out of the question, I have advised the others to lose not an hour in trying to escape and, by this time, they are all on the road. Two are making for Bristol, one for Southampton, and two for London. It would be too dangerous to attempt to escape by one of the northern ports. But, though force cannot succeed, we may be able to effect your father's escape by other means, and it is for this purpose that I am determined to stay, and I shall do so until all hope is gone. Alone you could effect nothing; but I, knowing who are our secret friends, may be able to use them to advantage.

"We will stay here tonight, but tomorrow we must change our quarters, for the search will be a close one. During the day we will go far up over the hills, but tomorrow night we will make for Lancaster. I have warned friends there to expect us, and it is the last place where they would think of searching for us."

"You will take me with you, too, father?" Harry exclaimed eagerly; while Charlie expressed his gratitude to Mr. Jervoise, for thus determining to risk his own life in the endeavour to effect the escape of Sir Marmaduke.

"Yes, I intend to take you with me, Harry. They will pretend, of course, that, in spite of our assertions of innocence, our flight is a confession of guilt, and you may be sure that we shall be condemned in our absence, and our estates declared confiscated, and bestowed upon some of William's minions. There will be no place for you here.

"My own plans are laid. As you know, your mother came from the other side of the border, and a cousin of hers, with whom I am well acquainted, has gone over to Sweden, and holds a commission in the army that the young king is raising to withstand Russia and Saxony; for both are thinking of taking goodly slices of his domains. I could not sit down quietly in exile, and, being but forty, I am not too old for service, and shall take a commission if I can obtain it. There are many Scottish Jacobites who, having fled rather than acknowledge Dutch William as their king, have taken service in Sweden, where their fathers fought under the great Gustavus Adolphus; and, even if I cannot myself take service, it may be that I shall be able to obtain a commission for you. You are nearly sixteen, and there are many officers no older.

"Should evil befall your father, Charlie, which I earnestly hope will not be the case, I shall regard you as my son, and shall do the same for you as for Harry.

"And now, I will to rest, for I have scarce slept the last two nights, and we must be in the saddle long before daybreak."

The little bedroom, that Charlie had used the two previous nights, was given up to Mr. Jervoise; while Harry and Charlie slept on some sheep skins, in front of the kitchen fire. Two hours before daybreak they mounted and, guided by the farmer, rode to a shepherd's hut far up among the hills. Late in the afternoon, a boy came up from the farm, with the news that the place had been searched by a party of troopers. They had ridden away without discovering that the fugitives had been at the farm, but four of the party had been left, in case Mr. Jervoise should come there. The farmer, therefore, warned them against coming back that way, as had been intended, naming another place where he would meet them.

As soon as the sun was setting they mounted and, accompanied by the shepherd on a rough pony, started for Lancaster. After riding for three hours, they stopped at a lonely farm house, at which Mr. Jervoise and his friends had held their meeting on the previous day. Here they changed their clothes for others that had been sent for their use from Lancaster. Mr. Jervoise was attired as a small trader, and the lads in garb suitable to boys in the same rank of life. They still, however, retained their swords, and the pistols in their holsters.

Three miles farther they met their host, as arranged, at some crossroads, and rode on until within three miles of Lancaster. They then dismounted, placed their pistols in their belts, and handed their horses to the two men, who would take them back to the hut in the hills, where they would remain until required.

It was two o'clock in the morning when they entered Lancaster and, going up to a small house, standing in a garden in the outskirts of the town, Mr. Jervoise gave three low knocks in quick succession. The door was opened almost immediately. No light was shown, and they entered in the dark, but as soon as the door was closed behind them, a woman came out with a candle from an inner room.

"I am glad to see you safe, Mr. Jervoise," a man said. "My wife and I were beginning to be anxious, fearing that you might have fallen into the hands of your enemies."

"No, all has gone well, Herries; but it is a long ride from the hills here, and we walked the last three miles, as we wanted to get the horses back again before daylight. We are deeply grateful to you for giving us shelter."

"I would be ready to do more than that," the man said, "for the sake of the good cause. My wife's father and mine both fell at Naseby, and we are as loyal to the Stuarts as they were. You are heartily welcome, sir, and, as we keep no servant, there will be none to gossip. You can either remain in the house, in which case none will know of your presence here; or, if you wish to go abroad in the town, I will accompany you, and will introduce you to any acquaintance I may meet as a cousin of my wife who, with his two sons, has come over from Preston to pay us a visit. I don't think that anyone would know you, in that attire."

"I will run no more risks than are necessary, Herries. Those I wish to see will visit me here, and, if I go out at all, it will not be until after dark."

For a fortnight they remained at the house. After dark each day, a man paid Mr. Jervoise a visit. He was the magistrates' clerk, and had an apartment in the castle. From him they learned that a messenger had been despatched to London, with an account of the evidence taken in Sir Marmaduke's case; and that, at the end of twelve days, he had returned with orders that all prisoners and witnesses were to be sent to town, where they would be examined, in the first place, by his majesty's council; and where Sir Marmaduke's trial for high treason would take place. They were to be escorted by a party of twelve troopers, under the command of a lieutenant.

The fugitives had, before, learned that the search for Mr. Jervoise had been given up; it being supposed that he, with his son and young Carstairs had, with their accomplices, all ridden for the coast at the first alarm, and had probably taken ship for France before the orders had arrived that all outgoing vessels should be searched.

Harry and Charlie had both been away for two or three days, and had been occupied in getting together ten young fellows, from the two estates, who would be willing and ready to attempt to rescue Sir Marmaduke from his captors' hands. They were able to judge, with tolerable accuracy, when the messenger would return from London and, two days previously, the men had been directed to ride, singly and by different roads, and to put up at various small inns in Manchester, each giving out that he was a farmer in from the country, either to purchase supplies, or to meet with a customer likely to buy some cattle he wished to dispose of. Charlie had paid a visit to Lynnwood, and had gone by the long passage into the Priest's Chamber, and had carried off the gold hidden there.

As soon as it was known that the messenger had returned, Herries had borrowed a horse, and had ridden with a note to the farmer, telling him to go up to the hills and bring the horses down, with one of his own, to the place where he had parted from them, when they entered Lancaster. There he was met by Mr. Jervoise and the lads and, mounting, they started with the spare horse for Blackburn, choosing that line in preference to the road through Preston, as there were troops stationed at the latter town.

The next day they rode on to Manchester. They went round, that evening, to the various inns where the men had put up, and directed them to discover whether, as was probable, the escort was to arrive that night. If so, they were to mount at daybreak, and assemble where the road crossed the moor, three miles north of Chapel le Frith, where they would find Mr. Jervoise awaiting them.

At nine o'clock that evening the troop rode in and, at daybreak, Mr. Jervoise and the boys started. Two of the men were already at the spot indicated, and, half an hour later, the whole of them had arrived.

Mr. Jervoise led them back to a spot that he had selected, where the road dipped into a deep valley, in which, sheltered from the winds, was a small wood. Leaving one at the edge, to give warning directly the escort appeared on the road over the brow, he told the rest to dismount. Most of them were armed with pistols. All had swords.

"Do you," he said, "who are good shots with your pistols, fire at the men when I give the word--let the rest aim at the horses. The moment you have opened fire, dash forward and fall on them. We are already as numerous as they are, and we ought to be able to dismount or disable four or five of them, with our first fire. I shall give the order as Sir Marmaduke arrives opposite me. Probably the officer will be riding. I shall make the officer my special mark, for it may be that he has orders to shoot the prisoner, if any rescue is attempted.

"I don't suppose they will be at all prepared for an attack. They were vigilant, no doubt, for the first two days but, once out of Lancashire, they will think that there is no longer any fear of an attempt at rescue. Pursue those that escape for half a mile or so, and then draw rein, and, as soon as they are out of sight, strike due north across the fells. Keep to the east of Glossop, and then make your way singly to your homes. It will be better for you to travel up through Yorkshire, till you are north of Ingleborough, so as to come down from the north to your farms.

"I know that you have all engaged in this affair for love of Sir Marmaduke or myself, and because you hate to see a loyal gentleman made the victim of lying knaves; but when we come back with the king, you may be sure that Sir Marmaduke and I will well reward the services you have rendered."

It was an hour before the man on the lookout warned them that the troop had just appeared over the hill. They mounted now, and, pistol in hand, awaited the arrival of the party. Two troopers came first, trotting carelessly along, laughing and smoking. A hundred yards behind came the main body, four troopers first, then the lieutenant and Sir Marmaduke, followed by the other six troopers.

With outstretched arm, and pistol pointed through the undergrowth, Mr. Jervoise waited till the officer, who was riding on his side of the road, came abreast of him. He had already told the boys that he intended to aim at his shoulder.

"They are the enemies of the king," he said, "but I cannot, in cold blood, shoot down a man with whom I have no cause for quarrel. I can depend upon my aim, and he will not be twelve paces from the muzzle of my pistol."

He fired. The officer gave a sudden start, and reeled on his horse, and, before he could recover himself, the band, who had fired at the flash of the first pistol, dashed out through the bushes and fell upon the troopers. Four men had dropped, one horse had fallen, and two others were plunging wildly as, with a shout, their assailants dashed upon them. All who could turn their horse's head rode furiously off, some along the road forward, others back towards Manchester. The lieutenant's horse had rolled over with him, as that of Mr. Jervoise struck it on the shoulder, with the full impetus of its spring.

"It is all over, Sir Marmaduke, and you are a free man. We have nothing to do now but to ride for it."

And, before the knight had fairly recovered from his astonishment, he found himself riding south across the moor, with his son on one side of him, and Mr. Jervoise and Harry on the other.

"You have saved my life, Jervoise," he said, holding out his hand to his friend. "They had got me so firmly in their clutches, that I thought my chances were at an end.

"How are you, Charlie? I am right glad to see you, safe and sound, for they had managed to include you in their pretended plot, and, for aught I knew, you had been all this time lying in a cell next mine in Lancaster Castle.

"But who are the good fellows who helped you?"

Mr. Jervoise briefly gave an account of the affair.

"They are only keeping up a sham pursuit of the soldiers, so as to send them well on their way. I told them not to overtake them, as there was no occasion for any further bloodshed, when you were once out of their hands. By tomorrow morning they will all be at work on their farms again, and, if they keep their own counsel, need not fear."

Suddenly Sir Marmaduke reined in his horse.

"We are riding south," he said.

"Certainly we are," Mr. Jervoise said. "Why not? That is our only chance of safety. They will, in the first place, suspect us of having doubled back to the hills, and will search every farmhouse and cottage. Our only hope of escape is to ride either for Bristol, or one of the southern ports."

"I must go back," Sir Marmaduke said doggedly. "I must kill that scoundrel John Dormay, before I do anything else. It is he who has wound this precious skein, in order to entrap us, expecting, the scoundrel, to have my estates bestowed on him as a reward."

"It were madness to ride back now, Sir Marmaduke. It would cost you your life, and you would leave Charlie here fatherless, and with but little chance of ever regaining the estate. You have but to wait for a time, and everything will right itself. As soon as the king comes to his own, your estates will be restored, and then I would not seek to stay your hand, if you sought vengeance upon this cunning knave."

"Besides, father," Charlie put in, "much as he deserves any punishment you can give him, you would not kill cousin Celia's husband and Ciceley's father. When the truth is all made known, his punishment will be bitter enough, for no honest man would offer him a hand, or sit down to a meal with him.

"Ciceley has been as a young sister to me, and her mother has ever been as kind as if she had been my aunt. I would not see them grieved, even if that rogue came off scot free from punishment; but, at any rate, father, I pray you to let it pass at present. This time we have happily got you out of the clutches of the Whigs, but, if you fell into them again, you may be sure they would never give us another chance."

Sir Marmaduke still sat irresolute, and Charlie went on:

"Besides, father, Mr. Jervoise has risked his life in lingering in Lancashire to save you, and the brave fellows who aided us to rescue you have risked theirs, both in the fray and afterwards, if their share in it should ever be known; and it would not be fair to risk failure, after all they have done. I pray you, father, be guided by the opinion of your good friend, Mr. Jervoise."

Sir Marmaduke touched his horse's flank with his heel.

"You have prevailed, Charlie. Your last argument decided me. I have no right to risk my life, after my good friends have done so much to save me. John Dormay may enjoy his triumph for a while, but a day of reckoning will surely come.

"Now, tell me of the others, Jervoise. Have all escaped in safety?"

"All. Your boy brought me the news of your arrest, and that we were charged with plotting William's assassination. I rode that night with the news, and next day all were on the road to the coast, and were happily on board and away before the news of their escape could be sent to the ports."

"And now, what are your plans, Jervoise--that is, if you have any plans, beyond reaching a port and taking ship for France?"

"I am going to Sweden," Mr. Jervoise said, and then repeated the reasons that he had given Charlie for taking this step.

"I am too old for the wars," Sir Marmaduke said. "I was sixty last birthday, and though I am still strong and active, and could strike a shrewd blow in case of need, I am too old for the fatigues and hardships of campaigning. I could not hope, at my age, to obtain a commission in the Swedish service."

"No, I did not think of your joining the army, Sir Marmaduke, though I warrant you would do as well as most; but I thought that you might take up your residence at Stockholm, as well as at Saint Germains. You will find many Scottish gentlemen there, and not a few Jacobites who, like yourself, have been forced to fly. Besides, both the life and air would suit you better than at Saint Germains, where, by all accounts the life is a gay one, and men come to think more of pleasure than of duty. Moreover, your money will go much further in Sweden than in France."

Sir Marmaduke, checking the horse's speed, said, "I have not so much as a penny in my pocket, and methinks I am like to have some trouble in getting at the hoard I have been collecting, ever since Dutch William came to the throne, for the benefit of His Majesty when he arrives."

"You will have no trouble in getting at that, father," Charlie said laughing, "seeing that you have nothing to do but to lean over, and put your hand into my holsters, which are so full, as you see, that I am forced to carry my pistols in my belt."

"What mean you, lad?"

"I mean, father, that I have the whole of the hoard, that was stowed away in the priest's hiding place;" and he then related how Banks had revealed to him the secret of the hiding place, and how he had, the night before Sir Marmaduke was removed from Lancaster Castle, visited the place and carried away the money.

"I could not see Banks," he said, "but I left a few words on a scrap of paper, saying that it was I who had taken the money. Otherwise he would have been in a terrible taking, when he discovered that it was gone."

"That is right good news, indeed, lad. For twelve years I have set aside half my rents, so that in those bags in your holsters there are six years' income, and the interest of that money, laid out in good mortgages, will suffice amply for my wants in a country like Sweden, where life is simple and living cheap. The money itself shall remain untouched, for your use, should our hopes fail and the estates be lost for all time. That is indeed a weight off my mind.

"And you are, I hope, in equally good case, Jervoise, for if not, you know that I would gladly share with you?"

"I am in very good case, Sir Marmaduke, though I none the less thank you for your offer. I too have, as you know, put aside half my income. My estates are not so large as those of Lynnwood. Their acreage may be as large, but a good deal of it is mountain land, worth but little. My fund, therefore, is not as large as yours, but it amounts to a good round sum; and as I hope, either in the army or in some other way, to earn an income for myself, it is ample. I shall be sorry to divert it from the use for which I intended it, but that cannot now be helped. I have had the pleasure, year by year, of putting it by for the king's use, and, now that circumstances have changed, it will be equally useful to myself."

"Do you know this country well, Jervoise?"

"Personally I know nothing about it, save that the sun tells me that, at present, I am travelling south, Sir Marmaduke. But, for the last few days I have been so closely studying a map, that I know the name of every town and village on the various routes."

"And whither think you of going?"

"To London or Southampton. Strangers are far less noticed in large towns than in small, and we could hardly hope to find a ship, bound for Sweden, in any of the Dorset or Devon ports."

Chapter 4: In Sweden.

After much discussion, the party agreed that it would be best to make for Southampton. The road thither was less frequented than that leading to London, and there were fewer towns to be passed, and less chance of interruption. Mr. Jervoise had brought with him a valise and suit of clothes for Sir Marmaduke, of sober cut and fashion. They avoided all large towns and, at the places where they put up, represented themselves as traders travelling from the Midlands to the southern coast, and they arrived at Southampton without having excited the smallest suspicion. Indeed, throughout the journey, they had heard no word of the affray near Chapel le Frith, and knew, therefore, that the news had not travelled as fast as they had.

At Southampton, however, they had scarcely put up at an inn when the landlord said:

"I suppose, gentlemen, they are talking of nothing else, in London, but the rescue of a desperate Jacobite by his friends. The news only reached here yesterday."

"It has occasioned a good deal of scare," Mr. Jervoise replied. "I suppose there is no word of the arrest of the man, or his accomplices? We have travelled but slowly, and the news may have passed us on the way."

"Not as yet," the landlord replied. "They say that all the northern and eastern ports are watched, and they make sure of catching him, if he presents himself there. The general opinion is that he will, for a time, go into hiding with his friends, in the hills of Cumberland or Westmoreland, or perhaps on the Yorkshire moors; but they are sure to catch him sooner or later."

"It is a bad business altogether," Mr. Jervoise said, "and we can only hope that all guilty persons will in time get the punishment they so well deserve. How can trade be carried on, if the country is to be disturbed by plots, and conspiracies?"

"How, indeed?" the landlord repeated heartily. "I do not meddle in politics, being content to earn my living by my business, and to receive all who can pay their reckoning, without caring a jot whether they be Whigs or Tories."

The next morning Mr. Jervoise and Sir Marmaduke went down to the port, leaving the lads to wander about the town at their pleasure, as two persons were likely to attract less attention than four. They found that there were two vessels in port, loading with munitions of war for Sweden, and that one of them would sail shortly. They at once went on board her, and saw the captain.

"Do you carry any passengers?"

"None have applied so far," the captain said; "but, if they were to offer, I should not say no to them."

"We want to take passage for Sweden," Mr. Jervoise said. "The King of that country is, as they say, fitting out an army. Clothes are as necessary for troops as swords and guns, and we think we could obtain a contract for these goods. There is no hope of doing so, unless we ourselves go over, and, though sorely loath to do so, for neither of us have ever before set foot on board a ship, we determined on making the journey, together with our two clerks, for whom we will take passage at the same rate as for ourselves, seeing that they are both related to us."

"Have you any goods with you?"

"We shall take over but a bale or two of cloth, as samples of the goods we can supply; but, beyond that, we have but little luggage, seeing that our stay may be a very short one."

There was a little haggling for terms, as the two gentlemen did not wish to appear eager to go; but the matter was finally settled to the satisfaction of both parties.

On their return to the inn, Mr. Jervoise took the host aside.

"We have business connected with our trade in cloth in Sweden, where we hope to obtain a large contract. The matter may occupy us a week, or a month or two for aught we know, and we do not want our horses to be eating their heads off, here, while we are away. Besides, we may be able, on our return, to take a passage to one of the Devonshire ports, which would suit us much better. But we should not be able to do so, if there were need for returning here for our horses. Therefore, we would fain dispose of them, and, if you can find us a purchaser by tomorrow night, we will pay you a fair commission on the money we receive."

"I doubt not that I can do that readily enough," the landlord said. "Three of them are fine animals, fit for any gentleman's riding. The other is a stout hackney. Trust me, I will get the best price I can for them."

The next day he came up to their room.

"I have had a good offer for the horses," he said. "Two gentlemen, who arrived yesterday from France, and are staying at the inn of a friend of mine, are requiring horses for themselves and their servants, and I have promised my friend a slice of my commission, if he will bring them round hither. Will you name your price for them?"

"No, I would rather not," Mr. Jervoise said cautiously. "If we asked too high a figure, we might frighten the purchasers away. If we should ask too little, we should be the losers. I daresay they have named, to your friend, the price they are willing to give. You had better ask from them a good bit above that, then you can come down little by little, and maybe, seeing the horses are really good ones, they may advance a bit. I am not used to a horse deal, and will leave it to you to make the bargain. We are sorry to part with the animals, but they might die on the voyage, or get so injured as to be worthless; and, moreover, we shall have no use for them there. Therefore, as we must sell, we are ready to take the best terms we can get."

When they returned to the inn, after an absence of two hours, they found that the landlord had sold the horses, for a sum nearly approaching their value, the gentlemen being as anxious to purchase them as they were to sell. The next day, they bought three or four rolls of west country cloth, and a supply of clothes suitable to their condition, together with trunks for their carriage. All these were sent down to the ship, in the course of the afternoon, and they themselves embarked late in the evening, as she was to set sail at daybreak.

The lads, accustomed to spacious and airy rooms, were quite taken aback at the small and stuffy cabin allotted to their joint use, and slept but badly, for the loading of the ship continued by torchlight, until within an hour of the time of their departure. After tossing about for some hours in their narrow beds, they were glad to go on deck, and to plunge their heads into a pail of water, and were then, after combing their long hair, able to take an interest in what was passing round them.

The sailors were busy; stowing away the cargo last received, tidying the decks, and coiling down the ropes. There were but few persons on the quay, for those who had been engaged in loading the cargo had gone off to bed, as soon as the last bale was on board.

In half an hour the sailors began to hoist the sails, the hawsers were thrown off, and, with a gentle wind blowing aft, the ship glided along past the shore, being helped by the tide, which had begun to ebb half an hour before. The lads were greatly interested in watching the well-wooded slope on the left, with the stately ruins of Tintern Abbey rising above the trees. Then they passed the round fort, at the water's edge, on their right, and issued out from Southampton Water into the broad sheet between the island and the mainland.

It was dotted with sails; fishing craft and coasters for the most part, but with some larger ships bound from the east to Southampton, and others that had come in through the Solent. This was very entertaining to the boys, and they were still more pleased when they saw the fortifications of Portsmouth, with cannon pointing seaward, and with many vessels riding in the strait by the side of the town.

"That fort would give the French or the Dutch a hot reception, were they at any time to think to capture the dockyard and shipping," Sir Marmaduke said.

"The Dutch have already captured the place, and that without shedding a drop of blood," Mr. Jervoise remarked.

"'That is true enough," the knight said, stamping his foot angrily on the deck, "but what has been won so easily may be lost as quickly. I have seen several changes since I can first remember, and I hope I may live to see another. However, we need not talk of that now."

"No, indeed," Mr. Jervoise agreed. "It may be, Sir Marmaduke, that it would be better if we had talked and thought less of it, during the last twelve years; better for ourselves, and for these lads. We might still have been ready to join His Majesty as soon as he landed, but as, till then, we could do nothing, it seems to me now that it would have been wiser had we gone about our business without worrying our heads, to say nothing of risking them, about a matter that may not take place during our lives; as we know, well enough, the King of France uses the Stuarts only for his own convenience, and at heart cares nothing for them or their cause. It is convenient to have the means of creating trouble here, and of so weakening William; and it may be that, some day or other, it may suit him to send over an army here to fight William, with the aid of the Stuarts' friends, instead of fighting him in Holland or elsewhere. But whether he may think fit to do so in one year, or in twenty years hence, who can say? It is a question solely of military policy.

"The Stuarts are simply used, by the French king, to pull English chestnuts out of the fire. I would that they had established themselves anywhere rather than in France. It does them harm with vast numbers who would otherwise be their friends, at any rate in England. In Scotland it is otherwise, for Scotland has always been in alliance with France; but in England it is different. France has always been the national foe; and, had not Charles and James proved themselves so subservient to Louis, William of Orange would never have been crowned king. There are vast numbers in England who would rather see a Stuart than a Dutchman on the throne, but who will never strike a blow to replace them there, and that because they will come over backed up by French bayonets.

"Well, let us talk of something else. If the time ever comes to act, we shall be ready, but till then we can let the matter sleep, the more so as we have a new life before us, and plenty of other things to occupy our thoughts."

"What is it, father," Harry asked, "that the Swedes and Danes are going to fight about?"

"It is a difficult question, Harry; but there can be little doubt that Denmark is in the wrong. The King of Sweden died in April, 1697. His death was unfortunate, for the powers contending in Europe had all agreed to refer their quarrels to his mediation. At his death, Denmark endeavoured to obtain the honour, but failed; and by the mediation, chiefly, of the Swedish regency, peace was concluded between France, England, and Holland, in the autumn of that year; and, shortly afterwards, the struggle between the German Emperor, France, and Spain was also concluded, but not at all to the satisfaction of the Swedish mediators.

"While Sweden was occupied in this matter of the pacification of Europe, the King of Denmark thought to take advantage of the fact that Charles of Sweden was but a minor, to press Frederick, Duke of Holstein, who was in close alliance with him.

"There had long been serious differences between the rulers of Denmark and Holstein, both of whom were branches of the Oldenburg family, and this in reference to the Duchy of Schleswig. The quarrel had arisen from the act of Christian the Third, of Denmark, who decreed that the descendants of his brother Adolphus should govern Holstein, jointly with the King of Denmark, and that Holstein and Schleswig should belong to them in common, neither making any change in Holstein without the consent of the other A more foolish arrangement could not have been conceived, for anyone might have foreseen that it would lead to disputes and troubles. In fact, quarrels continually arose, until, at the Peace of Rosahild, in 1658, the duchy was adjudged to Denmark.

"Holstein, however, never acquiesced in this, and in 1675 there was war, when, Holstein being defeated, the Danes imprisoned its duke, Christian Albertus, until he signed a renunciation of all his rights.

"His troops were disarmed, and all his towns and fortresses garrisoned by Danish troops. On his release, the duke went to Hamburg, where he remained till, at the Peace of Fontainebleau, four years later, he was replaced in possession of his estates and rights of sovereignty.

"But this did not last long. New troubles arose, but Sweden, England, and Holland interested themselves in favour of the duke, and a peace was concluded in 1689, by which he was confirmed in the rights given him, ten years before, with full liberty to raise a certain number of troops, and of building fortresses, on the condition that he should raise none to the prejudice of Denmark.

"This was another of those stipulations which inevitably lead to trouble, for it afforded to Denmark a pretext for continual complaint and interference. When Frederick the Fourth succeeded his father as Duke of Holstein, in 1694, the quarrel grew so hot that Denmark would have invaded Holstein, had not the parties to the Treaty of '89 interfered, and brought about a conference. This lasted all through the year 1696, but the negotiators appointed to settle the matter were unable to arrive at any conclusion.

"The following year, Charles of Sweden, who had just succeeded his father, furnished the duke with some troops, to help him to build some forts that were intended to protect the frontier, in case of invasion by Denmark. Christian of Denmark at once attacked and captured these forts, and levelled them to the ground. The duke, being too weak to engage in a war with his powerful neighbour, did not resent this attack, and the negotiations were continued as before. In view of the danger of the situation, and the necessity for a monarch at the head of affairs, the Swedish Diet met, at Stockholm, to take part in the funeral of the late king, which was to be performed on the 24th of November, and to deliberate upon the situation.

"By the will of the late king, Charles was not to ascend the throne until he reached the age of eighteen, but the diet passed a vote overruling this, and, as the regency concurred, he was at once crowned, and the alliance with Holstein was cemented by the marriage, that had been previously arranged between Charles's eldest sister and the Duke of Holstein, being celebrated at Stockholm. Charles the Twelfth at once concluded treaties with France, England, and Holland; while Denmark is reported to have prepared for war by making a secret alliance with Augustus of Saxony, King of Poland, and the Czar of Russia. Both these monarchs were doubtless desirous of extending their dominions, at the cost of Sweden, whose continental possessions are considerable.

"Augustus is not yet very firmly seated on the throne of Poland. There are several parties opposed to him, and these united in obtaining, from the diet, a refusal to pay the Saxon troops Augustus had brought with him. The king, no doubt, considered that these could be employed for the conquest of Livonia, and that the addition of so large a territory to Poland would so add to his popularity, that he would have no further troubles in his kingdom.

"Charles the Twelfth, being in ignorance of this secret agreement, sent an embassy to Russia, to announce his accession to the throne. The ambassadors were kept a long time waiting for an audience, as the czar was bringing a war with the Turks to a conclusion, and did not wish to throw off the mask until he was free to use his whole force against Sweden. The ambassadors were, at last, received civilly, but the czar evaded taking the usual oaths of friendship, and, after long delays, the embassy returned to Sweden, feeling somewhat disquieted as to the intentions of the czar, but having no sure knowledge of them.

"The King of Poland was more successful in disguising his leaning towards Denmark, sending the warmest assurances to Charles, requesting him to act as mediator in the quarrel between himself and the Duke of Brandenburg, and signing a treaty of alliance with Sweden. But, while Sweden had no idea of the triple alliance that had been formed against her, the intention of Denmark to make war was evident enough, for King Christian was gathering a great naval armament.

"The Duke of Holstein, becoming much alarmed at these preparations, hastened on the fortifications of Tonningen, on the Eider, three leagues from its mouth. The garrison of the place was a weak one, and a thousand Swedish troops were thrown in to strengthen it. The King of Denmark complained that this was a breach of the treaty, but, as his own preparations for war were unmistakable, no one could blame the Duke of Holstein for taking steps to defend his territories.

"As you know, Christian of Denmark died about this time, and was succeeded by his son Frederick the Fourth.

"Last August, he commenced the war, by sending a naval squadron to cover the passage of four regiments into Pomerania. Charles of Sweden, seeing that Holstein must be crushed by its powerful neighbour, called upon Holland and the Duke of Lunenburg, who were with Sweden guarantors of the treaty, to enforce its provisions; and a joint protest was sent to the King of Denmark, who was informed that, if he invaded Holstein, they should consider it a breach of the Treaty of Altena, and treat him as a common enemy. Frederick replied by sending some troops into the duchy.

"No active operations took place, until the beginning of this year. Up to that time, Sweden had not doubted the friendship of the King of Poland, and Charles, at first, could hardly believe the reports he received from the governor of Livonia, that the Saxon troops were approaching the frontier.

"A few days later, however, came the news that they were advancing against Riga. The governor prepared for defence, and hastily mounted cannon on the walls. His powers of resistance, however, were lessened by the fact that the river Duna was frozen over. Fleming, who commanded the Saxon troops, arrived before the town, early in February, with four thousand men. The governor had set fire to the suburbs on the previous day; and Fleming was surprised to find that, instead of taking it by surprise, as he had hoped, the place was in a position to offer a stout resistance. However, he attacked the fort of Cobrun, on the opposite side of the river, and carried it by assault.

"The news was brought to young Charles the Twelfth when he was out hunting, a sport of which he is passionately fond. By all accounts, he is an extraordinary young fellow. He is not content with hunting bears and shooting them, but he and his followers engage them armed only with forked sticks. With these they attack the bears, pushing and hustling the great creatures, with the forks of their sticks, until they are completely exhausted, when they are bound and sent away. In this hunt Charles took fourteen alive, one of which nearly killed him before it was captured. He did not break up the hunting party, but continued his sport to the end, sending off, however, orders for the concentration of all the troops, in Livonia and Finland, to act against the Saxons.

"As soon as the King of Denmark heard of the siege of Riga, he ordered the Duke of Wurtemberg-Neustadt, his commander-in-chief, to enter Holstein with his army, sixteen thousand strong. All of that country was at once overrun, the ducal domains seized, and great contributions exacted from Schleswig and Holstein. Fleming and the Saxons, after one severe repulse, forced the garrison of the fort of Dunamund, commanding the mouth of the Duna, to surrender. Tonningen is the only fortress that now holds out in Holstein. So you see, lads, there is every chance of there being brisk fighting, and I warrant the young King of Sweden will not be backward in the fray. A man who is fond of engaging with bears, armed with nothing but a forked stick, is not likely to hang back in the day of battle.

"But, at present, we will say no more on the matter. Now that we have got beyond the shelter of the island, the waves are getting up, and the vessel is beginning to toss and roll. I see that Sir Marmaduke has retired to his cabin. I mean to remain here as long as I can, and I should advise you both to do the same. I have always heard that it is better to fight with this sickness of the sea, as long as possible, and that it is easier to do so in fresh air than in a close cabin."

The lads quite agreed with this opinion, but were, in spite of their efforts, presently prostrate. They remained on deck for some hours, and then crawled to their cabin, where they remained for the next three days, at the end of which time they came on deck again, feeling better, but as weak as if they had suffered from a long illness.

Mr. Jervoise had been in frequently to see them, having escaped the malady, from which, as he told them, Sir Marmaduke was suffering to the full as severely as they were.

"So you have found your feet again," the captain said, when they appeared on deck. "You will be all right now."

"We feel much better," Harry said, "now that the storm is over."

"Storm! What storm? The weather has been splendid. We cannot wish for anything better. It has been just as you see it now--a bright sun, and just enough wind for her to carry whole sail."

The lads both looked astonished.

"Then why should we roll and toss about so much?" Harry asked.

"Roll and toss! Nonsense, lad! There has been a little movement, of course, as there always must be when there is a brisk wind; but as for rolling and tossing, you must wait till you see a storm, then you will begin to have an idea of what the sea is."

The boys both felt rather crestfallen, for they had flattered themselves that their sufferings were caused by something quite out of the ordinary way, and it was mortifying to know that the weather had been really fine, and there had been nothing even approaching a storm.

The rest of the voyage was a pleasant one. They found they had regained their appetites, and were able to enjoy their meals; still they were not sorry when they saw the coast of Sweden, and, a few hours later, entered the port of Gottenburg, where Sir Marmaduke, for the first time, came on deck--looking a mere shadow of his former jovial self.

"Well, lads," he said, "I was glad to hear that you got through this business quicker than I did. Here we are in Sweden, and here I, at least, am likely to stay, unless I can pass by land through Holland, France, and across from Calais, for never again will I venture upon a long voyage. I have been feeling very ungrateful, for, over and over again, I wished that you had not rescued me, as death on Tower Hill would have been nothing to the agonies that I have been enduring!"

As soon as the vessel was warped alongside the quay, they landed, and put up at an hotel, Sir Marmaduke insisting that the ground was as bad as the sea, as it kept on rising and falling beneath his feet. Mr. Jervoise agreed to return on board the following day, to fetch the luggage, which would by that time have been got up from the hold.

At the hotel, they met several persons able to speak English, and from them learnt how matters had been going on since they had last heard. The town and fortress of Tonningen had fallen, after a vigorous defence; it had been bombarded for eight days, and had repulsed one assault, but had been captured at the second attack. England and Holland had agreed to furnish fleets, and an army of twelve thousand

Swedes were in readiness to march, at once, while other armies were being formed. The king had, the week before, reviewed the army gathered at Malmoe; and had, on the previous day, arrived at Gottenburg, accompanied by the Duke of Holstein.

Mr. Jervoise went, the same afternoon, to find out some of his friends who resided at Gottenburg. He was fortunate enough to find one of them, who was able to inform him that his wife's cousin was now a major, in one of the newly-raised regiments stationed at Gottenburg.

He found him without difficulty. Major Jamieson was delighted at the coming of his former friend.

"You are the last person I expected to see here, Jervoise. It is true that, when we met last, you said that if matters went wrong in England you should come out here, instead of taking refuge in France; but, as everything is quiet, I had little hope of seeing you again, until I paid another visit to Scotland, of which at present there is but little prospect. Have you grown tired of doing nothing, and is it a desire to see something of a stirring life that has brought you over here?"

Mr. Jervoise related, shortly, the events by which he had been driven into exile, and expressed his desire to serve in the army of Sweden, and that his son and young Carstairs should also enter the army.

"They are but sixteen yet," he said, "but are stout, active fellows, and could hold their own in a day's march or in a stout fight with many men. Of course, if I could obtain commissions for them, all the better, but if not they are ready to enlist in the ranks. Roughing it will do them no harm."

"Their age is no drawback," Major Jamieson said. "There are many no older, both in the ranks and as officers. Men in Sweden of all ages and of all ranks are joining, for this unprovoked attack, on the part of Poland, has raised the national spirit to boiling heat. The chief difficulty is their and your ignorance of the language. Were it not for that, I could obtain, from the minister of war, commissions for you at once."

He sat thinking for some minutes, in silence.

"I think I see how it can be managed, Jervoise. I have some twenty or thirty Scotchmen in my regiment, and I know a colonel who has as many in his, and these I could manage to get, in exchange for an equal number of my Swedes. Ships are coming daily from Scotland, and most of them bring young fellows who have come out to join the army.

"You know how the Scots fought, under Gustavus Adolphus, and there is scarce a glen in Scotland where there are not traditions of fathers, or grandfathers, who fought in Hepburn's Green Brigade. Therefore, it is natural that, seeing there is no chance of military service at home, there should be many young fellows coming out to join.

"I can go across this evening to the minister of war, who is a personal friend of mine, and get him to give you permission to raise a company of Scotchmen for service. I shall, of course, point out to him that you will enlist them here. I shall show him the advantage of these men being gathered together, as their ignorance of the language makes them, for some time, useless as soldiers if enrolled in a Swedish regiment. I shall mention that I have twenty in my own corps, who are at present positively useless, and in fact a source of great trouble, owing to their understanding nothing that is said to them, and shall propose that they be at once handed over to you. As to the exchange, we can manage that quietly between ourselves. You would have no difficulty with fresh-landed men, as these will naturally be delighted at joining a company of their own countrymen."

"Thank you very heartily, Jamieson. This altogether exceeds my hopes, but I fear that I know nothing of drilling them."

"Two of my men are sergeants, and, having been in the army for some years, speak Swedish well. They will do the drilling at first. The manoeuvres are not complicated, and, for a pound or two, they will be glad to teach you all the orders necessary. I don't know how you are situated as to money, but I can assure you my purse is at your service."

"Thank you; I am, in that respect, excellently well provided, as is my friend Sir Marmaduke. We have both made provision for unexpected contingencies."

"Then, if you will call tomorrow after breakfast, I shall probably have your commission ready. As a matter of course, you will have the appointment of your own officers, and will only have to send in their names. Each company is from a hundred and forty to a hundred and fifty strong, and has a captain, two lieutenants, and two ensigns."

Mr. Jervoise's news was, on his return to the inn, received with delight by the two lads; and Sir Marmaduke said:

"I wish I could shake off twenty of my years, Jervoise, and join also. Well, well, I daresay I shall get on comfortably enough. I know there are a good many English and Scotch Jacobites settled in the town or neighbourhood, and I shall not be long before I meet someone I know.

"As the matter seems settled, I should advise you lads to go down, the first thing in the morning, to the wharves. There is no saying when ships may come in. Moreover, it is likely enough that you may light upon young fellows who have landed within the last few weeks, and who have been kept so far, by their ignorance of the language, from enlisting."

"That is a very good idea," Mr. Jervoise said. "They will be delighted to hear a friendly voice, and be only too glad to enlist in a Scottish company. You can say that each man will have a free outfit given him."

Accordingly, the next morning early, the two lads went down to the wharf. Presently they saw three young fellows, who were evidently Scotch by their dress and caps, talking together. They strolled up near enough to catch what they were saying.

"It is hard," one said, "that, now we are here, we can make no one understand us, and it seems to me we had far better have stayed at home."

"We shall find some one who speaks our language presently, Jock," another said more cheerfully. "The old man, where we lodged last night, said in his broken tongue, that we had but to go over to Malmoe, or some such place as that, where there is a big camp, and walk up to an officer and say we wish to enlist."

"Oh, that is all very well," the other grumbled; "but, if he did not understand us, we should be no better off than before."

"Are you wanting to enlist?" Harry said, going up to them.

The men gave an exclamation of pleasure, at being addressed in their own tongue.

"That we do, sir. If you can put us in the way, we shall be grateful."

"That I can do easily," Harry said. "My father is raising a company of Scotch and Englishmen, for the regiment commanded by Colonel Jamieson. This will be far better than joining a Swedish company, where no one will understand your language, and you will not be able to make out the orders given. My father will give each man who joins a free outfit."

"That is the very thing for us, sir. We expected to find Scotch regiments here, as there were in the old times, and we had hoped to join them; but whether it is a company or regiment, it makes but little difference, so that we are with those who speak our tongue."

"Very well, then. If you come to the Lion Inn, at nine o'clock, you will see my father there. If you know of any others in the same mind as yourselves, and willing to join, bring them with you."

"There are ten or twelve others who came over in the ship with us, two days since, and I have no doubt they will be fine and glad to join."

"Well, see if you can hunt them up, and bring them with you."

On returning to the inn, they found that Mr. Jervoise had already received his commission as captain, and, by ten o'clock, fifteen young Scotchmen had been sworn in. All of them had brought broadswords and dirks, and Captain Jervoise at once set to work buying, at various shops, iron head pieces, muskets, and other accoutrements.

During the next three days ten other English and Scotchmen had joined, and then a ship came in, from which they gathered another four-and-twenty recruits. Arms had already been purchased for them, and, on the following day, Captain Jervoise marched off to Malmoe with his forty-nine recruits. Harry accompanied them, Charlie being left behind, with his father, to gather another fifty men as the ships arrived.

A week later this number was obtained, and Charlie started with them for the camp, Sir Marmaduke accompanying them on horseback, in order to aid Charlie in maintaining order among his recruits. He had already fixed upon a small house, just outside the town, and, having met two or three old friends, who had been obliged to leave England at William's accession, he already began to feel at home.

"Don't you fidget about me, Charlie," he said. "Ferrers tells me that there are at least a score of Jacobites here, and that they form quite a society among themselves. Living is very cheap, and he will introduce me to a man of business, who will see that my money is well invested."

Chapter 5: Narva.

For the next fortnight, drilling went on from morning till night, the officers receiving instructions privately from the sergeants, and further learning the words of command by standing by while the men were being drilled. At the end of that time, both officers and men were sufficiently instructed to carry out the simple movements which were, alone, in use in those days.

It was not, however, until two months later that they were called upon to act. The English and Dutch fleets had arrived, and effected a junction with that of Sweden, and the Danish fleet had shut themselves up in the port of Copenhagen, which was closely blockaded. A large army had crossed to Zeeland, and repulsed the Danes, who had endeavoured to prevent their landing, and had then marched up to within sight of the walls of Copenhagen, which they were preparing to besiege; when the King of Denmark, alarmed at this unexpected result of his aggression on Holstein, conceded every point demanded, and peace was signed.

The negotiations were carried on in Holland, and the Swedes were extremely angry, when they found that they were baulked of their expected vengeance on their troublesome neighbours. The peace, however, left Charles the Twelfth at liberty to turn his attention to his other foes, and to hurry to the assistance of Riga, which was beleaguered by the Saxons and Poles; and of Narva, against which city the Russians had made several unsuccessful assaults.

Without losing an hour, the king crossed to Malmoe. The troops there were ordered to embark, immediately, in the vessels in the harbour. They then sailed to Revel, where the Swedish commander, Welling, had retired from the neighbourhood of Riga, his force being too small to meet the enemy in the open field.

No sooner had the troops landed than the king reviewed them, and General Welling was ordered, at once, to march so as to place himself between the enemy and Wesenberg, where a large amount of provisions and stores for the use of the army had been collected.

The two lieutenants, in the company of Captain Jervoise, were young Scotchmen of good family, who had three months before come over and obtained commissions, and both had, at the colonel's request, been transferred to his regiment, and promoted to the rank of lieutenants. Captain Jervoise and his four officers messed together, and were a very cheerful party; indeed, their commander, to the surprise both of his son and Charlie, had quite shaken off his quiet and somewhat gloomy manner, and seemed to have become quite another man, in the active and bracing life in which he was now embarked. Cunningham and Forbes were both active young men, full of life and energy, while the boys thoroughly enjoyed roughing it, and the excitement and animation of their daily work.

Sometimes they slept in the open air, sometimes on the floor of a cottage. Their meals were rough but plentiful. The king's orders against plundering were very severe, and, even when in Denmark, the country people, having nothing to complain of, had brought in supplies regularly. Here in Linovia they were in Swedish dominions, but there was little to be purchased, for the peasantry had been brought to ruin by the foraging parties of the Russians and Poles.

There was some disappointment, that the enemy had fallen back at the approach of Welling's force, but all felt sure that it would not be long before they met them, for the king would assuredly lose no time in advancing against them, as soon as his army could be brought over. They were not, however, to wait for the arrival of the main force, although the cavalry only took part in the first affair. General Welling heard that a force of three thousand Circassians had taken up their quarters in a village, some fifteen miles away, and sent six hundred horse, under Majors Patkul and Tisenbausen, to surprise them. They were, at first, successful and, attacking the Circassians, set fire to the village, and were engaged in slaughtering the defenders, when twenty-one squadrons of Russian cavalry came up and fell upon them, attacking them on all sides, and posting themselves so as to cut off their retreat. The Swedes, however, gathered in a body, and charged the Russians so furiously that they cut a way through their ranks, losing, however, many of their men, while Major Patkul and another officer were made prisoners.

The king was at Revel when this engagement took place, and, although but few of the troops had arrived, he was too impatient for action to wait until the coming of the fleet. He therefore marched to Wesenberg, with his bodyguard and a few troops from Revel. He at once despatched a thousand men, to cover the frontier, and issued orders for the rest of the troops to leave the whole of their baggage behind them, to take three days' provision in their haversacks, and to prepare to march the next morning.

Major Jamieson came into the cottage, occupied by Captain Jervoise and his officers, late in the evening. They had a blazing fire, for it was now the middle of November, and the nights were very sharp.

"Well, Jervoise, what do you think of the orders?" he asked, as he seated himself on a log that had been brought in for the fire.

"I have not thought much about them, except that we are going to do a long and quick march somewhere."

"And where is that somewhere, do you think?"

"That, I have not the slightest idea."

"You would not say that it was to Narva?"

"I certainly should not, considering that we have but five thousand infantry, and three thousand cavalry, and of these a large number have been so weakened, by fever, as to be unfit for fighting; while at Narva, report says there are eighty thousand Russians, in a strongly intrenched camp."

"Well, that is where we are going, Jervoise, nevertheless. At least, that is what the colonel has told me."

"He must have been surely jesting, major. We may be going to push forward in that direction, and occupy some strong position until the army comes up, but it would be the height of madness to attack an enemy, in a strong position, and just tenfold our force."

"Well, we shall see," Jamieson said coolly. "It is certain that Narva cannot hold out much longer, and I know that the king has set his heart on relieving it; but it does seem somewhat too dangerous an enterprise to attack the Russians. At any rate, that is the direction in which we are going, tomorrow. It is a good seventy miles distant, and, as they say that the whole country has been devastated, and the villagers have all fled, it is evident that when the three days' bread and meat we carry are exhausted we shall have to get some food, out of the Russian camp, if nowhere else."

Captain Jervoise laughed, as did the others.

"We can live for a short time on the horses, Jamieson, if we are hard pushed for it, though most of them are little beyond skin and bone."

"That is true. The cavalry are certainly scarcely fit for service. Welling's troops have had a very hard time of it, and we may thank our stars, though we did not think so at the time, that we were kept nearly three months at Malmoe, instead of being here with Welling."

"But do you seriously think, major, that the king means to attack the Russians?" Cunningham asked.

"My own idea is that he does, Cunningham. I cannot see what else there is for us to do. At any rate, if he does, you may be sure that we shall make a tough fight for it. The cavalry showed, the other day, that they can stand up against many times their number of the Russians, and if they can do it, I fancy we can. There is one thing, the very audacity of such an attempt is in its favour."

"Well, we will all do our best, you may be sure; but since Thermopylae, I doubt if men have fought against longer odds."

The next morning the men fell in. Captain Jervoise, who, like all of his rank, was mounted, took his place at the head of his company, and the little army marched away from Wesenberg. It was a dreary march to Purts, but the sight of the ruined villages, and devastated fields, aroused a feeling of indignation and fury among the troops, and a fierce longing to attack men who had so ruthlessly spread ruin through a fertile country. Orders were issued, that evening, that the men were to husband their provisions as much as possible, and the order was more strictly obeyed than such orders usually are, for the men saw, for themselves, that there was no possibility of obtaining fresh supplies in the wasted country, and were well aware that there existed no train of waggons and horses capable of bringing up stores from Wesenberg.

There were a few aged men and women remaining at Purts, and from these they learned that their next day's march would take them to a very difficult pass, which was held by six hundred of the Russian cavalry, together with a force of infantry and some guns. It was the intention of the king to encamp that evening near the pass, and, when within three or four miles of it, General Meidel, who had with him the quartermaster of the army, and four hundred cavalry, rode on ahead to choose a site for the camp. He presently saw a large body of Russian foragers in front of him, and sent back to the king for permission to attack them. Charles ordered the army to continue its march, and, hurrying forward with some of his officers, joined General Meidel and charged the foragers, killing many, taking others prisoners, and putting the rest to flight. He followed close upon their heels, and rode right up to the mouth of the pass, in spite of the heavy fire of artillery and musketry opened by the Russians.

He at once determined to take advantage of the alarm produced by the defeat of the Russian cavalry, and, although darkness was now drawing on, brought up some of his infantry and artillery, and attacked with such vigour that the Russians fled, after offering a very feeble resistance.

A battalion of foot were ordered to occupy the pass, while the rest of the army piled their arms, and lay down where they stood. In the morning, they were astonished at the strength of the position that had been gained so easily. The defile was deep and narrow, a rapid stream ran through it, and the ground was soft and marshy. A few determined men should have been able to bar the advance of an army.

The troops were in high spirits at the result of this, their first action against the enemy, and were the more pleased that they found, in the Russian camp, sufficient provisions to replace those they had used. After a hearty meal, they again advanced at a brisk march. The defile was captured on the evening of the 17th November, and, early in the morning of the 20th, the army reached Lagena, a league and a half from Narva, and, ordering the troops to follow, the king rode forward to reconnoitre the Russian position.

The troops were weary with their long marches, and many of those who had, but recently, recovered from fever were scarce able to drag themselves along, while great numbers were unfit to take part in a battle, until after two or three days of rest. The officers of the Malmoe Regiment, for it had taken its name from the camp where it had been formed, were gathered in a group at its head, discussing the situation. Most of the officers were of opinion that, to attack at once, with men and horses worn out with fatigue, was to ensure destruction; but there were others who thought that, in face of so great an army as that gathered in front of them, the only hope was in an immediate attack. Major Jamieson was one of these.

"The king is right," he said. "If the Russian army have time to form, and to advance against us in order of battle, we must be annihilated. At present, their camp is an extensive one, for, as I hear, it extends in a great semi-circle four or five miles long, with the ends resting on the river. They cannot believe that we intend to attack them, and, if we go straight at them, we may possibly gain a footing in their intrenchments, before the whole army can gather to aid those at the point of attack. It will be almost a surprise, and I think the king is right to attempt it, for it is only by a quick and sudden stroke that we can gain a success over so great an army."

The halt was but a short one and, as soon as the regiments had arrived at the positions assigned to them, they advanced. As soon as they appeared, on a rise of ground facing the intrenchments, the enemy opened fire. The king had already reconnoitred a portion of their position, exposing himself recklessly to their shot, and, as soon as the troops came up, he issued orders for them to prepare to attack in two columns. First, however, several of the regiments were ordered to fall out, and to cut down bushes and make fascines, to enable the troops to cross the ditches.

The intrenchment was a formidable one, being provided with parapets armed with chevaux de frise, and flanked by strong exterior works, while several batteries had been placed to sweep the ground across which an enemy must advance.

The right column, under General Welling, was to march to a point nearly in the centre of the great semicircle; while the left, under General Rhenschild, was to assault a point about halfway between the centre and the river, where one of the largest and most powerful of the enemy's batteries was placed. The king himself was with this wing, with his bodyguard, and he hoped that here he might meet the czar commanding in person. The Russian emperor had, however, left the camp that morning, to fetch up forty thousand men who were advancing from Plescow, and the command of the army had been assumed by the Duke of Croy.

The Swedish left wing had with it a battery of twenty-one guns, while sixteen guns covered the attack on the right. It was two o'clock in the afternoon when two guns gave the signal for the advance. Hitherto the weather had been fine, but it had become gradually overcast, and, just as the signal was given, a tremendous storm of snow and hail began. It set right in the face of the Russians, and concealed from them the movement of the Swedes, for which, indeed, they were wholly unprepared, believing that the small force they saw was but the advance guard of a great Swedish army, and that no attack need be expected until the main body arrived.

The consequence was, the Swedes were almost at the edge of the ditch before they were perceived, and both columns attacked with such vigour and courage that, in a quarter of an hour, they had gained a footing in the intrenchments, and had so filled up the ditch with the fascines that the cavalry were able to follow them.

The Russians were so astounded at this sudden attack that they lost heart altogether. The Swedish left, as soon as it entered the intrenchments, swept along them, the Russians abandoning their guns and batteries, and making for their bridge across the river. Unfortunately for them, their huts were built close behind the works, and in rear was another intrenchment, designed to repel assaults from the town; and the terrified crowd, unable to make their way rapidly along, over ground encumbered by their huts, crossed the interior intrenchments, thinking to make their way faster through the fields to the bridge.

The Swedish king, however, placed himself at the head of his bodyguard, and, followed by the rest of his horse, charged right upon them, cutting down great numbers, and driving the rest before them towards the river, while the infantry kept up a heavy fire upon the fugitives in the intrenchments.

The panic had spread quickly, and the Russian troops nearest to the bridge were already pouring over, when the mass of the fugitives arrived. These pressed upon the bridge in such numbers that it speedily gave way, cutting off the retreat of their comrades behind. Ignorant of the result, the terrified crowd pushed on, pressing those in front of them into the river, and the number of drowned was no less than that of those who fell beneath the bullets, pikes, and sabres of the Swedes.

In their despair the Russians, rallied by some of their generals, now attempted to defend themselves, and, by occupying some houses and barracks, and barricading the passages between these with overturned waggons, they fought bravely, and repulsed, for some time, every effort of the Swedes.

Darkness was now falling, and the king hastened to the spot where the battle was fiercely raging. As he ran towards it, he fell into a morass, from which he was rescued with some difficulty, leaving his sword and one boot behind him. However, he at once pushed on, and placed himself at the head of the infantry engaged in the assault. But even his presence and example did not avail. The Russians maintained their position with desperate courage, and, when it became quite dark, the assault ceased.

The right column had met with equal success. It had penetrated the intrench-ments, defeated all the Russians who opposed it, and now moved to assist the left wing.

The king, however, seeing that the Russian defences could not be carried, by a direct assault, without great loss, gathered the army in the space between the town and the Russian intrenchments, and placed them in a position to repel an attack, should the Russians take the offensive; giving orders that, at daylight, the hill on which the enemy had their principal battery should be assaulted. The guns here commanded all the intrenchments, and the capture of that position would render it impossible for the Russians to continue their defence, or for the now separated wings of the army to combine.

The officers in command of the Russian right wing, finding themselves unable to cross the river on their broken bridge, and surrounded by the Swedes, sent in to surrender in the course of the evening, and two battalions of the Swedish Guards took possession of the post that had been so gallantly defended. The king granted them permission to retire with their arms, the colours and standards being given up, and the superior officers being retained as prisoners of war.

The broken bridge was repaired and, early the next morning, the Russian troops passed over. Their left wing was, after the surrender of their right, in a hope-less position, for on that side no bridge had been thrown over the river, and their retreat was wholly cut off. On learning, before daybreak, that the right wing had surrendered, they too sent in to ask for terms. The king granted them freedom to return to their country, but without their standards or arms. They filed off before him, officers and soldiers bareheaded, and passed over the bridge, their numbers being so great that all had not crossed until next morning.

The Russians lost over 18,000 men killed or drowned, a hundred and forty-five cannon, and twenty-eight mortars, all of which were new, besides vast quanti-ties of military stores and provisions. A hundred and fifty-one colours, and twenty standards, and the greater proportion of their muskets, together with the military chest, the Duke of Croy, their commander-in-chief, and the whole of their gener-als, colonels, majors, and captains, fell into the hands of the Swedes, as prisoners of war. The total loss in killed and wounded of the Swedes was under two thousand, the chief loss being due to the desperate resistance of the Russians, after the battle was irretrievably lost. It may be doubted whether so complete and surprising a victory, between armies so disproportionate in force, was ever before gained.

The king had exposed himself, throughout the day, most recklessly, and was everywhere in the thick of the Russian bullets, and yet he escaped without so much as a scratch. The Malmoe Regiment had been with the left wing, but suffered comparatively little loss, as they were one of the last to enter the intrenchments, and it was only when darkness was closing in that they were called up to take a part in the attack on the position held by the Russians.

"Never was the saying, that fortune favours the brave, more signally verified, Jervoise," Major Jamieson said, as he sat down to a rough breakfast with the officers of the Scottish company, on the morning after the Russian surrender.

"That's true enough, but Russians are brave, too, as they showed at the end of the day. I fancy you have a scotch proverb to the effect that 'fou folk come to no harm.' I think that is more applicable in the present case."

The major laughed.

"The fou folk relates rather to drunkenness than madness, Jervoise. But, of course, it would do for both. I own that the whole enterprise did seem, to me, to be absolute madness, but the result has justified it. That sudden snowstorm was the real cause of our victory, and, had it not been for that, I still think that we could not have succeeded. The Russian cannon certainly continued to fire, but it was wholly at random, and they were taken by surprise when we suddenly appeared at the side of the ditch, while we were across before they could gather any force sufficient to defend it.

"After that, panic did the rest. The commander in chief fell early into our hands. There was no one to give orders, no one to rally them, and I expect the Russian soldiers gave us credit for having brought on that storm, to cover our assault, by the aid of malign spirits.

"Well, lads, and how did you feel when the shots were whistling about?"

"I did not like it at all, major," Charlie said. "It seemed such a strange thing, marching along in the thick of that snowstorm, hearing the rush of cannonballs overhead, and the boom of guns, and yet be unable to see anything but the rear files of the company in front."

"It was an uncanny feeling, Charlie. I felt it myself, and was very grateful that we were hidden from the enemy, who, of course, were blazing away in the direction in which they had last seen us. We only lost three killed and twelve wounded, altogether, and I think those were, for the most part, hit by random shots.

"Well, if this is the way the king means to carry on war, we shall have enough of it before we are done."

The sick and wounded were sent into the town, the first thing, but it was not until the Russians had all crossed the river that the king, himself, rode triumphantly into the place, surrounded by his staff, amid the wild enthusiasm of the inhabitants, whom his victory had saved from ruin and massacre.

The town, although strongly fortified, was not a large one, and its houses were so dilapidated, from the effects of the Russian bombardment, that but few of the troops could be accommodated there. The rest were quartered in the Russian huts. On the 26th, a solemn service of thanksgiving for the victory was celebrated, with a salute from all the cannon of the town and camp, and by salvos of musketry from the troops.

The question of provisions was the most important now. It was true that large quantities had been captured in the Russian camp, but, beyond a magazine of corn, abandoned by the fugitives at Tama and brought in, there was no prospect of replenishing the store when exhausted, for the whole country, for a great distance round, had been completely devastated by the Russians. These had not retreated far, having been rallied by the czar at Plescow, and quartered in the towns of the frontier of Livonia, whence they made incursions into such districts as had not been previously wasted.

"This is dull work," Archie Cunningham said, one day. "The sooner we are busy again, the better. There is nothing to do, and very little to eat. The cold is bitter, and fuel scarce. One wants something to warm one's blood."

"You are not likely to have anything of that kind, for some months to come," Major Jamieson replied dryly. "You don't suppose we are going to have a battle of Narva once a week, do you? No doubt there will be a few skirmishes, and outpost encounters, but beyond that there will be little doing until next spring. You can make up your mind, for at least five months, of the worst side of a soldier's life--dull quarters, and probably bad ones, scanty food, cold, and disease."

"Not a very bright lookout, major," Forbes laughed. "I hope it won't be as bad as that."

"Then I advise you to give up hoping, and to make up your mind to realities, Forbes. There is a good deal of illness in the camp now, and there will be more and more as the time goes on. There is nothing like inaction to tell upon the health of troops. However, we certainly shall not stay here. It would be impossible to victual the army, and I expect that, before long, we shall march away and take up quarters for the winter.

"As to operations on a great scale, they are out of the question. After the thrashing they have had, the Russians will be months before they are in a condition to take the offensive again; while we are equally unable to move because, in the first place, we are not strong enough to do so, and in the second we have no baggage train to carry provisions with us, and no provisions to carry if we had it."

On the 13th of December, the king quitted Narva with the army, and on the 19th arrived at Lais, an old castle six miles from Derpt, and here established his headquarters. A few of the troops were stationed in villages, but the greater part in rough huts in the neighbourhood, and along the frontier.

It was not long before Major Jamieson's predictions were verified. A low fever, occasioned by the fatiguing marches and the hardships they had endured, added to the misery from the cold and wet that penetrated the wretched huts, spread rapidly through the army. Many died, and great numbers were absolutely prostrated.

The king was indefatigable in his efforts to keep up the spirits of the troops. He constantly rode about from camp to camp, entering the huts, chatting cheerfully with the soldiers, and encouraging them by kind words and assurances that, when the spring came, they would soon gain strength again.

At Narva the four young officers had all purchased horses. Most of the Swedish officers were mounted; and the king encouraged this, as, on occasion, he could thereby collect at once a body of mounted men ready for any enterprise; but their own colonel preferred that, on the march, the lieutenants and ensigns should be on foot with their men, in order to set them an example of cheerful endurance. Those who wished it, however, were permitted to have horses, which were, on such occasions, led in the rear of the regiment.

Captain Jervoise had approved of the purchase of the horses, which were got very cheaply, as great numbers had been captured.

"If we can get over the difficulty of the forage," he said, "you will find them very useful for preserving your health during the winter. A ride will set your blood in motion, and, wherever we are quartered, there are sure to be camps within riding distance. The king approves of officers taking part in dashing expeditions, so you may be able to take a share in affairs that will break the monotony of camp life."

They found great benefit from being able to ride about. Forage was indeed very scarce. They had no means of spending their pay on luxuries of any kind, their only outlay being in the purchase of black bread, and an occasional load of forage from the peasants. Their regiment was with the force under the command of Colonel Schlippenbach, which was not very far from Marienburg, a place open to the incursions of the Russians. Baron Spens was at Signiz, and Colonel Alvedyhl at Rounenberg, and to both these places they occasionally paid a visit.

In order to keep the company in health, Captain Jervoise encouraged the men to get up games, in which the four young officers took part. Sometimes it was a snowball match in the open; at other times a snow fort was built, garrisoned, and attacked. Occasionally there were matches at hockey, while putting the stone, throwing the caber, running and wrestling matches, were all tried in turn; and the company suffered comparatively little from the illness which rendered so large a proportion of the Swedish army inefficient.

Colonel Schlippenbach was an energetic officer, and had, several times, ridden past when the men were engaged in these exercises. He expressed to Captain Jervoise his approval of the manner in which he kept his men in strength and vigour.

"I shall not forget it," he said, one day, "and if there is service to be done, I see that I can depend upon your company to do it."

In January, he took a party of horse, and reconnoitred along the River Aa, to observe the motions of the Saxons on the other side; and, hearing that a party of them had entered Marienburg, he determined to take possession of that place, as, were they to fortify it, they would be able greatly to harass the Swedes. Sending word to the king of his intention, and asking for an approval of his plan of fortifying the town, he took three companies of infantry and four hundred horse, made a rapid march to Marienburg, and occupied it without opposition.

He had not forgotten his promise, and the company of Captain Jervoise was one of those selected for the work. Its officers were delighted at the prospect of a change, and, when the party started, Captain Jervoise was proud of the show made by his men, whose active and vigorous condition contrasted strongly with the debility and feebleness evident, so generally, among the Swedish soldiers.

As soon as Marienburg was entered, the men were set to work, to raise and strengthen the rampart and to erect bastions; and they were aided, a few days later, by a reinforcement of two hundred infantry, sent by the king, with some cannon, from the garrison of Derpt. As the place was surrounded by a morass, it was, ere long, put into a position to offer a formidable defence against any force that the Russians or Saxons might bring against it.

The Swedes engaged on the work gained strength rapidly, and, by the time the fortifications were finished, they had completely shaken off the effects of the fever.

Chapter 6: A Prisoner.

A fortnight after the fortifications of Marienburg were completed, Colonel Schlippenbach sent off Lieutenant Colonel Brandt, with four hundred horse, to capture a magazine at Seffwegen, to which the Saxons had forced the inhabitants of the country round to bring in their corn, intending later to convey it to the headquarters of their army. The expedition was completely successful. The Saxon guard were overpowered, and a thousand tons of corn were brought, in triumph, into Marienburg. Some of it was sent on to the army, abundance being retained for the use of the town and garrison, in case of siege.

It was now resolved to surprise and burn Pitschur, a town on the frontier from which the enemy constantly made incursions. It was held by a strong body of Russians.

Baron Spens was in command of the expedition. He had with him both the regiments of Horse Guards. Much excitement was caused, in Marienburg, by the issue of an order that the cavalry, and a portion of the infantry, were to be ready to march at daylight; and by the arrival of a large number of peasants, brought in by small parties of the cavalry. Many were the surmises as to the operation to be undertaken, its object being kept a strict secret.

Captain Jervoise's company was one of those in orders, and paraded at daybreak, and, after a march of some distance, the force joined that of Baron Spens. The troops were halted in a wood, and ordered to light fires to cook food, and to prepare for a halt of some hours. Great fires were soon blazing and, after eating their meal, most of the troops wrapped themselves in the blankets that they carried, in addition to their greatcoats, and lay down by the fires.

They slept until midnight, and were then called to arms again. They marched all night, and at daybreak the next morning, the 13th of February, were near Pitschur, and at once attacked the Russian camp outside the town. Taken completely by surprise, the Russians fought feebly, and more than five hundred were killed before they entered the town, hotly pursued by the Swedes. Shutting themselves up in the houses, and barricading the doors and windows, they defended themselves desperately, refusing all offers of surrender.

The Livonian peasants were, however, at work, and set fire to the town in many places. The flames spread rapidly. Great stores of hides and leather, and a huge magazine filled with hemp, added to the fury of the conflagration, and the whole town was burned to the ground; numbers of the Russians preferring death by fire, in the houses, to coming out and surrendering themselves.

Many of the fugitives had succeeded in reaching a strong position on the hill commanding the town. This consisted of a convent, surrounded by strong walls mounted with cannon, which played upon the town while the fight there was going on. As Baron Spens had no guns with him, he was unable to follow up his advantage by taking this position, and he therefore gave orders to the force to retire, the peasants being loaded with booty that they had gathered before the fire spread.

The loss of the Swedes was thirty killed and sixty wounded, this being a small amount of loss compared with what they had inflicted upon the enemy.

"I call that a horrible business, Captain Jervoise," Charlie said, when the troops had returned to Marienburg. "There was no real fighting in it."

"It was a surprise, Charlie. But they fought desperately after they gained the town."

"Yes, but we did nothing there beyond firing away at the windows. Of course, I had my sword in my hand; but it might as well have been in its sheath, for I never struck a blow, and I think it was the same with most of our men. One could not cut down those poor wretches, who were scarce awake enough to use their arms. I was glad you held our company in rear of the others."

"Yes; I asked the colonel before attacking to put us in reserve, in case the enemy should rally. I did it on purpose, for I knew that our men, not having, like the Swedes, any personal animosity against the Russians, would not like the work. If it had come to storming the convent, I would have volunteered to lead the assault. At any rate, I am glad that, although a few of the men are wounded, no lives are lost in our company."

Harry cordially agreed with his friend. "I like an expedition, Charlie, if there is fighting to be done; but I don't want to have anything more to do with surprises. However, the cavalry had a good deal more to do with it than we had; but, as you say, it was a ghastly business. The only comfort is they began it, and have been robbing the peasants and destroying their homes for months."

Many small expeditions were sent out with equally favourable results; but Captain Jervoise's company took no part in these excursions.

Charles the Twelfth was passionately fond of hunting and, in spite of his many occupations, found time occasionally to spend a day or two in the chase. A few days after the attack upon Pitschur, he came to Marienburg to learn all particulars of the Russian position from Colonel Schlippenbach, as he intended, in the spring, to attack the triangle formed by three fortresses, in order to drive the Russians farther back from the frontier.

"I hear that there are many wolves and bears in the forest, five leagues to the north. I want a party of about fifty footmen to drive the game, and as many horse, in case we come across one of the parties of Russians. I want some hearty, active men for the march. I will send the foot on this afternoon, and ride with the horse so as to get there by daybreak. Which is your best company of infantry?"

"My best company is one composed chiefly of Scotchmen, though there are some English among them. It belongs to the Malmoe Regiment, and is commanded by Captain Jervoise, an Englishman. I do not say that they are braver than our Swedes; they have not been tested in any desperate service; but they are healthier and more hardy, for their officers, since the battle of Narva, have kept them engaged in sports of all kinds--mimic battles, foot races, and other friendly contests. I have marked them at it several times, and wondered sometimes at the rough play. But it has had its effect. While the rest of Suborn's regiment suffered as much from fever as the other troops, scarce a man in this company was sick, and they have, all the winter, been fit for arduous service at any moment."

"That is good indeed, and I will remember it, and will see that, another winter, similar games are carried on throughout the army. Let the company be paraded at once. I will, myself, inspect them."

The company's call was sounded, and, surprised at a summons just as they were cooking their dinners, the troops fell in, in front of their quarters, and the officers took their places in front of them, and waited for orders.

"I wonder what is up now," Nigel Forbes said to Harry. "You have not heard anything, from your father, of our being wanted, have you?"

"No; he was just as much surprised as I was, when a sergeant ran up with Schlippenbach's order that the company were to fall in."

Five minutes after they had formed up, three officers were seen approaching on foot.

"It is the colonel himself," Forbes muttered, as Captain Jervoise gave the word to the men to stand to attention.

A minute later, Captain Jervoise gave the order for the salute, and Harry saw that the tall young officer, walking with the colonel, was the king. Without speaking a word, Charles walked up and down the line, narrowly inspecting the men, then he returned to the front.

"A fine set of fellows, Schlippenbach. I wish that, like my grandfather, I had some fifteen thousand of such troops under my orders. Present the captain to me."

The officers were called up, and Captain Jervoise was presented.

"Your company does you great credit, Captain Jervoise," the king said. "I would that all my troops looked in as good health and condition. Colonel Schlippenbach tells me that you have kept your men in good health, all through the winter, by means of sports and games. It is a good plan. I will try to get all my officers to adopt it another winter. Do the men join in them willingly?"

Captain Jervoise and his officers had all, during the nine months that had passed since they landed in Sweden, done their best to acquire the language, and could now speak and understand it thoroughly.

"They like it, your majesty. Our people are fond of games of this kind. My four officers take part in them with the men."

The king nodded.

"That is as it should be. It must create a good feeling on both sides. Present your officers to me, Captain Jervoise."

This was done, and the king spoke a few words to each. Charlie had often seen the king at a distance, but never before so close as to be able to notice his face particularly. He was a tall young fellow, thin and bony. His face was long, and his forehead singularly high and somewhat projecting. This was the most noticeable feature of his face. His eyes were quick and keen, his face clean-shaven, and, had it not been for the forehead and eyes, would have attracted no attention. His movements were quick and energetic, and, after speaking to the officers, he strode a step or two forward and, raising his voice, said:

"I am pleased with you, men. Your appearance does credit to yourselves and your officers. Scottish troops did grand service under my grandfather, Gustavus Adolphus, and I would that I had twenty battalions of such soldiers with me. I am going hunting tomorrow, and I asked Colonel Schlippenbach for half a company of men who could stand cold and fatigue. He told me that I could not do better than take them from among this company, and I see that he could not have made a better choice. But I will not separate you, and will therefore take you all. You will march in an hour, and I will see that there is a good supper ready for you, at the end of your journey."

Colonel Schlippenbach gave Captain Jervoise directions as to the road they were to follow, and the village, at the edge of the forest, where they were to halt for the night. He then walked away with the king. Highly pleased with the praise Charles had given them, the company fell out.

"Get your dinners as soon as you can, men," Captain Jervoise said. "The king gave us an hour. We must be in readiness to march by that time."

On arriving at the village, which consisted of a few small houses only, they found two waggons awaiting them, one with tents and the other with a plentiful supply of provisions, and a barrel of wine. The tents were erected, and then the men went into the forest, and soon returned with large quantities of wood, and great fires were speedily lighted. Meat was cut up and roasted over them, and, regarding the expedition as a holiday, the men sat down to their supper in high spirits.

After it was eaten there were songs round the fires, and, at nine o'clock, all turned into their tents, as it was known that the king would arrive at daylight. Sentries were posted, for there was never any saying when marauding parties of Russians, who were constantly on the move, might come along.

Half an hour before daybreak, the men were aroused. Tents were struck and packed in the waggon, and the men then fell in, and remained until the king, with three or four of his officers and fifty cavalry, rode up. Fresh wood had been thrown on the fires, and some of the men told off as cooks.

"That looks cheerful for hungry men," the king said, as he leaped from his horse.

"I did not know whether your majesty would wish to breakfast at once," Captain Jervoise said; "but I thought it well to be prepared."

"We will breakfast by all means. We are all sharp set already. Have your own men had food yet?"

"No, sir. I thought perhaps they would carry it with them."

"No, no. Let them all have a hearty meal before they move, then they can hold on as long as may be necessary."

The company fell out again, and, in a quarter of an hour, they and the troopers breakfasted. A joint of meat was placed, for the use of the king and the officers who had come with him, and Captain Jervoise and those with him prepared to take their meal a short distance away, but Charles said:

"Bring that joint here, Captain Jervoise, and we will all take breakfast together. We are all hunters and comrades."

In a short time, they were all seated round a fire, with their meat on wooden platters on their knees, and with mugs of wine beside them; Captain Jervoise, by the king's orders, taking his seat beside him. During the meal, he asked him many questions as to his reasons for leaving England, and taking service with him.

"So you have meddled in politics, eh?" the king laughed, when he heard a brief account of Captain Jervoise's reason for leaving home. "Your quarrels, in England and Scotland, have added many a thousand good soldiers to the armies of France and Sweden, and, I may say, of every country in Europe. I believe there are some of your compatriots, or at any rate Scotchmen, in the czar's camp. I suppose that, at William's death, these troubles will cease."

"I do not know, sir. Anne was James' favourite daughter, and it may be she will resign in favour of her brother, the lawful king. If she does so, there is an end of trouble; but, should she mount the throne, she would be a usurper, as Mary was up to her death in '94. As Anne has been on good terms with William, since her sister's death, I fear she will act as unnatural a part as Mary did, and, in that case, assuredly we shall not recognize her as our queen."

"You have heard the news, I suppose, of the action of the parliament last month?"

"No, sir, we have heard nothing for some weeks of what is doing in England."

"They have been making an Act of Settlement of the succession. Anne is to succeed William, and, as she has no children by George of Denmark, the succession is to pass from her to the Elector of Hanover, in right of his wife Sophia, as the rest of the children of the Elector of the Palatinate have abjured Protestantism, and are therefore excluded. How will that meet the views of the English and Scotch Jacobites?"

"It is some distance to look forward to, sire. If Anne comes to the throne at William's death, it will, I think, postpone our hopes, for Anne is a Stuart, and is a favourite with the nation, in spite of her undutiful conduct to her father. Still, it will be felt that for Stuart to fight against Stuart, brother against sister, would be contrary to nature. Foreigners are always unpopular, and, as against William, every Jacobite is ready to take up arms. But I think that nothing will be done during Anne's reign. The Elector of Hanover would be as unpopular, among Englishmen in general, as is William of Orange, and, should he come to the throne, there will assuredly ere long be a rising to bring back the Stuarts."

Charles shook his head.

"I don't want to ruffle your spirit of loyalty to the Stuarts, Captain Jervoise, but they have showed themselves weak monarchs for a great country. They want fibre. William of Orange may be, as you call him, a foreigner and a usurper, but England has greater weight in the councils of Europe, in his hands, than it has had since the death of Elizabeth."

This was rather a sore point with Captain Jervoise, who, thorough Jacobite as he was, had smarted under the subservience of England to France during the reigns of the two previous monarchs.

"You Englishmen and Scotchmen are fighting people," the king went on, "and should have a military monarch. I do not mean a king like myself, who likes to fight in the front ranks of his soldiers; but one like William, who has certainly lofty aims, and is a statesman, and can join in European combinations."

"William thinks and plans more for Holland than for England, sire. He would join a league against France and Spain, not so much for the benefit of England, which has not much to fear from these powers, but of Holland, whose existence now, as of old is threatened by them."

"England's interest is similar to that of Holland," the king said. "I began this war, nominally, in the interest of the Duke of Holstein, but really because it was Sweden's interest that Denmark should not become too powerful.

"But we must not waste time in talking politics. I see the men have finished their breakfast, and we are here to hunt. I shall keep twenty horse with me; the rest will enter the forest with you. I have arranged for the peasants here to guide you. You will march two miles along by the edge of the forest, and then enter it and make a wide semicircle, leaving men as you go, until you come down to the edge of the forest again, a mile to our left.

"As soon as you do so, you will sound a trumpet, and the men will then move forward, shouting so as to drive the game before them. As the peasants tell me there are many wolves and bears in the forest, I hope that you will inclose some of them in your cordon, which will be about five miles from end to end. With the horse you will have a hundred and thirty men, so that there will be a man every sixty or seventy yards. That is too wide a space at first, but, as you close in, the distances will rapidly lessen, and they must make up, by noise, for the scantiness of their numbers. If they find the animals are trying to break through, they can discharge their pieces; but do not let them do so otherwise, as it would frighten the animals too soon, and send them flying out all along the open side of the semicircle."

It was more than two hours before the whole of the beaters were in position. Just before they had started, the king had requested Captain Jervoise to remain with him and the officers who had accompanied him, five in number. They had been posted, a hundred yards apart, at the edge of the forest. Charlie was the first officer left behind as the troop moved through the forest, and it seemed to him an endless time before he heard a faint shout, followed by another and another, until, at last, the man stationed next to him repeated the signal. Then they moved forward, each trying to obey the orders to march straight ahead.

For some time, nothing was heard save the shouts of the men, and then Charlie made out some distant shots, far in the wood, and guessed that some animals were trying to break through the lines. Then he heard the sound of firing directly in front of him. This continued for some time, occasionally single shots being heard, but more often shots in close succession. Louder and louder grew the shouting, as the men closed in towards a common point, and, in half an hour after the signal had been given, all met.

"What sport have you had, father?" Harry asked, as he came up to Captain Jervoise.

"We killed seventeen wolves and four bears, with, what is more important, six stags. I do not know whether we are going to have another beat."

It soon turned out that this was the king's intention, and the troops marched along the edge of the forest. Charlie was in the front of his company, the king with the cavalry a few hundred yards ahead, when, from a dip of ground on the right, a large body of horsemen suddenly appeared.

"Russians!" Captain Jervoise exclaimed, and shouted to the men, who were marching at ease, to close up.

The king did not hesitate a moment, but, at the head of his fifty cavalry, charged right down upon the Russians, who were at least five hundred strong. The little body disappeared in the melee, and then seemed to be swallowed up.

"Keep together, shoulder to shoulder, men. Double!" and the company set off at a run.

When they came close to the mass of horsemen, they poured in a volley, and then rushed forward, hastily fitting the short pikes they carried into their musket barrels; for, as yet, the modern form of bayonets was not used. The Russians fought obstinately, but the infantry pressed their way step by step through them, until they reached the spot where the king, with his little troop of cavalry, were defending themselves desperately from the attacks of the Russians.

The arrival of the infantry decided the contest, and the Russians began to draw off, the king hastening the movement by plunging into the midst of them with his horsemen.

Charlie was on the flank of the company as it advanced, and, after running through a Russian horseman with the short pike that was carried by officers, he received a tremendous blow on his steel cap, that stretched him insensible on the ground. When he recovered, he felt that he was being carried, and soon awoke to the fact that he was a prisoner.

After a long ride, the Russians arrived at Plescow. They had lost some sixty men in the fight. Charlie was the only prisoner taken. He was, on dismounting, too weak to stand, but he was half carried and half dragged to the quarters of the

Russian officer in command. The latter addressed him, but, finding that he was not understood, sent for an officer who spoke Swedish.

"What were the party you were with doing in the wood?"

"We were hunting wolves and bears."

"Where did you come from?"

"From Marienburg."

"How strong were you?"

"Fifty horse and a hundred and forty foot," Charlie replied, knowing there could be no harm in stating the truth.

"But it was a long way to march, merely to hunt, and your officers must have been mad to come out, with so small a party, to a point where they were likely to meet with us."

"It was not too small a party, sir, as they managed to beat off the attack made upon them."

The Russian was silent for a moment, then he asked:

"Who was the officer in command?"

"The officer in command was the King of Sweden," Charlie replied.

An exclamation of surprise and anger broke from the Russian general, when the answer was translated to him.

"You missed a good chance of distinguishing yourself," he said to the officer in command of the troops. "Here has this mad King of Sweden been actually putting himself in your hands, and you have let him slip through your fingers. It would have got you two steps in rank, and the favour of the czar, had you captured him, and now he will be in a rage, indeed, when he hears that five hundred cavalry could do nothing against a force only a third of their number."

"I had no idea that the King of Sweden was there himself," the officer said humbly.

"Bah, that is no excuse. There were officers, and you ought to have captured them, instead of allowing yourself to be put to flight by a hundred and fifty men."

"We must have killed half the horsemen before the infantry came up."

"All the worse, colonel, that you did not complete the business. The infantry would not have been formidable, after they discharged their pieces. However, it is your own affair, and I wash my hands of it. What the czar will say when he hears of it, I know not, but I would not be in your shoes for all my estates."

As Charlie learned afterwards, the colonel was degraded from his rank by the angry czar, and ordered to serve as a private in the regiment he commanded. The officer who acted as translator said something in his own tongue to the general, who then, through him, said:

"This officer tells me that by your language you are not a Swede."

"I am not. I am English, and I am an ensign in the Malmoe Regiment."

"All the worse for you," the general said. "The czar has declared that he will exchange no foreign officers who may be taken prisoners."

"Very well, sir," Charlie said, fearlessly. "He will be only punishing his own officers. There are plenty of them in the King of Sweden's hands."

The general, when this reply was translated to him, angrily ordered Charlie to be taken away, and he was soon lodged in a cell in the castle. His head was still swimming from the effects of the blow that had stricken him down, and, without even trying to think over his position, he threw himself down on the straw pallet, and was soon asleep.

It was morning when he woke and, for a short time, he was unable to imagine where he was, but soon recalled what had happened. He had been visited by some-one after he had lain down, for a platter of bread and meat stood on the table, and a jug of water. He was also covered with two thick blankets. These had not been there when he lay down, for he had wondered vaguely as to how he should pass the night without some covering.

He took a long draught of water, then ate some food. His head throbbed with the pain of the wound. It had been roughly bandaged by his captors, but needed surgical dressing.

"I wonder how long I am likely to be, before I am exchanged," he said to him-self. "A long time, I am afraid; for there are scores of Russian officers prisoners with us, and I don't think there are half a dozen of ours captured by the Russians. Of course, no exchange can take place until there are a good batch to send over, and, it may be, months may pass before they happen to lay hands on enough Swedish officers to make it worth while to trouble about exchanging them."

An hour later the door opened, and an officer entered, followed by a soldier with a large bowl of broth and some bread.

"I am a doctor," he said in Swedish. "I came in to see you yesterday evening, but you were sound asleep, and that was a better medicine than any I can give; so I told the man to throw those two barrack rugs over you, and leave your food in case you should wake, which did not seem to me likely. I see, however, that you did wake," and he pointed to the plate.

"That was not till this morning, doctor. It is not an hour since I ate it."

"This broth will be better for you, and I daresay you can manage another breakfast. Sit down and take it, at once, while it is hot. I am in no hurry."

He gave an order in Russian to the soldier, who went out, and returned in a few minutes with a small wooden tub, filled with hot water. By this time Charlie had finished the broth. The doctor then bathed his head for some time in hot water, but was obliged to cut off some of his hair, in order to remove the bandage. As he examined the wound, Charlie was astounded to hear him mutter to himself:

"It is a mighty nate clip you have got, my boy; and, if your skull had not been a thick one, it is lying out there on the turf you would be."

Charlie burst into a fit of laughter.

"So you are English, too," he exclaimed, as he looked up into the surgeon's face.

"At laste Irish, my boy," the doctor said, as surprised as Charlie had been. "To think we should have been talking Swedish to each other, instead of our native tongue. And what is your name? And what is it you are doing here, as a Swede, at all?"

"My name is Charles Carstairs. I come from Lancashire, just on the borders of Westmoreland. My father is a Jacobite, and so had to leave the country. He went over to Sweden, and I, with some friends of his, got commissions."

"Then our cases are pretty much alike," the doctor said. "I had gone through Dublin University, and had just passed as a surgeon, when King James landed. It didn't much matter to me who was king, but I thought it was a fine opportunity to study gunshot wounds, so I joined the royal army, and was at the battle of the Boyne. I had plenty of work with wounds, early in the day, but when, after the Irish had fairly beat the Dutchman back all day, they made up their minds to march away at night, I had to lave my patients and be off too. Then I was shut up in Limerick; and I was not idle there, as you may guess. When at last the surrender came, I managed to slip away, having no fancy for going over with the regiments that were to enter the service of France. I thought I could have gone back to Dublin, and that no one would trouble about me; but someone put them up to it, and I had to go without stopping to ask leave. I landed at Bristol, and there, for a time, was nearly starving.

"I was well nigh my wits' end as to what to do for a living, and had just spent my last shilling, when I met an English captain, who told me that across at Gottenburg there were a good many Irish and Scotchmen who had, like myself, been in trouble at home. He gave me a passage across, and took me to the house of a man he knew. Of course, it was no use my trying to doctor people, when they could not tell me what was the matter with them, and I worked at one thing and another, doing anything I could turn my hands to, for four or five months. That is how I got to pick up Swedish. Then some people told me that Russia was a place where a doctor might get on, for that they had got no doctors for their army who knew anything of surgery, and the czar was always ready to take on foreigners who could teach them anything. I had got my diploma with me, and some of my friends came forward and subscribed enough to rig me out in clothes and pay my passage. What was better, one of them happened to have made the acquaintance of Le Ford, who was, as you may have heard, the czar's most intimate friend.

"I wished myself back a hundred times before I reached Moscow, but when I did, everything was easy for me. Le Ford introduced me to the czar, and I was appointed surgeon of a newly-raised regiment, of which Le Ford was colonel. That was eight years ago, and I am now a sort of surgeon general of a division, and am at the head of the hospitals about here. Till the war began I had not, for five years, done any military work, but had been at the head of a college the czar has established for training surgeons for the army. I was only sent down here after that business at Narva.

"So, you see, I have fallen on my feet. The czar's is a good service, and we employ a score or two of Scotchmen, most of them in good posts. He took to them because a Scotchman, General Gordon, and other foreign officers, rescued him from his sister Sophia, who intended to assassinate him, and established him firmly on the throne of his father.

"It is a pity you are not on this side. Perhaps it isn't too late to change, eh?"

Charlie laughed.

"My father is in Sweden, and my company is commanded by a man who is as good as a father to me, and his son is like my brother. If there were no other reason, I could not change. Why, it was only yesterday I was sitting round a bivouac fire with King Charles, and nothing would induce me to fight against him."

"I am not going to try to persuade you. The czar has treated me well, and I love him. By the way, I have not given you my name after all. It's Terence Kelly."

"Is not the czar very fierce and cruel?"

"Bedad, I would be much more cruel and fierce if I were in his place. Just think of one man, with all Russia on his shoulders. There is he trying to improve the country, working like a horse himself, knowing that, like every other Russian, he is as ignorant as a pig, and setting to improve himself--working in the dockyards of Holland and England, attending lectures, and all kinds of subjects. Why, man, he learnt anatomy, and can take off a leg as quickly as I can. He is building a fleet and getting together an army. It is not much good yet, you will say, but it will be some day. You can turn a peasant into a soldier in six months, but it takes a long time to turn out generals and officers who are fit for their work.

"Then, while he is trying everywhere to improve his country, every man jack of them objects to being improved, and wants to go along in his old ways. Didn't they get up an insurrection, only because he wanted them to cut off their beards? Any other man would have lost heart, and given it up years ago. It looks as hopeless a task as for a mouse to drag a mountain, but he is doing it.

"I don't say that he is perfect. He gets into passions, and it is mighty hard for anyone he gets into a passion with. But who would not get into passions, when there is so much work to be done, and everyone tries to hinder instead of to help? It would break the heart of Saint Patrick! Why, that affair at Narva would have broken down most men. Here, for years, has he been working to make an army, and the first time they meet an enemy worthy of the name, what do they do? Why, they are beaten by a tenth of their number of half-starved men, led by a mad-brained young fellow who had never heard a shot fired before, and lose all their cannon, guns, ammunition, and stores. Why, I was heartbroken, myself, when I heard of it; but Peter, instead of blowing out his brains, or drowning himself, set to work, an hour after the news reached him, to bring up fresh troops, to re-arm the men, and to prepare to meet the Swedes again, as soon as the snow is off the ground.

"If James of England had been Peter of Russia, he would be ruling over Ireland now, and England and Scotland, too.

"But now, I must be off. Don't you worry about your head. I have seen as bad a clip given by a blackthorn. I have got to go round now and see the wounded, and watch some operations being done, but I will come in again this evening. Don't eat any more of their messes, if they bring them in. You and I will have a snug little dinner together. I might get you put into a more dacent chamber, but the general is one of the old pig-headed sort. We don't pull together, so I would rather not ask any favours from him.

"The czar may come any day--he is always flying about. I will speak to him when he comes, and see that you have better entertainment."

Chapter 7: Exchanged.

Late in the afternoon, Doctor Kelly came in again to the cell.

Come along," he said; "I have got lave for you to have supper with me, and have given my pledge that you won't try to escape till it is over, or make any onslaught on the garrison, but will behave like a quiet and peaceable man."

"You are quite safe in giving the pledge, doctor," Charlie laughed.

"Come along then, me boy, for they were just dishing up when I came to fetch you. It is cold enough outside, and there is no sinse in putting cold victuals into one in such weather as this."

They were not long in reaching a snugly-furnished room, where a big fire was burning. Another gentleman was standing, with his back to it. He was a man of some seven or eight and twenty, with large features, dark brown hair falling in natural curls over his ears, and large and powerful in build.

"This is my friend, Charlie Carstairs," the doctor said.

"This, Carstairs, is Peter Michaeloff, a better doctor than most of those who mangle the czar's soldiers."

"Things will better in time," the other said, "when your pupils begin to take their places in the army."

"I hope so," the doctor said, shrugging his shoulders. "There is one comfort, they can't be much worse."

At this moment a servant entered, bearing a bowl of soup and three basins. They at once seated themselves at the table.

"So you managed to get yourself captured yesterday," Doctor Michaeloff said to Charlie. "I have not had the pleasure of seeing many of you gentlemen here."

"We don't come if we can help it," Charlie laughed. "But the Cossacks were so pressing, that I could not resist. In fact, I did not know anything about it, until I was well on the way."

"I hope they have made you comfortable," the other said, sharply.

"I can't say much for the food," Charlie said, "and still less for the cell, which was bitterly cold. Still, as the doctor gave me two rugs to wrap myself up in, I need not grumble."

"That is not right," the other said angrily. "I hear that the King of Sweden treats our prisoners well.

"You should have remonstrated, Kelly."

The Irishman shrugged his shoulders.

"I ventured to hint to the general that I thought an officer had a right to better treatment, even if he were a prisoner, but I was told sharply to mind my own business, which was with the sick and wounded. I said, as the prisoner was wounded, I thought it was a matter that did come to some extent under my control."

"What did the pig say?"

"He grumbled something between his teeth, that I did not catch, and, as I thought the prisoner would not be kept there long, and was not unaccustomed to roughing it, it was not worthwhile pressing the matter further."

"Have you heard that an officer has been here this afternoon, with a flag of truce, to treat for your exchange?" Doctor Michaeloff said, turning suddenly to Charlie.

"No, I have not heard anything about it," Charlie said.

"He offered a captain for you, which you may consider a high honour."

"It is, no doubt," Charlie said, with a smile. "I suppose his majesty thought, as it was in his special service I was caught, he was bound to get me released, if he could."

"It was a hunting party, was it not?"

"Yes. There was only the king with four of his officers there, and my company of foot, and fifty horse. I don't think I can call it an escort, for we went principally as beaters."

"Rustoff missed a grand chance there, Kelly.

"What regiment do you belong to?"

And he again turned to Charlie.

"The Malmoe Regiment. The company is commanded by an English gentleman, who is a neighbour and great friend of my father. His son is an ensign, and my greatest friend. The men are all either Scotch or English, but most of them Scotch."

"They are good soldiers, the Scotch; none better. There are a good many in the Russian service, also in that of Austria and France. They are always faithful, and to be relied upon, even when native troops prove treacherous. And you like Charles of Sweden?"

"There is not a soldier in his army but likes him," Charlie said enthusiastically. "He expects us to do much, but he does more himself. All through the winter, he did everything in his power for us, riding long distances from camp to camp, to visit the sick and to keep up the spirits of the men. If we live roughly, so does he, and, on the march, he will take his meals among the soldiers, and wrap himself up in his cloak, and sleep on the bare ground, just as they do. And as for his bravery, he exposes his life recklessly--too recklessly, we all think--and it seemed a miracle that, always in the front as he was, he should have got through Narva without a scratch."

"Yes, that was a bad bit of business, that Narva," the other said thoughtfully. "Why do you think we were beaten in the horrible way we were?--because the Russians are no cowards."

"No; they made a gallant stand when they recovered from their surprise," Charlie agreed. "But in the first place, they were taken by surprise."

"They ought not to have been," the doctor said angrily. "They had news, two days before, brought by the cavalry, who ought to have defended that pass, but didn't."

"Still, it was a surprise when we attacked," Charlie said, "for they could not suppose that the small body they saw were going to assail them. Then, we had the cover of that snowstorm, and they did not see us, until we reached the edge of the ditch. Of course, your general ought to have made proper dispositions, and to have collected the greater part of his troops at the spot facing us, instead of having them strung out round that big semicircle, so that, when we made an entry they were separated, and each half was ignorant of what the other was doing. Still, even then they might have concentrated between the trenches and the town. But no orders had been given. The general was one of the first we captured. The others waited for the orders that never came, until it was too late. If the general who commanded on the left had massed his troops, and marched against us as we were attacking the position they held on their right, we should have been caught between two fires."

"It was a badly managed business, altogether," Doctor Michaeloff growled; "but we shall do better next time. We shall understand Charles's tactics better. We reckoned on his troops, but we did not reckon on him.

"Kelly tells me that you would not care to change service."

"My friends are in the Swedish army, and I am well satisfied with the service. I daresay, if Russia had been nearer England than Sweden is, and we had landed there first, we should have been as glad to enter the service of the czar as we were to join that of King Charles. Everyone says that the czar makes strangers welcome, and that he is a liberal master to those who serve him well. As to the quarrel between them, I am not old enough to be able to give my opinion on it, though, as far as I am concerned, it seems to me that it was not a fair thing for Russia to take advantage of Sweden's being at war with Denmark and Augustus of Saxony, to fall upon her without any cause of quarrel."

"Nations move less by morality than interest," Doctor Michaeloff said calmly. "Russia wants a way to the sea--the Turks cut her off to the south, and the Swedes from the Baltic. She is smothered between them, and when she saw her chance, she took it. That is not good morality. I admit that it is the excuse of the poor man who robs the rich, but it is human nature, and nations act, in the long run, a good deal like individuals."

"But you have not told me yet, doctor," Charlie said, turning the conversation, "whether the proposal for an exchange was accepted."

"The general had no power to accept it, Carstairs. It had to be referred to the czar himself."

"I wish his majesty could see me, then," Charlie laughed. "He would see that I am but a lad, and that my release would not greatly strengthen the Swedish army."

"But then the czar may be of opinion that none of his officers, who allowed themselves to be captured by a handful of men at Narva, would be of any use to him," Doctor Michaeloff laughed.

"That may, doubtless, be said of a good many among them," Charlie said, "but, individually, none of the captains could be blamed for the mess they made of it."

"Perhaps not, but if all the men had been panic stricken, there were officers enough to have gathered together and cut their way through the Swedes."

"No doubt there were; but you must remember, Doctor Michaeloff, that an officer's place is with his company, and that it is his duty to think of his men, before thinking of himself. Supposing all the officers of the left wing, as you say, had gathered together and cut their way out, the czar would have had a right to blame them for the capture of the whole of the men. How could they tell that, at daybreak, the general would not have given orders for the left wing to attack the Swedes? They were strong enough still to have eaten us up, had they made the effort, and had the czar been there in person, I will warrant he would have tried it."

"That he would," Doctor Michaeloff said warmly. "You are right there, young sir. The czar may not be a soldier, but at least he is a man, which is more than can be said for the officer who ordered sixty thousand men to lay down their arms to eight thousand."

"I am sure of that," Charlie said. "A man who would do as he has done, leave his kingdom, and work like a common man in dockyards, to learn how to build ships, and who rules his people as he does, must be a great man. I don't suppose he would do for us in England, because a king has no real power with us, and Peter would never put up with being thwarted in all his plans by parliament, as William is. But for a country like Russia, he is wonderful. Of course, our company being composed of Scotchmen and Englishmen, we have no prejudices against him. We think him wrong for entering upon this war against Sweden, but we all consider him a wonderful fellow, just the sort of fellow one would be proud to serve under, if we did not serve under Charles of Sweden.

"Well, Doctor Kelly, when do you think the czar will be here?"

The doctor did not reply, but Michaeloff said quietly:

"He arrived this afternoon."

"He did!" Charlie exclaimed excitedly.

"Why did you not tell me before, Doctor Kelly? Has he been asked about my exchange, and is the Swedish officer still here?"

"He is here, and you will be exchanged in the morning.

"I have other things to see about now, and must say goodnight; and if you should ever fall into the hands of our people again, and Doctor Kelly does not happen to be near, ask for Peter Michaeloff, and he will do all he can for you."

"Then I am really to be exchanged tomorrow, doctor?" Charlie said, as Doctor Michaeloff left the room.

"It seems like it."

"But did not you know?"

"No, I had heard nothing for certain. I knew the czar had come, but I had not heard of his decision. I congratulate you."

"It is a piece of luck," Charlie said. "I thought it might be months before there was an exchange. It is very good of the king to send over so quickly."

"Yes; and of the czar to let you go."

"Well, I don't see much in that, doctor, considering that he gets a captain in exchange for me; still, of course, he might have refused. It would not have been civil, but he might have done it."

"What did you think of my friend, Charlie?"

"I like him. He has a pleasant face, though I should think he has got a temper of his own. He has a splendid figure, and looks more like a fighting man than a doctor. I will write down his name, so as not to forget it, as he says he might be able to help me if I am ever taken prisoner again, and you did not happen to be with the army. It is always nice having a friend. Look at the difference it has made to me, finding a countryman here."

"Yes, you may find it useful, Carstairs; and he has a good deal of influence. Still, I think it probable that if you ever should get into a scrape again, you will be able to get tidings of me, for I am likely to be with the advanced division of our army, wherever it is, as I am in charge of its hospitals.

"You had better turn in now, for I suppose you will be starting early, and I have two or three patients I must visit again before I go to bed. This is your room, next to mine. I managed, after all, to get it changed."

"That is very good of you, doctor, but it really would not have mattered a bit for one night. It does look snug and warm, with that great fire."

"Yes, the stoves are the one thing I don't like in Russia. I like to see a blazing fire, and the first thing I do, when I get into fresh quarters, is to have the stove opened so that I can see one. This is a second room of mine. There were three together, you see, and as my rank is that of a colonel, I was able to get them, and it is handy, if a friend comes to see me, to have a room for him."

An hour later, just as Charlie was dozing off to sleep, the doctor put his head in to the door.

"You are to start at daybreak, Carstairs. My servant will call you an hour before that. I shall be up. I must put a fresh bandage on your head before you start."

"Thank you very much, doctor. I am sorry to get you up so early."

"That is nothing. I am accustomed to work at all hours. Good night."

At eight o'clock, having had a bowl of broth, Charlie descended to the court-yard in charge of an officer and two soldiers, the doctor accompanying him. Here he found a Swedish officer belonging to the king's personal staff. The Russian handed the lad formally over to his charge, saying:

"By the orders of the czar, I now exchange Ensign Carstairs for Captain Potoff, whom you, on your part, engage to send off at once."

"I do," the Swede said; "that is, I engage that he shall be sent off, as soon as he can be fetched from Revel, where he is now interned, and shall be safely delivered under an escort; and that if, either by death, illness, or escape, I should not be able to hand him over, I will return another officer of the same rank."

"I have the czar's commands," the Russian went on, "to express his regret that, owing to a mistake on the part of the officer commanding here, Ensign Carstairs has not received such worthy treatment as the czar would have desired for him, but he has given stringent orders that, in future, any Swedish officers who may be taken prisoners shall receive every comfort and hospitality that can be shown them."

"Goodbye, Doctor Kelly," Charlie said, as he mounted his horse, which had been saddled in readiness for him. "I am greatly obliged to you for your very great kindness to me, and hope that I may some day have an opportunity of repaying it."

"I hope not, Carstairs. I trust that we may meet again, but hope that I sha'n't be in the position of a prisoner. However, strange things have happened already in this war, and there is no saying how fortune may go. Goodbye, and a pleasant journey."

A Russian officer took his place by the side of the Swede, and an escort of twenty troopers rode behind them, as they trotted out through the gate of the convent.

"It was very kind of the king to send for me," Charlie said to the Swede, "and I am really sorry that you should have had so long a ride on my account, Captain

Pradovich."

"As to that, it is a trifle," the officer said. "If I had not been riding here, I should be riding with the king elsewhere, so that I am none the worse. But, in truth, I am glad I came, for yesterday evening I saw the czar himself. I conversed with him for some time. He expressed himself very courteously with respect to the king, and to our army, against whom he seems to bear no sort of malice for the defeat we inflicted on him at Narva. He spoke of it himself, and said, 'you will see that, some day, we shall turn the tables upon you.'

"The king will be pleased when I return with you, for we all feared that you might be very badly hurt. All that we knew was that some of your men had seen you cut down. After the battle was over, a search was made for your body. When it could not be found, questions were asked of some of our own men, and some wounded Russians, who were lying near the spot where you had been seen to fall.

"Our men had seen nothing, for, as the Russians closed in behind your company as it advanced, they had shut their eyes and lay as if dead, fearing that they might be run through, as they lay, by the Cossack lances. The Russians, however, told us that they had seen two of the Cossacks dismount, by the orders of one of their officers, lift you on to a horse, and ride off with you. There was therefore a certainty that you were still living, for the Russians would assuredly not have troubled to carry off a dead body. His majesty interested himself very much in the matter, and yesterday morning sent me off to inquire if you were alive, and if so, to propose an exchange.

"I was much pleased, when I reached Plescow yesterday, to learn that your wound is not a serious one. I saw the doctor, who, I found, was a countryman of yours, and he assured me that it was nothing, and made some joke that I did not understand about the thickness of North Country skulls.

"The czar arrived in the afternoon, but I did not see him until late in the evening, when I was sent for. I found him with the general in command, and several other officers, among whom was your friend the doctor. The czar was, at first, in a furious passion. He abused the general right and left, and I almost thought, at one time, that he would have struck him. He told him that he had disgraced the Russian name, by not treating you with proper hospitality, and especially by placing you in a miserable cell without a fire.

"'What will the King of Sweden think?' he said. 'He treats his prisoners with kindness and courtesy, and after Narva gave them a banquet, at which he himself was present. The Duke of Croy writes to me, to say he is treated as an honoured guest rather than as a prisoner, and here you disgrace us by shutting your prisoner in a cheerless cell, although he is wounded, and giving him food such as you might give to a common soldier. The Swedes will think that we are barbarians. You are released from your command, and will at once proceed to Moscow and report yourself there, when a post will be assigned to you where you will have no opportunity of showing yourself ignorant of the laws of courtesy.

"'Doctor,' he went on, 'you will remember that all prisoners, officers and men, will be henceforth under the charge of the medical department, and that you have full authority to make such arrangements as you may think necessary for their comfort and honourable treatment. I will not have Russia made a byword among civilized peoples.'

"Then he dismissed the rest of them, and afterwards sat down and chatted with me, just as if we had been of the same rank, puffing a pipe furiously, and drinking amazing quantities of wine. Indeed, my head feels the effects of it this morning, although I was quite unable to drink cup for cup with him, for, had I done so, I should have been under the table long before he rose from it, seemingly quite unmoved by the quantity he had drank. I have no doubt he summoned me especially to hear his rebuke to the general, so that I could take word to the king how earnest he was, in his regrets for your treatment."

"There was nothing much to complain of," Charlie said; "and, indeed, the cell was a palace after the miserable huts in which we have passed the winter. I am glad, however, the czar gave the general a wigging, for he spoke brutally to me on my arrival. You may be sure, now, that any prisoners that may be taken will be well treated; for Doctor Kelly, who has been extremely kind to me, will certainly take good care of them. As to my wound, it is of little consequence. It fell on my steel cap, and I think I was stunned by its force, rather than rendered insensible by the cut itself."

After three hours' riding they came to a village. As soon as they were seen approaching, there was a stir there. A man riding ahead waved the white flag that he carried, and, when they entered the village, they found a party of fifty Swedish cavalry in the saddle.

The Russian escort, as soon as the Swedish officer and Charlie had joined their friends, turned and rode off. A meal was in readiness, and when Charlie, who was still feeling somewhat weak from the effects of his wound, had partaken of it, the party proceeded on their way, and rode into Marienburg before nightfall.

Two or three miles outside the town, they met Harry Jervoise. Two soldiers had been sent on at full speed, directly Charlie reached the village, to report that he had arrived there and was not seriously wounded, and, knowing about the time they would arrive, Harry had ridden out to meet his friend.

"You are looking white," he said, after the first hearty greeting.

"I am feeling desperately tired, Harry. The wound is of no consequence, but I lost a good deal of blood, and it is as much as I can do to keep my saddle, though we have been coming on quietly on purpose. However, I shall soon be all right again, and I need hardly say that I am heartily glad to be back."

"We have all been in a great way about you, Charlie, for we made sure that you were very badly wounded. I can tell you, it was a relief when the men rode in three hours ago, with the news that you had arrived, and were not badly hurt. The men seemed as pleased as we were, and there was a loud burst of cheering when we told them the news. Cunningham and Forbes would have ridden out with me; but Cunningham is on duty, and Forbes thought that we should like to have a chat together."

On his arrival, Charlie was heartily welcomed by Captain Jervoise and the men of the company, who cheered lustily as he rode up.

"You are to go and see the king at once," Captain Jervoise said as he dismounted. "I believe he wants to hear, especially, how you were treated. Make the best of it you can, lad. There is no occasion for the feeling of Charles against the Russians being embittered."

"I understand," Charlie said. "I will make things as smooth as I can."

He walked quickly to the little house where the king had taken up his quarters. There was no sentry at the door, or other sign that the house contained an occupant of special rank. He knocked at the door, and hearing a shout of "Enter," opened it and went in.

"Ah, my young ensign; is it you?" the king said, rising from a low settle on which he was sitting by the fire, talking with Colonel Schlippenbach.

"Hurt somewhat, I see, but not badly, I hope. I was sure that you would not have been taken prisoner, unless you had been injured."

"I was cut down by a blow that clove my helmet, your majesty, and stunned me for some time; but, beyond making a somewhat long gash on my skull, it did me no great harm."

"That speaks well for the thickness of your skull, lad, and I am heartily glad it is no worse. Now, tell me, how did they treat you?"

"It was a somewhat rough cell into which I was thrown, sir, but I was most kindly tended by an Irish doctor high in the czar's service, and, when the czar himself arrived, and learned that I had not been lodged as well as he thought necessary, I hear he was so angered that he disgraced the general, deprived him of his command, and sent him to take charge of some fortress in the interior of Russia; and I was, by his orders, allowed to occupy the doctor's quarters, and a bedroom was assigned to me next to his. I heard that the czar spoke in terms of the warmest appreciation of your treatment of your prisoners, and said that any of your officers who fell into his hands should be treated with equal courtesy."

Charles looked gratified.

"I am glad to hear it," he said. "In the field, if necessary, blood must flow like water, but there is no reason why we should not behave towards each other with courtesy, when the fighting is over. You know nothing of the force there, at present?"

"No, sir, I heard nothing. I did not exchange a word with anyone, save the doctor and another medical man; and as the former treated me as a friend, rather than as an enemy, I did not deem it right to question him, and, had I done so, I am sure that he would have given me no answer."

"Well, you can return to your quarters, sir. Your company did me good service in that fight, and Colonel Schlippenbach did not speak in any way too warmly in their favour. I would that I had more of these brave Englishmen and Scotchmen in my service."

Charlie's head, however, was not as hard as he had believed it to be; and the long ride brought on inflammation of the wound, so that, on the following morning, he was in a high state of fever. It was a fortnight before he was convalescent, and the surgeon then recommended that he should have rest and quiet for a time, as he was sorely pulled down, and unfit to bear the hardships of a campaign; and it was settled that he should go down with the next convoy to Revel, and thence take ship for Sweden.

He was so weak, that although very sorry to leave the army just as spring was commencing, he himself felt that he should be unable to support the fatigues of the campaign, until he had had entire rest and change. A few hours after the decision of the surgeon had been given, Major Jamieson and Captain Jervoise entered the room where he was sitting, propped up by pillows.

"I have a bit of news that will please you, Charlie. The king sent for the major this morning, and told him that he intended to increase our company to a regiment, if he could do so. He had heard that a considerable number of Scotchmen and Englishmen had come over, and were desirous of enlisting, but, from their ignorance of the language, their services had been declined. He said that he was so pleased, not only with the conduct of the company in that fight, but with its discipline, physique, and power of endurance, that he had decided to convert it into a regiment. He said he was sorry to lose its services for a time; but, as we lost twenty men in the fight, and have some fifteen still too disabled to take their places in the ranks, this was of the less importance.

"So we are all going to march down to Revel with you. Major Jamieson is appointed colonel, and I am promoted to be major. The king himself directed that Cunningham and Forbes shall have commissions as captains, and you and Harry as lieutenants. The colonel has authority given him to nominate Scotch and English gentlemen of good name to make up the quota of officers, while most of our own men will be appointed non-commissioned officers, to drill the new recruits. The king has been good enough, at Colonel Jamieson's request, to say that, as soon as the regiment is raised and organized, it shall be sent up to the front."

"That is good news, indeed," Charlie said, with more animation than he had evinced since his illness. "I have been so accustomed to be attended to, in every way, that I was quite looking forward with dread to the journey among strangers. Still, if you are all going, it will be a different thing altogether. I don't think you will be long in raising the regiment. We only were a week in getting the company together, and, if they have been refusing to accept the services of our people, there must be numbers of them at Gottenburg."

Early on the following morning, Charlie and the men unable to march were placed in waggons, and the company started on its march to Revel. It was a heavy journey, for the frost had broken up, and the roads were in a terrible state from the heavy traffic passing. There was no delay when they reached the port, as they at once marched on board a ship, which was the next day to start for Sweden. Orders from the king had already been received that the company was to be conveyed direct to Gottenburg, and they entered the port on the fifth day after sailing.

The change, the sea air, and the prospect of seeing his father again greatly benefited Charlie, and, while the company was marched to a large building assigned to their use, he was able to make his way on foot to his father's, assisted by his soldier servant, Jock Armstrong.

"Why, Charlie," Sir Marmaduke Carstairs exclaimed as he entered, "who would have thought of seeing you? You are looking ill, lad; ill and weak. What has happened to you?"

Charlie briefly related the events that had brought about his return to Gottenburg, of which Sir Marmaduke was entirely ignorant. Postal communications were rare and uncertain, and Captain Jervoise had not taken advantage of the one opportunity that offered, after Charlie had been wounded, thinking it better to delay till the lad could write and give a good account of himself.

"So Jervoise, and his son, and that good fellow Jamieson are all back again? That is good news, Charlie; and you have been promoted? That is capital too, after only a year in the service. And you have been wounded, and a prisoner among the Russians? You have had adventures, indeed! I was terribly uneasy when the first news of that wonderful victory at Narva came, for we generally have to wait for the arrival of the despatches giving the lists of the killed and wounded. I saw that the regiment had not been in the thick of it, as the lists contained none of your names. I would have given a limb to have taken part in that wonderful battle. When you get as old as I am, my boy, you will feel a pride in telling how you fought at Narva, and helped to destroy an entire Russian army with the odds ten to one against you.

"Of course, you will stay here with me. I suppose you have leave at present?"

"Yes, father, Colonel Jamieson told me that my first duty was to get strong and well again, and that I was to think of no other until I had performed that. And how have you been getting on, father?"

"Very well, lad. I don't pretend that it is not a great change from Lynnwood, but I get along very well, and thank heaven, daily, that for so many years I had set aside a portion of my rents, little thinking that the time would come when they would prove my means of existence. My friends here have invested the money for me, and it bears good interest, which is punctually paid. With the English and Scotch exiles, I have as much society as I care for, and as I find I am able to keep a horse--for living here is not more than half the cost that it would be in England--I am well enough contented with my lot.

"There is but one thing that pricks me. That villain John Dormay has, as he schemed for, obtained possession of my estates, and has been knighted for his distinguished services to the king. I heard of this some time since, by a letter from one of our Jacobite friends to whom I wrote, asking for news. He says that the new knight has no great cause for enjoyment in his dignity and possessions, because, not only do the Jacobite gentry turn their backs upon him, when they meet him in the town, but the better class of Whigs hold altogether aloof from him, regarding his elevation, at the expense of his wife's kinsman, to be disgraceful, although of course they have no idea of the evil plot by which he brought about my ruin. There is great pity expressed for his wife, who has not once stirred beyond the grounds at Lynnwood since he took her there, and who is, they say, a shadow of her former self. Ciceley, he hears, is well. That cub of a son is in London, and there are reports that he is very wild, and puts his father to much cost. As to the man himself, they say he is surrounded by the lowest knaves, and it is rumoured that he has taken to drink for want of better company. It is some comfort to me to think that, although the villain has my estates, he is getting no enjoyment out of them.

"However, I hope some day to have a reckoning with him. The Stuarts must come to their own, sooner or later. Until then I am content to rest quietly here in Sweden."

Chapter 8: The Passage of the Dwina.

A few hours after Charlie's arrival home, Major Jervoise and Harry came round to the house. I congratulate you, Jervoise, on your new rank," Sir Marmaduke said heartily, as he entered; "and you, too, Harry. It has been a great comfort to me, to know that you and Charlie have been together always. At present you have the advantage of him in looks. My lad has no more strength than a girl, not half the strength, indeed, of many of these sturdy Swedish maidens."

"Yes, Charlie has had a bad bout of it, Carstairs," Major Jervoise said cheerfully; "but he has picked up wonderfully in the last ten days, and, in as many more, I shall look to see him at work again. I only wish that you could have been with us, old friend."

"It is of no use wishing, Jervoise. We have heard enough here, of what the troops have been suffering through the winter, for me to know that, if I had had my wish and gone with you, my bones would now be lying somewhere under the soil of Livonia."

"Yes, it was a hard time," Major Jervoise agreed, "but we all got through it well, thanks principally to our turning to at sports of all kinds. These kept the men in health, and prevented them from moping. The king was struck with the condition of our company, and he has ordered that, in future, all the Swedish troops shall take part in such games and amusements when in winter quarters. Of course, Charlie has told you we are going to have a regiment entirely composed of Scots and Englishmen. I put the Scots first, since they will be by far the most numerous. There are always plenty of active spirits, who find but small opening for their energy at home, and are ready to take foreign service whenever the chance opens. Besides, there are always feuds there. In the old days, it was chief against chief. Now it is religion against religion; and now, as then, there are numbers of young fellows glad to exchange the troubles at home for service abroad. There have been quite a crowd of men round our quarters, for, directly the news spread that the company was landing, our countrymen flocked round, each eager to learn how many vacancies there were in the ranks, and whether we would receive recruits. Their joy was extreme when it became known that Jamieson had authority to raise a whole regiment. I doubt not that many of the poor fellows are in great straits."

"That I can tell you they are," Sir Marmaduke broke in. "We have been doing what we can for them, for it was grievous that so many men should be wandering, without means or employment, in a strange country. But the number was too great for our money to go far among them, and I know that many of them are destitute and well-nigh starving. We had hoped to ship some of them back to Scotland, and have been treating with the captain of a vessel sailing, in two or three days, to carry them home."

"It is unfortunate, but they have none to blame but themselves. They should have waited until an invitation for foreigners to enlist was issued by the Swedish government, or until gentlemen of birth raised companies and regiments for service here. However, we are the gainers, for I see that we shall not have to wait here many weeks. Already, as far as I can judge from what I hear, there must be well-nigh four hundred men here, all eager to serve.

"We will send the news by the next ship that sails, both to Scotland and to our own country, that men, active and fit for service, can be received into a regiment, specially formed of English-speaking soldiers. I will warrant that, when it is known in the Fells that I am a major in the regiment, and that your son and mine are lieutenants, we shall have two or three score of stout young fellows coming over."

The next day, indeed, nearly four hundred men were enlisted into the service, and were divided into eight companies. Each of these, when complete, was to be two hundred strong. Six Scottish officers were transferred, from Swedish regiments, to fill up the list of captains, and commissions were given to several gentlemen of family as lieutenants and ensigns. Most of these, however, were held over, as the colonel wrote to many gentlemen of his acquaintance in Scotland, offering them commissions if they would raise and bring over men. Major Jervoise did the same to half a dozen young Jacobite gentlemen in the north of England, and so successful were the appeals that, within two months of the return of the company to Gottenburg, the regiment had been raised to its full strength.

A fortnight was spent in drilling the last batch of recruits, from morning till night, so that they should be able to take their places in the ranks; and then, with drums beating and colours flying, the corps embarked at Gottenburg, and sailed to join the army.

They arrived at Revel in the beginning of May. The port was full of ships, for twelve thousand men had embarked, at Stockholm and other ports, to reinforce the army and enable the king to take the field in force; and, by the end of the month, the greater portion of the force was concentrated at Dorpt.

Charlie had long since regained his full strength. As soon as he was fit for duty, he had rejoined, and had been engaged, early and late, in the work of drilling the recruits, and in the general organization of the regiment. He and Harry, however, found time to take part in any amusement that was going on. They were made welcome in the houses of the principal merchants and other residents of Gottenburg, and much enjoyed their stay in the town, in spite of their longing to be back in time to take part in the early operations of the campaign.

When they sailed into the port of Revel, they found that the campaign had but just commenced, and they marched with all haste to join the force with which the king was advancing against the Saxons, who were still besieging Riga. Their army was commanded by Marshal Steinau, and was posted on the other side of the river Dwina, a broad stream. Charles the Twelfth had ridden up to Colonel Jamieson's regiment upon its arrival, and expressed warm gratification at its appearance, when it was paraded for his inspection.

"You have done well, indeed, colonel," he said. "I had hardly hoped you could have collected so fine a body of men in so short a time."

At his request, the officers were brought up and introduced. He spoke a few words to those he had known before, saying to Charlie:

"I am glad to see you back again, lieutenant. You have quite recovered from that crack on your crown, I hope. But I need not ask, your looks speak for themselves. You have just got back in time to pay my enemies back for it."

The prospect was not a cheerful one, when the Swedes arrived on the banks of the Dwina. The Saxons were somewhat superior in force, and it would be a desperate enterprise to cross the river, in the teeth of their cannon and musketry. Already the king had caused a number of large flat boats to be constructed. The sides were made very high, so as to completely cover the troops from musketry, and were hinged so as to let down and act as gangways, and facilitate a landing.

Charlie was standing on the bank, looking at the movements of the Saxon troops across the river, and wondering how the passage was to be effected, when a hand was placed on his shoulder. Looking round, he saw it was the king, who, as was his custom, was moving about on foot, unattended by any of his officers.

"Wondering how we are to get across, lieutenant?"

"That is just what I was thinking over, your majesty."

"We want another snowstorm, as we had at Narva," the king said. "The wind is blowing the right way, but there is no chance of such another stroke of luck, at this time of year."

"No, sir; but I was thinking that one might make an artificial fog."

"How do you mean?" the king asked quickly.

"Your majesty has great stacks of straw here, collected for forage for the cattle. No doubt a good deal of it is damp, or if not, it could be easily wetted. If we were to build great piles of it, all along on the banks here, and set it alight so as to burn very slowly, but to give out a great deal of smoke, this light wind would blow it across the river into the faces of the Saxons, and completely cover our movements."

"You are right!" the king exclaimed. "Nothing could be better. We will make a smoke that will blind and half smother them;" and he hurried away.

An hour later, orders were sent out to all the regiments that, as soon as it became dusk, the men should assemble at the great forage stores for fatigue duty. As soon as they did so, they were ordered to pull down the stacks, and to carry the straw to the bank of the river, and there pile it in heavy masses, twenty yards apart. The whole was to be damped, with the exception of only a small quantity on the windward side of the heaps, which was to be used for starting the fire.

In two hours, the work was completed. The men were then ordered to return to their camps, have their suppers, and lie down at once. Then they were to form up, half an hour before daybreak, in readiness to take their places in the boats, and were then to lie down, in order, until the word was given to move forward.

This was done, and just as the daylight appeared the heaps of straw were lighted, and dense volumes of smoke rolled across the river, entirely obscuring the opposite shore from view. The Saxons, enveloped in the smoke, were unable to understand its meaning. Those on the watch had seen no sign of troops on the bank, before the smoke began to roll across the water, and the general was uncertain whether a great fire had broken out in the forage stores of the Swedes, or whether the fire had been purposely raised, either to cover the movements of the army and enable them to march away and cross at some undefended point, or whether to cover their passage.

The Swedish regiments, which were the first to cross, took their places at once in the boats, the king himself accompanying them. In a quarter of an hour the opposite bank was gained. Marshal Steinau, an able general, had called the Saxons under arms, and was marching towards the river, when the wind, freshening, lifted the thick veil of smoke, and he saw that the Swedes had already gained the bank of the river, and at once hurled his cavalry against them.

The Swedish formation was not complete and, for a moment, they were driven back in disorder, and forced into the river. The water was shallow, and the king, going about among them, quickly restored order and discipline, and, charging in solid formation, they drove the cavalry back and advanced across the plain. Steinau recalled his troops and posted them in a strong position, one flank being covered by a marsh and the other by a wood. He had time to effect his arrangements, as Charles was compelled to wait until the whole of his troops were across. As soon as they were so, he led them against the enemy.

The battle was a severe one, for the Swedes were unprovided with artillery, and the Saxons, with the advantages of position and a powerful artillery, fought steadily. Three times Marshal Steinau led his cavalry in desperate charges, and each time almost penetrated to the point where Charles was directing the movements of his troops; but, at last, he was struck from his horse by a blow from the butt end of a musket; and his cuirassiers, with difficulty, carried him from the field. As soon as his fall became known, disorder spread among the ranks of the Saxons. Some regiments gave way, and, the Swedes rushing forward with loud shouts, the whole army was speedily in full flight.

This victory laid the whole of Courland at the mercy of the Swedes, all the towns opening their gates at their approach.

They were now on the confines of Poland, and the king, brave to rashness as he was, hesitated to attack a nation so powerful. Poland, at that time, was a country a little larger than France, though with a somewhat smaller population, but in this respect exceeding Sweden. With the Poles themselves he had no quarrel, for they had taken no part in the struggle, which had been carried on solely by their king, with his Saxon troops.

The authority of the kings of Poland was much smaller than that of other European monarchs. The office was not a hereditary one; the king being elected at a diet, composed of the whole of the nobles of the country, the nobility embracing practically every free man; and, as it was necessary, according to the constitution of the country, that the vote should be unanimous, the difficulties in the way of election were very great, and civil wars of constant occurrence.

Charles was determined that he would drive Augustus, who was the author of the league against him, from the throne; but he desired to do this by means of the Poles themselves, rather than to unite the whole nation against him by invading the country. Poland was divided into two parts, the larger of which was Poland proper, which could at once place thirty thousand men in the field. The other was Lithuania, with an army of twelve thousand. These forces were entirely independent of each other. The troops were for the most part cavalry, and the small force, permanently kept up, was composed almost entirely of horsemen. They rarely drew pay, and subsisted entirely on plunder, being as formidable to their own people as to an enemy.

Lithuania, on whose borders the king had taken post with his army, was, as usual, harassed by two factions, that of the Prince Sapieha and the Prince of Oginski, between whom a civil war was going on.

The King of Sweden took the part of the former, and, furnishing him with assistance, speedily enabled him to overcome the Oginski party, who received but slight aid from the Saxons. Oginski's forces were speedily dispersed, and roamed about the country in scattered parties, subsisting on pillage, thereby exciting among the people a lively feeling of hatred against the King of Poland, who was regarded as the author of the misfortunes that had befallen the country.

From the day when Charlie's suggestion, of burning damp straw to conceal the passage of the river, had been attended with such success, the king had held him in high favour. There was but a few years' difference between their ages, and the suggestion, so promptly made, seemed to show the king that the young Englishman was a kindred spirit, and he frequently requested him to accompany him in his rides, and chatted familiarly with him.

"I hate this inactive life," he said one day, "and would, a thousand times, rather be fighting the Russians than setting the Poles by the ears; but I dare not move against them, for, were Augustus of Saxony left alone, he would ere long set all Poland against me. At present, the Poles refuse to allow him to bring in reinforcements from his own country; but if he cannot get men he can get gold, and with gold he can buy over his chief opponents, and regain his power. If it costs me a year's delay, I must wait until he is forced to fly the kingdom, and I can place on the throne someone who will owe his election entirely to me, and in whose good faith I can be secure.

"That done, I can turn my attention to Russia, which, by all accounts, daily becomes more formidable. Narva is besieged by them, and will ere long fall; but I can retake Narva when once I can depend upon the neutrality of the Poles. Would I were king of Poland as well as of Sweden. With eighty thousand Polish horse, and my own Swedish infantry, I could conquer Europe if I wished to do so.

"I know that you are as fond of adventure as I am, and I am thinking of sending you with an envoy I am despatching to Warsaw.

"You know that the Poles are adverse to business of all kinds. The poorest noble, who can scarcely pay for the cloak he wears, and who is ready enough to sell his vote and his sword to the highest bidder, will turn up his nose at honest trade; and the consequence is, as there is no class between the noble and the peasant, the trade of the country is wholly in the hands of Jews and foreigners, among the latter being, I hear, many Scotchmen, who, while they make excellent soldiers, are also keen traders. This class must have considerable power, in fact, although it be exercised quietly. The Jews are, of course, money lenders as well as traders. Large numbers of these petty nobles must be in their debt, either for money lent or goods supplied.

"My agent goes specially charged to deal with the archbishop, who is quite open to sell his services to me, although he poses as one of the strongest adherents of the Saxons. With him, it is not a question so much of money, as of power. Being a wise man, he sees that Augustus can never retain his position, in the face of the enmity of the great body of the Poles, and of my hostility. But, while my agent deals with him and such nobles as he indicates as being likely to take my part against Augustus, you could ascertain the feeling of the trading class, and endeavour to induce them, not only to favour me, but to exert all the influence they possess on my behalf. As there are many Scotch merchants in the city, you could begin by making yourself known to them, taking with you letters of introduction from your colonel, and any other Scotch gentleman whom you may find to have acquaintanceship, if not with the men themselves, with their families in Scotland. I do not, of course, say that the mission will be without danger, but that will, I know, be an advantage in your eyes. What do you think of the proposal?"

"I do not know, sire," Charlie said doubtfully. "I have no experience whatever in matters of that kind."

"This will be a good opportunity for you to serve an apprenticeship," the king said decidedly. "There is no chance of anything being done here, for months, and as you will have no opportunity of using your sword, you cannot be better employed than in polishing up your wits. I will speak to Colonel Jamieson about it this evening. Count Piper will give you full instructions, and will obtain for you, from some of our friends, lists of the names of the men who would be likely to be most useful to us. You will please to remember that the brain does a great deal more than the sword, in enabling a man to rise above his fellows. You are a brave young officer, but I have many a score of brave young officers, and it was your quick wit, in suggesting the strategy by which we crossed the Dwina without loss, that has marked you out from among others, and made me see that you are fit for something better than getting your throat cut."

The king then changed the subject with his usual abruptness, and dismissed Charlie, at the end of his ride, without any further allusion to the subject. The young fellow, however, knew enough of the king's headstrong disposition to be aware that the matter was settled, and that he could not, without incurring the king's serious displeasure, decline to accept the commission. He walked back, with a serious face, to the hut that the officers of the company occupied, and asked Harry Jervoise to come out to him.

"What is it, Charlie?" his friend said. "Has his gracious majesty been blowing you up, or has your horse broken its knees?"

"A much worse thing than either, Harry. The king appears to have taken into his head that I am cut out for a diplomatist;" and he then repeated to his friend the conversation the king had had with him.

Harry burst into a shout of laughter.

"Don't be angry, Charlie, but I cannot help it. The idea of your going, in disguise, I suppose, and trying to talk over the Jewish clothiers and cannie Scotch traders, is one of the funniest things I ever heard. And do you think the king was really in earnest?"

"The king is always in earnest," Charlie said in a vexed tone; "and, when he once takes a thing into his head, there is no gainsaying him."

"That is true enough, Charlie," Harry said, becoming serious. "Well, I have no doubt you will do it just as well as another, and after all, there will be some fun in it, and you will be in a big city, and likely to have a deal more excitement than will fall to our lot here."

"I don't think it will be at all the sort of excitement I should care for, Harry. However, my hope is, that the colonel will be able to dissuade him from the idea."

"Well, I don't know that I should wish that if I were in your place, Charlie. Undoubtedly, it is an honour being chosen for such a mission, and it is possible you may get a great deal of credit for it, as the king is always ready to push forward those who do good service. Look how much he thinks of you, because you made that suggestion about getting up a smoke to cover our passage."

"I wish I had never made it," Charlie said heartily.

"Well, in that case, Charlie, it is likely enough we should not be talking together here, for our loss in crossing the river under fire would have been terrible."

"Well, perhaps it is as well as it is," Charlie agreed. "But I did not want to attract his attention. I was very happy as I was, with you all. As for my suggestion about the straw, anyone might have thought of it. I should never have given the matter another moment's consideration, and I should be much better pleased if the king had not done so, either, instead of telling the colonel about it, and the colonel speaking to the officers, and such a ridiculous fuss being made about nothing."

"My dear Charlie," Harry said seriously, "you seem to be forgetting that we all came out here, together, to make our fortune, or at any rate to do as well as we could till the Stuarts come to the throne again, and our fathers regain their estates, a matter concerning which, let me tell you, I do not feel by any means so certain as I did in the old days. Then, you know, all our friends were of our way of thinking, and the faith that the Stuarts would return was like a matter of religion, which it was heresy to doubt for an instant. Well, you see, in the year that we have been out here one's eyes have got opened a bit, and I don't feel by any means sanguine that the Stuarts will ever come to the throne of England again, or that our fathers will recover their estates.

"You have seen here what good soldiers can do, and how powerless men possessing but little discipline, though perhaps as brave as themselves, are against them. William of Orange has got good soldiers. His Dutch troops are probably quite as good as our best Swedish regiments. They have had plenty of fighting in Ireland and elsewhere, and I doubt whether the Jacobite gentlemen, however numerous, but without training or discipline, could any more make head against them than the masses of Muscovites could against the Swedish battalions at Narva. All this means that it is necessary that we should, if possible, carve out a fortune here. So far, I certainly have no reason to grumble. On the contrary, I have had great luck. I am a lieutenant at seventeen, and, if I am not shot or carried off by fever, I may, suppose the war goes on and the army is not reduced, be a colonel at the age of forty.

"Now you, on the other hand, have, by that happy suggestion of yours, attracted the notice of the king, and he is pleased to nominate you to a mission in which there is a chance of your distinguishing yourself in another way, and of being employed in other and more important business. All this will place you much farther on the road towards making a fortune, than marching and fighting with your company would be likely to do in the course of twenty years, and I think it would be foolish in the extreme for you to exhibit any disinclination to undertake the duty."

"I suppose you are right, Harry, and I am much obliged to you for your advice, which certainly puts the matter in a light in which I had not before seen it. If I thought that I could do it well, I should not so much mind, for, as you say, there will be some fun to be got out of it, and some excitement, and there seems little chance of doing anything here for a long time. But what am I to say to the fellows? How can I argue with them? Besides, I don't talk Polish."

"I don't suppose there are ten men in the army who do so, probably not five. As to what to say, Count Piper will no doubt give you full instructions as to the line you are to take, the arguments you are to use, and the inducements you are to hold out. That is sure to be all right."

"Well, do not say anything about it, Harry, when you get back. I still hope the colonel will dissuade the king."

"Then you are singularly hopeful, Charlie, that is all I can say. You might persuade a brick wall to move out of your way, as easily as induce the King of Sweden to give up a plan he has once formed. However, I will say nothing about it."

At nine o'clock, an orderly came to the hut with a message that the colonel wished to speak to Lieutenant Carstairs. Harry gave his friend a comical look, as the latter rose and buckled on his sword.

"What is the joke, Harry?" his father asked, when Charlie had left. "Do you know what the colonel can want him for, at this time of the evening? It is not his turn for duty."

"I know, father; but I must not say."

"The lad has not been getting into a scrape, I hope?"

"Nothing serious, I can assure you; but really, I must not say anything until he comes back."

Harry's positive assurance, as to the impossibility of changing the king's decision, had pretty well dispelled any hopes Charlie might before have entertained, and he entered the colonel's room with a grave face.

"You know why I have sent for you, Carstairs?"

"Yes, sir; I am afraid that I do."

"Afraid? That is to say, you don't like it."

"Yes, sir; I own that I don't like it."

"Nor do I, lad, and I told his majesty so. I said you were too young for so risky a business. The king scoffed at the idea. He said, 'He is not much more than two years younger than I am, and if I am old enough to command an army, he is old enough to carry out this mission. We know that he is courageous. He is cool, sharp, and intelligent. Why do I choose him? Has he not saved me from the loss of about four or five thousand men, and probably a total defeat? A young fellow who can do that, ought to be able to cope with Jewish traders, and to throw dust in the eyes of the Poles.

"I have chosen him for this service for two reasons. In the first place, because I know he will do it well, and even those who consider that I am rash and headstrong, admit that I have the knack of picking out good men. In the next place, I want to reward him for the service he has done for us. I cannot, at his age, make a colonel of him, but I can give him a chance of distinguishing himself in a service in which age does not count for so much, and Count Piper, knowing my wishes in the matter, will push him forward. Moreover, in such a mission as this, his youth will be an advantage, for he is very much less likely to excite suspicion than if he were an older man.'

"The king's manner did not admit of argument, and I had only to wait and ask what were his commands. These were simply that you are to call upon his minister tomorrow, and that you would then receive full instructions.

"The king means well by you, lad, and on turning it over, I think better of the plan than I did before. I am convinced, at any rate, that you will do credit to the king's choice."

"I will do my best, sir," Charlie said. "At present, it all seems so vague to me that I can form no idea whatever as to what it will be like. I am sure that the king's intentions are, at any rate, kind. I am glad to hear you say that, on consideration, you think better of the plan. Then I may mention the matter to Major Jervoise?"

"Certainly, Carstairs, and to his son, but it must go no farther. I shall put your name in orders, as relieved from duty, and shall mention that you have been despatched on service, which might mean anything. Come and see me tomorrow, lad, after you have received Count Piper's instructions. As the king reminded me, there are many Scotchmen at Warsaw, and it is likely that some of them passed through Sweden on the way to establish themselves there, and I may very well have made their acquaintance at Gottenburg or Stockholm.

"Once established in the house of one of my countrymen, your position would be fairly safe and not altogether unpleasant, and you would be certainly far better off than a Swede would be engaged on this mission. The Swedes are, of course, regarded by the Poles as enemies, but, as there is no feeling against Englishmen or Scotchmen, you might pass about unnoticed as one of the family of a Scottish trader there, or as his assistant."

"I don't fear its being unpleasant in the least, colonel. Nor do I think anything one way or the other about my safety. I only fear that I shall not be able to carry out properly the mission intrusted to me."

"You will do your best, lad, and that is all that can be expected. You have not solicited the post, and as it is none of your choosing, your failure would be the fault of those who have sent you, and not of yourself; but in a matter of this kind there is no such thing as complete failure. When you have to deal with one man you may succeed or you may fail in endeavouring to induce him to act in a certain manner, but when you have to deal with a considerable number of men, some will be willing to accept your proposals, some will not, and the question of success will probably depend upon outside influences and circumstances over which you have no control whatever. I have no fear that it will be a failure. If our party in Poland triumph, or if our army here advances, or if Augustus, finding his position hopeless, leaves the country, the good people of Warsaw will join their voices to those of the majority. If matters go the other way, you may be sure that they will not risk imprisonment, confiscation, and perhaps death, by getting up a revolt on their own account. The king will be perfectly aware of this, and will not expect impossibilities, and there is really no occasion whatever for you to worry yourself on that ground."

Upon calling upon Count Piper the next morning, Charlie found that, as the colonel had told him, his mission was a general one.

"It will be your duty," the minister said, "to have interviews with as many of the foreign traders and Jews in Warsaw as you can, only going to those to whom you have some sort of introduction from the persons you may first meet, or who are, as far as you can learn from the report of others, ill disposed towards the Saxon party. Here is a letter, stating to all whom it may concern, that you are in the confidence of the King of Sweden, and are authorized to represent him.

"In the first place, you can point out to those you see that, should the present situation continue, it will bring grievous evils upon Poland. Proclamations have already been spread broadcast over the country, saying that the king has no quarrel with the people of Poland, but, as their sovereign has, without the slightest provocation, embarked on a war, he must fight against him and his Saxon troops, until they are driven from the country. This you will repeat, and will urge that it will be infinitely better that Poland herself should cast out the man who has embroiled her with Sweden, than that the country should be the scene of a long and sanguinary struggle, in which large districts will necessarily be laid waste, all trade be arrested, and grievous suffering inflicted upon the people at large.

"You can say that King Charles has already received promises of support from a large number of nobles, and is most desirous that the people of the large towns, and especially of the capital, should use their influence in his favour. That he has himself no ambition, and no end to serve save to obtain peace and tranquillity for his country, and that it will be free for the people of Poland to elect their own monarch, when once Augustus of Saxony has disappeared from the scene.

"In this sealed packet you will find a list of influential citizens. It has been furnished me by one well acquainted with the place. The Jews are to be assured that, in case of a friendly monarch being placed on the throne, Charles will make a treaty with him, insuring freedom of commerce to the two countries, and will also use his friendly endeavours to obtain, from the king and Diet, an enlargement of the privileges that the Jews enjoy. To the foreign merchants you will hold the same language, somewhat altered, to suit their condition and wants.

"You are not asking them to organize any public movement, the time has not yet come for that; but simply to throw the weight of their example and influence against the party of the Saxons. Of course our friends in Warsaw have been doing their best to bring round public opinion in the capital to this direction, but the country is so torn by perpetual intrigues, that the trading classes hold aloof altogether from quarrels in which they have no personal interest, and are slow to believe that they can be seriously affected by any changes which will take place.

"Our envoy will start tomorrow morning. His mission is an open one. He goes to lay certain complaints, to propose an exchange of prisoners, and to open negotiations for peace. All these are but pretences. His real object is to enter into personal communication with two or three powerful personages, well disposed towards us.

"Come again to me this evening, when you have thought the matter over. I shall then be glad to hear any suggestion you may like to make."

"There is one thing, sir, that I should like to ask you. It will evidently be of great advantage to me, if I can obtain private letters of introduction to Scotch traders in the city. This I cannot do, unless by mentioning the fact that I am bound for Warsaw. Have I your permission to do so, or is it to be kept a close secret?"

"No. I see no objection to your naming it to anyone you can implicitly trust, and who may, as you think, be able to give you such introductions, but you must impress upon them that the matter must be kept a secret. Doubtless the Saxons have in their pay people in our camp, just as we have in theirs, and were word of your going sent, you would find yourself watched, and perhaps arrested. We should, of course wish you to be zealous in your mission, but I would say, do not be over anxious. We are not trying to get up a revolution in Warsaw, but seeking to ensure that the feeling in the city should be in our favour; and this, we think, may be brought about, to some extent, by such assurances as you can give of the king's friendship, and by such expressions of a belief in the justice of our cause, and in the advantages there would be in getting rid of this foreign prince, as might be said openly by one trader to another, when men meet in their exchanges or upon the street. So that the ball is once set rolling, it may be trusted to keep in motion, and there can be little doubt that such expressions of feeling, among the mercantile community of the capital, will have some effect even upon nobles who pretend to despise trade, but who are not unfrequently in debt to traders, and who hold their views in a certain respect."

"Thank you, sir. At what time shall I come this evening?"

"At eight o'clock. By that time, I may have thought out farther details for your guidance."

Chapter 9: In Warsaw.

Upon leaving the quarters of Count Piper, Charlie returned to the camp, and, after discussing the matter with Major Jervoise, proceeded with him to the colonel's hut. Well, you look brighter this morning, Carstairs. Are you better pleased, now you have thought the matter over?" "Yes, sir. What you said last night has been quite confirmed by Count Piper, and the matter does not really seem so difficult. I am merely, as a foreigner in the employment of the King of Sweden, to talk with foreigners in Warsaw, to assure them that the king is sincere in his desire to avoid war with Poland, and will gladly make a lasting peace between the two countries, to urge upon them to show themselves favourable to his project for securing such a peace, by forcing Augustus to resign the crown, and to use what influence they can in that direction, both upon their fellow traders and upon the Poles."

"There is nothing very difficult about that," Colonel Jamieson said cheerfully, "as it happens to be quite true; and there can be no real question as to the true interest of Poland, and especially of the trading classes in the great towns, from whom heavy contributions towards the expenses of war are always exacted by their own rulers, and who have to pay a ruinous ransom in case of their city being captured by the enemy. The traders of Warsaw will need no reminder of such well-known facts, and will be only too glad to be assured that, unless as a last resource, our king has no intention of making war upon Poland, and they will certainly be inclined to bestir themselves to avert such a possibility. You have, I suppose, a list of names of the people with whom you had best put yourself into communication?"

"Yes, sir. Here is a list. There are, I see, ten Scotchmen, fifteen Frenchmen, and about as many Jews."

"I know nothing of the Frenchmen, and less of the Jews," the colonel said, taking the list; "but I ought to know some of the Scotchmen. They will hail from

Dundee and Glasgow, and, it may be, Dumfries."

He ran his eye down the list.

"Aha! Here is one, and we need go no further. Allan Ramsay; we were lads together at the High School of Glasgow, and were classmates at the College. His father was a member of the city council, and was one of the leading traders in the city. Allan was a wild lad, as I was myself, and many a scrape did we get into together, and had many a skirmish with the watch. Allan had two or three half brothers, men from ten to twenty years older than himself, and, a year or two after I came out to Sweden and entered the army as an ensign, who should I meet in the streets of Gottenburg, but Allan Ramsay.

"We were delighted to see each other, and he stopped with me nearly a week. He had, after leaving the College, gone into his father's business, but when the old man died he could not get on with his half brothers, who were dour men, and had little patience with Allan's restlessness and love of pleasure. So, after a final quarrel, they had given him so much money for his share of the business, and a letter of introduction to a trader in Poland, who had written to them saying that he wanted a partner with some capital; and Allan was willing enough to try the life in a strange country, for he was a shrewd fellow, with all his love of fun.

"Five years afterwards, he came through Gottenburg again. I did not see him, for my regiment was at Stockholm at the time, but he wrote me a letter saying that he had been in Scotland to marry and bring back one Janet Black, the daughter of a mercer, whom I remember well enough as an old flame of his.

"He reported that he was doing well, and that the Poles were not bad fellows to live among, though less punctual in their payments than might be wished. He said he did not suppose that, as a Swedish officer, I should ever be in Poland, unless Sweden produced another Gustavus Adolphus; but if I was, he would be delighted to welcome me, and that anyone I asked in Warsaw would direct me to his shop. I wonder that I did not think of him before; but that is ten years ago, and it had altogether passed out of my mind, till I saw his name here. Unless he is greatly changed, you may be sure of a hearty welcome from Allan Ramsay, for my sake. We need not trouble about the other names. He will know all about them, and will be able to put you in the way of getting at them."

This was a great relief to Charlie, who felt that it would be an immense advantage to have the house of someone, from whom he might expect a welcome, to go to on his arrival in Warsaw; and he was able, during the day, to talk over the prospects of the journey, with Harry Jervoise, with a real sense of interest and excitement in his mission.

In the evening, he again went to the house of the minister. The latter, a close observer of men, saw at once that the young officer was in much better spirits than he had been in the morning.

"Have you obtained information respecting any of the persons whose names I gave you?" he asked.

"Yes, sir. It seems that, most fortunately, the trader named Allan Ramsay is an old friend of Colonel Jamieson, and the colonel has given me a letter to him which will, he assures me, procure me a hearty welcome."

"And have you thought anything more of your best plan of action?"

"Yes, sir. It seems to me that I had better dress myself in an attire such as might be worn by a young Scotchman, journeying through the country to place himself with a relation established in business. I could ride behind the royal envoy, as if I had received permission to journey under the protection of his escort, and could drop behind a few miles from the capital, and make my way in alone. I could not, of course, inquire for Allan Ramsay in Polish, but I know enough French to ask for him at any shop having a French name over it, if I did not happen to light upon one kept by a Scotchman."

"Yes, that plan will do very well. But you will have no difficulty in finding the house, as I have arranged that a man shall accompany you as servant. He is a Lithuanian, and is the grandson of a soldier of Gustavus Adolphus, who married and settled there. His grandfather kept up his connection with his native country, and the young fellow speaks Swedish fairly, and, of course, Polish. For the last three weeks I have employed him in various matters, and find him shrewd and, I believe, faithful. Such a fellow would be of great use to you, and could, if necessary, act as your interpreter in any interviews you may have with Polish Jews, although you will find that most of these men speak other languages besides their own."

He touched a bell, and on a servant entering, said:

"Bring Stanislas Bistron here."

An active, well-built young fellow of some four and twenty years of age entered the room a minute later. His fair hair and blue eyes showed that he took after his Swedish ancestors.

"This is the gentleman, Stanislas, that you are to accompany to Warsaw, as his servant. You will obey him, in all respects, as if he had hired you in his service, and, should he arrive at any situation of danger or difficulty, I trust that you will not be found wanting."

The man had looked closely at Charlie.

"I will do my best, sir, and I doubt not that the gentleman's service will suit me. He has the look of one who would be kind to his servants."

"Wait at the outside door," the count said. "Captain Carstairs will speak to you as he leaves."

The man bowed and went out, and the count then said, with a smile at the look of surprise on Charlie's face:

"It was not a slip of the tongue. Here is a commission, signed by his majesty, appointing you to the rank of captain, as he has long considered that you had well won your promotion, by your suggestion which enabled him to cross the Dwina without loss; but he thought there would be a difficulty in placing you over the heads of so many officers senior to yourself. This inconvenience no longer exists, now that you have what may be considered a staff appointment, and the rank may, moreover, add to your weight and influence in your interviews with persons at Warsaw.

"You will need money. Here is a purse for your expenses. You may meet with some of these men, especially among the Jewish traders, who may need a bribe. Bribery is common, from the highest to the lowest, in Poland. You will find, in this letter of instructions, that you are authorized to promise sums of money to men whose assistance may be valuable. It is impossible to fix the sums. These must depend upon the position of the men, and the value of their services; and I can only say do not be lavish, but at the same time do not hesitate to promise a sum that will secure the services of useful men. Your best plan will be to find out, if you are able, what each man expects, and to make what abatement you can. The only limit placed is that you must not commit the royal treasury to a total sum exceeding ten thousand crowns. You will, I hope, find a smaller sum suffice.

"The envoy will start at six tomorrow morning. I do not know that there are any further instructions to give you. You will find details, in these written instructions, as to the manner in which you are to communicate, from time to time, the result of your mission, and you will receive orders when to return."

Outside the house, Charlie saw his new servant waiting him.

"You have a horse, Stanislas?"

"Yes, sir, I have been provided with one. I have also a brace of pistols, and a sword."

"I hope you will not have to use them, but in these disturbed times they are necessaries."

"I have better clothes than these, sir, if you wish me to look gay."

"By no means," Charlie replied. "I am going in the character of a young Scotchman, on my way to join a relative in business in Warsaw, and you accompany me in the capacity of guide and servant. As I should not be in a position to pay high wages, the more humble your appearance, the better. We start at six in the morning. The envoy will leave the royal quarters at that hour, and we travel with his escort. Join me a quarter of an hour before that at my hut. You had better accompany me there now, so that you may know the spot. I shall not require your services before we start, as my soldier servant will saddle my horse, and have all in readiness."

Harry came to the door of the hut, as he saw his friend approaching.

"Well, Charlie, is all satisfactorily settled?

"Yes, quite satisfactorily, I think. That is my new servant. Count Piper has appointed him. He speaks Swedish and Polish."

"That will be a great comfort to you, Charlie. Jock Armstrong, who has not picked up ten words of Swedish since he joined, would have been worse than useless."

"I have another piece of news, Harry, that I am in one way very glad of, and in another sorry for. I had always hoped that we should keep together, and that, just as we joined together, and were made lieutenants at the same time, it would always be so."

"You have got another step?" Harry exclaimed. "I am heartily glad of it. I thought very likely you might get it. Indeed, I was surprised that you did not get it, at once, after our fight with the Saxons. I am sure you deserved it, if ever a fellow did, considering what it saved us all."

"Of course it is for that," Charlie replied, "though I think it is very absurd. Count

Piper said the king would have given it to me at once, only it would have taken me over the heads of so many men older than myself; but he considered that, now I am going on a sort of staff work, away from the regiment, I could be promoted, and he thought, too, that the title of Captain would assist me in my mission."

"Of course it will," Harry said, warmly. "That is just what I told you, you know. This business was not quite to your liking, but it was a good long step towards making your fortune. Don't you think that I shall be jealous of your going ahead, for I am not in the least. I am sorry you are going away, for I shall miss you terribly; but I am quite content to be with the regiment, and to work my way up gradually. As it is, I am senior lieutenant in the regiment, and the first battle may give me my company; though I don't expect it, for I do not think my father would wish the colonel to give me the step, if it occurred, for all the other lieutenants are older than we are, though they are junior to us in the regiment, and I feel sure that he would prefer me to remain for another two or three years as lieutenant. In fact, he said as much to me, a short time ago. Still, when I am fit to command a company, there is no doubt I shall get it.

"Of course, I am sorry you are going, very sorry, Charlie; but, even if you go altogether on to the staff, I shall see a good deal of you, for, as the king is always with the army, this must be your headquarters still.

"I wonder how long you will be away. I like the look of the fellow who is going with you. It was an honest, open sort of face, as far as I saw it. At any rate, it is a comfort to think that you won't be absolutely alone, especially among people whose language you don't know. Mind, if you are sending letters to Count Piper, be sure you send a few lines, by the same messenger, to let me know how you are going on. Not long letters, you know; I expect you will have your hands pretty well full; but just enough to give me an idea of how you are, and what you are doing."

The following morning, Charlie started. He had said goodbye to no one, except the colonel, Major Jervoise, and Harry, as it was not considered advisable that his departure with the envoy for Warsaw should be talked about. He only joined the party, indeed, after they had ridden out of the camp. He had laid aside his uniform, and was dressed in clothes which Major Jervoise had procured for him, from one of the last-joined recruits who had but just received his uniform. The lieutenant commanding the escort of twenty troopers rode up to him, as he joined the party.

"Baron Seckers informs me that he has given permission to a young Scotchman and his servant, travelling to Warsaw, to ride under his protection. Are you the person in question, sir?"

"It is all right, Lieutenant Eberstein," Charlie said, with a smile. "Don't you recognize me?"

"Of course--Lieutenant Carstairs. I was at the hunt where you were taken prisoner; but I did not expect to see you in this garb."

"I am going on duty," Charlie said, "and am dressed according to orders. Do not address me by my name. I am at present Sandy Anderson, going to join a relation in Warsaw."

"Ah, ah! Is that so? Going to put your head into the den of the Lion Augustus. Well, I rather envy you, for it is likely, by all accounts, to be dull work here for some time. It is hard to be sitting idle, while the Russian guns are thundering round Narva. Now, I must join the baron again. Where would you rather ride--after us, or behind the escort?"

"Behind the escort. I think it will be more natural, and I can chat more freely with my servant. He is a Lithuanian, but speaks Swedish, and I hope to get some information from him."

The lieutenant rode on, and, as he passed the troopers, he told them that the two men behind had the baron's permission to ride with them, in order that they might have protection from the bands of pillagers who were roaming through the country.

"Now, Stanislas," Charlie said. "We can talk freely together. Do you know Warsaw?"

"I have been there several times, sir, but I never stopped there long. Still, I can find my way about the town."

"When were you there last?"

"Some two months ago. It was just before I entered the Swedish service."

"And what do the people say about the war?"

"They are bitterly opposed to it. The king entered upon it without consulting the diet, which was altogether contrary to the constitution. It is true that the king may do so, in cases of emergency, and obtain the sanction of the diet afterwards. There was no urgency here, and the king made his agreement with the czar and the king of Denmark without anyone knowing of it. He certainly obtained a sort of sanction from the diet afterwards, but everyone knows how these things are worked. He has a strong party, of course, because it is the interest of a great many people to retain him in power, as no one can say who would be chosen to succeed him. But among the people in general, the traders and the peasants, he is hated, and so are his Saxon soldiers.

"Suppose he had gained a slice of Swedish territory. It would not have benefited them; while, as it is, all sorts of misfortunes and troubles have come upon the country, and none can say how much greater may ensue.

"Poland is always split up into parties. They used to unite against the Turk, and they would unite again against the Swedes, if their country was invaded; but as long as King Charles keeps his army beyond the frontier, they are too deeply engaged in their own quarrels to think of anything else."

"Then, even if I were known, in the city, to be in the Swedish service, there would be little danger, Stanislas?"

"I do not say that, at all," the man said gravely. "In the first place, Warsaw is held by Saxon soldiers, who would show you but scant mercy, were you known to be a Swedish officer; and, in the second place, the lower classes are ever ready to make tumults; and, if worked upon by the archbishop, or the nobles of the king's party, they would readily enough tear a stranger to pieces.

"Going as you do as a Scotchman, there is, I hope, little danger, especially if you are received into a Scottish household."

The journey passed without incident, until they were within a few miles of Warsaw, when Charlie, after formally thanking Baron Seckers for the protection his escort had afforded him, fell behind with his servant. Several parties of armed men had been met with, but they knew better than to interfere with the little body of Swedish cavalry; while, in the towns through which they passed, the baron was respectfully received as the envoy of the dreaded King of Sweden.

"Is there another gate to the city, on this side of the town, beside that by which the Swedes will enter? If so, it would be as well to use it, so that there should seem to be no connection between us and them," said Charlie.

There was another gate, and by this they rode into Warsaw, at that time a city of far greater importance than it is at present. The gate was unguarded, and they passed through without question. The citizens were talking excitedly in groups, evidently discussing the question of the arrival of the Swedish envoy, and the chances of peace; and no attention was paid to the travellers, whose appearance denoted them to be persons of no importance. Richly-attired nobles, in costumes of almost oriental magnificence, galloped through the streets on splendid horses, scattering the groups of citizens, and paying no attention whatever to the angry murmurs that followed them.

Charlie stopped at a small inn, and there the horses were put up. Stanislas made inquiries for the shop of Allan Ramsay, mentioning that his employer was a relation of the Scottish merchant, and had come out to be with him, until he had learned the language.

"The Scots know their business," the landlord grumbled. "They and the French and the Jews, together, have their hand in everyone's pocket. They buy the cattle and grain of the peasants, for what they choose to give for them, and send them out of the country, getting all the profits of the transaction; while, as to the nobles, there is scarce one who is not deep in their books."

"Still, you could not do without them," Stanislas said. "There must be somebody to buy and to sell, and as the nobles won't do it, and the peasants can't, I don't see that the foreigners are to be blamed for coming in and taking the trade."

"That is true enough," the landlord admitted reluctantly. "Still, there is no doubt the country is kept poor, while, between them, these men gather up the harvest."

"Better that than let it rot upon the ground," Stanislas said unconcernedly; and then, having obtained the name of the street where several of the Scottish traders had places of business, he and Charlie started on foot. They were not long in finding the shop with the sign of the merchant swinging over the door.

"You had better wait outside, Stanislas, while I go in and see the master. No; if he is not in the shop, his men will not understand me, so come in with me till you see that I have met him, and then go back to the inn for the night. Whether I join you there will depend upon the warmth of my welcome."

Two or three young Poles were in the shop. Stanislas asked them for Allan Ramsay, and they replied that he was taking his evening meal upstairs, whereupon Charlie produced the letter from Colonel Jamieson, and Stanislas requested one of them to take it up to the merchant. Three minutes later the inner door opened, and a tall man with a ruddy face and blue eyes entered, holding the open letter in his hand. Charlie took a step forward to meet him.

"So you are Sandy Anderson," he said heartily, with a merry twinkle in his eye, "my connection, it seems, and the friend of my dear classmate Jamieson? Come upstairs. Who is this Scotch-looking lad with you?"

"He is my servant and interpreter. His grandfather was a Swede, and to him he owes his fair hair and complexion. He is a Lithuanian. He is to be trusted, I hope, thoroughly. He was sent with me by--"

"Never mind names," the Scotchman said hastily. "We will talk about him afterwards. Now come upstairs. Your letter has thrown me quite into a flutter.

"Never say anything in English before those Poles," he said, as he left the shop; "the fellows pick up languages as easily as I can drink whisky, when I get the chance. One of them has been with me two years, and it is quite likely he understands, at any rate, something of what is said.

"Here we are."

He opened a door, and ushered Charlie into a large room, comfortably furnished. His wife, a boy eight years of age, and a girl a year older, were seated at the table.

"Janet," the merchant said, "this is Captain Carstairs, alias Sandy Anderson, a connection of ours, though I cannot say, for certain, of what degree."

"What are you talking of, Allan?" she asked in surprise; for her husband, after opening and partly reading the letter, had jumped up and run off without saying a word.

"What I say, wife. This gentleman is, for the present, Sandy Anderson, who has come out to learn the business and language, with the intent of some day entering into partnership with me; also, which is more to the point, he is a friend of my good friend Jock Jamieson, whom you remember well in the old days."

"I am very glad, indeed, to see any friend of Jock Jamieson," Janet Ramsay said warmly, holding out her hand to Charlie, "though I do not in the least understand what my husband is talking about, or what your name really is."

"My name is Carstairs, madam. I am a captain in the Swedish service, and am here on a mission for King Charles. Colonel Jamieson, for he is now colonel of the regiment to which I belong--"

"What!" the merchant exclaimed. "Do you mean to say that our Jock Jamieson is a colonel? Well, well, who would have thought he would have climbed the tree so quickly?"

"It is a regiment entirely of Scotch and Englishmen," Charlie said; "and he was promoted, to take its command, only a short time since."

"Well, please to sit down and join us," Mrs. Ramsay said. "It is bad manners, indeed, to keep you talking while the meat is getting cold on the table. When you have finished, it will be time enough to question you."

While the meal was going on, however, many questions were asked as to Colonel Jamieson, the regiment, and its officers.

"As soon as matters are more settled," the merchant said, "I will give myself a holiday, and Janet and I will go and spend a few days with Jock. Many of the names of the officers are well known to me, and two or three of the captains were at Glasgow College with Jock and myself. It will be like old times, to have four or five of us talking over the wild doings we had together."

The supper over, the children were sent off to bed. Allan Ramsay lit a long pipe. A bottle of wine and two glasses were placed on the table, and Mrs. Ramsay withdrew, to see after domestic matters, and prepare a room for Charlie.

"Now, lad, tell me all about it," Allan Ramsay said. "Jock tells me you are here on a mission, which he would leave it to yourself to explain; but it is no business of mine, and, if you would rather keep it to yourself, I will ask no questions."

"There is no secret about it, as far as you are concerned, Mr. Ramsay, for it is to you and to other merchants here that I have come to talk it over;" and he then went fully into the subject.

The Scotchman sat, smoking his pipe in silence, for some minutes after he had concluded.

"We do not much meddle with politics here. We have neither voice nor part in the making of kings or of laws, and, beyond that we like to have a peace-loving king, it matters little to us whom the diet may set up over us. If we were once to put the tips of our fingers into Polish affairs, we might give up all thought of trade. They are forever intriguing and plotting, except when they are fighting; and it would be weary work to keep touch with it all, much less to take part in it. It is our business to buy and to sell, and so that both parties come to us, it matters little; one's money is as good as the other. If I had one set of creditors deeper in my books than another, I might wish their party to gain the day, for it would, maybe, set them up in funds, and I might get my money; but, as it is, it matters little. There is not a customer I have but is in my debt. Money is always scarce with them; for they are reckless and extravagant, keeping a horde of idle loons about them, spending as much money on their own attire and that of their wives as would keep a whole Scotch clan in victuals. But, if they cannot pay in money, they can pay in corn or in cattle, in wine or in hides.

"I do not know which they are fondest of--plotting, or fighting, or feasting; and yet, reckless as they are, they are people to like. If they do sell their votes for money, it is not a Scotchman that should throw it in their teeth; for there is scarce a Scotch noble, since the days of Bruce, who has not been ready to sell himself for English gold. Our own Highlanders are as fond of fighting as the Poles, and their chiefs are as profuse in hospitality, and as reckless and spendthrift.

"But the Poles have their virtues. They love their country, and are ready to die for her. They are courteous, and even chivalrous, they are hospitable to an excess, they are good husbands and kindly masters, they are recklessly brave; and, if they are unduly fond of finery, I, who supply so many of them, should be the last to find fault with them on that score. They are proud, and look down upon us traders, but that does not hurt us; and, if they were to take to trading themselves, there would be no place for us here. But this has nothing to do with our present purpose.

"Certainly, if it was a question of Polish affairs, neither the foreign nor the Jewish merchants here would move a finger one way or the other. We have everything to lose, and nothing to gain. Suppose we took sides with one of the parties, and the other got the upper hand. Why, they might make ordinances hampering us in every way, laying heavy taxes on us, forbidding the export of cattle or horses, and making our lives burdensome. True, if they drove us out they would soon have to repeal the law, for all trade would be at an end. But that would be too late for many of us.

"However, I do not say that, at the present time, many would not be disposed to do what they could against Augustus of Saxony. We are accustomed to civil wars; and, though these may cause misery and ruin, in the districts where they take place, they do not touch us here in the capital. But this is a different affair. Augustus has, without reason or provocation, brought down your fiery King of Sweden upon us;

and, if he continues on the throne, we may hear the Swedish cannon thundering outside our walls, and may have the city taken and sacked. Therefore, for once, politics become our natural business.

"But, though you may find many well wishers, I doubt if you can obtain any substantial aid. With Saxon troops in the town, and the nobles divided, there is no hope of a successful rising in Warsaw."

"The king did not think of that," Charlie said. "His opinion was, that were it evident that the citizens of Warsaw were strongly opposed to Augustus of Saxony, it would have a great moral effect, and that, perhaps, they might influence some of the nobles who, as you say, are deeply in their books, or upon whose estates they may hold mortgages, to join the party against the king."

"They might do something that way," Allan Ramsay agreed. "Of course, I have no money out on mortgages. I want badly enough all the money I can lay hands on in my own business. Giving credit, as we have to, and often very long credit, it requires a large capital to carry on trade. But the Jews, who no doubt do hold large mortgages on the land, cannot exert much power. They cannot hold land themselves, and, were one of them to venture to sell the property of any noble of influence, he would be ruined. The whole class would shrink from him, and, like enough, there would be a tumult got up, his house would be burned over his head, and he and his family murdered.

"Still, as far as popular opinion goes, something might be done. At any rate, I will get some of my friends here tomorrow, and introduce you to them and talk it over. But we must be careful, for Augustus has a strong party here, and, were it suspected that you are a Swedish officer, it would go very hard with you.

"Tomorrow you must fetch your servant here. I have already sent round to the inn, and you will find your valises in your room. You said you could rely thoroughly upon him?"

"Yes, he was handed over to me by Count Piper himself; and moreover, from what I have seen of him, I am myself confident that he can be trusted. He is of Swedish descent, and is, I think, a very honest fellow."

For a fortnight, Charlie remained at Allan Ramsay's, and then, in spite of the pressing entreaties of his host and hostess, took a lodging near them. He had, by this time, seen a good many of the leading traders of the town. The Scotch and Frenchmen had all heartily agreed with his argument, that it was for the benefit of Poland, and especially for that of Warsaw, that Augustus of Saxony should be replaced by another king, who would be acceptable to Charles of Sweden; but all were of opinion that but little could be done, by them, towards bringing about this result.

With the Jewish traders his success was less decided. They admitted that it would be a great misfortune, were Warsaw taken by the Swedes, but, as Poles, they retained their confidence in the national army, and were altogether sceptical that a few thousand Swedes could withstand the host that could be put in the field against them.

Several of them pointedly asked what interest they had in the matter, and, to some of these, Charlie was obliged to use his power of promising sums of money, in case of success.

There were one or two, however, of whom he felt doubtful. Chief among these was Ben Soloman Muller, a man of great influence in the Jewish community. This man had placed so large a value upon his services, that Charlie did not feel justified in promising him such a sum. He did not like the man's face, and did not rely upon the promises of silence he had given, before the mission was revealed to him. It was for this reason, principally, that he determined to go into lodgings. Should he be denounced, serious trouble might fall upon Allan Ramsay, and it would at least minimize this risk, were he not living at his house when he was arrested. Ramsay himself was disposed to make light of the danger.

"I believe myself that Ben Soloman is an old rogue, but he is not a fool. He cannot help seeing that the position of the king is precarious, and, were he to cause your arrest, he might get little thanks and no profit, while he would be incurring the risk of the vengeance of Charles, should he ever become master of the town. Did he have you arrested, he himself would be forced to appear as a witness against you, and this he could hardly do without the matter becoming publicly known.

"I do not say, however, that, if he could curry favour with the king's party by doing you harm, without appearing in the matter, he would hesitate for a moment.

"Even if you were arrested here, I doubt whether any great harm would befall me, for all the Scotch merchants would make common cause with me, and, although we have no political power, we have a good deal of influence one way or another, and Augustus, at this time, would not care to make fresh enemies. However, lad, I will not further dispute your decision. Were I quite alone, I would not let you leave me, so long as you stop in this city, without taking great offence; but, with a wife and two children, a man is more timid than if he had but himself to think of."

Charlie therefore moved into the lodging, but every day he went for three or four hours to the shop, where he kept up his assumed character by aiding to keep the ledgers, and in learning from the Polish assistants the value of the various goods in the shop.

One evening, he was returning after supper to his lodging, when Stanislas met him.

"I observed three or four evil-looking rascals casting glances at the house today, and there are several rough-looking fellows hanging about the house this evening. I do not know if it means anything, but I thought I would let you know."

"I think it must be only your fancy, Stanislas. I might be arrested by the troops, were I denounced, but I apprehend no danger from men of the class you speak of. However, if we should be interfered with, I fancy we could deal with several rascals of that sort."

At the corner of his street, three or four men were standing. One of them moved, as he passed, and pushed rudely against him, sending his hat into the gutter. Then, as his face was exposed, the fellow exclaimed:

"It is he, death to the Swedish spy!"

They were the last words he uttered. Charlie's sword flew from its scabbard, and, with a rapid pass, he ran the man through the body. The others drew instantly, and fell upon Charlie with fury, keeping up the shout of, "Death to the Swedish spy!" It was evidently a signal--for men darted out of doorways, and came running down the street, repeating the cry.

"Go, Stanislas!" Charlie shouted, as he defended himself against a dozen assailants. "Tell Ramsay what has happened; you can do no good here."

A moment later, he received a tremendous blow on the back of the head, from an iron-bound cudgel, and fell senseless to the ground.

Chapter 10: In Evil Plight.

When Charlie recovered his senses, he found himself lying bound in a room lighted by a dim lamp, which sufficed only to show that the beams were blackened by smoke and age, and the walls constructed of rough stone work. There was, so far as he could see, no furniture whatever in it, and he imagined that it was an underground cellar, used perhaps, at some time or other, as a storeroom. It was some time before his brain was clear enough to understand what had happened, or how he had got into his present position. Gradually the facts came back to him, and he was able to think coherently, in spite of a splitting headache, and a dull, throbbing pain at the back of his head.

"I was knocked down and stunned," he said to himself, at last. "I wonder what became of Stanislas. I hope he got away.

"This does not look like a prison. I should say that it was a cellar, in the house of one of the gang that set upon me. It is evident that someone has betrayed me, probably that Jew, Ben Soloman. What have they brought me here for? I wonder what are they going to do with me."

His head, however, hurt him too much for him to continue the strain of thought, and, after a while, he dozed off to sleep. When he awoke, a faint light was streaming in through a slit, two or three inches wide, high up on the wall. He still felt faint and dizzy, from the effects of the blow. Parched with thirst, he tried to call out for water, but scarce a sound came from his lips.

Gradually, the room seemed to darken and become indistinct, and he again lapsed into insensibility. When he again became conscious, someone was pouring water between his lips, and he heard a voice speaking loudly and angrily. He had picked up a few words of Polish from Stanislas--the names of common things, the words to use in case he lost his way, how to ask for food and for stabling for a horse, but he was unable to understand what was said. He judged, however, that someone was furiously upbraiding the man who was giving him water, for the latter now and then muttered excuses.

"He is blowing the fellow up, for having so nearly let me slip through their fingers," he said to himself. "Probably they want to question me, and find out who I have been in communication with. They shall get nothing, at present, anyhow."

He kept his eyes resolutely closed. Presently, he heard a door open, and another man come in. A few words were exchanged, and, this time, wine instead of water was poured down his throat. Then he was partly lifted up, and felt a cooling sensation at the back of his head. Some bandages were passed round it, and he was laid down again. There was some more conversation, then a door opened and two of the men went out; the third walked back to him, muttering angrily to himself.

Charlie felt sure that he had been moved from the place in which he had been the evening before. His bonds had been loosed, and he was lying on straw, and not on the bare ground. Opening his eyelids the slightest possible degree, he was confirmed in his belief, by seeing that there was much more light than could have entered the cellar. He dared not look farther, and, in a short time, fell into a far more refreshing sleep than that he before had.

The next time he woke his brain was clearer, though there was still a dull sense of pain where he had been struck. Without opening his eyes, he listened attentively. There was some sound of movement in the room, and, presently, he heard a faint regular breathing. This continued for some time, and he then heard a sort of grunt.

"He is asleep," he said to himself, and, opening his eyes slightly looked round. He was in another chamber. It was grimy with dirt, and almost as unfurnished as the cellar, but there was a window through which the sun was streaming brightly. He, himself, lay upon a heap of straw. At the opposite side of the room was a similar heap, and upon this a man was sitting, leaning against the wall, with his chin dropped on his chest.

The thought of escape at once occurred to Charlie. Could he reach the window, which was without glass and a mere opening in the wall, without awakening his guard, he could drop out and make for Allan Ramsay's. As soon as he tried to move, however, he found that this idea was for the present impracticable. He felt too weak to lift his head, and, at the slight rustle of straw caused by the attempt, the man opposite roused himself with a start.

He gave another slight movement, and then again lay quiet with his eyes closed. The man came across and spoke, but he made no sign. Some more wine was poured between his lips, then the man returned to his former position, and all was quiet.

As he lay thinking his position over, Charlie thought that those who had set his assailants to their work must have had two objects--the one to put a stop to his efforts to organize an agitation against the king, the second to find out, by questioning him, who were those with whom he had been in communication, in order that they might be arrested, and their property confiscated. He could see no other reason why his life should be spared by his assailants, for it would have been easier, and far less troublesome, to run him through as he lay senseless on the ground, than to carry him off and keep him a prisoner.

This idea confirmed the suspicion he had first entertained, that the assault had been organized by Ben Soloman. He could have no real interest in the king, for he was ready to join in the organization against him, could he have obtained his own terms. He might intend to gain credit with the royal party, by claiming to have stopped a dangerous plot, and at the same time to benefit himself, by bringing about the expulsion or death of many of his foreign trade rivals. For this end, the Jew would desire that he should be taken alive, in order to serve as a witness against the others.

"He will not get any names from me," he said. "Besides, none of them have promised to take any active measures against Augustus. I did not ask them to do so. There is no high treason in trying to influence public opinion. Still, it is likely enough that the Jew wants to get me to acknowledge that an insurrection was intended, and will offer me my freedom, if I will give such testimony. As I am altogether in his power, the only thing to do is to pretend to be a great deal worse than I am, and so to gain time, till I am strong enough to try to get away from this place."

All this was not arrived at, at once, but was the result of half-dreamy cogitation extending over hours, and interrupted by short snatches of sleep. He was conscious that, from time to time, someone came into the room and spoke to his guard; and that, three or four times, wine was poured between his lips. Once he was raised up, and fresh cloths, dipped in water, and bandages applied to his head.

In the evening, two or three men came in, and he believed that he recognized the voice of one of them as that of Ben Soloman. One of the men addressed him suddenly and sharply in Swedish.

"How are you feeling? Are you in pain? We have come here to give you your freedom."

Charlie was on his guard, and remained silent, with his eyes closed.

"It is of no use," Ben Soloman said in his own language. "The fellow is still insensible. The clumsy fool who hit him would fare badly, if I knew who he was. I said that he was to be knocked down, silenced, and brought here; and here he is, of no more use than if he were dead."

"He will doubtless come round, in time," another said in an apologetic tone. "We will bring him round, if you will have patience, Ben Soloman."

"Well, well," the other replied, "a few days will make no difference; but mind that he is well guarded, directly he begins to gain strength. I will get him out of the town, as soon as I can. Allan Ramsay has laid a complaint, before the mayor, that his countryman has been attacked by a band of ruffians, and has been either killed or carried off by them. It is a pity that servant of his was not killed."

"We thought he was dead. Two or three of us looked at him, and I could have sworn that life was out of him."

"Well, then, you would have sworn what was not true, for he managed to crawl to Ramsay's, where he lies, I am told, dangerously ill, and an official has been to him, to obtain his account of the fray. It was a bungled business, from beginning to end."

"We could not have calculated on the fellows making such a resistance," the other grumbled. "This one seemed but a lad, and yet he killed three of our party, and the other killed one. A nice business that; and you will have to pay their friends well, Ben Soloman, for I can tell you there is grumbling at the price, which they say was not enough for the work, which you told them would be easy."

"It ought to have been," the Jew said sullenly. "Fifteen or twenty men to overpower a lad. What could have been more easy? However, I will do something for the friends of the men who were fools enough to get themselves killed, but if I hear any grumbling from the others, it will be worse for them; there is not one I could not lay by the heels in jail.

"Well, as to this young fellow, I shall not come again. I do not want to be noticed coming here. Keep a shrewd lookout after him."

"There is no fear about that," the man said. "It will be long ere he is strong enough to walk."

"When he gets better, we will have him taken away to a safe place outside the town. Once there, I can make him say what I like."

"And if he does not get well?"

"In that case, we will take away his body and bury it outside. I will see to that myself."

"I understand," the other sneered. "You don't want anyone to know where it is buried, so as to be able to bring it up against you."

"You attend to your own business," the Jew said angrily. "Why should I care about what they say? At any rate, there are some matters between you and me, and there is no fear of your speaking."

"Not until the time comes when I may think it worth my while to throw away my life, in order to secure your death, Ben Soloman."

"It is of no use talking like that," the Jew said quietly. "We are useful to each other. I have saved your life from the gibbet, you have done the work I required. Between us, it is worse than childish to threaten in the present matter. I do not doubt that you will do your business well, and you know that you will be well paid for it; what can either of us require more?"

Charlie would have given a good deal to understand the conversation, and he would have been specially glad to learn that Stanislas had escaped with his life; for he had taken a great fancy to the young Lithuanian, and was grieved by the thought that he had probably lost his life in his defence.

Three days passed. His head was now clear, and his appetite returning, and he found, by quietly moving at night, when his guard was asleep, that he was gaining strength. The third day, there was some talking among several men who entered the room; then he was lifted, wrapt up in some cloths, and put into a large box. He felt this being hoisted up, it was carried downstairs, and then placed on something. A minute afterwards he felt a vibration, followed by a swaying and bumping, and guessed at once that he was on a cart, and was being removed, either to prison or to some other place of confinement. The latter he considered more probable.

The journey was a long one. He had no means of judging time, but he thought that it must have lasted two or three hours. Then the rumbling ceased, the box was lifted down, and carried a short distance, then the lid was opened and he was again laid down on some straw. He heard the sound of cart wheels, and knew that the vehicle on which he had been brought was being driven away.

He was now so hungry that he felt he could no longer maintain the appearance of insensibility. Two men were talking in the room, and when, for a moment, their conversation ceased, he gave a low groan, and then opened his eyes. They came at once to his bedside, with exclamations of satisfaction.

"How do you feel?" one asked in Swedish.

"I do not know," he said in a low tone. "Where am I, how did I get here?"

"You are with friends. Never mind how you got here. You have been ill, but you will soon get well again. Someone hit you on the head, and we picked you up and brought you here."

"I am weak and faint," Charlie murmured. "Have you any food?"

"You shall have some food, directly it is prepared. Take a drink of wine, and see if you can eat a bit of bread while the broth is preparing."

Charlie drank a little of the wine that was put to his lips, and then broke up the bread, and ate it crumb by crumb, as if it were a great effort to do so, although he had difficulty in restraining himself from eating it voraciously. When he had finished it, he closed his eyes again, as if sleep had overpowered him. An hour later, there was a touch on his shoulder.

"Here is some broth, young fellow. Wake up and drink that, it will do you good."

Charlie, as before, slowly sipped down the broth, and then really fell asleep, for the jolting had fatigued him terribly.

It was evening when he awoke. Two men were sitting at a blazing fire. When he moved, one of them brought him another basin of broth, and fed him with a spoon.

Charlie had been long enough in the country to know, by the appearance of the room, that he was in a peasant's hut. He wondered why he had been brought there, and concluded that it must be because Allan Ramsay had set so stringent a search on foot in the city, that they considered it necessary to take him away.

"They will not keep me here long," he said to himself. "I am sure that I could walk now, and, in another two or three days, I shall be strong enough to go some distance. That soup has done me a deal of good. I believe half my weakness is from hunger."

He no longer kept up the appearance of unconsciousness, and, in the morning, put various questions, to the man who spoke Swedish, as to what had happened and how he came to be there. This man was evidently, from his dress and appearance, a Jew, while the other was as unmistakably a peasant, a rough powerfully-built man with an evil face. The Jew gave him but little information, but told him that in a day or two, when he was strong enough to listen, a friend would come who would tell him all about it.

On the third day, he heard the sound of an approaching horse, and was not surprised when, after a conversation in a low tone outside, Ben Soloman entered. Charlie was now much stronger, but he had carefully abstained from showing any marked improvement, speaking always in a voice a little above a whisper, and allowing the men to feed him, after making one or two pretended attempts to convey the spoon to his mouth.

"Well, Master Englishman," Ben Soloman said, as he came up to his bedside, "what do you think of things?"

"I do not know what to think," Charlie said feebly. "I do not know where I am, or why I am here. I remember that there was a fray in the street, and I suppose I was hurt. But why was I brought here, instead of being taken to my lodgings?"

"Because you would be no use to me in your lodging, and you may be a great deal of use to me here," Ben Soloman said. "You know you endeavoured to entrap me into a plot against the king's life."

Charlie shook his head, and looked wonderingly at the speaker.

"No, no," he said, "there was no plot against the king's life. I only asked if you would use your influence among your friends to turn popular feeling against Augustus."

"Nothing of the kind," the Jew said harshly. "You wanted him removed by poison or the knife. There is no mistake about that, and that is what I am going to swear, and what, if you want to save your life, you will have to swear too; and you will have to give the names of all concerned in the plot, and to swear that they were all agreed to bring about the death of the king. Now you understand why you were brought here. You are miles away from another house, and you may shout and scream as loud as you like. You are in my power."

"I would die rather than make a false accusation."

"Listen to me," the Jew said sternly. "You are weak now, too weak to suffer much. This day week I will return, and then you had best change your mind, and sign a document I shall bring with me, with the full particulars of the plot to murder the king, and the names of those concerned in it. This you will sign. I shall take it to the proper authorities, and obtain a promise that your life shall be spared, on condition of your giving evidence against these persons."

"I would never sign such a villainous document," Charlie said.

"You will sign it," Ben Soloman said calmly. "When you find yourself roasting over a slow charcoal fire, you will be ready to sign anything I wish you to."

So saying, he turned and left the room. He talked for some time to the men outside, then Charlie heard him ride off.

"You villain," he said to himself. "When you come, at the end of a week, you will not find me here; but, if I get a chance of having a reckoning with you, it will be bad for you."

Charlie's progress was apparently slow. The next day he was able to sit up and feed himself. Two days later he could totter across the room, and lie down before the fire. The men were completely deceived by his acting, and, considering any attempt to escape, in his present weak state, altogether impossible, paid but little heed to him, the peasant frequently absenting himself for hours together.

Looking from his window, Charlie saw that the hut was situated in a thick wood, and, from the blackened appearance of the peasant's face and garments, he guessed him to be a charcoal burner, and therefore judged that the trees he saw must form part of a forest of considerable extent.

The weather was warm, and his other guard often sat, for a while, outside the door. During his absence, Charlie lifted the logs of wood piled beside the hearth, and was able to test his returning strength, assuring himself that, although not yet fully recovered, he was gaining ground daily. He resolved not to wait until the seventh day; for Ben Soloman might change his mind, and return before the day he had named. He determined, therefore, that on the sixth day he would make the attempt.

He had no fear of being unable to overcome his Jewish guard, as he would have the advantage of a surprise. He only delayed as long as possible, because he doubted his powers of walking any great distance, and of evading the charcoal burner, who would, on his return, certainly set out in pursuit of him. Moreover, he wished to remain in the hut nearly up to the time of the Jew's return, as he was determined to wait in the forest, and revenge himself for the suffering he had caused him, and for the torture to which he intended to put him.

The evening before the day on which he decided to make the attempt, the charcoal burner and the Jew were in earnest conversation. The word signifying brigand was frequently repeated, and, although he could not understand much more than this, he concluded, from the peasant's talk and gestures, that he had either come across some of these men in the forest, or had gathered from signs he had observed, perhaps from their fires, that they were there.

The Jew shrugged his shoulders when the narration was finished. The presence of brigands was a matter of indifference to him. The next day, the charcoal burner went off at noon.

"Where does he go to?" Charlie asked his guard.

"He has got some charcoal fires alight, and is obliged to go and see to them. They have to be kept covered up with wet leaves and earth, so that the wood shall only smoulder," the man said, as he lounged out of the hut to his usual seat.

Charlie waited a short time, then went to the pile of logs, and picked out a straight stick about a yard long and two inches in diameter. With one of the heavier ones he could have killed the man, but the fellow was only acting under the orders of his employer, and, although he would doubtless, at Ben Soloman's commands, have roasted him alive without compunction, he had not behaved with any unkindness, and had, indeed, seemed to do his best for him.

Taking the stick, he went to the door. He trod lightly, but in the stillness of the forest the man heard him, and glanced round as he came out.

Seeing the stick in his hand he leaped up, exclaiming, "You young fool!" and sprang towards him.

He had scarce time to feel surprise, as Charlie quickly raised the club. It described a swift sweep, fell full on his head, and he dropped to the ground as if shot.

Charlie ran in again, seized a coil of rope, bound his hands and feet securely, and dragged him into the hut. Then he dashed some cold water on his face. The man opened his eyes, and tried to move.

"You are too tightly bound to move, Pauloff," he said. "I could have killed you if I had chosen, but I did not wish to. You have not been unkind to me, and I owe you no grudge; but tell your rascally employer that I will be even with him, some-day, for the evil he has done me."

"You might as well have killed me," the man said, "for he will do so when he finds I let you escape."

"Then my advice to you is, be beforehand with him. You are as strong a man as he is, and if I were in your place, and a man who meant to kill me came into a lonely hut like this, I would take precious good care that he had no chance of carrying out his intentions."

Charlie then took two loaves of black bread and a portion of goat's flesh from the cupboard; found a bottle about a quarter full of coarse spirits, filled it up with water and put it in his pocket, and then, after taking possession of the long knife his captive wore in his belt, went out of the hut and closed the door behind him.

He had purposely moved slowly about the hut, as he made these preparations, in order that the Jew should believe that he was still weak; but, indeed, the effort of dragging the man into the hut had severely taxed his strength, and he found that he was much weaker than he had supposed.

The hut stood in a very small clearing, and Charlie had no difficulty in seeing the track by which the cart had come, for the marks of the wheels were still visible in the soft soil. He followed this until, after about two miles' walking, he came to the edge of the wood. Then he retraced his steps for a quarter of a mile, turned off, and with some difficulty made his way into a patch of thick undergrowth, where, after first cutting a formidable cudgel, he lay down, completely exhausted.

Late in the afternoon he was aroused from a doze by the sound of footsteps, and, looking through the screen of leaves, he saw his late jailers hurrying along the path. The charcoal burner carried a heavy axe, while the Jew, whose head was bound up with a cloth, had a long knife in his girdle. They went as far as the end of the forest, and then retraced their steps slowly. They were talking loudly, and Charlie could gather, from the few words he understood, and by their gestures, something of the purport of their conversation.

"I told you it was of no use your coming on as far as this," the Jew said. "Why, he was hardly strong enough to walk."

"He managed to knock you down, and afterwards to drag you into the house," the other said.

"It does not require much strength to knock a man down with a heavy club, when he is not expecting it, Conrad. He certainly did drag me in, but he was obliged to sit down afterwards, and I watched him out of one eye as he was making his preparations, and he could only just totter about. I would wager you anything he cannot have gone two hundred yards from the house. That is where we must search for him. I warrant we shall find him hidden in a thicket thereabouts."

"We shall have to take a lantern then, for it will be dark before we get back."

"Our best plan will be to leave it alone till morning. If we sit outside the hut, and take it in turns to watch, we shall hear him when he moves, which he is sure to do when it gets dark. It will be a still night, and we should hear a stick break half a mile away. We shall catch him, safe enough, before he has gone far."

"Well, I hope we shall have him back before Ben Soloman comes," the charcoal burner said, "or it will be worse for both of us. You know as well as I do he has got my neck in a noose, and he has got his thumb on you."

"If we can't find this Swede, I would not wait here for any money. I would fly at once."

"You would need to fly, in truth, to get beyond Ben Soloman's clutches," the charcoal burner said gruffly. "He has got agents all over the country."

"Then what would you do?"

"There is only one thing to do. It is our lives or his. When he rides up tomorrow, we will meet him at the door as if nothing had happened, and, with my axe, I will cleave his head asunder as he comes in. If he sees me in time to retreat, you shall stab him in the back. Then we will dig a big hole in the wood, and throw him in, and we will kill his horse and bury it with him.

"Who would ever be the wiser? I was going to propose it last time, only I was not sure of you then; but, now that you are in it as deep as I am--deeper, indeed, for he put you here specially to look after this youngster--your interest in the matter is as great as mine."

The Jew was silent for some time, then he said:

"He has got papers at home which would bring me to the gallows."

"Pooh!" the other said. "You do not suppose that, when it is found that he does not return, and his heirs open his coffers, they will take any trouble about what there may be in the papers there, except such as relate to his money. I will warrant there are papers there which concern scores of men besides you, for I know that Ben Soloman likes to work with agents he has got under his thumb. But, even if all the papers should be put into the hands of the authorities, what would come of it? They have got their hands full of other matters, for the present, and with the Swedes on their frontier, and the whole country divided into factions, who do you think is going to trouble to hunt up men for affairs that occurred years ago? Even if they did, they would not catch you. They have not got the means of running you down that Ben Soloman has.

"I tell you, man, it must be done. There is no other way out of it."

"Well, Conrad, if we cannot find this fellow before Ben Soloman comes, I am with you in the business. I have been working for him on starvation pay for the last three years, and hate him as much as you can."

When they reached the hut they cooked a meal, and then prepared to keep alternate watch.

Charlie slept quietly all night, and, in the morning, remained in his hiding place until he heard, in the distance, the sound of a horse's tread. Then he went out and sat down, leaning against a tree by the side of the path, in an attitude of exhaustion.

Presently he saw Ben Soloman approaching. He got up feebly, and staggered a few paces to another tree, farther from the path. He heard an angry shout, and then Ben Soloman rode up, and, with a torrent of execrations at the carelessness of the watchers, leapt from his horse and sprang to seize the fugitive, whom he regarded as incapable of offering the slightest resistance.

Charlie straightened himself up, as if with an effort, and raised his cudgel.

"I will not be taken alive," he said.

Ben Soloman drew his long knife from his girdle. "Drop that stick," he said, "or it will be worse for you."

"It cannot be worse than being tortured to death, as you said."

The Jew, with an angry snarl, sprang forward so suddenly and unexpectedly that he was within the swing of Charlie's cudgel before the latter could strike. He dropped the weapon at once, and caught the wrist of the uplifted hand that held the knife.

The Jew gave a cry of astonishment and rage, as they clasped each other, and he found that, instead of an unresisting victim, he was in a powerful grasp. For a moment there was a desperate struggle.

The Jew would, at ordinary times, have been no match for Charlie, but the latter was far from having regained his normal strength. His fury at the treatment he had received at the man's hands, however, enabled him, for the moment, to exert himself to the utmost, and, after swaying backwards and forwards in desperate strife for a minute, they went to the ground with a crash, Ben Soloman being undermost.

The Jew's grasp instantly relaxed, and Charlie, springing to his feet and seizing his cudgel, stood over his fallen antagonist. The latter, however, did not move. His eyes were open in a fixed stare. Charlie looked at him in surprise for a moment, thinking he was stunned, then he saw that his right arm was twisted under him in the fall, and at once understanding what had happened, turned him half over. He had fallen on the knife, which had penetrated to the haft, killing him instantly.

"I didn't mean to kill you," Charlie said aloud, "much as you deserve it, and surely as you would have killed me, if I had refused to act as a traitor. I would have broken your head for you, but that was all. However, it is as well as it is. It adds to my chance of getting away, and I have no doubt there will be many who will rejoice when you are found to be missing.

"Now," he went on, "as your agents emptied my pockets, it is no robbery to empty yours. Money will be useful, and so will your horse."

He stooped over the dead man, and took the purse from his girdle, when suddenly there was a rush of feet, and in a moment he was seized. The thought flashed through his mind that he had fallen into the power of his late guardians, but a glance showed that the men standing round were strangers.

"Well, comrade, and who are you?" the man who was evidently the leader asked. "You have saved us some trouble. We were sleeping a hundred yards or two away, when we heard the horseman, and saw, as he passed, he was the Jew of Warsaw, to whom two or three of us owe our ruin, and it did not need more than a word for us to agree to wait for him till he came back. We were surprised when we saw you, still more so when the Jew jumped from his horse and attacked you. We did not interfere, because, if he had got the best of you, he might have jumped on his horse and ridden off, but directly he fell we ran out, but you were so busy in taking the spoil that you did not hear us.

"I see the Jew is dead; fell on his own knife. It is just as well for him, for we should have tied him to a tree, and made a bonfire of him, if we had caught him."

Charlie understood but little of this, but said when the other finished:

"I understand but little Polish."

"What are you then--a Russian? You do not look like one."

"I am an Englishman, and am working in the house of Allan Ramsay, a Scotch trader in Warsaw."

"Well, you are a bold fellow anyhow, and after the smart way in which you disposed of this Jew, and possessed yourself of his purse, you will do honour to our trade."

"I hope you will let me go," Charlie said. "My friends in Warsaw will pay a ransom for me, if you will let me return there."

"No, no, young fellow. You would of course put down this Jew's death to our doing, and we have weight enough on our backs already. He is a man of great influence, and all his tribe would be pressing on the government to hunt us down. You shall go with us, and the purse you took from Ben Soloman will pay your footing."

Charlie saw that it would be useless to try and alter the man's decision, especially as he knew so little of the language. He therefore shrugged his shoulders, and said that he was ready to go with them, if it must be so.

The Jew's body was now thoroughly searched. Various papers were found upon him, but, as these proved useless to the brigands, they were torn up.

"Shall we take the horse with us?" one of the men asked the leader.

"No, it would be worse than useless in the forest. Leave it standing here. It will find its way back in time. Then there will be a search, and there will be rejoicing in many a mansion throughout the country, when it is known that Ben Soloman is dead. They say he has mortgages on a score of estates, and, though I suppose these will pass to others of his tribe, they can hardly be as hard and mercenary as this man was.

"I wonder what he was doing in this forest alone? Let us follow the path, and see where he is going.

"Honred, you have a smattering of several languages, try then if you can make our new comrade understand."

The man tried in Russian without success, then he spoke in Swedish, in which language Charlie at once replied.

"Where does this pathway lead to?"

"To a hut where a charcoal burner lives. I have been imprisoned there for the last fortnight. It was all the Jew's doing. It was through him that I got this knock here;" and he pointed to the unhealed wound at the back of his head.

"Well, we may as well pay them a visit," the chief said, when this was translated to him. "We are short of flour, and they may have some there, and maybe something else that will be useful."

Chapter 11: With Brigands.

The man who had spoken to Charlie drew the long knife from the back of the Jew, wiped it on the grass, and handed it to him. That ought to be your property," he said. "It has done you good service." Not sorry to have a weapon in addition to his cudgel, Charlie placed it in his belt, and then started with the bandits. He would not have cared to face the charcoal burner alone; but now that the band regarded him as enrolled among their number, he felt no uneasiness respecting him.

When they issued from the trees, the Jew was seen standing at the door of the hut. He at once ran in on seeing them, and came out again, accompanied by the charcoal burner, who carried his axe on his shoulder. The Jew started, on catching sight of Charlie among the ranks of the brigands, and said a word or two to his companion.

"Well, Master Charcoal Burner," the leader of the party said, "how is it that honest woodmen consort with rogues of the town?"

"I don't know that they do so, willingly," the man said gruffly. "But some of us, to our cost, have put our heads into nooses, and the rogues of the town have got hold of the other end of the ropes, and we must just walk as we are told to."

"Well, that is true enough," the brigand said.

"And you, Jew, what are you doing here?"

"I am like Conrad," he replied, sulkily. "It is not only countrymen who have their necks in a noose, and I have to do what I am ordered."

"By a bigger rogue than yourself?"

"That is so; bigger and cleverer."

"You are expecting him here now, our new comrade tells us. Well, you need expect him no longer. He will not come. If you will go along the path, you will come upon his body, and may bury him if you like to take the trouble."

An exclamation of satisfaction broke from the two men.

"You have done us a service, indeed," the charcoal burner said. "We had thought to do it for ourselves, this morning, for after the escape of him you call your new comrade, he would have shown us no mercy."

"You may thank our new comrade, and not us," the brigand said. "We only arrived on the spot when it was all over."

The Jew looked at Charlie in astonishment.

"What! Did he kill Ben Soloman?"

"That did he; or rather, the Jew killed himself. There was a grapple hand to hand, and a wrestle. The Jew fell undermost, and was pierced with his own knife."

"But the lad is but just out of a sickbed, and has no strength for a struggle, and Ben Soloman, though past middle life, was strong and active."

"Neither strong enough nor active enough," the man laughed. "You have been nicely taken in. Who would have thought that two Jews and a Pole would have been cheated by an English lad? His face shows that he has been ill, and doubtless he has not yet recovered his full strength, but he was strong enough, anyhow, to overthrow Ben Soloman.

"Now, what have you in the hut? We are in need of provisions."

The hut was ransacked; the flour, two bottles of spirits, and a skin of wine seized, and the meat cut up and roasted over the fire. After the meal was eaten, the captain called upon Charlie to tell his story more fully, and this he did, with the aid of the man who spoke Swedish; starting, however, only at the point when he was attacked in the street, as he felt it better to remain silent as to his connection with the Swedish army.

"But what was the cause of Ben Soloman's hostility to you?"

"There are some in Warsaw who are of opinion that Augustus of Saxony has done much harm to Poland, in engaging without cause in the war against Charles of Sweden, and who think that it would be well that he should be dethroned, and some other prince made king in his place. To this party many of the traders belong, and the Jew had reason to think that I was acquainted with the design, and could give the names of those concerned in it. There was really no plot against Augustus, but it was only intended that a popular demonstration against his rule should be made. But Soloman wanted me to give evidence that there was a conspiracy against the king's life, so that he might gain great credit by exposing it, and might at the same time rid himself of many of his rivals in the trade."

"He was an artful fox," the leader of the brigands said, when this had been translated to him. "But where is the Jew he put over you?"

Three or four of the men sprang to their feet and ran out, but the Jew was nowhere to be seen. The captain was furious, and abused his men right and left, while his anger was in no way mitigated when one of them told him that, if he had wanted the Jew kept, he should have given one of them orders to look after him. This was so evident that the chief was silenced for a moment.

"How long is it since any of you saw him last?"

"He went round with the wineskin, and filled our cups just as we sat down to breakfast," one of the men said. "I have not noticed him since."

Nor had any of the others.

"Then it will be no use to pursue. He has had more than half an hour's start, and long before this he will have mounted Ben Soloman's horse, and have ridden off.

"Well, comrade," he said, turning to Charlie, "this settles your movements. I was but half in earnest before as to your joining us; but it is clear now that there's nothing else for you to do, for the present. This fellow will, directly he gets to Warsaw, denounce you as the murderer of his master. That he is sure to do to avert suspicion from himself, and, if you were to return there, it would go hard with you. So, for a time, you must throw in your lot with us."

When this was translated to Charlie, he saw at once the force of the argument. He could not have denied that the Jew had fallen in a hand-to-hand struggle with himself, and, were he to appear in Warsaw, he might be killed by the co-religionists of Ben Soloman; or, if he escaped this, might lie in a dungeon for months awaiting his trial, and perhaps be finally executed. There was nothing for him now but to rejoin the Swedes, and it would be some time, yet, before he would be sufficiently recovered to undertake such a journey.

"I should not mind, if I could send a letter to Allan Ramsay, to tell him what has befallen me. He will be thinking I am dead, and will, at any rate, be in great anxiety about me."

"I have taken a liking to you, young fellow," the leader said, "and will send in one of my men to Warsaw with a letter; that is, if you can write one."

"Yes, I can write. Fortunately there are paper, pen, and an ink horn on that shelf. Ben Soloman brought them the last time he came, to write down the lies he wanted me to testify to. I am greatly obliged to you, and will do it at once."

As he had, only the day before he was attacked, sent off a messenger to Count Piper, telling him all he had done the previous week, there was no occasion to repeat this, and he had only to give an account of his capture, and the events that had since occurred.

"You see," he said, "I cannot return to Warsaw. The Jew who was here unfortunately heard that it was in a struggle with me Ben Soloman was killed, and he will, of course, denounce me as his murderer, though the deed was done in fair fight. I should have all his tribe against me, and might be imprisoned for months awaiting trial. I am still very weak, and could not attempt the journey to the frontier. I am, however, gaining strength, and, as soon as I am quite recovered, I shall take the first opportunity of leaving the men I am with, and making for the Swedish camp. Please forward this news by a sure hand to Count Piper, and express my sorrow that my mission has not been completed, although, indeed, I do not think that my further stay at Warsaw would have been any great service, for it is clear that the great majority of the traders will not move in the matter until the Swedes advance, and, from their point of view, it is not to their interest to do so.

"I know but little of the men I am with at present, beyond the fact that they are bandits, nor can I say whether they are disbanded soldiers, or criminals who have escaped from justice; but at any rate they show me no ill will. I have no doubt I shall be able to get on fairly with them, until I am able to make my escape. I wish I had poor Stanislas with me. Only one of the men here speaks Swedish, and he does not know very much of the language. I cannot say, at present, whether the twenty men here are the whole of the band, or whether they are only a portion of it. Nor do I know whether the men subsist by plundering the peasants, or venture on more serious crimes. Thanking you for your great kindness during my stay at Warsaw, I remain, yours gratefully--

"Charlie Carstairs."

While he was occupied in writing this letter, an animated conversation was going on between the bandits. Charlie gathered that this related to their future operations, but more than this he could not learn. In a postscript to the letter, he requested Allan Ramsay to hand over to the bearer some of the clothes left in his lodgings, and to pay him for his trouble.

"As to the money I left in your hands, I do not think it worth while for you to send it. However much these men may consider me a comrade, I have not sufficient faith in their honesty to believe that money would reach me safely; but, if you send me a suit of clothes, two or three gold pieces might be wrapped up in a piece of cloth and shoved into the toe of a shoe. The parcel must be a small one, or there would be little chance of the man carrying it far. I will ask him, however, to bring me a sword, if you will buy one for me, and my pistols."

He folded up the letter and gave it to the captain. There was no means of fastening it, but this mattered little, because, being written in English, there was no chance of its being read. The captain handed it to one of the men, with instructions for its delivery. The messenger started at once. The others, after remaining a short time in the hut, set out through the forest.

After an hour's walking, Charlie was unable to go further. The captain, seeing this, ordered four of the men to stop with him, and to follow the next morning. As soon as he had gone on with the rest of the band, the men set about collecting sticks and making a fire. Charlie, who was utterly exhausted, threw himself on the ground, and was not long before he fell sound asleep.

When he awoke, the shades of evening were already falling, and the men were sitting over the fire, roasting a portion of a goat, one of a flock they had fallen in with in the wood, where large numbers roamed about in a semi-wild state.

The man who could speak Swedish was one of those who had remained with him, and, from him, he learnt that the present headquarters of the band were some six miles farther away. This distance was performed next morning, frequent halts being made to enable him to sit down and rest; and it was not till five hours after the start that they arrived.

Overgrown as it now was, with trees and undergrowth, he could see that a village once stood there. It must, however, have been abandoned a very long time, as trees of considerable size grew among the low walls and piles of stones that marked where cottages had stood. The place occupied by the brigands had, in former times, been a castellated building of some strength, standing on a knoll in the middle of the village, which had probably been inhabited by the retainers of its owner. Part of the wall had fallen, but a large arched room, that had doubtless been the banqueting hall of the castle, remained almost intact, and here the brigands had established themselves. Several fires burned on the flagged floors, the smoke finding its way out through holes and crevices in the roof. Some fifty men were gathered round these, and were occupied in cooking their midday meal.

"I am glad to see that you have arrived," the captain said, coming across to Charlie. "I expected you two hours ago, and intended, as soon as we had finished our meal, to send out another four men to meet you and help to carry you in."

"Thank you," Charlie said. "It is not the men's fault we are late, but the last part of the way we came on very slowly. I was getting so exhausted that I had to stop every few hundred yards."

"Well, you had better eat something, and then lie down for a sleep. Meat is plentiful with us, for there are thousands of goats in the forest, and occasionally we get a deer or wild boar. If we had but bread and wine we should live like nobles. Our supplies, however, are low at present, and we shall have to make an expedition, tomorrow or next day, to replenish them."

Charlie ate a few mouthfuls of meat, and then lay down and slept, for some hours, on a bed of leaves. He was awoke by loud and excited talking among the men, and learnt from Honred that one of the men, who had been left on watch at the mouth of the path by which he had entered the forest, had just brought in the news that a party of a hundred infantry, led by the Jew, had arrived with a cart. In this the body of Ben Soloman had been sent off, while the troops had established themselves in the little clearing round the hut.

"This comes of letting that Jew escape," the captain said. "No doubt he told the story his own way, and the Jewish traders went to the governor and asked that troops should be sent to root us out. Well, they are far enough away at present, and I have sent off to have their movements watched. It is a good nine miles, from here to the hut, and they may look for a week before they find this place, unless that rascally Jew has heard of it from the woodman, or they get hold of the fellow himself, though I should think they will hardly do that. I fancy he has some cause of quarrel with the authorities, and will not put himself in the way of being questioned closely, if he can help it."

The next morning when Charlie awoke, two men were standing beside him.

His eyes first fell on the one who had been to the town, and who held a large bundle in his hand. Then he turned his eyes to the other, and gave an exclamation of pleasure, as he saw that it was Stanislas. He looked pale and weak, and was evidently just recovering from a severe illness.

"Why, Stanislas!" he exclaimed. "This is a pleasure, indeed. I never for a moment dreamt of seeing you. I heard from the Jew who guarded me that you got away, but I was afraid that you had been badly wounded. Why, my brave fellow, what brings you here?"

"I have come to be with your honour," the man said. "It was, of course, my duty to be by your side. I was very ill for a week, for I had half a dozen wounds, but I managed, after the assailants left me, to crawl back to Mr. Ramsay's to tell him what had happened. I don't remember much about the next few days. Since then I have been mending rapidly. None of the wounds were very serious, and it was more loss of blood, than anything else, that ailed me. Mr. Ramsay searched high and low for you, and we had all given you up for dead, till a few hours before this man arrived with your letter.

"We heard you had killed Ben Soloman. I had a long talk with your messenger, who received a handsome present from Mr. Ramsay, and he agreed to conduct me here, upon my solemn promise that, if the captain would not receive me, I would not give any information, on my return, as to the whereabouts of the band. Mr. Ramsay hired a light cart, and that brought us yesterday far into the forest. We camped there, and I had not more than a couple of miles to walk to get here this morning."

"Have you seen the captain?" Charlie asked eagerly.

"Yes. I was stopped by some sentries, a quarter of a mile away, and was kept there while my guide came on and got permission of the captain for me to be brought in. When I met him, I had no great difficulty in persuading him to let me stop, for Mr. Ramsay had given me fifty rix-dollars to give him; and so, your honour, here I am, and here is a letter from Mr. Ramsay himself."

"I cannot tell you how glad I am to have you, Stanislas. I am getting better, but I am so weak that I took five hours, yesterday, to get six miles. Now I have got you to talk to, I shall pick up strength faster than I have been doing, for it has been very dull work having no one who could understand me. There is only one man here who understands a word of Swedish."

"We will soon get you round, sir, never fear. I have brought with me four casks of wine. They were left at the place where the cart stopped last night, but the captain has sent off men already to bring them in. You will be all the better for a suit of clean clothes."

"That I shall. It is a month now since I had a change, and my jerkin is all stained with blood. I want a wash more than anything; for there was no water near the hut, and the charcoal burner used to bring in a small keg from a spring he passed on his way to his work. That was enough for drinking, but not enough for washing--a matter which never seemed to have entered into his head, or that of the Jew, as being in the slightest degree necessary."

"There is a well just outside," Stanislas said. "I saw them drawing water in buckets as we came in. I suppose it was the well of this castle, in the old time."

"I will go and have a wash, and change my clothes the first thing," Charlie said. "Mr. Ramsay's letter will keep till after that."

They went out to the well together.

"So you heard the story, that I had killed Ben Soloman, before you left?"

"Yes; before your letter arrived, Mr. Ramsay sent for me, and told me a Jewish trader had just informed him that news had come that Ben Soloman had been murdered, and the deed had been done by the young Scotchman who had been with him. Mr. Ramsay did not believe the story in the slightest. He admitted that Ben Soloman might have been murdered, and even said frankly that, hated as he was, it was the most natural end for him to come to; but that you should have done so was, he said, absurd. In the first place, he did not think that you were alive; and in the second, it was far more probable that you had been murdered by Ben Soloman, than that he should have been murdered by you.

"However, even before your letter came, three or four hours later, there seemed no longer any doubt that you had killed the Jew. By that time, there was quite an uproar among his people. He was the leader of their community, and had dealings with so many nobles that his influence was great; and, although he was little liked, he was regarded as an important person, and his loss was a very heavy one to the Jewish community. A deputation went to the governor, and we heard that troops would be at once sent out to capture you, and the band of brigands you had joined.

Mr. Ramsay told me that it was fortunate, indeed, that you had not returned to the city. But, no doubt, he has told you all that in the letter."

"I feel quite another man, Stanislas," Charlie said, when he had changed his garments. "Now I can read the letter you brought me."

After expressing the great satisfaction he felt, at the news that Charlie was alive, Mr. Ramsay went on to say that, even were he well, he could not return to Warsaw in the present state of public feeling.

"Your story that you were attacked, grievously wounded, and, after being confined here for some days, carried away and confined in the wood, by order of Ben Soloman, and that he visited you there, would be treated with derision. The version given by the man who brought in the story of the Jew's death was that he himself was staying in the cottage of a charcoal burner, an acquaintance of his, and that a party of brigands, of whom you were one, arrived there, and that they were boasting of having caused the death of Ben Soloman, who had fallen by your hand. He managed to escape from the brigands, and on the road found the dead body of his employer, who was, he knew, that morning coming out to give him some instructions. My opinion, and that of my friends who knew you, was that the fellow had himself killed and robbed his master; but your letter, of course, showed that his account was true to some extent--that Ben Soloman had fallen in a struggle with you, and that you yourself were a prisoner in the hands of these bandits. Still, as it would be next to impossible for you to prove the truth of your story, and as the Jews of the place, who are numerous and influential, are dead against you, your life would certainly be forfeited were you to be captured.

"I know your story to be true, but it would appear wildly improbable, to others, that this wealthy Jew should have conspired, in the first place, to cause an attack to be made upon an unknown young stranger, still less that he should have had him carried off to the forest, and should have gone to visit him there. The explanation that you were a Swedish officer in disguise would not benefit you in any way, while it would involve us who knew you in your danger, and would cause the Jew to be regarded as a man who had lost his life in endeavouring to unmask a plot against Poland. Therefore, I think it is extremely fortunate that you are, for the present, safe in the hands of these brigands, and should certainly advise you to make no attempt to leave them, until you are perfectly well and strong.

"I have, as you directed me, hidden a few pieces of gold in your shoe, and have handed the rest of your money to your man, who is starting to join you. He will conceal it about him. I have just heard that a body of troops are starting at once for the forest, and that orders have been sent to other towns, to send detachments into it at different points, so it is evident the authorities are determined to catch you, if possible. If you had killed half a dozen traders in a smaller way, they would have cared little about it; but just at present, pressed as the king is by want of money, he is bound to do everything he can to please the Jewish traders, as it is upon them that he must rely for loans for the payment of his troops.

"In this matter, then, he will leave no stone unturned to gratify them, and I should strongly advise your band to move away from the neighbourhood, at any rate for a time. They may plunder whole villages with impunity, but what is regarded as the murder of the richest citizen of Warsaw, a man mixed up in business and politics with half the principal nobles of the land, is a different matter altogether. Do not think of trying to traverse the country until you are perfectly strong. It will be a dangerous business at the best, but with your man with you, to bear the brunt of replying to questions, I have every confidence that you will succeed in making your way through. As to this, I can give no advice, as there is no saying as to the point from which you may start, or the directions in which you may travel.

"Should you, at any time, find yourself in a town in which there are any of my countrymen established in trade, and you will find them nearly everywhere, use my name. I think it is pretty generally known to Scotchmen in Poland. You will see I have inclosed a note that will be useful to you."

The inclosure contained only a few words:

"I, Allan Ramsay, merchant of Warsaw, do declare the bearer of this note to be my friend, and beg any countrymen of mine, to whom he may present himself, to assist him in every way, and, should he require money, to furnish him with it, I undertaking to make myself responsible for the same, and to pay all monies and other charges that he may incur."

"The first thing to do," Charlie said, as he placed the letters in his doublet, "is to let the leader of our band know that other bodies of troops, besides that at the hut, are about to enter the forest. He may decide that it is necessary to march away at once."

As soon, indeed, as the outlaw received the tidings, he issued orders for the band to prepare for instant departure.

"A party of five or six men together," he said to Charlie, "might hide in this forest for years. But a band of fifty is too large to be long concealed. To begin with, they must get food, and must either buy it or hunt for it; and in the second, there are a considerable number of men living in the forest, charcoal burners and herders of goats and swine, and any of these, if questioned by the troops, might mention that they had seen a considerable number of men passing. As it is, we will break up into parties of seven or eight, and appoint a rendezvous where we may meet again."

The band was speedily mustered, for, with the exception of those who were watching the forest through which the troops at the hut must march to reach them, the whole were close at hand. A messenger was sent off to call in the scouts. Then the booty that had been taken during their late excursions was brought out, and emptied on the ground. It consisted of money and jewellery. It was divided into equal portions, of which each member took one, the lieutenants of the band two, and the captain three.

"You don't share this time," the latter said to Charlie; "but next time, of course, you and your comrade will each have your portion."

When this was done, the men were told off in parties of six or seven, and instructions given as to the point of rendezvous. Each band chose its own leader, and, in an hour from the reception of the news, the place was deserted, and the parties were making their way in different directions through the forest.

Charlie and Stanislas formed part of the captain's own force, which numbered ten in all.

"Do you think they will all turn up at the meeting place?" Charlie asked the leader, whose name he now ascertained was Ladislas Koffski.

"They may," he said. "But it is seldom that bands, when they once disperse like this, ever come together again. It is impossible to content everyone, and any man who is chosen leader of a party may, if he is dissatisfied, persuade those with him to join some other band. Even if they do not go in a body, many are sure to break off and make for their homes, to enjoy the booty they have gathered.

"But, upon the other hand, as we go we shall gather up fresh recruits. With so many disbanded soldiers and discontented men roaming the country, there is no difficulty in getting as many men as one cares to keep together.

"Fifty is the outside that is advisable, for with more, even if one makes a good haul, it comes to so little, a head, that the men are dissatisfied. Of course they work in small parties, but this does not succeed so well as when a small band are under a single leader."

"How long have you been at this work?"

"Since last autumn."

"And you find it pay?"

"We do not get much in money. As you saw, there were but four rix dollars a head, and that is the result of a month's work. Still, that is not bad for men who might otherwise starve. Sometimes we do worse and sometimes better, but that is about the average. Still, the life is a pleasant one, and unless we disbanded soldiers took to it, what would there be for us to do? If government would keep us on regular pay, there would soon be no brigands left, except the men who have escaped from justice. But the treasury is empty, and, even at the best of times, the troops are badly and irregularly paid, and are forced to plunder to keep life together. They are almost in rags, and though we Poles do not mind fighting, there is generally a difficulty in getting sufficient infantry. As for the cavalry, they are nobles, and draw no pay.

"How do you feel today?"

"Better. The night's rest, and a wash and change of clothes this morning, have made me feel another man. How far do you intend to march?"

"We shall go slowly for a day or two. The other parties have all pushed on ahead fast, but by taking matters quietly, and by keeping a sharp lookout, we need have no great fear of being surprised. I know the forest well, and its thickest hiding places, so we can afford to travel slowly, and as you become accustomed to it you will be able to make longer journeys."

For ten days they travelled through the forest, increasing their distance daily, as Charlie regained his strength. The last day or two they did not make less than twenty miles a day. Their faces were turned steadily east. Occasionally they passed large tracts of cleared land, villages, and cultivated fields. At some of these they stopped and replenished their stock of flour, which they took without paying for it, but did no farther damage.

Of meat they had abundance. Two or three men started each day as soon as they halted, and, in a short time, returned with a goat or young pig.

"We are now close to the Bug River," Ladislas said at their last halting place. "Tomorrow we shall meet some, at least, of our comrades. I do not expect a great many, for we were pretty equally divided as to the direction we should travel in. Practically, we were safe from pursuit when we had gone fifteen miles, for the forest there spreads out greatly, and those in search of us would know that further pursuit would be useless. Many of my men did not care about going farther, but all this part of the country has been so harried, for the last two or three years, that we thought it best to try altogether new ground. When we have crossed the Bug we shall be beyond the forest, but there are great swamps and morasses, and hills with patches of wood. Many streams take their rise there, all meeting farther on, and forming the Dnieper. We must keep north of that river, for to the south the country is thinly populated, and we should have difficulty in maintaining ourselves."

Charlie made no comment, but he was glad to hear that the band intended to keep to the north of the Dnieper, for that river would have formed a serious obstacle to his making his way to rejoin the Swedes. The next day, they reached the bank of the Bug, and, following the river down, came after an hour's walking upon a great fire, round which fifteen men were stretched. These, as the captain's party approached, rose to their feet with a shout of welcome.

"That is better than I expected," Ladislas said, as they came up to them. "Five and twenty is quite enough for work here. In the forests one can do with more, but, moving steadily on, as we mean to do, till we get pretty near the eastern frontier, five and twenty is ample. It is enough, when together, to surprise a village; and it is not too many, travelling in twos and threes, to attract attention. Things always go on better, too, after a dispersal. Many who are discontented, or who want to command a band of their own, break off, and one starts fresh, with just the men one likes best to keep."

"We had begun to give you up, captain," one of the men said, as he joined the other party. "We have been here six days."

"We travelled but slowly, at first, and it is only the last two days we have really made fair journeys; but there was no reason for any great haste. The world is all our own, and, at any rate, as long as we were in the forest, there was no fear of wanting food.

"So I see some of our comrades have left us."

"We can do very well without them, captain. There were thirty of us here two days ago. Essos and Polinski quarrelled, and Essos was killed. Then Polinski wanted us to elect him captain, and to move away at once. Four or five, who have always been grumblers, joined him at once, and persuaded some of the others, till we were about equally divided. It came pretty nearly to a fight; but neither liked to begin, and they moved away."

"There are quite enough of us left," Ladislas said. "As to Essos and Polinski, I am heartily glad that they have gone. I know they have both been scheming for the leadership for some time. Most of the others can be very well spared, too. There are plenty of us here for travel. There is no doubt, as we agreed before starting, that there is not much more to be done in this part of the country. What with the civil wars, and the bands of soldiers without a leader, and others like ourselves who do not mean to starve, the peasants have been wrought up into a state of desperation. They have little left to lose, but what they have got they are ready to fight to the death for, and, lately, at the first alarm they have sounded the bells and assembled for miles round, and, equipped with scythes and flails, routed those who meddled with them. We had more than one hot fight, and lost many good men. Besides, many of the nobles who have suffered have turned out, with their followers, and struck heavy blows at some of the bands; so that the sooner we get out of this country, which is becoming a nest of hornets, the better, for there is little booty and plenty of hard blows to be got.

"We will go on, as we agreed, till near the eastern frontier. The country is well covered with forest there, and we can sally out on which side we like, for, if there is not much gold to be had in the Russian villages, there is plenty of vodka, and sometimes things worth taking in their churches. The priests and headmen, too, have generally got a little store, which can be got at with the aid of a few hot coals, or a string twisted tight enough round a thumb. At any rate we sha'n't starve; but we must move on pretty fast, for we shall have to get up a warm hut in the forest, and to lay in a stock of provisions before the winter sets in. So we must only stop to gather a little plunder when a good opportunity offers."

Chapter 12: Treed By Wolves.

Charlie and Stanislas were, that evening, sitting apart from the rest, at a short distance from the fire, talking over the future. They agreed that it would be comparatively easy to withdraw from the band as they journeyed forward, if, as seemed likely, they travelled in very small parties. If, indeed, they found themselves with two others, they could leave openly, for these would scarcely care to enter upon a desperate struggle, merely for the sake of retaining two unwilling companions in the band.

The difficulties would only begin when they started alone. As they were talking, the captain came across to them.

"I can guess," he said, "that you are talking together as to the future. I like you, young Englishman, and I like your companion, who seems an honest fellow, but I would not keep you with me by force. I understand that you are not placed as we are. We have to live. Most of us would live honestly if we could, but at present it is the choice of doing as we do, or starving. We occasionally take a few crowns, if we come across a fat trader, or may ease a rich farmer of his hoard, but it is but seldom such a chance comes in our way. As a rule, we simply plunder because we must live. It is different with you. Your friends may be far away, but if you can get to them you would have all that you need. Therefore, this life, which is hard and rough, to say nothing of its danger, does not suit you; but for all that, you must stay with us, for it would be madness for you to attempt to escape.

"As I told you, the peasants are maddened, and would kill any passing stranger as they would a wild beast. They would regard him as a spy of some band like ours, or of a company of disbanded soldiers, sent forward to discover which houses and villages are best worth plundering. In your case, you have other dangers to fear. You may be sure that news has been sent from Warsaw to all the different governors, with orders for your arrest for killing Ben Soloman, and these orders will be transmitted to every town and village. Your hair and eyes would at once betray you as strangers, and your ignorance of the language would be fatal to you. If, therefore, you escaped being killed as a robber by the peasants, you would run the risk of arrest at the first town or village you entered.

"Translate that to him, Stanislas. He is learning our language fast, but he cannot understand all that."

"That is just what we were talking about," Charlie said, when Stanislas had repeated the captain's speech, "and the danger seems too great to be risked. Think you, that when we get farther to the east, we shall be able to make our way more easily up into Livonia?"

"Much more easily, because the forest is more extensive there; but not until the winter is over. The cold will be terrible, and it would be death to sleep without shelter. Besides, the forests are infested with wolves, who roam about in packs, and would scent and follow and devour you. But when spring comes, you can turn your faces to the north, and leave us if you think fit, and I promise you that no hindrance shall be thrown in your way. I only ask you not to risk your lives by trying now to pass through Poland alone."

"I think you are right, Ladislas, and I promise you that we will not attempt to leave you during our journey east. As you say, it would be impossible for us to travel after winter had once set in. It is now the end of September."

"And it will be November before we reach our destination. We shall not travel fast. We have no motive for doing so. We have to live by the way, and to gather a little money to help us through the winter. We may shoot a bear or an elk sometimes, a few deer, and hares, but we shall want two or three sacks of flour, and some spirits. For these we must either get money, or take the goods. The first is the best, for we have no means of dragging heavy weights with us, and it would not do to infuriate the peasants by plundering any of them within twenty miles of the place where we mean to winter. That would set them all against us."

"I tell you frankly, Ladislas, that we shall not be willing to aid in any acts of robbery. Of course, when one is with an army one has to plunder on a large scale, and it has often gone terribly against the grain, when I have had to join parties sent out to forage. But it has to be done. I would rather not join men in taking food, yet I understand that it may be necessary. But as to taking money, I will have nothing to do with it. At the same time, I understand that we cannot share your food, and be with you, without doing something. Stanislas has brought me a little money from Warsaw, and I shall be ready to pay into the common treasury a sum sufficient to pay for our share of the food. As to money taken, we shall not expect any share of it. If you are attacked, we shall of course fight, and shall be ready to do our full share in all work. So, at any rate, you will not be losers by taking us with you."

"That is fair enough," the captain said, when Stanislas had translated what Charlie said, suppressing, however, his remarks about foraging with the army, as the brigands were ignorant that Charlie and he had any connection with the Swedes, or that he was not, as he had given out, a young Englishman come out to set up as a trader.

The band now journeyed slowly on, keeping near the north bank of the Dnieper. They went by twos and threes, uniting sometimes and entering a village or surrounding a farmhouse at night, and taking what they wanted. The people were, however, terribly poor, and they were able to obtain but little beyond scanty supplies of flour, and occasionally a few gold or silver trinkets. Many other bands of plunderers had passed along, in the course of the summer, and the robbers themselves were often moved to pity by the misery that they everywhere met with.

When in small parties they were obliged to avoid entering any villages, for once or twice furious attacks were made upon those who did so, the women joining the men in arming themselves with any weapon that came to hand, and in falling upon the strangers.

Only once did they succeed in obtaining plunder of value. They had visited a village, but found it contained nothing worth taking. One of the women said:

"Why do you trouble poor people like us? There is the count's chateau three miles away. They have every luxury there, while we are starving."

After leaving the village, the man to whom she had spoken repeated what she had said, and it was agreed to make the attempt. At the first cottage they came to they made further inquiries, and found that the lord of the soil was very unpopular; for, in spite of the badness of the times, he insisted on receiving his rents without abatement, and where money was not forthcoming, had seized cattle and horses, assessing them at a price far below what they would have fetched at the nearest market.

They therefore marched to the house. It was a very large one. The captain thoughtfully placed Charlie and Stanislas among the six men who were to remain without, to prevent any of the inmates leaving the chateau. With the rest, he made a sudden attack on the great door of the house, and beat it down with a heavy sledge hammer. Just as it gave way, some shots were fired from the inside, but they rushed in, overpowered the servants, and were soon masters of the place.

In half an hour they came out again, laden with booty. Each man carried half a dozen bottles of choice wine, from the count's cellar, slung at his belt. On their shoulders they carried bundles containing silver cups and other valuables; while six of them had bags of silver money, that had been extracted from the count by threats of setting fire to the chateau, and burning him and his family.

A halt was made two or three miles away, when the silver was divided into shares as usual, the men being well satisfied when they learned that Charlie and his companion claimed no part of it. Some of the provisions they had also taken were eaten. Each man had a flask of wine, with which the count's health was derisively drunk.

"This has been a good night's work," the leader said, "and you have each sixty rix dollars in your pockets, which is more than you have had for months past. That will keep us in provisions and spirits all through the winter; but mind, although we took it without much trouble, we have not heard the last of the business. No doubt, by this time, the count has sent off a messenger to the nearest town where there are troops, and, for a day or two, we shall have to march fast and far. It is one thing to plunder villages, and another to meddle with a rich nobleman."

For the next forty-eight hours they marched by night instead of by day, keeping always together, and prepared to resist an attack. One morning they saw, from their hiding place among some high reeds near the river, a body of about sixty horsemen ride past at a distance. They were evidently searching for something, for parties could be seen to break off several times, and to enter woods and copses, the rest halting till they came out again.

As the band had with them enough food for another three days, they remained for thirty-six hours in their hiding place, and then, thinking the search would by that time be discontinued, went on again. The next day they killed two or three goats from a herd, the boy in charge of them making off with such speed that, though hotly pursued and fired at several times, he made his escape. They carried the carcasses to a wood, lit a fire, and feasted upon them. Then, having cooked the rest of the flesh, they divided it among the band.

By this time the wine was finished. The next day they again saw horsemen in the distance, but remained in hiding till they had disappeared in the afternoon. They then went into a village, but scarcely had they proceeded up the street when the doors were opened, and from every house men rushed out armed with flails, clubs, and axes, and fell upon them furiously, shouting "Death to the robbers!"

They had evidently received warning that a band of plunderers were approaching, and everything had been prepared for them. The band fought stoutly, but they were greatly outnumbered, and, as but few of them carried firearms, they had no great advantage in weapons. Charlie and Stanislas, finding that their lives were at stake, were forced to take part in the fray, and both were with the survivors of the band, who at last succeeded in fighting their way out of the village, leaving half their number behind them, while some twenty of the peasants had fallen.

Reduced now to twelve men and the captain, they thought only of pushing forward, avoiding all villages, and only occasionally visiting detached houses for the sake of obtaining flour. The country became more thinly populated as they went on, and there was a deep feeling of satisfaction when, at length, their leader pointed to a belt of trees in the distance, and said:

"That is the beginning of the forest. A few miles farther, and we shall be well within it."

By nightfall they felt, for the first time since they had set out on their journey, that they could sleep in safety. A huge fire was lit, for the nights were now becoming very cold, and snow had fallen occasionally for the last four or five days, and in the open country was lying some inches deep. The next day they journeyed a few miles farther, and then chose a spot for the erection of a hut. It was close to a stream, and the men at once set to work, with axes, to fell trees and clear a space.

It was agreed that the captain and two of the men, of the most pacific demeanour, should go to the nearest town, some forty miles away, to lay in stores. They were away five days, and then returned with the welcome news that a cart, laden with flour and a couple of barrels of spirits, was on a country track through the forest a mile and a half away.

"How did you manage, captain?" Charlie asked.

"We went to the house of a well-to-do peasant, about a mile from the borders of the wood. I told him frankly that we belonged to a band who were going to winter in the forest, that we would do him no harm if he would give us his aid, but that if he refused he would soon have his place burnt over his head. As we said we were ready to pay a fair sum for the hire of his cart, he did not hesitate a moment about making the choice. The other two remained at his cottage, so as to keep his family as hostages for his good faith, and I went with him to the town, where we bought six sacks of good flour and the two barrels of spirits. We got a few other things--cooking pots and horns, and a lot of coarse blankets, and a thick sheepskin coat for each man. They are all in the car. I see that you have got the hut pretty nearly roofed in, so, in a day or two, we shall be comfortable."

They went in a body to the place where the cart had been left, but it required two journeys before its contents were all transported to the hut. Another three days and this was completed. It was roughly built of logs, the interstices being filled in with moss. There was no attempt at a door, an opening being left four feet high and eighteen inches wide for the purpose of an entry. The skin of a deer they had shot, since they arrived, was hung up outside; and a folded rug inside. There was no occasion for windows. A certain amount of light made its way in by an orifice, a foot square, that had been left in the roof for the escape of smoke. The hut itself consisted of one room only, about eighteen feet square.

When this was finished, all hands set to work to pile up a great stack of firewood, close to the door, so as to save them from the necessity of going far, until snow had ceased falling, and winter had set in in earnest.

The cart had brought six carcasses of sheep, that had been purchased from a peasant; these were hung up outside the hut to freeze hard, and the meat was eaten only once a day, as it would be impossible to obtain a fresh supply, until the weather became settled enough to admit of their hunting.

The preparations were but just finished when the snow began to fall heavily. For a week it came down without intermission, the wind howled among the trees, and even Charlie, half stifled as he was by the smoke, felt no inclination to stir out, except for half an hour's work to clear away the snow from the entrance, and to carry in wood from the pile.

The time passed more cheerfully than might have been expected. He had by this time begun to talk Polish with some facility, and was able to understand the stories that the men told, as they sat round the fire; sometimes tales of adventures they themselves had gone through, sometimes stories of the history of Poland, its frequent internal wars, and its struggles with the Turks.

Making bread and cooking occupied some portion of the time, and much was spent in sleep. At the end of a week the snow ceased falling and the sun came out, and all were glad to leave the hut and enjoy the clear sky and the keen air.

While they had been confined to the hut, two of the men had made a large number of snares for hares, and they at once started into the forest, to set these in spots where they saw traces of the animals' passage over the snow. The rest went off in parties of twos and threes in search of other game.

With the exception of Charlie, all were accustomed to the woods; but, as Stanislas had much less experience than the others, the captain decided to go with them.

"It is easy for anyone to lose his way here," he said. "In fact, except to one accustomed to the woods, it would be dangerous to go far away from the hut. As long as it is fine, you will find your way back by following your own tracks, but if the weather changed suddenly, and it came on to snow, your case would be hopeless. One of the advantages of placing our hut on a stream is that it forms a great aid to finding one's way back. If you strike it above, you follow it down; if below, upwards, until you reach the hut. Of course you might wander for days and never hit it, still it is much more easy to find than a small object like the hut, though even when found, it would be difficult to decide whether it had been struck above or below the hut.

"Now, there is one rule if, at any time, you get lost. Don't begin to wander wildly about, for, if you did, you would certainly walk in a circle, and might never be found again. Sit down quietly and think matters over, eat if you have got any food with you; then examine the sky, and try to find out from the position of the sun, or the direction in which the clouds are going, which way the hut ought to lie. Always take with you one of your pistols; if you fire it three times, at regular intervals, it will be a signal that you want help, and any of us who are within hearing will come to aid you."

With the exception of hares, of which a good many were snared, the hunting was not productive. Tracks of deer were seen not unfrequently, but it was extremely difficult, even when the animals were sighted, to get across the surface of the snow to within range of the clumsy arquebuses that two or three of the men carried. They did, however, manage to shoot a few by erecting a shelter, just high enough for one man to lie down under, and leaving it until the next snowstorm so covered it that it seemed but a knoll in the ground, or a low shrub bent down and buried under the weight of the snow. These shelters were erected close to paths taken by the deer, and, by lying patiently all day in them, the men occasionally managed to get a close shot.

Several bears were killed, and two elks. These afforded food for a long time, as the frozen flesh would keep until the return of spring. Holes were made in the ice on the stream, and baited hooks being set every night, it was seldom that two or three fish were not found fast on them in the morning.

Altogether, therefore, there was no lack of food; and as, under the teaching of the captain, Charlie in time learnt to be able to keep his direction through the woods, he was often able to go out, either with Stanislas or alone, thus keeping clear of the close smoky hut during the hours of daylight. Upon the whole he found the life by no means an unpleasant one.

Among the articles purchased by the captain were high boots, lined with sheepskin, coming up to the thigh. With these and the coats, which had hoods to pull over the head, Charlie felt the cold but little during the day; while at night he found the hut often uncomfortably warm, sleeping, as they all did, in the same attire in which they went out.

In February the weather became excessively severe, more so, the peasants and charcoal burners they occasionally met with declared, than they ever remembered. The wild animals became tamer, and in the morning when they went out, they frequently found tracks of bears that had been prowling round the hut in search of offal, or bones thrown out. They were now obliged to hang their supply of meat, by ropes, from boughs at some distance from the ground, by which means they were enabled to prevent the bears getting at it.

They no longer dared to venture far from the hut, for large packs of wolves ranged through the forest, and, driven by hunger, even entered villages, where they attacked and killed many women and children, made their entrance into sheds, and tore dogs, horses, and cattle to pieces, and became at last so dangerous that the villagers were obliged to keep great fires burning in the streets at night, to frighten them away. Several times the occupants of the hut were awakened by the whining and snarling of wolves outside. But the walls and roof were alike built of solid timber, and a roughly-made door of thick wood was now fastened, every night, against the opening, and so stoutly supported by beams behind it as to defy assault. Beyond, therefore, a passing grumble at being awakened by the noise, the men gave themselves no trouble as to the savage animals outside.

"If these brutes grow much bolder," the captain said one day, "we shall be prisoners here altogether. They must have come down from the great forest that extends over a large part of Russia. The villages are scarce there, and the peasants take good care to keep all their beasts in shelter, so no doubt they are able to pick up more at the edge of the forest here."

"How far are we from the Russian frontier?"

"I do not think anyone could tell you. For aught I know, we may be in Russia now. These forests are a sort of no man's land, and I don't suppose any line of frontier has ever been marked. It is Russia to the east of this forest, some thirty miles away, and it is Poland to the west of it. The forest is no good to anyone except the charcoal burners. I have met both Russians and Poles in the wood, and, as there is plenty of room for all--ay, and would be were there a thousand to every one now working in it--they are on friendly terms with each other, especially as the two nations are, at present, allied against Sweden."

In spite of the wolves, Charlie continued his walks in the forest, accompanied always by Stanislas. Both carried axes and pistols, and, although Charlie had heard many tales of solitary men, and even of vehicles, being attacked by the wolves in broad daylight, he believed that most of the stories were exaggerations, and that the chances of two men being attacked in daylight were small, indeed.

He had found that the track, by which the cart had brought the stores, was a good deal used, the snow being swept away or levelled by the runners of sledges, either those of peasants who came into the forest for wood or charcoal, or of travellers journeying between Russia and Poland. He generally selected this road for his walk, both because it was less laborious than wading through the untrodden snow, and because there was here no fear of losing his way, and he was spared the incessant watchfulness for signs that was necessary among the trees. At first he had frequently met peasants' carts on the road, but, since the cold became more severe and the wolves more numerous and daring, he no longer encountered them. He had indeed heard, from some of the last he saw, that they should come no more, for that the charcoal burners were all abandoning their huts, and going into the villages.

One afternoon, when they had, on their return, nearly reached the spot where they left the road to strike across the forest to the hut, they heard a noise behind them.

"That is a pack of wolves, in full cry!" Stanislas exclaimed. "You had better get up into a tree. They are after something."

They hastily clambered into a tree, whose lower branches were but six or seven feet from the ground. A moment later two horses, wild with fright, dashed past, while some twenty yards behind them came a pack of fifty or sixty wolves. They were almost silent now, with their red tongues hanging out.

"The brutes have been attacking a sledge," Stanislas said in a low tone. "You saw the horses were harnessed, and their broken traces were hanging by their side. It is easy to read the story. The sledge was attacked; the horses, mad with fear, broke their traces and rushed off, or perhaps the driver, seeing at the last moment that escape was impossible, slashed the ropes with his knife, so as to give the horses a chance. I expect they got a start, for the wolves would be detained a little at the sledge."

"Do you think the poor beasts will get safe out of the forest, Stanislas?"

"I don't think so, but they may. The chase has evidently been a long one, and the wolves have tired themselves with their first efforts to come up to them. It did not seem to me that they were gaining when they passed us. It is simply a question of endurance, but I fancy the wolves will last longest.

"See, here is a party of stragglers. I suppose they stopped longer at the sledge."

"It seems to me they are on our scent, Stanislas. Do you see, they are coming along at the side of the road where we walked, with their heads down."

"I am afraid they are. Well, we shall soon see. Yes, they are leaving the road where we did."

A moment later a dozen wolves ran up to the trunk of the tree, and there gathered snuffing and whining. Presently one caught sight of the two figures above them, and with an angry yelp sprang up in the air, and immediately all were growling, snarling, and leaping. Charlie laughed out loud at their impotent efforts.

"It is no laughing matter, sir," Stanislas said gravely.

"They cannot climb up here, Stanislas."

"No, but they can keep us here. It will be dark in an hour, and likely enough they will watch us all night."

"Then we had better shoot two of them, and jump down with our hatchets. Keeping back to back, we ought to be able to face ten wolves."

"Yes, if that were all; but see, here come three or four more, and the dozen will soon swell to a score. No, we shall have to wait here all night, and probably for some time tomorrow, for the men are not likely to find us very early, and they will hardly hear our pistols unless some of them happen to come in this direction."

"Do you think, if we shoot two or three of them, the rest will go?"

"Certainly not. It will be all the worse. Their comrades would at once tear them to pieces and devour them, and the scent of blood would very soon bring others to the spot."

"Well, if we have got to wait here all night, Stanislas, we had better choose the most comfortable place we can, at once, before it gets dark. We must mind we don't go to sleep and tumble off."

"There will be no fear of our sleeping," Stanislas said. "The cold will be too great for that. We shall have to keep on swinging our hands and feet, and rubbing our noses, to prevent ourselves from getting frostbitten."

"Well, I have never felt the cold in these clothes," Charlie said.

"No, sir, but you have never been out at night, sitting cramped on a tree."

Hour after hour passed. Even in the darkness they could see the wolves lying in the snow below them, occasionally changing their position, keeping close together for warmth, and often snarling or growling angrily, as one or two shifted their position, and tried to squeeze in so as to get into a warm spot.

The cold was intense and, in spite of swinging his legs and arms, Charlie felt that his vital heat was decreasing.

"This is awful, Stanislas. I do not think we can last on till morning."

"I begin to have doubts myself, sir. Perhaps it would be better to leap down and make a fight of it."

"We might shoot some of them first," Charlie said. "How many charges have you?"

"I have only two, besides one in the barrel."

"And I have only three," Charlie said. "Powder has run very short. The captain was saying, yesterday, that we must send to the village and try to get some more. Still, six shots will help us."

"Not much, sir. There must be thirty or forty of them now. I have seen some come from the other way. I suppose they were part of the pack that followed the horses."

Charlie sat for some time thinking. Then he exclaimed:

"I think this is a dead tree."

"It is, sir. I noticed it when we climbed up. The head has gone, and I think it must have been struck with lightning last summer."

"Then I think we can manage."

"Manage what, sir?" the man asked in surprise.

"Manage to make a fire, Stanislas. First of all, we will crawl out towards the ends of the branches as far as we can get, and break off twigs and small boughs. If we can't get enough, we can cut chips off, and we will pile them all where these three big boughs branch off from the trunk. We have both our tinderboxes with us, and I see no reason why we should not be able to light a fire up here."

"So we might," Stanislas said eagerly. "But if we did, we might set the whole tree on fire."

"No bad thing, either," Charlie rejoined. "You may be sure the fire will keep the wolves at a respectful distance, and we could get down and enjoy the heat without fear."

"I believe your idea will save our lives, sir. Ten minutes ago I would not have given a crown for our chances."

They at once crawled out upon two of the great branches, and a renewed chorus of snarls from below showed that their foes were watchful. The snapping of the small branches excited a certain amount of uneasiness among them, and they drew off a short distance. In ten minutes Charlie and his companion worked themselves back to the main trunk, each carrying an armful of twigs. They first cut off a number of small dry chips, and made a pile of these at the junction of one of the branches with the trunk. They then got out their tinderboxes and bunches of rags, shook a few grains of powder from one of the horns among the chips, and then got the tinder alight. A shred of rag, that had been rubbed with damp powder, was applied to the spark and then placed among the shavings. A flash of light sprang up, followed by a steady blaze, as the dried chips caught. One by one at first, and then, as the fire gained strength, several sticks at a time were laid over the burning splinters, and in five minutes a large fire was blazing.

Charlie and his companion took their seats where the other two big branches shot out from the trunk. These were two or three feet higher than that on which the fire had been lighted, and, ere long, a sensation of genial warmth began to steal over them. Fresh sticks were lighted as the first were consumed, and before long the trunk, where the flames played on it, began to glow. Light tongues of flame rose higher and higher, until the trunk was alight ten or twelve feet up.

"The wolves are all gone," Charlie said, looking down.

"I don't suppose they have gone very far, sir. But when the tree once gets fairly alight, you may be sure they won't venture anywhere near it."

They had already been forced to move some little distance away from the trunk, by the heat, and as the flames rose higher and higher, embracing in the course of half an hour the whole of the trunk and upper branches, they felt that it was perfectly safe to drop off into the snow beneath them.

Blazing brands soon began to fall. They stood a short distance away, so as to be beyond the risk of accident, but, at Charlie's suggestion, they ran in from time to time, gathered up the brands and laid them at the foot of the trunk, and in a short time a second fire was kindled here.

The tree was now a pyramid of fire, lighting up the snow for a long distance round. Outside this circle the wolves could be heard whining and whimpering, occasionally uttering a long-drawn howl.

"They know that they are baulked of their prey," Stanislas said. "We shall have some of the big branches falling soon, and shall be able to keep up a roaring fire, that will last until daylight. I should think by that time the wolves will be tired of it, and will make off; but if not, the captain will be sure to send men out to search for us. He will guess we have been treed by wolves, and we have only to get into another tree, and fire our pistols, to bring them in this direction."

"But they may be attacked, too," Charlie remarked.

"There are ten of them, and they are sure to come armed with axes and swords. They ought to be able to fight their way through a good-sized pack. Besides, the wolves will be so cowed by this great fire, that I don't think they will have the courage to meddle with so strong a party."

One by one the arms of the tree fell, burnt through at the point where they touched the trunk. They would have been far too heavy to be dragged, but three or four of them fell across the lower fire, and there lay blazing. Not knowing which way the tree itself would fall, Charlie and his companion were obliged to remain at some distance off, but the heat there was amply sufficient for them. At last the trunk fell with a crash, and they at once established themselves as near the fire as they could sit, without being scorched, and there chatted until morning began to break.

They felt sure that some, at least, of the wolves were around them, as they occasionally caught sight of what looked like two sparks among the undergrowth; these being, as they knew, the reflection of the fire in the eyes of a wolf. There was a tree hard by in which they could, if necessary, take refuge, and they therefore resolved to stay near the fire.

Fortunately the night had been perfectly still, and, as the tree they had fired was a detached one, the flames had not spread, as Charlie had at one time been afraid they would do.

Half an hour after daylight had fairly broken, they discharged three shots at regular intervals with their pistols, then they waited half an hour.

"Shall we fire again?"

"No. Not until we hear shots from them," Charlie replied. "We have but four charges left, and if the wolves made a sudden rush, we might want to use them."

After a time, both thought they heard the distant report of a musket. Stanislas looked at Charlie inquiringly. The latter shook his head.

"No, no! Stanislas. That gun would be heard twice as far as one of these pistols. Let us wait until we are pretty sure that they are near. I don't like leaving ourselves without other protection than our axes."

Chapter 13: A Rescued Party.

After a considerable pause, a gun was again fired, this time much nearer to them. Charlie drew out his pistol and was about to reply, when his companion touched his arm. Look!" he said.

Charlie turned in time to see several gray forms flit rapidly between the bushes. He stepped to the edge of the road, and saw some wolves spring out through the bushes, and go straight along the road.

"What can have scared them?" he asked, in surprise. "The gun was not near enough for that."

"No, besides they would have fled deeper into the forest, instead of taking to the road. Perhaps they hear something coming."

Almost at the same moment, two shots were heard in the direction towards which the wolves were making.

"That is it!" Charlie excitedly exclaimed. "Another body of wolves have attacked a passing traveller. Heap the wood on, Stanislas. If we make a great fire, and they get as far as this, possibly they could spring off and take refuge here. At any rate, the brands will be better weapons even than our axes."

The ends of such branches as they were able to move were brought together, and a few blows with their axes speedily broke off several of the outer ends of charred wood. These were thrown on, and the fire soon blazed up high again.

Two more shots were heard, this time close at hand.

They ran into the road. A sledge, with several figures in it, was coming along at full speed. It was almost surrounded by wolves, and, as they looked, two of them sprang at the horses' heads; but two shots again rung out, and they dropped backwards among their companions, many of whom threw themselves at once upon their bodies, while the sledge continued on its headlong course.

"Here! here!" Charlie shouted at the top of his voice, waving his hands to show the direction which they were to take.

A moment later the sledge dashed past them, and swept up to the fire.

"Seize the blazing brands!" Charlie shouted, as those in the sledge threw themselves out.

He and Stanislas rolled the two first wolves over with their pistols, and then joined the others.

The driver had run at once to the horses, and had muffled them, by throwing his coat over the head of one, and a rug over the head of the other, and, though snorting and trembling in every limb, they stood quiet until he had thrown a head rope round each of their necks, and fastened them to the heaviest of the branches. Then he seized a handful of fallen leaves, which were exposed by the melting of the snow above them, and threw them into the fire, whence a dense smoke poured out.

The wolves had again stopped to devour the two animals that had been shot, and this gave time to the men, by their united efforts, to move a heavy branch and place it across two others, whose ends lay in the fire, so as to form with them a sort of triangular breastwork, the face of which, next to them, was manned by the two travellers, their servants, Charlie, and Stanislas, with blazing brands.

Charlie and his companion hastily loaded their pistols again. The two gentlemen had each rifles and a brace of pistols, as had their servants. A lady and child had been lifted from the sledge, and these crouched down at the angle by the fire. The sledge and the two horses protected one of the faces of the position, and the driver, at his master's orders, took his position on the front seat again, so as to shoot down any wolf that might try to attack the flank of the outside horse.

The wolves looked doubtful at the appearance of the dense smoke rising up, but, after a little hesitation, they rushed to the attack. Four were rolled over by bullets from the rifles, and, as they came within a few yards, the pistols cracked out in rapid succession. As soon as these were all emptied, the six men caught up the blazing brands, and struck full in the faces of the wolves, shouting loudly as they did so.

Seized with a momentary panic, the animals turned and fled, and then a fierce fight took place between the injured wolves and their companions. There was but just time to recharge the rifles and pistols, when they came on again. Although the

fire of the defenders was as deadly as before, the wolves seemed this time determined to get at their victims. In vain were blows showered on their heads, while
those who first sprang on the tree were stabbed with the knives the defenders held
in their left hands.

The contest could have had but one termination, when suddenly two shots
were heard, and then, with loud shouts, a party of men burst through the forest,
and with pistol and axe fell on the wolves. This unexpected onslaught had a decisive
effect, and, with loud howls and yelps, the wolves turned and fled.

Up to this time, not a word had been exchanged by the defenders, beyond
Charlie's first shout of "Lay this branch across those two," and the order of one of
the gentlemen to the coachman to take his place in the sledge--where he had done
his work well, for four wolves lay dead by the flank of the outside horse. Several of
those that had sprung at the heads of the horses had been shot or cut down by the
master, who had placed himself close to them, and the horses' thick mufflings had
saved them from any serious injury.

As soon as the wolves fled, the gentleman turned to Charlie, and, flinging down
his weapons, threw his arms round his neck.

"You have preserved us from death, sir. You have saved my wife and child from
being torn to pieces. How can I express my thanks to you?"

"It was fortunate that we happened to be here," Charlie said, "and that we had
this fire handy."

A cry from the child called off the gentleman's attention, and he ran to his
wife, who had sunk fainting on the ground; and Charlie, not a little pleased at this
diversion, turned to Ladislas and his men, who were looking on with the most intense astonishment at the scene. Charlie leapt over the branch, and grasped Ladislas
by the hand.

"You have arrived at the nick of time, Ladislas. Another three minutes, and it
would have been all over with us."

"Yes, I could see it was a close thing as soon as I caught sight of you. We have
been wondering all night what became of you, and set out as soon as it was light.
We fired a shot occasionally, but we listened in vain for your three shots."

"We fired them half an hour after daylight," Charlie said; "but, as we had then
only five charges left between us, and there were wolves all round, we dared not

waste them."

"We heard firing at last," the captain went on. "First two shots faintly, then two nearer, and a minute later two others. We knew then that you must be engaged with wolves, and we were running as hard as we could in the direction of the shots, when we heard a number fired close together. Of course we could make nothing of it, but on we ran. Then there was another outbreak of firing, this time quite close. A moment later we caught sight of a confused mass. There was a fire, and a sledge with two horses, and a man standing up in it shooting; and we could see a desperate fight going on with the wolves in front, so Alexander and Hugo fired their pieces into the thick of them. We set up a yell, and went at them with our axes, yet I did not feel by any means sure that they would not be too many for us.

"But what on earth does it all mean? And how is it that you have lived through the night? We had no expectation of finding you alive. However, that fire tells its own tale, as though nothing less than burning up a big tree would content you."

"I will tell you all, presently. It is too long a story now. Let us help these travellers to go their way, before the wolves rally again."

"They will not do that," the captain said confidently. "If it was night, they might hang about the neighbourhood, but they are cowardly beasts in the daytime, and easily scared. They are still going away at their best pace, I will be bound."

While Charlie was speaking to Ladislas, one of the travellers had been talking to Stanislas, who, in answer to his question, had informed him that he was in Charlie's service, and that the latter was an English gentleman, who had, from a variety of circumstances, especially the suspicion with which all strangers were regarded, been unable to travel through the country, and had therefore been passing the winter hunting, with this company of disbanded soldiers who had so opportunely arrived to their assistance.

The other traveller had, by this time, carried his wife beyond the heat of the fire, and had applied some snow to her forehead, pouring a little brandy from the flask between her lips. She had now begun to revive, and, leaving her, he approached the party. His brother met him, and in a few words told him what he had learned from Stanislas.

"My friends," he said, "my brother tells me that you are a party of discharged soldiers, who are passing the winter in a hut here in the forest, supporting yourselves by shooting and fishing. I have to thank Providence for the thought that sent you here. I have to thank you for your prompt assistance, to which we are indebted for our lives.

"I am Count Nicholas Staroski, and can at least make a substantial return for the service you have done me. My estates lie some sixty miles to the north. You will have no difficulty in finding me. Present yourselves there at Easter. I shall certainly be at my chateau then. I will then talk over what can be done for you. Those who like to settle down on land shall have land, those who would like employment in my household shall have it, those who would prefer money to go their own way and settle in their own villages shall each have a heavy purse."

Then he turned to Charlie.

"You, sir, as my brother has learned from your brave follower here, are an English gentleman. To you I owe far heavier obligation than to these soldiers, for you and your man incurred a terrible risk, and well-nigh sacrificed your lives for ours. I pray you come with us, and stay with us for a time. I shall then hear your plans, and your object in visiting this country, and if I can in any way further them, you may be sure I will do so to the utmost; for the present, I can promise you at least excellent hunting, and the heartiest welcome."

"I thank you very heartily, Count Staroski, and accept gladly your invitation; but I must first speak to the captain of these men, to whom I am much beholden for the kindness he has shown me."

He went across to Ladislas, who had heard what was said.

"You will not think it ungrateful for me to quit you so suddenly, Ladislas," he said in a low voice.

"Assuredly not. You have done us a service, indeed, in thus enabling us to obtain favour with the count. He is one of our richest and most powerful nobles, and our fortunes are as good as made."

"I will introduce you to him personally," Charlie said.

"This, count, is the leader of the party. He has shown me very great kindness, and has proved a true friend. From what I have seen of him, I have no doubt whatever that, in spite of certain acts of lawlessness to which he and his friends have been driven of late, you will find him, in any position you may be good enough to give him, an honest and thoroughly trustworthy man."

"I will bear it in mind," the count said. "Now, the sooner we are off, the better. How far is it to the next village?"

"About seven miles, count."

The count gave orders for the sledge to be taken on to the road again.

"One moment," the captain said, taking Charlie aside. "Pray tell us, in a few words, what has happened. The burning of the tree is a mystery to us, and we shall die of curiosity if we have to remain here for another two months with the matter unexplained."

In as few words as possible, Charlie related to the men the story of the preceding night, which was greeted with exclamations of surprise and admiration.

"Truly, you have your wits about you," the captain said. "I should have been frozen to death, if I had been in your position, for I should certainly never have thought of lighting a fire up in a tree.

"Well, goodbye, if we do not see you again, may all good fortune attend you, and may the saints protect you from all danger."

Charlie shook hands with the men all round, and then hurried down to the sledge. The coachman was already in the front seat, the countess and her child had taken their places, and the two armed servants and Stanislas were standing behind, in readiness to jump on to a board fastened above the runners.

"I must apologize for keeping you waiting, countess," Charlie said as he ran up. "I had to explain to my friends, in a few words, how this had all come about."

"We are also longing to know," the count said. "But I have not yet introduced you to my wife, nor have I learned the name of the gentleman to whom I owe so much."

"Ah, sir," the young countess said, holding out her hand after Charlie had given his name, "what do we not owe you? I shall never forget it all, never."

"We will talk when we have started, Feodora. Let us get out of this forest as soon as we can."

He took his place beside his wife, and set the child on his knees; his brother and Charlie sitting opposite to him. The servants spread a bearskin rug over their knees, and then jumped into their places, as the driver cracked his whip, and the horses started.

"You must think us almost mad to be driving through the forest, at this time of the year," the count said to Charlie. "But the countess is a Russian. We have been staying two months at her father's place, a hundred miles to the east. My two youngest children are at home, and two days since a message arrived, saying that one of them was dangerously ill. We had heard, of course, many tales of the numbers and fierceness of the wolves, but we hoped that, by travelling only by day and with excellent horses, there was not much to fear, especially as we were five armed men.

"We fell in with a few wolves yesterday, but beat them off easily enough. Last night, we stopped at a little village in the forest. They certainly made me feel uneasy there, with their tales about the wolves, but there was no help for it. We started as soon as day broke, and had driven some fifteen miles, before we came up to you. We had not gone five when the wolves began to show themselves.

"At first, they kept well behind us, but presently we came upon a large number, who joined in near where we saw an overturned sledge, with the snow stained with blood all round it. From there we kept up a running fight, and must have killed a score; but their numbers increased, rather than diminished, and when a fresh pack came up from ahead, a quarter of a mile before we saw you, it looked as if our case was hopeless; for the horses, which had been going at the top of their speed from the time we started, were beginning to flag, while the wolves were fast closing in upon us, and were just beginning to attack the horses, when I saw you in the road.

"And now, pray tell us how you came to be there so opportunely, and how it was that you had that great fire blazing."

Charlie gave the full history of the previous night's adventure.

"Wonderful!" the count and his brother exclaimed; and the former went on: "I have heard many stories of escapes from wolves, but never one like yours. It was an admirable thought, indeed, that of at once obtaining heat and frightening the wolves away, by setting the tree on fire. That thought saved our lives as well as your own, for our fate would have been the same as those unfortunate travellers, whose horses you saw, and who brought the wolves upon you.

"And now, sir, would it be impertinent to ask for what purpose you have come to Poland? Believe me, I only put the question in order to see if I can in any way be of assistance to you."

"I do not know, count, whether my avowal will affect you unfavourably, but

I know that it will make no difference in your conduct towards me. I am, as my servant told you, an Englishman by birth; but I and my father were obliged, in consequence of political opinions, to leave the country, and I am now a captain in the service of Charles of Sweden."

Exclamations of surprise broke from his hearers.

"Well, sir," the count said, smiling, "as his majesty King Charles, although not yet one-and-twenty, is one of the greatest generals in Europe, I cannot consider it strange that you, who appear to me to be no older, should be a captain in his service. But I own that I pictured, to myself, that the officers of these wonderful soldiers were fierce-looking men, regular iron veterans."

"I am but eighteen," Charlie said, "and I myself feel it absurd that I should be a captain. It is but two years since I was appointed an ensign, and the king happening to be with my company, when we had a sharp fight with the Russians, he rewarded us by having us made into a regiment; so each of us got promotion. I was appointed captain last May, as a reward for a suggestion that turned out useful."

"May I ask what it was, Captain Carstairs, for it seems to me that you are full of happy ideas?"

"King Charles, as you may have heard, speaks freely to officers and soldiers as he moves about the camp. I was standing on the edge of the river, looking across at the Saxons, on the day before we made the passage, when the king came up and spoke to me. He said there was no hope of our passage being covered--as our advance against the Russians at Narva had been--by a snowstorm; and I said that, as the wind was at our backs, if we were to set fire to the great straw stacks the smoke would hide our movements from the Saxons. The idea was a very simple one, and would no doubt have occurred to the king himself; however, he put it into execution with success, and was good enough, afterwards, to promote me to the rank of captain."

"So it was owing to you that our army--or rather the Saxon army, for but few Poles were engaged in the battle--was defeated," the count said, smiling. "Well, sir, it will do you no harm with us, for personally we are entirely opposed to Augustus of Saxony. But you have not yet explained how you, an officer in the Swedish service, came to be here."

"I was sent by King Charles to Warsaw, to ascertain the feeling of the trading

classes there. I had an introduction to a Scottish merchant, and I passed as a countryman of his, who had come out to enter his business. One of the objects of my
mission was to endeavour to induce the foreign merchants in Warsaw to do what
they could to promote a feeling in favour of peace with the Swedes, and the substi-
tution of another king in place of Augustus."

"It is not very clear, Captain Carstairs, how you can be fulfilling that object by
passing your winter with a party of robbers--for I suppose your disbanded soldiers
were little better--in a forest on the confines of Russia."

Charlie laughed.

"It is rather a long story, count. Perhaps you will kindly tell me the news about
public affairs, first."

"By no means," the count said. "That is a long story, too, and my wife would
much rather hear yours than listen to it. She has not yet recovered from the events
of this morning. But we will wait until we are at the village. We have left the forest
behind us, and another half hour will take us to Stromoff, where we can get pretty
good accommodation."

The horses, a splendid pair of animals, had, during their passage through the
forest, shown every sign of fear; starting nervously, swerving, and going in sharp,
sudden rushes, and always needing a constant strain on the reins to keep them from
bolting. Once away from the trees, however, they settled down into a fast trot, and
the seven miles to Stromoff were done in less than half an hour.

No sooner did the landlord of the inn learn the name of his guest, than he,
his wife, and sons bustled about in the greatest haste to make things comfortable
for them. Huge fires were lighted in the guest rooms, and the common room was
cleared of the other customers, until the chamber should be sufficiently warmed
for occupation; while in the kitchen preparations were made for a meal, to which,
in half an hour from their arrival, the party in the sledge sat down. When this was
over, settles were placed round the fire, and Charlie then gave a full account of his
adventures, from the time he was attacked in the streets of Warsaw.

"So it was you, Captain Carstairs, after whom there was so keen a search in September. The death of Ben Soloman made a great stir, and I can assure you that there
are a great many people who owe you a debt of gratitude. The man had no sons,
and all his property passed to his widow, whom he had, it seems, treated harshly

during his lifetime. She was from Holland, and wished to return to her people, so, as his means were very large, she made the easiest terms with all those on whose estates her husband had held mortgages, in order to wind up her affairs as soon as possible. Thus, his death was the subject of wide rejoicings. However, if you had been caught at the time, I fear it would have gone hard with you; for the Jews were all very keen about it--as the man, rascal though he was, was one of the chief heads of their religion--and were you to fall into their hands in any of the towns, they would either kill you or send you to Warsaw."

"And now, sir, will you tell me what has taken place since September?"

"Things have moved slowly. Augustus endeavoured, after his defeat on the Dwina, to make peace with Charles on his own account, and without the knowledge of the diet, but Charles refused to give audience to any of his agents, and would not even see the beautiful Countess of Konigsmark, who is, you know, herself a Swede, and whom Augustus sent, thinking that her blandishments might win over the young king. It was useless. Charles maintained the ground that he took up from the first--namely, that he would treat with the diet, but would have nothing whatever to say to Augustus. So the diet sent an embassy of four senators.

"Instead of receiving them with every pomp and ceremony, as they expected, the king met them on horseback. He demanded that, as a first condition, they should dethrone Augustus. Parties in the diet were pretty equally divided; but the proposal was rejected, for even those most hostile to Augustus resented the proposal that we, a free and unconquered people, should be ordered by a foreign prince to change our king. So nothing came of it.

"The Swedish army advanced a certain distance into Poland, and there were a great number of skirmishes, but there has been no serious fighting, nor is there much chance of any, until the snow has gone and the country dried up in the spring. At present, Augustus is quarrelling with the diet, who still set themselves against the importation of more Saxon troops. But doubtless, before the campaign begins in earnest, he will have settled matters with the senators, and will have his own way in that respect. There is, however, little chance of the diet agreeing to call out the whole forces of the country, and the next battle will, like the last, be between the Swedes and the Saxons, who may have with them perhaps a few thousand Poles, belonging to the king's party."

"You don't belong to the king's party, count?"

"No. I, like the majority of our nobles, have no interest whatever in the war, for we were never consulted before it began. It is an affair between Saxony and the Swedes. Let them fight it out. It would be a bad day for Poland, if Augustus and the Russians were to overcome and despoil Sweden. We want no addition of territory, for that would be to strengthen our kings against us. We see the trouble caused by Augustus having Saxony at his command, and if he had other territory, the country would be divided into two parts, one of which would have nothing in common with the other.

"Still less do we wish to see Russia gain territory to the north of us. Hitherto we have thought but little of the Muscovites, but this war has shown that they can put great armies into the field, and the czar is making them into a nation which may some day be formidable to us.

"Charles has sent every assurance that he has no ill will towards Poland, and is an enemy not of the country but of its king--who had formed a coalition against him in a time of profound peace--and that his hostility will altogether cease with the overthrow and expulsion of Augustus. So you see, we who live at a distance from the capital, and hold ourselves altogether aloof from the intrigues of court, look on at the fray as if it were one in which we have no part or lot. If Augustus drives out the Swedes, we shall probably have trouble with him afterwards. If Charles drives out Augustus, we shall have a fresh king, and shall no doubt choose one upon the recommendation of Charles, who will then march away again, leaving us to manage our own affairs. Therefore, we have no animosity whatever against you as a Swedish officer, but for comfort's sake it is better that nothing should be said of this, and that I should introduce you to my friends simply as an English gentleman, who has rendered me the greatest possible service."

The countess retired to bed, a short time after they had finished their meal, and the others sat up talking until late in the evening. Charlie learnt that the country was still in a greatly disturbed state. Parties of disbanded soldiers and others, rendered desperate by cold and hardship, were everywhere plundering the peasantry, and many encounters had taken place between them and the nobles, who, with their retainers, had marched against them. Travel would be dangerous for a long time to come.

"Therefore, until the spring, you must not think of moving," the count said. "Indeed, I think that your best plan, when you start, will be to work due north, and join the Swedish forces near Narva. It will be shorter as well as less dangerous. Still, we can talk of that later on."

The next morning they started early, and arrived in the afternoon at the chateau of the count. It was not a fortified building, for the Poles differed from the western nations, abstaining from fortifying their towns and residences, upon the ground that they were a free people, capable of defending their country from foreign invasion, and therefore requiring no fortified towns, and that such places added to the risks of civil war, and enabled factions to set the will of the nation at defiance.

The building was a large one, but it struck Charlie as being singularly plain and barn-like in comparison with the residences of country gentlemen in England. A number of retainers ran out as they drove up into the courtyard, and exclamations of surprise and dismay rose, as the wounds on the horses' flanks and legs were visible; and when, in a few words, the count told them that they had been attacked by wolves, and had been saved principally by the English gentleman and his follower, the men crowded round Charlie, kissed his hands, and in other ways tried to show their gratitude for his rescue of their master and mistress.

"Come along," the count said, taking his arm and leading him into the house. "The poor fellows mean well, and you must not be vexed with them."

The countess's first question had been for her child, and with an exclamation of thankfulness, when she heard that it was better, she had at once hurried into the house. As soon as they had entered, the count left Charlie in charge of his brother, and also hurried away. He was not long before he returned.

"The child is doing well," he said, "and now that it has got its mother again, it will, I think, improve rapidly. The doctor said this morning that he considered it out of danger, but that it needed its mother sorely, to cheer and pet it."

In a very short time the tables were laid. The count, his brother, and Charlie sat at an upper table, and the hall was filled with the various officers and retainers. The count's arrival was expected, for a horseman had been sent forward on their arrival at the inn the evening before. The dinner had therefore been cooked in readiness, and Charlie was astonished at the profusion with which it was served. Fish, joints, great pies, and game of many kinds were placed on the table in unlimited quantities;

the drink being a species of beer, although excellent wine was served at the high table. He could now understand how often the Polish nobles impoverished themselves by their unbounded hospitality and love of display.

"I suppose, for tomorrow, you will like to remain quiet," the count said, "but after that we will try to amuse you. There is game of all sorts to be shot, or if you have had enough sport, lately, there will be a sledge and horses at your disposal, whenever you choose to ride or drive, and in a few days we will give an entertainment, in honour at once of our return, your visit, and the child's restoration to health. Then you will have an opportunity of seeing our national dances."

Charlie had had enough shooting, but he greatly enjoyed the drives in the sledges, behind the spirited horses. The entertainment came off a fortnight after his arrival at the chateau. The guests, for the most part, arrived early in the afternoon, many having driven in from great distances. The preparations had been on an immense scale, and the scene at night was a brilliant one.

Never had Charlie seen anything like the magnificence of the dresses, not of the ladies only, but also of the gentlemen; the Poles having the true oriental love for rich costumes, a taste that their national dress permitted them to gratify to the utmost. Next to the splendour of the dresses, Charlie was surprised at the grace and spirit of the dancing, which was far more vivacious than that of western nations. The Poles were long considered to be the best dancers in the world. It was their great national amusement; and all danced, from noble to peasant, entering into it with spirit and enthusiasm, and uniting the perfection of rhythmical motion with the grace and ease peculiar to them, and to their kinsmen the Hungarians.

The dancing was kept up, with unflagging energy, during the whole night; and then, after a substantial breakfast, the men and women were muffled up in furs, and took their places in the sledges.

The count would gladly have had Charlie remain with him until spring began, but he was anxious to rejoin the army; and, seeing that this was so, the count did everything in his power to facilitate his journey, which, after talking it over, had been decided should be direct towards the royal camp. The count's brother insisted upon accompanying him on the journey, as in this way many of the difficulties would be avoided. Two sledges were prepared, the one for the use of Charlie and Count John, and the other for the two servants and baggage. Both were horsed by the fastest animals in the count's stables.

Charlie himself had been loaded with presents, which he had been obliged somewhat reluctantly to accept, as he saw that a refusal would hurt and mortify his kind hosts. He had, on his arrival, been provided with an ample wardrobe of clothes of all kinds, and to these were now added dolmans, cloaks, rugs, and most costly furs. A splendid gun, pistols, and a sword, with the hilt studded with gems, completed his outfit; while Stanislas had been presented with a heavy purse of money.

The whole of the retainers of the castle were assembled to see them start, and the count and countess, at parting, made him promise to come and pay them another visit, if the fortune of war should bring him within the possibility of reaching them.

The journey was a delightful one. Each night they put up at the chateau of some nobleman. To many of these Count John Staroski was personally known; at the others, his name secured at once a hearty welcome for himself and his companion. Travelling only by day, and at the full speed of the horses, they escaped interruption by the marauding bands, and in fourteen days after starting they drove into the town where Charles of Sweden had his headquarters, after being twice stopped and questioned by bodies of Swedish horse.

The town was crowded with troops, and they had some difficulty in finding a lodging for themselves, and stabling for the horses. As soon as this was done, Charlie proceeded alone to the quarters of Count Piper.

Chapter 14: The Battle Of Clissow.

Charlie sent in his name, and was shown in at once. I glad, indeed, to see you, Captain Carstairs," the minister said, as he entered. "We had given you up for lost. We heard first that you had been murdered in the streets of Warsaw. A month later, a man brought a letter to me from your Scotch friend Ramsay, to say that you were accused of the murder of a Jew trader, a man, it seems, of some importance in Warsaw. Ramsay said that you were in the company of a band of brigands, and that the man who went with you as your servant had joined you, and had taken you some money. He forwarded the letter you had sent him explaining your position, and said he thought that, upon the whole, it was the best thing you could have done, as a vigorous search had been set on foot, at the instance of the Jews, and there would have been but little chance of your making your way through the country alone. He added that he felt confident that, if alive, you would manage somehow to rejoin us before the campaign opened in the spring.

"I am glad that you have been able to do so, but your appearance, at present, is rather that of a wealthy Polish noble, than of a companion of brigands."

"I was able to do some service to Count Staroski, as, when travelling with his wife and child, and his brother, Count John, he was attacked by a pack of wolves. I have been staying with him for some weeks, and his brother has now had the kindness to accompany me here. He has thereby made my passage through the country easy, as we have travelled with fast horses in his sledge, and have always put up at the chateaux of nobles of his acquaintance. I have, therefore, avoided all risk of arrest at towns. In the letter forwarded to you I explained the real circumstances of the death of the Jew."

"Yes, we quite understood that, Captain Carstairs. You had a very narrow escape from death at his hands, and, as the danger was incurred purely in the king's service, it will not be forgotten. Up to the time when the Jew organized the attack upon you in Warsaw, I was well satisfied with your reports of your work. So far nothing has come of it, as Augustus has been too strong for any movement against him, but we hope, ere long, to defeat him so decisively that our friends will be able to declare against him. I will inform the king of your return, and I have no doubt he will be glad to hear your story from your own lips. He loves tales of adventure, and time hangs somewhat heavily on hand, as, until the frost breaks, nothing can be done in the field."

On the following day, indeed, Charlie was sent for to the royal quarters, and had to recount the story of his adventures in full to the king, who was highly interested in them, and at the conclusion requested him to introduce Count John Staroski, in order that he might express to him his obligation for the service he had rendered to one of his officers. This done, Charlie drove out with the count to the village where Colonel Jamieson's regiment was quartered, and where his return was received with delight by Harry, and with great pleasure by Major Jervoise and his fellow officers. He was obliged to give a short outline of what he had been doing since he left, but put off going into details for a future occasion.

"And are you coming back to us now, Charlie?" Harry asked.

"Certainly. My success in the diplomatic way was not sufficiently marked for them to be likely to employ me in that line again. We must return this afternoon, as the king has invited us both to sup with him tonight."

Two days later, Count John Staroski started upon his return journey, much pleased with the reception he had met with from the King of Sweden, and determined to work vigorously, among the nobles of his acquaintance, to bring about the dethronement of Augustus of Saxony. Charlie had already seen Count Piper, who had told him that, although the king and himself were both well satisfied with the work he had done, there was not at present any mission of the same sort on which he could be employed. Indeed, it was evident that, until the Saxons had been decisively defeated, political action would be useless, and that, therefore, for the present he could either remain at headquarters, or rejoin his regiment. Charlie at once chose the latter alternative.

"Very well, Captain Carstairs, you can rejoin when you like, but remember I may claim your services again. You see, now that you have acquired a knowledge of Polish, your value for this sort of work is largely increased."

As soon as the frost had broken, the Swedish army commenced its advance. Skirmishes frequently took place, but Augustus had, as yet, no army with which he could meet them in the field, and he summoned a diet at Warsaw, in hopes of persuading the Poles to decide upon calling out the whole national force.

In this he failed altogether. The citizens, led by the foreign traders, were already openly opposed to him, and their attitude so encouraged his opponents in the diet, that many of these rose and openly denounced the government, and the conduct of the king, that had brought the country into its present difficulties.

As the Swedish army advanced, they were joined by the Duke of Holstein, and, in spite of the efforts of a considerable body of the enemy, under Prince Wisniowiski, progressed steadily, crossed the river Memel, and, when near Grodno, were met by an embassy sent by the diet, to endeavour to persuade Charles not to advance further.

An interview took place between the king, the Poles, and his ministers, the conversation on both sides being in Latin. But as the ambassadors had no definite plans to propose, and their leaders were wholly devoted to Augustus, the king refused to allow his advance to be arrested, and continued his march. When near Praga they crossed the plain where Charles Gustavus, King of Sweden, had defeated the Polish army in a great battle, that had lasted for three days. The city was occupied, and a contribution of 20,000 crowns imposed upon it, in addition to food for the army while it remained there. Plundering, however, was strictly forbidden, and, as the king issued a proclamation declaring that he was no enemy of the Polish Republic, but simply of their king, the inhabitants were, on the whole, well satisfied with the conduct of the invaders.

A halt was made here for some time, and a bridge was thrown across the Vistula, while the army rested after the long and fatiguing marches it had made. A fresh attempt was made to arrest the advance of the Swedes, and the Cardinal Primate, himself, met the king; but nothing came of the negotiations, and the army entered Warsaw. Here they were warmly received, and great entertainments were given to the king.

Towards the end of June, they again advanced to meet the force that Augustus had gathered, and on the 6th of July the Swedes arrived within a few miles of Clissow. The next day some reinforcements arrived, and the king decided to give battle on the following day, which was the anniversary of the victory on the Dwina, the previous year.

His army was twelve thousand strong, while that of Augustus was nearly double that strength, and was very strongly posted, his camp being surrounded by morasses, although situated on rising ground which commanded the whole of the country round it. The bogs in the front were found to be so impassable, that the Swedes were forced to make a circuit to the left, where the ground was firmer. This movement obliged the enemy also to change front, a movement that caused considerable confusion, as they themselves were forced to traverse boggy ground, to take up a new position facing that by which the Swedes would now advance.

The attack was commenced by the division commanded by the Duke of Holstein, but, scarcely had he set his troops in motion than he was mortally wounded, by a ball from a falconet. His troops, however, pushed forward vigorously. The Polish division opposed to them resisted the two first assaults bravely, but gave way at the third attack, and were driven from the ground, in such confusion that they took no further part in the engagement.

While this was going on, the Saxon cavalry had been repulsed by that of Charles, and, passing in their retreat under the fire of three infantry regiments, suffered so heavily that they left the field. The Swedish foot now advanced all along the line, and in the centre destroyed several battalions of Saxons.

But the Swedish right was attacked so vigorously by the Saxon left, under Field Marshal Steinau, that for a time the conflict was doubtful. The Swedish horse guards and other cavalry, however, charged with such determination that the Saxon horse on this flank were also defeated, and driven off the field, while the Swedish infantry, advancing without firing, drove several battalions of Saxon foot into a village, where, being surrounded, almost all were killed or taken prisoners.

The Saxon horse, gathering once more, attempted bravely to retrieve the fate of the day, and engaged the Swedish horse with such desperate valour, that a considerable portion of the Saxon infantry were enabled, under cover of the conflict, to draw off, cross the morasses, and make their escape.

The battle lasted four hours, and had been, throughout, severely contested. The Saxons lost four thousand killed and wounded, and three thousand taken prisoners, while the Swedes had eleven hundred killed and wounded. Forty-eight cannon were captured by the victors, together with all the baggage and waggons. The death of the Duke of Holstein, a gallant prince who was exceedingly popular with the army, and beloved by the king, cast a gloom over this great victory, which virtually laid Poland at the feet of the victors, and insured the fulfilment of the object for which Charles had persisted in the war.

Jamieson's regiment had been on the left wing, but, as it had been held in reserve, to strengthen the line at any point at which it might give way, the Scotch had taken but a small share in the fighting, and had but thirty men killed and wounded by the shot and bullets that passed over the heads of the fighting line.

The captain of one of the companies was among those killed, and Charlie, who had, since he rejoined the regiment, been doing duty as lieutenant, now took the vacant place.

The army still advanced. Augustus sent in several proposals for peace, but these were all rejected. The Saxons had speedily rallied after the battle, but were not in a position to oppose the advance of the victorious Swedes, who occupied Cracow without meeting with any resistance. Seeing that Augustus would not be strong enough to hazard another pitched battle, Charles had, on the morning after the victory, ordered three of his regiments, of which Jamieson's was one, to march with all speed to reinforce Major General Schlippenbach, who had sent an urgent request for aid, as he heard that the Russian army, fifty thousand strong, was preparing to cross the frontier; and as he had but six thousand, he could not hope to oppose their advance successfully.

As the king's orders enjoined the troops to march with the greatest possible speed, they performed the journey back to Warsaw in four days, although the distance exceeded a hundred miles. Mounted messengers had been sent on before them, and, on reaching the town, they found boats already prepared to take them down the river to Danzic, where orders had already been sent for ships to be in readiness to convey them to Revel. The fatigues since the campaign opened had been severe, and the troops all enjoyed the long days of rest, while the craft that conveyed them dropped quietly down the Vistula. Then came the short sea passage.

On their arrival at Revel, bad news met them. They had come too late. On the 16th of July the Russian army had passed the frontier, and the Swedes had tried to oppose them at the passage of the river Embach; but the water was low, from the effects of a long drought, and the Russians were enabled to ford it at several points. The Swedes fell upon those who first crossed, and for two hours repulsed their attacks, obtaining at some points considerable advantage, and capturing some guns, but, as fresh reinforcements poured across the river, the tide of battle turned. The Russian cavalry drove back the Swedish horse, who, as they retreated, rode through the infantry and threw them into disorder. These were attacked by the Russians before they could recover from their confusion, and were almost entirely destroyed or taken prisoners.

The general, and many of the mounted officers, effected their escape, rallied the broken cavalry, and fell back towards Revel. The Russians spread over the country and plundered it, burning the little town of Valk, murdering its inhabitants, and carrying off into slavery the whole of the population who fell into their hands.

The arrival of the three regiments was hailed with much satisfaction by the people of Revel, who feared that the Russians might besiege the town. They did not, however, approach within many miles, but, after completely wasting the country, retired across the frontier.

The victory that had been gained over the Swedes at Embach, and the destruction of the greater part of General Schlippenbach's force, enabled the czar to turn his arms against Ingria, the extreme eastern province of Sweden, which included the shores of Lake Ladoga and the whole of the coast of the Baltic between Narva and Finland. Urgent messages were sent by the governor of that province to General Schlippenbach, requesting him to send him aid, as he had not even sufficient men to garrison the walled towns. The general was, however, afraid that Narva would be again besieged, and he therefore dared not reduce his small force to any considerable degree, but drew one company from each of the three regiments, and embarked them on board a ship for the mouth of the Neva.

As there seemed little prospect of service, for a time, near Revel, all the officers were eager that their company should be chosen for the service in Ingria. Colonel Jamieson therefore said:

"I do not wish to choose one company more than another; all can equally be depended upon. Therefore, I think the fairest way will be to draw lots as to which shall go."

The lot fell upon Charlie's company, which therefore formed part of the expedition. On reaching the mouth of the Neva, they heard that the town of Notteburg, situated at the point where the Neva issues from the lake, was already besieged by the Russians, and that the Swedish vessels on the lake had been obliged to come down the river. A fort had been raised by the Russians on the bank, to prevent succour being conveyed into the town, and two thousand men had crossed the river and occupied a small redoubt on the northern side, so that the town was completely invested.

The newly-arrived force was ordered to march, at once, with a hundred horse and four field pieces, the whole under the command of Major Sion, who was well acquainted with the country.

"What do you think of this expedition, Captain Carstairs?" his lieutenant, John Bowyer, asked him.

"I would rather be back with King Charles," Charlie replied. "Of course, I don't know the geography of the place, but if the Russians keep their eyes at all open, I don't see how a force like ours, with cavalry and guns, can hope to enter the town unnoticed. The addition of the horsemen seems to me altogether ridiculous, as they could be no good whatever, if they did enter the town. As for those four field pieces, they will hamper our march; and as they say the Russians have already some forty cannon in position about the town, those little pieces would be useless.

"Four hundred infantry, making the attempt at night under good guidance, might manage to slip into the place, but this procession of ours is, to my mind, tempting destruction, for we certainly cannot hope to cut our way, by force, through the whole Russian army.

"But even if we do get inside the town, our plight can be no better. The Russians' cannon are bombarding it, night and day, and more batteries are in course of erection, and Schlippenbach the governor, who is, I believe, a brother of the general, has but a few pieces to reply to them.

"Were there an army advancing to the relief of the place, it would be different altogether, for our reinforcement might be of vital importance in repelling assaults, until aid arrived. But there is no hope of aid. The king's army is some nine hundred miles away, and his hands are full. General Schlippenbach has sent as many men as he could spare. They say there are at least twenty thousand Russians round the town, and where is an army to come from that can compel them to raise the siege?

To my mind, we shall either be destroyed making our way into the town, or, if we do get in, shall be made prisoners of war, if not massacred--for the Russians have but vague ideas as to giving quarter--when the town falls, which may be a fortnight hence."

"It seems a bad lookout, altogether," the lieutenant remarked.

"Very much so. The best possible thing that could befall us would be for the Russians to make us out, before we get too far into their lines, in which case we may be able to fall back before they can gather in overwhelming strength, and may thus draw off without any very great loss."

Major Sion called the captains of the infantry companies, and the troop of horse, to a sort of council of war, when the little force halted for an hour at three o'clock in the afternoon.

"We have another ten miles to march, gentlemen, and I should like to ask your opinion as to whether it would be best to try to force our way in as soon as we get there, or to halt at a distance of three or four miles from the Russians, and make our effort at daybreak before they are fairly afoot."

The other three officers gave their opinion in order of seniority, and all advocated the plan of falling upon the Muscovites at daybreak.

"And what do you think, Captain Carstairs?" Major Sion asked Charlie.

"I regret to say, major, that my opinion differs from that of the other gentlemen, and this for several reasons. In the first place, if we halt so near the Russians, our presence in their neighbourhood may be betrayed by a peasant, and we may be surprised in the night. If no such mishap should take place, we should have to be on foot two hours before sunrise. I in no way doubt your knowledge of the road, but it is at all times difficult to make out a mere track, like that we are following, at night, and in the morning we might well find ourselves involved in the Russian intrenchments, from which we could not extricate ourselves before a large force had gathered round us, in which case we must be all either killed or taken prisoners. My own suggestion would be that we should remain here another two hours, and then continue our march so as to reach the spot, where we are to endeavour to break through their line, about sunset. Should we be observed, as we most likely should be, we might at that hour be taken for a freshly-arrived body of Russian troops. There would be no risk of losing our way, and we might hope to be close upon them before we were discovered to be enemies. If we succeed, as I trust we shall, in breaking our way through and reaching the town, well and good. If, on the other hand, we find greater obstacles than we expect, and are forced to fall back fighting, we shall have the advantage that darkness will be setting in. The Russians, the greater part of whom will be ignorant of our strength, will lose time before they move, fearing they may be assaulted in other quarters, and in the darkness we might be able to make good our escape, which it is certain none of us would do, should we meet with a repulse at daybreak."

"Your reasons are very just, Captain Carstairs. Though certainly my opinion was in accordance with that given by your fellow officers, I am bound to say that your argument seems unanswerable.

"What say you, gentlemen? I have two objects in view--the first to reinforce the garrison of Notteburg, the second to save the troops under my command, if I should fail in doing so. I know the country well, but its features will be considerably altered. Trees will have been cut down, houses levelled, intrenchments thrown up, camps scattered here and there, and I own that in the dark, I might, as Captain Carstairs says, very easily miss my way. I think his proposal therefore unites the greatest chances of getting through their line and entering the town, with a possibility of drawing off the troops without great loss, in case of failure."

The other three officers at once agreed, and orders were issued for the men to lie down until five o'clock and rest themselves before pursuing their march.

It was past that hour before they were in motion again. Major Sion, with a peasant from the neighbourhood of Notteburg, rode ahead. Then came the troop of cavalry, with the guns close behind them, followed by the infantry. As they approached the Russian lines, the peasant several times went on in advance, and presently a trooper rode down the line, with the order that the troops with firearms were to light their matches, and the spearmen to keep in a compact body.

They were now not far from the Russian lines, and the destruction that had been wrought during the last ten days was visible to them. Every tree and bush had been felled, for use in the intrenchments or for the erection of shelters. A few blackened walls alone showed where houses had stood. Gardens had been destroyed, and orchards levelled.

Light smoke could be seen rising at many points from the Russian fires, and, when the troops were halted, they were but half a mile from the intrenchments.

Word was passed down that the rapid Swedish march was to be moderated, and that they were to move carelessly and at a slow rate, as if fatigued by a long march, and that the spears were to be carried at the trail, as they were so much longer than those used by the Russians that their length would, if carried erect, at once betray the nationality of the troops. There was no attempt at concealment, for the cavalry would be visible for a considerable distance across the flat country. Considerable bodies of men could be seen, gathered round fires at a distance of not more than a quarter of a mile on either hand, but, as the column passed between them, there was no sign of any stir.

In a short time, the order was passed for the troops to form from column into line, and the cavalry officer who brought it said that there was a Russian battery erected right across the road, a little more than a quarter of a mile ahead.

"Things look better, Captain Carstairs," the lieutenant said, as the company, which happened to be leading, fell into line.

"Yes, I have no doubt we shall take their battery, coming down, as we do, upon its rear. The question is, are there any intrenchments ahead? Major Sion told us, when we halted, that the peasant assured him that there were no works beyond it, and that it was the weakest point of the line; but it is three days since he came out from Notteburg, and, working hard as the Russians evidently do, they may have pushed on their intrenchments far in advance of the battery by this time."

The force halted for a moment. The guns were unlimbered, turned round, and loaded. Then the line of cavalry opened right and left, the four pieces poured a discharge of grape into the Russians, clustered thickly in the battery four hundred yards away, and then, with a shout, the Swedish cavalry charged, the infantry coming on at a run behind them.

The surprise was complete. With cries of terror, the Russians for the most part leapt from the battery and fled, and the few who attempted to defend their guns were sabred by the cavalry.

"There are other works ahead!" Major Sion exclaimed, as, sitting on his horse, he looked over the parapet, "and bodies of troops scattered all about. Push forward, men, at a double, and do you, Captain Sherlbach, cut a way for us with your cavalry."

The sun had set a few minutes before the guns were fired, and Charlie, as he led his men over the earthwork, and saw the Russian lines in front, congratulated himself upon the fact that, in another half hour, it would be quite dark. As they approached the next line of works, a scattering fire of musketry opened upon them, but the aim was wide, and without loss they reached the work. The Russians, though inferior in numbers, defended themselves obstinately, and continually received reinforcements of bodies of men, running up from all sides. In five minutes the Swedes cleared the works of them, but, as they prepared to advance again, they saw a large body of horse riding down to bar their advance, while numbers of footmen were running to occupy some intrenchments ahead of them. Trumpets were sounding to the right, left, and rear.

"We cannot force our way farther," the major said to Charlie. "We knew nothing of these works, and they are fatal to our enterprise. We must retreat while we can. Do you not think so?"

"Yes, sir, I think the enterprise is quite hopeless."

The order was given. The troops faced about, formed into closer order, and at the double retraced their steps, the spearmen of each company forming its front line, and the musketeers the second.

Already it was growing dusk. The cavalry, riding ahead, scattered the small bodies of men who threw themselves in their way, and the battery they had first taken was entered without loss. There was a momentary halt here, for the men to recover their wind. Then the musketeers poured a volley into a dark line advancing upon them, the horsemen charged in among them, the long pikes of the front line cleared the way, and, with a shout, the Swedes passed through their foes and pressed forward.

But more troops were gathering to bar their way, and the major changed the line of march sharply to the right, sweeping along by the side of the force through which they had just cut their way, the musketeers on the flank firing into them as they passed. The movement was an adroit one, for in the gathering darkness the enemy in front would not be able to distinguish friends from foes, or to perceive the nature of the movement. For a few minutes they were unmolested, then the course was again changed, and Charlie was beginning to think that, in the darkness, they would yet make their escape, when a dull heavy sound was heard in their rear.

"That's the Russian cavalry, Bowyer. Take the musketeers on with you, and keep close to the company ahead. I will break them up with the pikemen. If they do come up to you, give them a volley and then continue your retreat with the rest."

While the captains of the other two companies had placed their pikemen in the front line, Charlie had placed his in the rear, in order to repel any attack of cavalry from that direction. He now formed them in a close clump, taking his place among them. The Russian squadrons came along with a deep roll like that of thunder. They were but thirty yards away when they perceived the little cluster of men with levelled lances. A few, unable to check their horses, rushed upon the points, but most of them reined in their little steeds in time. In a moment, the Swedes were surrounded by a wall of yelling horsemen, some of whom tried to break through the hedge of spears, while others discharged their pistols.

Charlie listened anxiously for the roll of a volley of musketry, but no sound came, and he felt sure that the whole body of cavalry had halted round him, and that his movement had saved the rest, who would now, if fortunate, be able to make their way off in the darkness. But the men were falling now from the pistol fire of the Cossacks, and, feeling that the work had been done, he determined to make one effort to save the men with him.

"Level your spears, and charge through them shoulder to shoulder," he said. "It is your only chance. Once through, throw away your spears, and break up in the darkness. Most of you may escape.

"Now!"

With a shout, the Swedes rushed forward in a body. Horses and riders went down before them. There was a rush from behind. Charlie shouted to the rear rank, to face about, but in the confusion and din his words were unheard. There was a brief struggle in the darkness. Charlie emptied his pistols, and cut down more than one of his opponents, then a sword fell on his shoulder, while at the same moment he was ridden over by a Cossack, and was stunned by the force of his fall.

When he recovered consciousness, several men with torches were moving about him, and, at the orders of an officer, were examining the bodies of the fallen. He saw them pass their swords through the bodies of three of his own men, who were lying near him, and as they came up to him he closed his eyes, expecting a similar fate.

"This is an officer, captain," one of the torch bearers said in Russian.

"Very well. Carry him to the camp, then. If he is alive, the general may want to question him."

Seeing that he breathed, four of the Russian soldiers took him upon their shoulders, and carried him away. The pain of his wound, caused by the movement, was acute, but he retained consciousness until, after what seemed to him a journey of immense length, he was again laid down on the ground, close to a large fire. Several officers stood round him, and he asked, first in Polish and then in Swedish, for water, and at the orders of one who seemed of superior rank to the others, some was at once brought to him.

"Your king treats his prisoners well," the officer said. "We will do everything we can for you."

Half an hour later, a doctor came to his side, and cutting open his coat, applied a bandage to his shoulder.

"Is it a serious wound?" Charlie asked in Swedish.

"It might be worse, but it will be a troublesome one; it is a sabre cut, and has cleft right through your shoulder bone. Are you hurt anywhere else?"

"No, I do not think so. I was knocked down in the dark, and I believe stunned, though I have a sort of recollection of being trampled on, and I feel sore all over."

The surgeon felt his ribs and limbs, repeatedly asking him if it hurt him. When he finished the examination, he said:

"You are doubtless badly bruised, but I don't think anything is broken. Our Cossack horses are little more than ponies. Had they been heavy horse, they would have trod your life out."

A few moments later there was a sound of trampling horses. They halted close by. The officers drew back, and a moment later Marshal Scheremetof, the commander of the Russian army, came up to Charlie's side.

"Which of you speaks Swedish?" he asked the officers, and one of them stepped forward.

"Ask him what force was this that attacked us, and with what object."

As Charlie saw no reason for concealment, he replied that it was a body of four hundred Swedish infantry, and a troop of horse, with four guns, and that their object was to enter the town.

"They must have been mad to attempt to cut their way through our whole army," the general said, when the answer was translated to him; "but, by Saint Paul, they nearly succeeded. The Swedes are mad, but this was too much even for madmen. Ask him whence the force came. It may be that a large reinforcement has reached Vyburg, without our knowing it."

"We arrived two days since," Charlie replied, when the question was put to him. "We came in a ship together from Revel."

"Did others come with you?" was next asked, at the general's dictation.

"No other ship but ours has arrived."

"But others are coming?"

As Charlie had no doubt that great efforts would be made to send further reinforcements, he replied:

"Many more troops are coming, but I cannot say when they will arrive."

"Will it be soon?"

"That I cannot say, but I don't think they will come from Revel. There was a talk of large reinforcements, but whether from Sweden or from the king's army, I cannot say."

"Are you a Swede?" the general asked.

"I am an Englishman in the Swedish service, general."

"We have many of your countrymen with us," the general said. "It would have been better for you, had you come to the czar.

"See that he is well treated," he said to the officers, and then mounted and rode away.

Chapter 15: An Old Acquaintance.

The next morning Charlie was placed in a tent, in which lay several officers who had been wounded, either the night before or by shots from the town. He learned with great pleasure, upon questioning the doctor, that the Swedes had got off safely in the darkness. Some eight or ten men only had straggled and been made prisoners, and not more than twenty had been left dead on the field. He had the satisfaction, therefore, of knowing that the defence made by his own pikemen had been the means of saving the whole force. In other respects he had nothing to complain of, for he was well attended to, and received the same treatment as the Russians.

For another ten days the roar of the cannon continued, some seventy guns keeping up an incessant fire on the town. At the end of that time the governor capitulated, and was allowed to march out with the honours of war.

Only forty out of the brave garrison remained unwounded at the end of the siege. They, as well as such of their comrades as were strong enough to travel, passed through the lines of the Russians, and marched to Vyburg.

Three weeks after being made a prisoner, Charlie's wound was so far healed that the surgeon pronounced him able to sit a horse, and, under the escort of an officer and four Cossacks, he was taken by easy stages to Bercov, a prison fortress a short distance from Moscow. He had inquired from the surgeon who attended him for Doctor Kelly. The doctor knew him, but said that he was not with the army, but was, he believed, away visiting some towns on the Volga, where a serious pestilence was raging.

Charlie remained but a short time at Bercov. His wound was healing rapidly, and the surgeon who attended him assured him that there was every prospect of his making a complete cure, if he would but keep his arm, for some weeks, in a sling.

He had nothing to complain of, either as to his comfort or food. The governor, who spoke a little Polish, visited him every day, and asked many questions as to his native country. On one of these visits he said to him:

"You asked me yesterday if I knew Doctor Kelly, one of the chief surgeons of the army, who, as you had heard, was at present on the Volga. You mentioned that he was a friend of yours, and that you had made his acquaintance, when you were unlucky enough before to be a prisoner in our hands. I am sorry to say that I have today seen an official report, in which his name appears among the list of those who have fallen victims to the pestilence."

"I am sorry to hear that," Charlie exclaimed; "both because he was very kind to me, and I liked him much, and because, in the second place, I was sure that he would have used his influence, with the czar, to obtain my exchange as soon as possible."

"It is very unfortunate," the governor said, "especially as these exchanges are of rare occurrence. A few officers may be taken prisoners on each side in the skirmishes, but the numbers are too small to make the loss of any importance, either to Russia or Sweden, and it is months since either have taken any steps to bring about exchanges. I myself have no influence. My appointment here is a sort of punishment, for having offended the czar by not having brought up my regiment in time to take part in the fight, when you attacked us at Narva. I saved the regiment, but that was not regarded as any excuse for having been three days longer on the march than the czar expected; so I was sent here, as a sort of dismissal from active service.

"You know no one else who could move in your matter?"

"No one. The governor of the castle at Plescow was a surly fellow, and was reprimanded by the czar, at least so I heard, for not having treated me sufficiently well. I was only three or four days there, and the only officer I saw besides Doctor Kelly was a friend of his, another doctor. He was at the table when I dined with Kelly. He seemed to me to be a fine fellow, and, by the by, he did say jokingly that, if I was ever made prisoner again, I was to ask for him, and that he would do anything he could for me."

"What was his name?" the governor asked.

"Peter Michaeloff.

"Do you know him?" he added, as he saw a look of surprise in the governor's face.

"I know one of that name," the governor said doubtfully, "I don't know that he is a doctor; though he may be, for he knows something of many things."

"Oh, he was a doctor," Charlie said confidently. "I know Kelly said he could take off a limb as well as he could do it, himself."

"What sort of man was he?"

"He was a tall, strong man, with black hair and gray eyes. He has rather a positive way of talking, and seemed to have very strong opinions about things. He looked good tempered, but I should say that he could be passionate enough, if he were put out."

"That might be the Peter Michaeloff I know," the governor said. "You are sure he said that you were to ask for him, if you were a second time taken prisoner?"

"I am quite certain he said so, though I don't know whether the promise meant much. But he certainly spoke as if he thought he might be able to help me, and, though it did not seem likely that I could have such bad luck twice, I think he meant at the time what he said, and I should think he was the sort of man who would keep his word."

"I will make some inquiries," the governor said, "and find out, if I can, where he is at present. Yes, I should think that he would be able to assist you, if he chose to interest himself in the matter."

Ten days later, the governor came into Charlie's room.

"An officer has arrived, with an order for your removal," he said. "You are to be taken up again to Notteburg."

"I am very sorry," Charlie said. "I have been very comfortable here. You have been very kind to me, and I feel sure the change will not be for the better. Besides, we are nearly into September now, and in that marshy country round the lake and river, the winter will be even more severe than it is here. The only thing I can think of is that the Swedes at Vyburg may have taken a Russian captain prisoner, and that they are going to exchange us."

The governor shook his head.

"There are no longer any Swedes at Vyburg. All Ingria is in our hands and the Swedes have retired into Finland. It may be that it is the work of your friend. I sent a message to Peter Michaeloff, should he be found in that neighbourhood, by an officer who was going there, telling him that you were here, and that, having met him when a prisoner at Plescow, you relied on his good offices. Should the officer have found him there, and have given him my message, he may probably have begged the field marshal to order you to be taken to the prison there, where he could be near you, and visit you sometimes."

"Your doctors must have a good deal more influence in your army than they have among the Swedes," Charlie remarked, "if that is how it has come about."

"It would be a matter of favour," the governor said. "If Michaeloff is acquainted with the field marshal, or had attended him when unwell, he could ask a little favour of that sort. If the field marshal sent you here, he could send for you again without more trouble than signing his name to the order."

"Well, if it is Michaeloff who has done this," Charlie grumbled; "no doubt he meant it kindly, but I would much rather that he left me here. A ride of two hundred and fifty miles, in August, is not pleasant to begin with, and the thought of winter in those swamps is enough to make one shiver."

"With a comfortable room and a warm stove, you will not find much to complain of, Captain Carstairs," the governor said with a smile; "and, no doubt, Michaeloff may be enabled to obtain leave for you to go out with him on parole. I was about myself to ask you, now that you are strong and well again, whether you would like to give your parole, and offer you the use of my horse for a ride, when inclined for it."

"Thank you, governor. If Michaeloff can do that, it will certainly be a boon, but I am not disposed to agree that the change can be his work. In the first place, we don't know that he is there. In the second, I can hardly think that he could have managed it; and, most of all, I do not see he could possibly have had a hand in the matter, for, even supposing the officer had found him directly he arrived, and then given him the message, and he had acted upon it at once, there would have been no time for the order to get here. It would have needed a messenger riding night and day, with frequent relays of horses, to have got to Notteburg and back since the day I spoke to you about the matter.

"When am I to start?"

"As soon as you have eaten your breakfast. The order says 'send at once,' and field marshals expect their orders to be attended to promptly."

On descending to the courtyard after breakfast, Charlie was surprised to see that, instead of a horse as he had expected, a well-appointed carriage, with an ample supply of rugs, was standing there. The governor was there to see him off.

"Well, sir," Charlie said. "If this is the way in which you convey prisoners from one place to another in Russia, I shall certainly be able, when I meet King Charles, to report to him most favourably as to the treatment of his officers who have fallen into the czar's hands. This will make the journey a very much more pleasant one than I had expected."

"I am glad you are pleased," the governor said, "and that you have no unpleasant recollection of your stay here."

A minute later, the carriage dashed out through the gate of the prison. An officer was seated by Charlie's side, two Cossacks galloping in front, while two others rode behind.

"It was worth making the change, if only for this drive," Charlie thought cheerfully, as the dust flew up in a cloud before the horses' hoofs, and he felt a sense of exhilaration from the keen air that blew in his face.

The journey was performed with great rapidity. One of the Cossacks galloped ahead, as soon as they arrived at the station where they changed horses, and had fresh ones in readiness at the next post house. The Cossacks themselves were changed at every other station, fresh relays from the men stationed there taking their place. Excellent meals were served three times a day, and each night a comfortable bed was provided, at the last post house where they stopped.

The officer was a pleasant fellow, but he spoke nothing except Russian, and, although Charlie fancied he understood him to some extent when he spoke to him in Polish, he shook his head and gave no answers in that language.

Late in the evening of the third day, they arrived at Notteburg. The building at which the carriage stopped was of considerable size. It stood in the heart of the town, and had no outward appearance of a prison. It was apparently at a side entrance at which they stopped. On the officer knocking at the door, it was opened by two Cossacks, who, after exchanging a few words in Russian with the officer, led Charlie along a passage and up a narrow staircase, which led into a somewhat spacious corridor. They opened a door, and he found himself in a comfortable room. A table laid for dinner with handsome silver and appointments stood in the middle of the room, which was carpeted with tartar rugs. One of the Cossacks opened an inner door, which led into a bedroom, snugly furnished.

"It must be the doctor, after all," Charlie murmured to himself, in great surprise. "I see now that there was plenty of time for a letter to come up here and have gone back again, and I suppose the good fellow has got leave for me to stay for a night in his quarters, before I am handed over to the prison. Well, for the last three days I have travelled like a prince, and this is the closing act of it."

He enjoyed a good wash, then returned to the other room, and sat down in a comfortable chair to wait for his host. He was on the point of dozing off, when the door opened, and Peter Michaeloff entered. Charlie sprang to his feet.

"Well, Captain Carstairs," the Russian said, holding out his hand, "so it seems you had bad luck again. You must have quite an affection for our prisons."

"I shall have, at least, a pleasant remembrance of the kindness shown to me as a prisoner," Charlie said; "and I am sure it is you that I have to thank for my transfer here, and for the pleasant journey I have had. I could not have travelled more comfortably, if I had been a Russian grandee."

"Well, I am glad to meet you again," the doctor said heartily. "Let me see, it is some twenty months since we supped together last at Kelly's quarters. Poor fellow! I shall miss him greatly. You have heard of his death?"

"The governor of Bercov told me of it, a fortnight ago. I was indeed sorry to hear it. I shall never forget his kindness to me."

"Yes, he was a good man, skilful in his profession, and full of zeal and energy. The blood runs faster somehow, in the veins of you islanders, than of us sluggish Muscovites. If we could but at one sweep banish every Russian official, from the highest to the lowest, and fill their places with men from your islands, what progress we should make, what work could we get done, what reforms could be carried out!

"However, at present," he went on, changing the subject abruptly, "the point is supper. I am as hungry as a bear, for I have been at work since daylight, and have eaten nothing since I broke my fast."

He rang a handbell placed on the table. Two Cossacks entered bearing dishes, and the doctor and his guest at once fell to on the supper, which was excellent.

"Hard work deserves good food," the Russian said, in reply to a remark of Charlie's as to the excellence both of the food and wine. "Your Charles does not think so, I hear, and lives on the roughest of food. What will be the consequence? He will wear himself out. His restless activity will exhaust his powers, and weaken his judgment. I can eat rough food if I can get no better, but I take the best, when opportunity offers.

"What have you been doing ever since you left Plescow? I inquired after you the other day, when our troops broke up Schlippenbach's force on the Embach. I found you were not among the prisoners, and I wondered if you were among the killed."

"I was not in Livonia at the time. I was with the king's army at Warsaw. Three regiments were sent off, the day after the battle of Clissow, by boats down the Vistula, and then by ship to Revel. Mine was one of them, but we arrived a fortnight too late."

"Then you were present at Charles' third victory? How that young fellow handles his troops, and what wonderful troops they are! Now we will get into our easy chairs again, and you shall tell me something about what you have been doing, since we last met."

Charlie gave a sketch of his adventures.

"So you fought at the Dwina, too? You have had luck in going through three battles without a wound."

When Charlie stated that he had gone to Warsaw on a private mission, whose nature was immaterial to the story, the doctor broke in:

"You need not tell me what it was, it was of course something to do with Augustus. The way Charles is hunting down that unfortunate king is shocking, it is downright malignity. Why, he has wasted fifteen months over it already, and it has cost him Ingria. He could have made any terms with Poland he liked, after his victory on the Dwina, and would then have been free to use all his forces against us. As it is, he has wasted two summers, and is likely to waste another, and that not for any material advantage, but simply to gratify his hatred against Augustus; and he has left us to take Ingria almost without a blow, and to gain what Russia has wanted for the last hundred years, a foothold on the Baltic. He may be a great general, but he is no politician. No real statesman would throw away solid advantages in order to gratify personal pique."

"He considers Augustus the author of this league against him," Charlie said.

"He and the czar had no grounds at all of quarrel against him."

"We talked over that, the last time we met," the doctor said with a laugh, "and I told you then that a foothold on the Baltic was so necessary to Russia, that she would have accepted the alliance of the Prince of Darkness himself to get it. As to Augustus, I don't defend him. He was ambitious, as I suppose most of us are. He thought he saw an opportunity of gaining territory. He has found that he has made a mistake, and will of course lose a province. But Charles' persecution of him goes beyond all bounds. Never before did a sovereign insist upon a nation consenting to dethrone its king at his dictation.

"But go on with your story."

He listened without remark, until Charlie concluded.

"I wish you had been in our service," he said, "instead of that of Sweden. You would have mounted fast. You have all the requisites for success, above all, promptitude of decision and quickness of invention. You did well in getting away from that Jewish scoundrel in the hut, and in killing his master, but it was your adventure with the wolves that showed your quality. That idea of setting fire to the tree in which you were sitting, in order at once to warm yourself and to frighten away the wolves, would never have occurred to a Russian, and the quickness with which you formed, with three logs, a redoubt against the wolves, showed a quick military eye, and the ability to think and act in a moment of danger.

"Now tell me how it was that you were the only officer captured the other day."

Charlie briefly related how he, with the pikemen of his company, had stayed behind to check the pursuit of the Russian horse, and to gain time for the main body to lose themselves in the darkness. The Russian struck his fist on the arm of his chair.

"It was well done," he said. "There is the difference. A Russian captain would have done it, if he had been ordered, and he and his men would, without a question, have sacrificed themselves to cover the retreat of the rest, but he would never have done it on his own initiative. The idea would never have struck him. He would have plodded along until the enemy's cavalry came up and annihilated them all. By the way, why did you not ask for me at once?"

"I had asked for Doctor Kelly the day after I was taken prisoner, and was told that he had gone to the Volga. I thought that he would be back before long, and it was only when I heard of his death that it occurred to me to endeavour to find one who had kindly promised, after a few hours' acquaintance only, to befriend me should I ever find myself in a similar scrape."

"It would have saved you the journey down to Moscow. I heard, of course, that a Swedish captain had been made prisoner that night, but I was myself at Moscow at the time, and did not happen to notice the name of the officer taken. Were you well treated at Bercov?"

"The governor there was most kind, and all the arrangements of the prison seem excellent. I had no reason whatever to complain. The governor was good enough to come frequently himself to talk to me. He is a fine soldierly man, and though he did not say much, I think he is eating his heart out at being laid on the shelf there, instead of aiding to fight the battles of his country."

The Russian took out a pocketbook and made a note, then he rose.

"It is time for bed," he said. "I am up at daybreak."

"I hope I shall see you often in the prison," Charlie said. "I suppose I shall go in there tomorrow morning. I am indebted to you, indeed, for the very great kindness you have shown me."

"No, you will not go in early. I have got leave for you for another day, and I am going to take you for a drive in the morning. You will be called an hour before sunrise. Take your breakfast as soon as you are dressed. Do not wait for me. I have work to do before I start, and shall breakfast elsewhere."

As soon as Charlie had breakfasted the next morning, a Cossack told him that the carriage was below, and he followed him to the door where he had entered on the previous evening. The carriage was a simple one, but the three horses harnessed abreast to it were magnificent animals. Charlie stood admiring them for some little time.

"I should think," he said to himself, "the doctor must be a man of large property, and most likely of noble family, who has taken up his profession from pure love of it. He is evidently full of energy, and has an intense desire to see Russia greater and higher in the rank of nations. I suppose that, like Kelly, he is one of the principal medical officers in the army. Certainly he must be a man of considerable influence to obtain my transfer here so easily, and to see that I travelled so comfortably. I wonder where he is going to take me this morning."

Four or five minutes later Charlie's friend appeared at the door. He was evidently out of temper. He sprung hastily into the vehicle, as if he had altogether forgotten that he had asked Charlie to accompany him.

Then, as his eye fell on him, he nodded and said briefly, "Jump in."

A little surprised at the unceremonious address, Charlie sprang into the seat beside him without hesitation, seeing that his companion was evidently so much out of temper that he was not thinking of what he was doing at the moment. The coachman cracked his whip, and the spirited horses went off, at a rate of speed that threatened danger to persons traversing the narrow streets of the town. The cracking of the coachman's whip, and an occasional loud shout and the jangling of the bells, gave, however, sufficient warning of their approach.

Charlie smiled at the alacrity with which every one sprang out of the way, and either leapt into doorways or squeezed themselves against the wall. He was surprised, however, to see that not only did the townspeople show no resentment, at the reckless pace at which the carriage was driven, but that the soldiers, officers as well as men, cleared out as quickly, and without any expression of indignation or anger.

Indeed, most of them, as soon as they gained a place of safety, saluted his companion.

"These Russians have evidently a higher respect for their doctors than have the Swedes," he said to himself. "I am sure that not even the chief surgeon of the army would be treated with anything like the same respect, and, indeed, no one would recognize him at all, if he were not in uniform."

The doctor seemed to pay no attention to what was passing round him, but was muttering angrily to himself. It was not until they dashed out into the open country that he seemed to remember Charlie's presence at his side.

"These people are enough to vex one of the saints, by their stupidity," he said. "Unless they have some one standing behind them with a whip, they cannot be trusted to do what they are told. It is not that they are not willing, but that they are stupid. No one would believe that people could be so stupid. They drive me well nigh to madness sometimes, and it is the more irritating because, against stupidity, one is powerless. Beating a man or knocking him down may do him good if he is obstinate, or if he is careless, but when he is simply stupid it only makes him more stupid than before. You might as well batter a stone wall.

"You slept well and breakfasted well, Captain Carstairs?"

"Excellently well, thank you. What superb horses you have, doctor."

"Yes. I like travelling fast. Life is too short to throw away time in travelling. A busy man should always keep good horses."

"If he can afford to do so," Charlie said with a laugh. "I should say that every one, busy or not, would like to sit behind such horses as these, and, as you say, it would save a good deal of time to one who travelled much. But three such horses as these would only be in the reach of one with a very long purse."

"They were bred here. Their sire was one of three given by the king of England to the czar. The dams were from the imperial stables at Vienna. So they ought to be good."

Charlie guessed that the team must have been a present from the czar, and, remembering what Doctor Kelly had said of the czar's personal communications with him, he thought that the ruler of Russia must have a particular liking for doctors, and that the medical profession must be a more honoured and profitable one in Russia than elsewhere.

After driving with great rapidity for upwards of an hour along the banks of the Neva, Charlie saw a great number of people at work on an island in the middle of the river, some distance ahead, and soon afterwards, to his surprise, observed a multitude on the flat, low ground ahead.

"This is what I have brought you to see," his companion said. "Do you know what they are doing?"

"It seems to me that they are building a fortress on that island."

"You are right. We have got a footing on the sea, and we are going to keep it. While Charles of Sweden is fooling away his time in Poland, in order to gratify his spite against Augustus, we are strengthening ourselves here, and never again will Sweden wrest Ingria from our hands."

"It is marvellous how much has been done already," Charlie said, as he looked at the crowd of workmen.

"Everything was prepared," his companion said. "While the army was invading Livonia, and driving the remnant of the Swedes into Revel, thousands of carts laden with piles of wood, stone, and cement were moving towards Ingria. Tens of thousands of workmen and peasants were in motion from every part of Russia towards this point, and, the day after Notteburg surrendered, they began their work here. It was the opportunity in the lifetime of a nation, and we have seized it. The engineers who had, in disguise, examined it months ago, had reported that the island was covered at high tides, and was unfit to bear the foundations of even the slightest buildings. Piles are being driven in, as close as they will stand, over every foot of ground in it. Over this a coating of concrete many feet thick will be laid, and on this the fortress, which is to be the centre and heart of Russia, will rise. In the fort will stand a pile, which will be the tomb of the future czars of Russia, and there in front of us, where you see fifty thousand peasants at work, shall be the future capital of the empire."

"But it is a swamp," Charlie said in astonishment, alike at the vastness of the scheme, and the energy with which it was being prosecuted.

"Nature has made it a swamp," his companion said calmly, "but man is stronger than nature. The river will be embanked, the morass drained, and piles driven everywhere, as has been done in the island, and the capital will rise here. The fort has already been named the Fortress of Saint Peter and Saint Paul. The capital will be named alike after the patron saint and its founder--Petersburg."

They had now reached the spot. The carriage stopped and they alighted. Charlie saw, with astonishment, that a wide deep cut had been driven, between the road and the river, in a straight line. Looking down into it, he saw that it was paved with the heads of piles, and that carts were already emptying loads of concrete down upon it.

"Every bag of cement, every stone that you see, has been brought from a great distance," his companion said. "There is not a stone to be had within fifty miles of this spot. The work would seem well-nigh impossible, but it is the work of a nation. In another month, there will be a hundred and fifty thousand peasants at work here, and well nigh as many carts, bringing materials for the work and provisions for the workers."

"It is stupendous! But it will take years to complete, and it will surely be terribly unhealthy here?"

"I calculate the work will occupy ten years, and will cost a hundred thousand, maybe two hundred thousand lives," the other said calmly; "but what is that to the making of a nation? Before, Russia was stifled, she could not grow. Now we have a communication with the world. The island that lies at the mouth of the Neva will be fortified, and become a great naval arsenal and fort. Along the walls which will rise here will be unloaded the merchandise of Europe, and in exchange the ships will carry away our products. Some day we shall have another port on the south, but for the present this must suffice. You will say that this is dangerously near our frontier, but that will soon be remedied. As we have pushed the Swedes out of Ingria, so in time shall we drive them from Livonia on the west, and from Finland on the north.

"But I must to work."

And he motioned to a group of five or six officers, who had been standing a short distance away, to approach him.

Charlie was struck with the air of humility with which they saluted his companion, who at once asked a number of questions as to the supplies that had arrived, the progress that had been made, at a point where they had met with a deep slough into which the piles had penetrated without meeting with any firm ground, the number of huts that had been erected during the past three days for the reception of labourers, the state of stocks of meat and flour, and other particulars. To each he gave short, sharp orders. When they had left, he turned to Charlie.

"You guess who I am, I suppose?"

"I guess now, your majesty," Charlie said respectfully, "but until now the idea that my kind friend was the czar himself never entered my mind. I understood, from Doctor Kelly, that you were a surgeon."

"I don't think he said so," the czar replied. "He simply said that I could perform an amputation as well as he could, which was not quite true. But I studied surgery for a time in Holland, and performed several operations under the eyes of the surgeons there.

"I saw that you did not recognize my name. It is known to every Russian, but doubtless you never heard of me save as Peter the Czar. Directly you mentioned it to the commandant at Bercov, and described my appearance, he knew who it was you were speaking of, and despatched a messenger at once to me. He will be here in the course of a week or so. Upon your report of the state of the prison, I at once despatched an order for him to hand over his command to the officer next in rank, and to proceed hither at once. He is evidently a good administrator, and heaven knows I have need of such men here.

"I was pleased with you, when I saw you with my friend Doctor Kelly. It was pleasant not to be known, and hear a frank opinion such as you gave me, and as you know, I sent you back on the following morning. I certainly told Kelly, at the time, not to mention who I was, but I did not intend that he should keep you in ignorance of it after I had left, and it was not until I heard, from your jailer at Bercov, that you were ignorant that Peter Michaeloff was the czar, that I knew that he had kept you in ignorance of it until the end.

"I should have liked to have kept you as my guest for a time, but winter comes on early and suddenly, and if you did not go now you might be detained here until the spring. I have therefore given orders that one of the Swedish vessels we captured on the lake should be got in readiness, and its crew placed on board again. You shall embark in an hour, and it shall carry you to any port in Sweden you may choose. The wind is from the east, and you have every chance of a quick run thither."

Charlie expressed his warm thanks to the czar for his thoughtful kindness.

"I have much to do now," the czar said, "and must hand you over to the care of one of my officers. He will accompany you, in my carriage, to the spot where the vessel is lying, near the mouth of the river, and will there see you on board. Should the fortune of war again throw you into our hands, do not lose an hour in sending a message to Peter Michaeloff."

So saying, the czar shook hands with Charlie, beckoned an officer to him and gave him instructions, and then moved away among the workmen, while Charlie, with his conductor, took their places in the vehicle and drove rapidly off.

An hour later, he was on board the Swedish vessel, whose master and crew were delighted at their sudden and unlooked for release. The former was overjoyed, for the vessel was his own property.

"You will find your things in your cabin, sir," he said. "They were sent on board this morning, together with food and wine sufficient for a month's voyage, whereas, with this wind, we ought not to be more than four days. At which port will you land?"

"I would rather go to Gottenburg, captain, though it is farther for you than

Stockholm."

"It shall be Gottenburg, sir. It is thanks to you that I have got my liberty and my ship, and a day or two can make no difference to me."

Charlie, indeed, had thought the matter over as he drove along. He would not be able to rejoin the army until it had gone into winter quarters, and therefore decided that he would go to Gottenburg, apply for six months' leave, and spend the winter with his father. Somewhat puzzled at the mention of his things having gone on board, he went into the cabin, and found there a handsome pelisse trimmed with costly furs, two robes composed of valuable skins, and a change of clothes.

The wind held fair, blowing strongly, and four days later he arrived at Gottenburg.

Chapter 16: In England Again.

Charlie was received with delight by his father, whom he had not seen since the spring of the previous year. Then you got my letter, Charlie?" Sir Marmaduke asked, when the first greetings were over. "And yet, I do not see how you could have done so. It is little over a fortnight since I wrote, and I had not looked for you for another month yet."

"I have certainly received no letter, father. A fortnight ago I was in a Russian prison, and my arrival here, in so short a time, seems to me almost miraculous;" and he then briefly related his singular experiences.

"Now about the letter, father," he said, as he concluded. "I suppose you must have written to ask me to get leave for a time, as it seems that you were expecting me shortly. I suppose you felt that you would like me with you, for a time."

"So I should, lad, of that you may be sure, but I should not have called you away for that. No, I had this letter the other day from old Banks. You know he writes to me once a year. His letters have been only gossip so far, for you know my precious cousin kicked him out of the house, as soon as he took possession; but this is a different matter. Read it for yourself."

Charlie took the letter, and with some trouble spelt through the crabbed handwriting.

It began:

"Honoured sir and master, I hope that this finds you and Captain Charles both well in health. I have been laid up with rhematis in the bones, having less comfort in my lodgings than I used to have at Lynnwood. Your honour will have heard that King William has fallen from his horse, and broken his collarbone, and died. May the Lord forgive him for taking the place of better men. Anne has come to the throne, and there were some hopes that she would, of herself, step aside and let him to whom the throne rightly belongs come to it. Such, however, has not been the case, and those who know best think that things are no forwarder for William's death, rather indeed the reverse, since the Princess Anne is better liked by the people than was her sister's husband.

"There is no sure news from Lynnwood. None of the old servants are there; and I have no one from whom I can learn anything for certain. Things however are, I hear, much worse since young Mr. Dormay was killed in the duel in London, of which I told you in my last letter.

"Dame Celia and Mistress Ciceley go but seldom abroad, and when seen they smile but little, but seem sad and downcast. The usurper has but small dealing with any of the gentry. There are always men staying there, fellows of a kind with whom no gentleman would consort, and they say there is much drinking and wild going on. As Captain Charles specially bade me, I have done all that I could to gather news of Nicholson. Till of late I have heard nothing of him. He disappeared altogether from these parts, just after your honour went away. News once came here from one who knew him, and who had gone up to London on a visit to a kinsman, that he had met him there, dressed up in a garb in no way according with his former position, but ruffling it at a tavern frequented by loose blades, spending his money freely, and drinking and dicing with the best of them.

"A week since he was seen down here, in a very sorry state, looking as if luck had gone altogether against him. Benjamin Haddock, who lives, as you know, close to the gate of Lynnwood, told me that he saw one pass along the road, just as it was dusk, whom he could swear was that varlet Nicholson. He went to the door and looked after him to make sure, and saw him enter the gate. Next day Nicholson was in Lancaster. He was spending money freely there, and rode off on a good horse, which looked ill assorted with his garments, though he purchased some of better fashion in the town. It seemed to me likely that he must have got money from the usurper. I do not know whether your honour will deem this news of importance, but I thought it well to write to you at once. Any further news I may gather, I will send without fail.

"Your humble servant,
"John Banks."

"There is no doubt that this is of importance," Charlie said, when he had read the letter through. "It is only by getting hold of this villain that there is any chance of our obtaining proof of the foul treachery of which you were the victim. Hitherto, we have had no clue whatever as to where he was to be looked for. Now, there can be little doubt that he has returned to his haunts in London. I understand now, father, why you wanted me to get leave. You mean that I shall undertake this business."

"That was my thought, Charlie. You are now well-nigh twenty, and would scarce be recognized as the boy who left four years ago. The fellow would know me at once, and I might be laid by the heels again under the old warrant; besides being charged with breaking away from the custody of the soldiers. Besides, in this business youth and strength and vigour are requisite. I would gladly take the matter in my own hands, but methinks you would have a better chance of bringing it to a favourable issue. Now that Anne is on the throne, she and her advisers will look leniently upon the men whose only fault was devotion to her father; and if we can once get this foul charge of assassination lifted from our shoulders, I and Jervoise and the others who had to fly at the same time, may all be permitted to return, and obtain a reversal of the decree of the Act of Confiscation of our estates.

"I have no friends at court, but I know that Jervoise was a close acquaintance, years ago, of John Churchill, who is now Duke of Marlborough, and they say high in favour with Anne. I did not think of it when I wrote to you, but a week later it came to my mind that his intervention might be very useful, and I took advantage of an officer, leaving here for the army, to send by him a letter to Jervoise, telling him that there was now some hope of getting at the traitor who served as John Dormay's instrument in his plot against us. I said that I had sent for you, and thought it probable you would take the matter in hand; and I prayed him to send me a letter of introduction for you to the duke, so that, if you could by any means obtain the proof of our innocence of this pretended plot, he might help you to obtain a reversal of the Act of Confiscation against us all. I have asked him to write at once, and I will send the letter after you, as soon as I get it.

"I know nothing of London, but I have heard of the Bull's Head, in Fenchurch Street, as being one frequented by travellers from the country. You had best put up there, and thither I will forward the note from Jervoise."

"The letter will be a useful one, indeed, father, when I have once wrung the truth from that villain Nicholson. It will be an expedition after my own heart.

There is first the chance of punishing the villain, and then the hope of restoring you to your place at dear old Lynnwood."

"You must be careful, Charlie. Remember it would never do to kill the rascal. That would be the greatest of misfortunes; for, with his death, any chance of unmasking the greater villain would disappear."

"I will be careful, father. I cannot say how I shall set about the matter, yet. That must depend upon circumstances; but, as you say, above all things I must be careful of the fellow's life. When is there a ship sailing, father?"

"The day after tomorrow, Charlie. You will want that time for getting clothes, suitable to a young gentleman of moderate condition, up from the country on a visit to London. You must make up your mind that it will be a long search before you light on the fellow, for we have no clue as to the tavern he frequents. As a roistering young squire, wanting to see London life, you could go into taverns frequented by doubtful characters, for it is probably in such a place that you will find him.

"However, all this I must leave to you. You showed yourself, in that Polish business, well able to help yourself out of a scrape, and if you could do that among people of whose tongues you were ignorant, you ought to be able to manage on English soil."

"At any rate, I will do my best, father, of that you may be sure. I have the advantage of knowing the fellow, and am pretty certain that he will not know me."

"Not he, Charlie," his father said confidently. "Even in the last two years, since you were here with Jervoise and the others, you have changed so much that I, myself, might have passed you in the street without knowing you.

"Now, you had better go off and see about your things. There is no time to be lost. I have drawn out a hundred guineas of my money, which will, I should say, serve you while you are away; but don't stint it, lad. Let me know if it runs short, and I will send you more."

"I have money, too, father. I have four months' pay due, besides money I have in hand, for there was but little need for us to put our hands in our pockets."

Ten days later, Charlie arrived in the Port of London, and took up his abode at the Bull's Head, where he found the quarters comfortable, indeed, after the rough work of campaigning. The next morning he took a waiter into his confidence.

"I have come to London to see a little life," he said, "and I want to be put into the way of doing it. I don't want to go to places where young gallants assemble. My purse is not deep enough to stand such society. I should like to go to places where I shall meet hearty young fellows, and could have a throw of the dice, or see a main fought by good cocks, or even sally out and have a little fun with the watch. My purse is fairly lined, and I want some amusement--something to look back upon when I go home again. What is the best way to set about it?"

"Well, sir, if that is your humour, I have a brother who is one of the mayor's tipstaffs. He knows the city well, ay, and Westminster, too, and the purlieus of Saint James's, and whether you want to meet young gallants or roistering blades, or to have a look in at places where you can hire a man to cut another's throat for a few crowns, he can show you them. He will be on duty now, but I will send him a message to come round this evening, and I warrant me he will be here. He has showed young squires from the country over the town before this, and will guess what is on hand when he gets my message."

Having nothing to do, Charlie sauntered about the town during the day, looking into the shops, and keeping a keen eye on passers by, with the vague hope that he might be lucky enough to come across his man.

After he had finished his supper, the waiter came up and told him that his brother was outside.

"I have spoken to him, sir, and he warrants that he can take you into the sort of society you want to meet, whatever it may be."

Charlie followed him out. A man was standing under the lamp that swung before the door.

"This is the gentleman I was speaking to you of, Tony."

As the man took off his cap, Charlie had a good view of his face. It was shrewd and intelligent.

"You understand what I want?" he asked, as the waiter ran into the house again, to attend to his duties.

"Yes, sir. So far as I understood him, you wish to go to taverns of somewhat inferior reputations, and to see something of that side of London life. If you will pardon my boldness, it is somewhat of a dangerous venture. In such places brawls are frequent, and rapiers soon out.

"You look to me like one who could hold his own in a fray," he added, as his eye ran over the athletic figure before him, "but it is not always fair fighting. These fellows hang together, and while engaged with one, half a dozen might fall upon you. As to your purse, sir, it is your own affair. You will assuredly lose your money, if you play or wager with them. But that is no concern of mine. Neither, you may say, is your life; but it seems to me that it is. One young gentleman from the country, who wanted, like you, to see life, was killed in a brawl, and I have never forgiven myself for having taken him to the tavern where he lost his life. Thus, I say that, though willing enough to earn a crown or two outside my own work, I must decline to take you to places where, as it seems to me, you are likely to get into trouble."

"You are an honest fellow, and I like you all the more, for speaking out frankly to me," Charlie said, "and were I, as I told your brother, thinking of going to such places solely for amusement, what you say would have weight with me. But, as I see that you are to be trusted, I will tell you more. I want to find a man who did me and mine a grievous ill turn. I have no intention of killing him, or anything of that sort, but it is a matter of great importance to lay hand on him. All I know of him is that he is a frequenter of taverns here, and those not of the first character. Just at present he is, I have reason to believe, provided with funds, and may push himself into places where he would not show himself when he is out of luck. Still, it is more likely he is to be found in the lowest dens, among rascals of his own kidney. I may lose a little money, but I shall do so with my eyes open, and solely to obtain a footing at the places where I am most likely to meet him."

"That alters the affair," the man said gravely. "It will add to your danger; for as you know him, I suppose he knows you, also."

"No. It is four years since we met, and I have so greatly changed, in that time, that I have no fear he would recognize me. At any rate, not here in London, which is the last place he would suspect me of being in."

"That is better. Well, sir, if that be your object, I will do my best to help you. What is the fellow's name and description?"

"He called himself Nicholson, when we last met; but like enough that is not his real name, and if it is, he may be known by another here. He is a lanky knave, of middle height; but more than that, except that he has a shifty look about his eyes, I cannot tell you."

"And his condition, you say, is changeable?"

"Very much so, I should say. I should fancy that, when in funds, he would frequent places where he could prey on careless young fellows from the country, like myself. When his pockets are empty, I should say he would herd with the lowest rascals."

"Well, sir, as you say he is in funds at present, we will this evening visit a tavern or two, frequented by young blades, some of whom have more money than wit; and by men who live by their wits and nothing else. But you must not be disappointed, if the search prove a long one before you run your hare down, for the indications you have given me are very doubtful. He may be living in Alsatia, hard by the Temple, which, though not so bad as it used to be, is still an abode of dangerous rogues. But more likely you may meet him at the taverns in Westminster, or near Whitehall; for, if he has means to dress himself bravely, it is there he will most readily pick up gulls.

"I will, with your permission, take you to the better sort to begin with, and then, when you have got more accustomed to the ways of these places, you can go to those a step lower, where, I should think, he is more likely to be found; for such fellows spend their money freely, when they get it, and unless they manage to fleece some young lamb from the country, they soon find themselves unable to keep pace with the society of places where play runs high, and men call for their bottles freely. Besides, in such places, when they become unable to spend money freely, they soon get the cold shoulder from the host, who cares not to see the money that should be spent on feasting and wine diverted into the pockets of others.

"I shall leave you at the door of these places. I am too well known to enter. I put my hand on the shoulder of too many men, during the year, for me to go into any society without the risk of someone knowing me again."

They accordingly made their way down to Westminster, and Charlie visited several taverns. At each he called for wine, and was speedily accosted by one or more men, who perceived that he was a stranger, and scented booty. He stated freely that he had just come up to town, and intended to stay some short time there. He allowed himself to be persuaded to enter the room where play was going on, but declined to join, saying that, as yet, he was ignorant of the ways of town, and must see a little more of them before he ventured his money, but that, when he felt more at home, he should be ready enough to join in a game of dice or cards, being considered a good hand at both.

After staying at each place about half an hour, he made his way out, getting rid of his would-be friends with some little difficulty, and with a promise that he would come again, ere long.

For six days he continued his inquiries, going out every evening with his guide, and taking his meals, for the most part, at one or other of the taverns, in hopes that he might happen upon the man of whom he was in search. At the end of that time, he had a great surprise. As he entered the hotel to take supper, the waiter said to him:

"There is a gentleman who has been asking for you, in the public room. He arrived an hour ago, and has hired a chamber."

"Asking for me?" Charlie repeated in astonishment. "You must be mistaken."

"Not at all, sir. He asked for Mr. Charles Conway, and that is the name you wrote down in the hotel book, when you came."

"That must be me, sure enough, but who can be asking for me I cannot imagine. However, I shall soon know."

And, in a state of utter bewilderment as to who could have learnt his name and address, he went into the coffee room. There happened, at the moment, to be but one person there, and as he rose and turned towards him, Charlie exclaimed in astonishment and delight:

"Why, Harry, what on earth brings you here? I am glad to see you, indeed, but you are the last person in the world I should have thought of meeting here in London."

"You thought I was in a hut, made as wind tight as possible, before the cold set in, in earnest. So I should have been, with six months of a dull life before me, if it had not been for Sir Marmaduke's letter. Directly my father read it through to me he said:

"'Get your valises packed at once, Harry. I will go to the colonel and get your leave granted. Charlie may have to go into all sorts of dens, in search of this scoundrel, and it is better to have two swords than one in such places. Besides, as you know the fellow's face you can aid in the search, and are as likely to run against him as he is. His discovery is as important to us as it is to him, and it may be the duke will be more disposed to interest himself, when he sees the son of his old friend, than upon the strength of a letter only.'

"You may imagine I did not lose much time. But I did not start, after all, until the next morning, for when the colonel talked it over with my father, he said:

"'Let Harry wait till tomorrow. I shall be seeing the king this evening. He is always interested in adventure, and I will tell him the whole story, and ask him to write a few lines, saying that Harry and Carstairs are young officers who have borne themselves bravely, and to his satisfaction. It may help with the duke, and will show, at any rate, that you have both been out here, and not intriguing at Saint Germains.'

"The colonel came in, late in the evening, with a paper, which the king had told Count Piper to write and sign, and had himself put his signature to it. I have got it sewn up in my doublet, with my father's letter to Marlborough. They are too precious to lose, but I can tell you what it is, word for word:

"'By order of King Charles the Twelfth of Sweden. This is to testify, to all whom it may concern, that Captain Charles Carstairs, and Captain Harry Jervoise--'"

"Oh, I am glad, Harry!" Charlie interrupted. "It was horrid that I should have been a captain, for the last year, and you a lieutenant. I am glad, indeed."

"Yes, it is grand, isn't it, and very good of the king to do it like that. Now, I will go on--

"'Have both served me well and faithfully during the war, showing great valour, and proving themselves to be brave and honourable gentlemen, as may be seen, indeed, from the rank that they, though young in years, have both attained, and which is due solely to their deserts.'

"What do you think of that?"

"Nothing could be better, Harry. Did you see my father at Gottenburg?"

"Yes. The ship I sailed by went to Stockholm, and I was lucky enough to find there another, starting for England in a few hours. She touched at Gottenburg to take in some cargo, and I had time to see Sir Marmaduke, who was good enough to express himself as greatly pleased that I was coming over to join you."

"Well, Harry, I am glad, indeed. Before we talk, let us go in and have supper, that is, if you have not already had yours. If you have, I can wait a bit."

"No; they told me you had ordered your supper at six, so I told them I would take mine at the same time; and, indeed, I can tell you that I am ready for it."

After the meal, Charlie told his friend the steps he was taking to discover Nicholson.

"Do you feel sure that you would know him again, Harry?"

"Quite sure. Why, I saw him dozens of times at Lynnwood."

"Then we shall now be able to hunt for him separately, Harry. Going to two or three places, of an evening, I always fear that he may come in after I have gone away. Now one of us can wait till the hour for closing, while the other goes elsewhere."

For another fortnight, they frequented all the places where they thought Nicholson would be most likely to show himself; then, after a consultation with their guide, they agreed that they must look for him at lower places.

"Like enough," the tipstaff said, "he may have run through his money the first night or two after coming up to town. That is the way with these fellows. As long as they have money they gamble. When they have none, they cheat or turn to other evil courses. Now that there are two of you together, there is less danger in going to such places; for, though these rascals may be ready to pick a quarrel with a single man, they know that it is a dangerous game to play with two, who look perfectly capable of defending themselves."

For a month, they frequented low taverns. They dressed themselves plainly now, and assumed the character of young fellows who had come up to town, and had fallen into bad company, and lost what little money they had brought with them, and were now ready for any desperate enterprise. Still, no success attended their search.

"I can do no more for you," their guide said. "I have taken you to every house that such a man would be likely to use. Of course, there are many houses near the river frequented by bad characters. But here you would chiefly meet men connected, in some way, with the sea, and you would be hardly likely to find your man there."

"We shall keep on searching," Charlie said. "He may have gone out of town for some reason, and may return any day. We shall not give it up till spring."

"Well, at any rate, sirs, I will take your money no longer. You know your way thoroughly about now, and, if at any time you should want me, you know where to find me. It might be worth your while to pay a visit to Islington, or even to go as far as Barnet. The fellow may have done something, and may think it safer to keep in hiding, and in that case Islington and Barnet are as likely to suit him as anywhere."

The young men had, some time before, left the inn and taken a lodging. This they found much cheaper, and, as they were away from breakfast until midnight, it mattered little where they slept. They took the advice of their guide, stayed a couple of nights at Islington, and then went to Barnet. In these places there was no occasion to visit the taverns, as, being comparatively small, they would, either in the daytime or after dark, have an opportunity of meeting most of those living there.

Finding the search ineffectual, Charlie proposed that they should go for a long walk along the north road.

"I am tired of staring every man I meet in the face, Harry. And I should like, for once, to be able to throw it all off and take a good walk together, as we used to do in the old days. We will go eight or ten miles out, stop at some wayside inn for refreshments, and then come back here for the night, and start back again for town tomorrow."

Harry at once agreed, and, taking their hats, they started.

They did not hurry themselves, and, carefully avoiding all mention of the subject that had occupied their thoughts for weeks, they chatted over their last campaign, their friends in the Swedish camp, and the course that affairs were likely to take. After four hours' walking they came to a small wayside inn, standing back twenty or thirty yards from the road.

"It is a quiet-looking little place," Charlie said, "and does but a small trade, I should say. However, no doubt they can give us some bread and cheese, and a mug of ale, which will last us well enough till we get back to Barnet."

The landlord placed what they demanded before them, and then left the room again, replying by a short word or two to their remarks on the weather.

"A surly ill-conditioned sort of fellow," Harry said.

"It may be, Harry, that badness of trade has spoiled his temper. However, so long as his beer is good, it matters little about his mood."

They had finished their bread and cheese, and were sitting idly, being in no hurry to start on their way back, when a man on horseback turned off from the road and came up the narrow lane in which the house stood. As Charlie, who was facing that way, looked at him he started, and grasped Harry's arm.

"It is our man," he said. "It is Nicholson himself! To think of our searching all London, these weeks past, and stumbling upon him here."

The man stopped at the door, which was at once opened by the landlord.

"All right, I suppose, landlord?" the man said, as he swung himself from his horse.

"There is no one here except two young fellows, who look to me as if they had spent their last penny in London, and were travelling down home again."

He spoke in a lowered voice, but the words came plainly enough to the ears of the listeners within. Another word or two was spoken, and then the landlord took the horse and led it round to a stable behind, while its rider entered the room. He stopped for a moment at the open door of the taproom, and stared at the two young men, who had just put on their hats again. They looked up carelessly, and Harry said:

"Fine weather for this time of year."

The man replied by a grunt, and then passed on into the landlord's private room.

"That is the fellow, sure enough, Charlie," Harry said, in a low tone. "I thought your eyes might have deceived you, but I remember his face well. Now what is to be done?"

"We won't lose sight of him again," Charlie said. "Though, if we do, we shall know where to pick up his traces, for he evidently frequents this place. I should say he has taken to the road. There were a brace of pistols in the holsters. That is how it is that we have not found him before. Well, at any rate, there is no use trying to make his acquaintance here. The first question is, will he stay here for the night or not--and if he does not, which way will he go?"

"He came from the north," Harry said. "So if he goes, it will be towards town."

"That is so. Our best plan will be to pay our reckoning and start. We will go a hundred yards or so down the road, and then lie down behind a hedge, so as to see if he passes. If he does not leave before nightfall, we will come up to the house and reconnoitre. If he does not leave by ten, he is here for the night, and we must make ourselves as snug as we can under a stack. The nights are getting cold, but we have slept out in a deal colder weather than this. However, I fancy he will go on. It is early for a man to finish a journey. If he does, we must follow him, and keep him in sight, if possible."

Two hours later they saw, from their hiding place, Nicholson ride out from the lane. He turned his horse's head in their direction.

"That is good," Charlie said. "If he is bound for London, we shall be able to get into his company somehow; but if he had gone up to some quiet place north, we might have had a lot of difficulty in getting acquainted with him."

As soon as the man had ridden past they leapt to their feet, and, at a run, kept along the hedge. He had started at a brisk trot, but when, a quarter of a mile on, they reached a gate, and looked up the road after him, they saw to their satisfaction that the horse had already fallen into a walk.

"He does not mean to go far from Barnet," Charlie exclaimed. "If he had been bound farther, he would have kept on at a trot. We will keep on behind the hedges as long as we can. If he were to look back and see us always behind him, he might become suspicious."

They had no difficulty in keeping up with the horseman. Sometimes, when they looked out, he was a considerable distance ahead, having quickened his pace; but he never kept that up long, and by brisk running, and dashing recklessly through the hedges running at right angles to that they were following, they soon came up to him again.

Once, he had gone so far ahead that they took to the road, and followed it until he again slackened his speed. They thus kept him in sight till they neared Barnet.

"We can take to the road now," Harry said. "Even if he should look round, he will think nothing of seeing two men behind him. We might have turned into it from some by-lane. At any rate, we must chance it. We must find where he puts up for the night."

Chapter 17: The North Coach.

Barnet was then, as now, a somewhat straggling place. Soon after entering it, the horseman turned off from the main road. His pursuers were but fifty yards behind him, and they kept him in sight until, after proceeding a quarter of a mile, he stopped at a small tavern, where he dismounted, and a boy took his horse and led it round by the side of the house.

"Run to earth!" Harry said exultantly. "He is not likely to move from there tonight."

"At any rate, he is safe for a couple of hours," Charlie said. "So we will go to our inn, and have a good meal. By that time it will be quite dark, and we will have a look at the place he has gone into; and if we can't learn anything, we must watch it by turns till midnight. We will arrange, at the inn, to hire a horse. One will be enough. He only caught a glimpse of us at that inn, and certainly would not recognize one of us, if he saw him alone. The other can walk."

"But which way, Charlie? He may go back again." "It is hardly likely he came here merely for the pleasure of stopping the night at that little tavern. I have no doubt he is bound for London. You shall take the horse, Harry, and watch until he starts, and then follow him, just managing to come up close to him as he gets into town. I will start early, and wait at the beginning of the houses, and it is hard if one or other of us does not manage to find out where he hides."

They had no difficulty in arranging with the landlord for a horse, which was to be left in a stable he named in town. They gave him a deposit, for which he handed them a note, by which the money was to be returned to them by the stable keeper, on their handing over the horse in good condition.

After the meal they sallied out again, and walked to the tavern, which was a small place standing apart from other houses. There was a light in the taproom, but they guessed that here, as at the other stopping place, the man they wanted would be in a private apartment. Passing the house, they saw a light in a side window, and, noiselessly opening a little wicket gate, they stole into the garden. Going a short distance back from the window, so that the light should not show their faces, they looked in, and saw the man they sought sitting by the fire, with a table on which stood a bottle and two glasses beside him, and another man facing him.

"Stay where you are, Harry. I will steal up to the window, and find out whether I can hear what they are saying."

Stooping close under the window, he could hear the murmur of voices, but could distinguish no words. He rejoined his companion.

"I am going to make a trial to overhear them, Harry, and it is better that only one of us should be here. You go back to the inn, and wait for me there."

"What are you going to do, Charlie?"

"I am going to throw a stone through the lower part of the window. Then I shall hide. They will rush out, and when they can find no one, they will conclude that the stone was thrown by some mischievous boy going along the road. When all is quiet again I will creep up to the window, and it will be hard if I don't manage to learn something of what they are saying."

The plan was carried out, and Charlie, getting close up to the window, threw a stone through one of the lowest of the little diamond-shaped panes. He heard a loud exclamation of anger inside, and then sprang away and hid himself at the other end of the garden. A moment later he heard loud talking in the road, and a man with a lantern came round to the window; but in a few minutes all was quiet again, and Charlie cautiously made his way back to the window, and crouched beneath it. He could hear plainly enough, now, the talk going on within.

"What was I saying when that confounded stone interrupted us?"

"You were saying, captain, that you intended to have a week in London, and then to stop the North coach."

"Yes, I have done well lately, and can afford a week's pleasure. Besides, Jerry Skinlow got a bullet in his shoulder, last week, in trying to stop a carriage on his own account, and Jack Mercer's mare is laid up lame, and it wants four to stop a coach neatly. Jack Ponsford is in town. I shall bring him out with me."

"I heard that you were out of luck a short time ago."

"Yes, everything seemed against me. My horse was shot, and, just at the time,

I had been having a bad run at the tables and had lost my last stiver. I was in hiding for a fortnight at one of the cribs; for they had got a description of me from an old gentleman, who, with his wife and daughter, I had eased of their money and watches. It was a stupid business. I dropped a valuable diamond ring on the ground, and in groping about for it my mask came off, and, like a fool, I stood up in the full light of the carriage lamp. So I thought it better, for all reasons, to get away for a month or so, until things quieted down. I wanted to visit my banker, and it was a good many miles to tramp."

"Oh, you have got a banker, captain?"

"I have one who is just as good, though I cannot say he shells out his money willingly--in fact he was rude enough to say, when I called this time, that if I ever showed my face to him again he would shoot me, even if he were hung for it. Bad taste, wasn't it? At any rate, I mustn't call on him again too soon."

"You haven't settled on the night yet, I suppose, captain?"

"About the end of next week. Friday will be a full moon, I think, and I like a moon for the work. It gives light enough to see what you are doing, and not light enough for them to see much of you. So I suppose I may as well fix Friday. I will send up a message for Jack Mercer and Jerry Skinlow to be here on Thursday evening. I will be here that afternoon, and settle matters with them as to where they shall meet me, and what each man shall do. Then I will ride back to town, and come out again just as it gets dark, with Jack Ponsford."

"I suppose you will do it north of here?"

"No, I will do it a mile or two out of town. The road north of this is getting rather a bad reputation, and in going out of Barnet the guard now looks to his blunderbuss, and the passengers get their pistols ready. It isn't once in a hundred times they have pluck enough to use them, but they always think they will, until the time comes. Near town we shall take them by surprise, and stop them before they have time to think of getting out their arms.

"Confound that window. Shove something into the hole, Johnson. I can feel the cold right down my back."

A cloth was pushed into the broken pane, and Charlie could hear no more of what was said inside. He had heard, indeed, enough for his purpose, but he had hoped to gather the name of the place at which the man would put up in London.

However, he was well satisfied with his success, and at once made his way back to the inn.

"Well, Charlie, how have you succeeded?" Harry asked, as he sat down at the table.

"Could not be better, Harry, though I did not find out where he puts up in London. However, that is of small consequence. In the first place, I found out that our suspicions were right, and that the fellow is a highwayman, and seems to be captain of a gang consisting anyhow of three, and perhaps of more, fellows like himself. In the second place, he intends, with his three comrades, to attack the coach on Friday week, two or three miles out of town. Nothing could better suit our purpose, even if we had planned the affair ourselves. Of course, we will be there. If we can capture him while engaged in that work, we can get anything out of him. He has either got to confess or be hanged."

"That is a stroke of good luck, indeed," Harry exclaimed. "It will be rather difficult to manage, though. The fellows will be sure to be masked; and, if we were to shoot him instead of one of the others, it would be fatal."

"Yes, that would be awkward. Besides," Charlie said, "even if we did recognize him and shot his horse, he might jump up behind one of the other men, or might make off across the country, and we might lose sight of him before we could get down from the top of the coach to pursue."

"It might be better if we were mounted, instead of being on the coach."

"Better in some ways, Harry; but if they heard two mounted men coming along beside the coach, they would probably take the alarm and not attack at all; while, if we were to keep a bit behind, and ride up as soon as we heard the firing--for they generally shoot one of the horses to bring the coach to a standstill--they might ride off as soon as they heard the sound of the horses on the road. Those fellows are splendidly mounted. Their lives depend upon it, and nothing we should be able to hire would be likely to have a chance with them."

"Well, we shall have plenty of time to think this over, Charlie. I suppose we shall carry out our plan tomorrow, as we arranged."

"Certainly. It is as important to find out where he lives in London as it was before, for if he gets away, we can then look him up there. We may as well go to bed at once, for I shall start at four, so as to get to town before him, however early he may be off. But as we know, now, he is going up on pleasure and not on business, I don't suppose he will be in any hurry in the morning."

Charlie arrived in town about eight o'clock, and, having breakfasted at the first tavern he came to, walked along for some distance, to decide upon the spot where he should take up his position. As Nicholson was going up, as he said, to enjoy himself, it was not likely that he would put up at Islington, but would take up his quarters in the centre of the town. He therefore decided to walk on, until he came to some junction of important roads; and there wait, as the man might make either for the city or Westminster, though the latter appeared the more probable direction.

Here he walked up and down for an hour, and then, entering a tavern, took his place at the window, where he could see up the street, called for a stoup of wine, and prepared for a long wait.

It was not, indeed, until three o'clock that he saw Nicholson coming along. He was more gaily dressed than he had been on the previous day. He had on a green cloth coat with gold braid round the cuffs, an embroidered waistcoat, yellow breeches, top boots, and three-cornered hat. He was riding at foot pace.

Charlie went to the door as soon as he passed, and saw that, as he expected, he took the road to Westminster. Looking round, he saw Harry riding about a hundred yards behind. Charlie had no difficulty in keeping up with Nicholson, and traced him to a house in a quiet street lying behind the Abbey. A boy came out and held the horse, while its rider dismounted, and then led it away to the stable of an inn a short distance away. Charlie turned at once, and joined Harry.

"I need not have taken all the trouble I have, Harry, still there was no knowing. Evidently the fellow has no fear of being detected, and is going to pass, for a week, as a gentleman from the country. I suppose he is in the habit of stopping at that house whenever he comes up with his pockets lined, and is regarded there as a respectable gentleman by the landlord. Now you had better take your horse to the stable, where you agreed to hand it over, and we will meet at our lodgings and plan what to do next."

The discussion did not lead to much. There did not seem, to them, anything to do until the day when the coach was to be attacked, but they agreed it would be well to take the advice of their friend the tipstaff. Hitherto, they had not told him more of their motive for desiring to find Nicholson, than Charlie had said at his first interview with him. They thought it would be better, now, to make him more fully acquainted with the facts, for they had found him shrewd, and eager to assist them to the best of his power. They therefore sent a boy with a note to him, at the court, and at seven o'clock he came to their lodgings.

"We have found our man," Charlie said as he entered.

"I am very glad to hear it, gentlemen. I had quite given up all hopes that you would be able to do so, and thought he must have left town altogether for a time."

"Sit down and take a glass of wine. We want your advice in this matter, and unless you know how much there is at stake, you will not be able to enter fully into the affair.

"Some four years ago, this fellow was concerned in a plot by which six gentlemen, among whom were our friends, were brought to ruin. They were in the habit of meeting together, being all of similar political opinions, and advantage was taken of this by a man, who hoped to profit largely by their ruin, especially by that of my father. In order to bring this about, he recommended this fellow we are in search of to my father, who happened, at the time, to be in want of a servant.

"The fellow undoubtedly acted as a spy, for I once caught him at it. But spying alone would have been of no use, for there was nothing at any time said that would have brought harm upon them. They simply discussed what thousands of other people have discussed, the measures that should be taken on behalf of the Stuarts, if one of them came over from France supported by a French force. The fellow, however, swore that the object of these meetings was to arrange for an assassination of William. He gave full details of the supposed plot, and in order to give substance to his statements, he hid, in a cabinet of my father's, a number of compromising papers, professing to be letters from abroad.

"These were found by the officers sent to arrest my father. He and his five friends managed to escape, but their estates were forfeited. Of course, what we want to prove is the connection between this spy and his employer, who, for his services in bringing this supposed plot to light, received as a reward my father's estates. There is no way of doing this, unless this man can be brought to confess his own villainy in the matter of the letters, and to denounce the scoundrel whose agent he was. Probably, by this time, he has got nearly all he can expect from his employer, and will at least feel no scruples in exposing him, if by so doing he can save his own neck.

"Now, we have not only discovered the man, but have found out that he is a notorious highwayman, and the leader of a gang; but more, I have found out the day and hour on which he proposes to stop and rob the North coach."

"Well, Mr. Carstairs, if you have done that," the man said, "you have done marvels. That you should find the man might be a piece of good luck, but that you should have learned all this about him seems to me wonderful."

"It was a lucky accident, altogether. We saw him, watched him, and managed to overhear a conversation from which we gathered these facts. It was all simple enough. Of course, our idea is that we should, if possible, catch him in the act of robbing the coach, bind and take charge of him, saying that we should hand him over to justice, when the coachman and passengers would, of course, appear to testify against him. Instead of doing this, we should take him somewhere, and then give him the option of either making a clean breast of the whole story, and remaining in our custody until called upon to testify to his statement in a court of justice, whenever required; or of being handed over to the authorities, to be tried and hung as a highwayman.

"One of our greatest difficulties is how to effect his capture. The attack will be made at night on the coach, and in the darkness we might shoot him, or he might get away. He is at present in London, at a lodging in a street behind the Abbey, where, doubtless, his real profession is altogether unsuspected by the people of the house.

"Now you know the whole affair. Let us have your opinion as to the manner in which we had best set about the business."

The man sat for some time, in silence.

"I can think of no better plan than yours, sir, and yet it seems to me that there is scarcely any chance of your catching him at the coach. Of course, it would be easy enough if you did not care whether you killed or caught him. All you would have to do would be to get half a dozen stout fellows, armed with pistols, on the coach with you instead of passengers, and then you would be pretty certain to kill some of them, perhaps all; but, as you can't do that, and are afraid to shoot lest you should kill him, it seems to me that you have a very small chance of catching him that way."

Charlie and his friend so thoroughly saw this, that they sat silent when he ceased speaking.

"We could not arrest him now, I suppose?" Harry said at last.

"Well, you see, you have got nothing against him. He may have been a Knight of the Road for the last five years, but you have no witnesses to prove it, and it is not much use to accuse him of intending to rob the North mail. You have no proofs, even of that. It is only your word against his.

"There is no doubt that, after they have robbed the coach, they will separate. They may go away in twos, or singly. Now, you see, we know three of this fellow's hiding places. He would hardly choose the one at Barnet. It is too close. It is more likely he would choose the next place, the little inn in which you saw him first; but I think it more likely still that he and his mates will divide the plunder, half a mile or so from the place where they stopped the coach, and will then separate, and I am inclined to think his most likely course is to strike off from the main road, make a long round, and come down before morning to where he is now. He may take his horse into its stable, or, more likely, he may leave it at some place he may know of on the road leading out through Putney, and then arrive at his lodgings just about daybreak. He would explain he had been at a supper, and had kept it up all night, and no one would even have a suspicion he had been engaged in the affair with the coach. I am sure that is his most likely plan."

"Then, what would you do?" Harry asked.

"What I should do is this. I will get two sharp active boys. I know of two who would just do, they have done jobs for us before now. I will give them the exact description of those two taverns, and send them down the day before the coach is to be attacked, and tell them that, that night, they are each to keep watch over one of them, see who goes in, watch till they come out, and then follow them, for days if necessary, and track them down. Then they can send word up by the guard of the coach, each day; so that, if we find our man does not come back here by Saturday morning, we shall have news that will put us on his track again, before long.

"However, I think he is sure to come back here. You had better point out to me, this evening, where he lodges, and I shall be able to find out, before long, whether they are respectable people, or whether they are likely to be pals of his.

"If they are respectable, I will see them on Friday evening, show them my badge, and tell them that the man who has been lodging here is a notorious high-wayman, and that I am going to arrest him. To prevent any chance of a mistake, I will put three or four of my mates round the house, to see that no one goes out to give him the alarm. I will come down and open the door for you, at two o'clock in the morning. You can then come up with me into his bedroom, and as he comes in, I will nab him.

"If, on the other hand, I find the people of the house have a doubtful reputation in the neighbourhood, we must simply hide in doorways, make a rush upon him as he goes up to the house, and overpower him there. If one stands in his doorway, and leaps out on him as he comes up, he won't have much chance of using a pistol. I will have a cart ready, close by. We will truss him up tightly, gag him and put him into it, and I will have some place ready for us to drive him to, if you think that plan is as good as any other."

"I think it is an excellent plan, and could not be better," Charlie exclaimed, and his friend heartily agreed with him.

"I think you will be able to get anything out of him, when you get him there," said the tipstaff. "He is sure to have some of the swag about him, and, even if none of the passengers of the coach are able to swear to him, that and the talk you over-heard would be sufficient to hang him."

"Can those boys you speak of write?"

"Not they, sir."

"There might be a difficulty about a verbal message."

"The guard will give it, all right, if he gets half a crown with it. You need not trouble about that, sir. I will have a man to meet each coach, as it comes in.

"And now we have arranged matters, sir, I will go with you to see the house, and will send a sharp fellow down tomorrow, to make inquiries about the people of the place."

When they returned, the friends sat for a long time, talking together. The suggested plan looked so hopeful that they felt confident of its success.

"I think, Charlie," Harry said, "it would be a good thing for us to present ourselves to the Duke of Marlborough. Then we shall see if he is disposed to take an interest in us, and help us. If he is, he will tell us what had best be done towards getting Nicholson's statement made in the presence of some sort of official who will act on it. If he gives us the cold shoulder, we shall have to do as best we can in some other direction, and it will be well to have the matter settled, if possible, before we catch the fellow."

"I think that will be a very good plan, Harry. I know where he lives. I inquired directly I came over. Tomorrow morning we can go there and inquire, at the door, at what hour he receives callers."

The next day at eleven o'clock the young men, dressed in their best attire, called at the duke's. They were informed that the great man was at home, and would be as likely to see them then as at any other hour. Accordingly they entered, and were shown into an anteroom, and sent their names in by a footman. He returned with a request that they would follow him, and were shown into a library, where a singularly handsome man, in the prime of life, was sitting at a desk. He looked at them in some surprise.

"Is there not some mistake, young gentlemen?" he asked. "My servant gave the names as Captain Jervoise, and Captain Carstairs. I do not recall the names as those of officers in her majesty's service."

"No, my lord, we have the honour to be captains in the service of King Charles of Sweden, as this document, signed both by his minister, Count Piper, and by the king himself, will testify."

The duke took the paper, and read it.

"The king of Sweden speaks very highly of you both, gentlemen," he said cordially. "It is no mean credit to have gained such warm praise from the greatest general of his time. What can I do for you? Do you wish to be transferred from the service of Sweden to that of her majesty? We have need of good officers, and I can promise that you shall receive the same rank that you now hold, and it is likely that, before long, you will have an opportunity of seeing some service under your national flag."

"I thank you warmly for your kindness, my lord, but it is not with that view that we have now come to you, though I am sure that we both should prefer to fight under our own flag, rather than under that of a foreign king, however kindly he may be disposed to us, personally. We have called upon a private matter, and I am the bearer of this letter from my father, who had once the honour of your lordship's friendship."

"Jervoise," the duke repeated, as he took the letter. "Not Mat Jervoise, surely?"

"That is my father's name, sir."

"Do I remember him? Why, he was one of my closest friends when I was a lad, and I once stayed with him at his father's place, for a fortnight, on a journey I took to the north. But I will read his letter--

"What changes happen," he said, as he laid it down. "To think that Mat Jervoise should be an exile, his old home in the hands of strangers, and he a major in the Swedish service; and that I should never have heard a word about it!

"Well, young sir," and he held out his hand to Harry, "I can promise you my aid and protection, to the utmost, in whatever matter you may be concerned. I seem to remember the name of your companion, too."

"His father, Sir Marmaduke, was a neighbour of ours. There has always been great friendship between the two families."

"Of course, I remember him now. He was some fifteen or twenty years older than your father. I remember that I went over with your father and grandfather, and dined at his place. He is still alive and well, I hope?"

"He is both, sir," Charlie said; "but, like Major Jervoise, an exile."

"You amaze me, but I will not ask you to tell me more, now. I have to be at Saint James's at twelve.

"Let me see, this evening I shall be engaged. Come tomorrow morning, at half past eight, and I shall then be able to give you an hour, or maybe two, if necessary, and will then hear the whole story fully."

The young men, on presenting themselves the next morning, at the hour named, were at once ushered in.

"Now, let us lose no time," the duke said, after shaking hands heartily. "Which of you will tell the story?"

"Carstairs will do so, my lord," Harry replied. "The mischief was hatched in his house, and my father, and six other gentlemen, were the victims of the treachery of a kinsman of his."

Charlie told the story of the events that had brought about the ruin of his father and friends.

"It is monstrous!" the duke exclaimed indignantly, when he had brought this part of his story to a conclusion. "That my old friend, Mat Jervoise, should be concerned in a plot for assassination, is, I would pledge my life, untrue; and Sir Marmaduke Carstairs was, I know, an honourable gentleman, who would be equally incapable of such an act. That they were both Jacobites, I can well believe, for the Jacobites are strong everywhere in the north, but, as half of us are or have been Jacobites, that can scarcely be counted as an offence. At any rate, a Stuart is upon the throne now, and, as long as she reigns, there is no fear that a civil war will be set up by another of the race. The story, as you have told it, sir, is, I doubt not for a moment, true, but at present it is unsupported; and though, on my assurance of their loyalty, I think I can promise that her majesty would extend a pardon to the gentlemen who have been so unjustly accused, I fear that she could not, by her own act, restore the estates that have been confiscated, unless you can bring some proof that this fellow you speak of was suborned to get up false evidence against them."

"That, sir, is what I shall have the honour to inform you now."

And Charlie then related the story of their quest for the man Nicholson, and its result.

"Rarely devised and carried out," the duke said warmly. "Do you lay the knave by the heels, and frighten him into confessing the truth, and I will see to the rest of the matter. I do not know that I ought to let the North coach be robbed, after the information you have given me, but, as we will hunt down all the other fellows, and shall probably recover the booty they carry off, the passengers will have no reason to grumble.

"Well, young sirs, the king of Sweden has given you a testimonial as to your bravery and conduct. If necessary, I will give you one for your ingenuity in planning and carrying out a difficult scheme.

"So you have both been with the Swedes through their campaign against the Russians and Poles. I envy you. King Charles' service is a grand school for soldiers, and that victory of Narva is the most extraordinary one ever seen. Had you the honour of any personal intercourse with the king?"

"Only during three days, when our company formed part of his escort at a hunting expedition," Harry, whom he addressed, replied. "But Carstairs spoke to him more frequently. He has been a captain nearly two years, while I only had my promotion two months ago. We were in the same regiment, and of the same rank, but Carstairs was promoted by the king, after the battle at the passage of the

Dwina, as a reward for the suggestion he made in conversation with him, that the passage might be made under the screen of smoke caused by the lighting of the forage stacks."

"I must have a long talk with you both. It is certain that, next spring, the campaign with France will re-open, and your experience in the field will be very useful to me. The Swedes are wonderful soldiers. The Muscovites, at present, are little better than barbarians carrying European arms, but the Saxons are good troops, and the Swedes have twice beaten them heavily, and they evidently retain the fighting qualities that, under Gustavus Adolphus, shook the imperial power to its centre.

"The trouble is to find time. I am pestered with men desirous of employment in the army, with persons who want favours at court, with politicians of both parties, with people with schemes and intrigues of all kinds. I have to be in attendance at the palace, and to see into the whole details of the organization of the army. I have no doubt that, at present, my antechamber is crowded with people who want to see me."

He looked at his tablets.

"Next Wednesday evening I am free, except for a reception at Lord Godolphin's, but I can look in there late. I will not ask you here, because I want you to myself. I will have a private room at Parker's coffee house in Covent Garden. We will sup at seven. When you go there, ask for Mr. Church's room, and make yourself comfortable there until I come, for I can never answer for my own hours. In that way, we shall be free from all chance of interruption, and I can pick your brains undisturbed. You will remember the day and hour. Should there be any change in this private matter of yours, do not hesitate to come to me here."

Tony Peters, their guide and adviser, reported favourably as to the people with whom the highwayman was lodging.

"The house is kept by the widow of an usher at the palace. She entertains gentlemen from the country, who come up on business at the courts of justice, or with people of influence at court. I have ascertained that our man passes as a well-to-do trader of Salisbury, who comes up, two or three times a year, to transact business, and to enjoy for a short time the pleasures of town. He is liberal in his payments, and is held in high respect by the woman, whose only objection to him, as a lodger, is the late hours he keeps. He is a crafty fellow this, for by always going to the same house, and comporting himself with moderation, he secures a place of retirement, where, however close the quest after him, there will be no suspicion whatever, as to his profession, on the part of the people he is with.

"My man found out all these matters from the servant wench. We shall have no difficulty in taking him quietly. The woman will be so terrified, when I tell her what he is wanted for, that she will do anything rather than have a scandal that would damage the reputation of the house."

He assured Charlie that he need give the matter no further thought. All the arrangements would be made, and, unless he heard farther from him, he and Harry would only have to present themselves, at the door of the house in question, at two o'clock on the morning of Saturday.

The evening with the duke passed off pleasantly. The general's questions turned, not so much upon the actual fighting, as upon the organization of the Swedes, their methods of campaigning, of victualling the army, of hutting themselves in winter, the maintenance of discipline in camp, and other military points that would be of service to him in his next campaign.

"Your king is very wise, in so strictly repressing all plundering and violence," he said. "Only so can a general maintain an army in an enemy's country. If the peasantry have confidence in him, and know that they will get a fair price for their produce, they will bring it into the market gladly, in spite of any orders their own government may issue to the contrary. I am determined that, if I again lead an English army in the field, I will follow King Charles' example; though I shall find it more difficult to enforce my orders than he does, for he is king as well as general, and his Swedes are quiet, honest fellows, while my army will be composed of ne'er-do-wells--of men who prefer to wear the queen's uniform to a prison garment, of debtors who wish to escape their creditors, and of men who find village life too quiet for them, and prefer to see the world, even at the risk of being shot, to honest labour on the farms. It requires a stern hand to make a disciplined army out of such materials, but when the time of fighting comes, one need wish for no better."

Before parting with them, the duke inquired farther into their arrangements for the arrest of the highwayman, and said he should expect to see them on Saturday, and that, if he heard that all had gone well, he would at once take steps for bringing the matter before a court that would deal with it.

The young men felt restless, as the day approached. They had seen no more of Tony, but they felt complete confidence in him, and were sure that they would hear if any difficulties arose; but though, throughout Friday, they did not quit their lodging, no message reached them.

Chapter 18: A Confession.

At the appointed hour, as the clock of the Abbey was striking, they gave three gentle knocks at the door of the house. It was immediately opened by Tony, who held a candle in his hand, closed the door quietly behind them, and then led them into a parlour.

"Well, Tony, I suppose all has gone well, as we have not heard from you."

"There was nothing to tell you, sir, and, indeed, I have been mightily busy. In the first place, I got two days' leave from the courts, and went down myself, in a light cart, with the boys and two men. That way I made sure that there should be no mistake as to the houses the boys were to watch. The two men I sent on, ten miles beyond the farthest tavern there to watch the road, and if any horseman goes by tonight, to track him down.

"This evening I came here. I brought with me one of my comrades from the courts, and we told the good woman the character of the lodger we had seen leave the house a quarter of an hour before. She almost fainted when we showed her our badges, and said we must arrest him, on his return, as a notorious highwayman and breaker of the laws. She exclaimed that her house would be ruined, and it took some time to pacify her, by saying that we would manage the job so quietly that no one in the house need know of it, and that we would, if possible, arrange it so that the place of his arrest should not be made public.

"At that, she at once consented to do all that we wished her. We searched his room carefully, and found some watches, rings, and other matters, that answered to the description of those stolen from a coach that was stopped near Dorking, three weeks ago. My mate has taken them away. As she was afraid that a scuffle in the bedroom might attract the attention of the four other gentlemen who are lodging here, I arranged that it should be done at the door. In that case, if there was any inquiry in the morning, she could say that it was some drunken fellow, who had come to the house by mistake, and had tried to force his way in.

"So she put this parlour at our disposal, and, as I have got the shutters up and the curtains drawn, there is no fear of his noticing the light, for, as we may have some hours to wait, it is more pleasant to have a candle, than to sit in the dark."

"Does she come down to let him in?" Harry asked.

"No, sir, the door is left on the latch. She says he finds his way up to his room, in the dark, and the candle and a tinderbox are always placed handy for him there. We will take our shoes off presently, and, when we hear footsteps come up to the door and stop, we will blow out the candle and steal out into the passage, so as to catch him directly he closes the door. I have got handcuffs here, some rope, and a gag."

"Very well, then. I will undertake the actual seizing of him," Charlie said. "You slip on the handcuffs, and you, Harry, if you can find his throat in the dark, grip it pretty tightly, till Tony can slip the gag into his mouth. Then he can light the candle again, and we can then disarm and search him, fasten his legs, and get him ready to put in the cart."

The hours passed slowly, although Tony did his best to divert them, by telling stories of various arrests and captures in which he had been concerned. The clock had just struck five, when they heard a step coming up the quiet street.

"That is likely to be the man," Tony said. "It is about the hour we expected him."

He blew out the candle and opened the door quietly, and they went out into the passage. A moment later the step stopped at the door, the latch clicked, and it was opened. A man entered, and closed the door behind him. As he did so Charlie, who had marked his exact position, made a step forward and threw his arms round him.

The man gave an exclamation of surprise and alarm, and then struggled fiercely, but he was in the hands of one far stronger than himself. A moment later, he felt that his assailant was not alone, for he was grasped by the throat, and at the same time he felt something cold close round his wrists. There was a sharp click, and he knew that he was handcuffed.

Then a low voice said, "I arrest you, in the name of the queen, for being concerned in the robbery of the Portsmouth coach at Dorking."

Then a gag was forced between his teeth. Bewildered at the suddenness of the attack, he ceased to struggle, and remained quiet, in the grasp of his captors, till there was the sound of the striking of flint and steel hard by. Then Tony came out of the parlour with a lighted candle, the highwayman was lifted into the room, and the door was shut.

He then saw that his captors were three in number. There were two young gentlemen, and a smaller man, who, as he looked at him, held out a badge, and showed that he was an officer of the law. His pistols and sword were removed, then his pockets were searched, and two watches and three purses, with some rings and bracelets, were taken out and laid on the table.

"It came off, you see," Tony said to Charlie.

"Well, Master Nicholson, to use one of your aliases, of which you have, no doubt, a score or more, you may consider yourself under arrest, not only for the robbery of the Portsmouth coach three weeks ago, but of the North coach last evening."

The prisoner started. It seemed impossible to him that that affair should be known yet, still less his connection with it.

"You know what that means?" Tony went on grimly. "Tyburn. Now I am going to make you a little safer still. You have been a hard bird to catch, and we don't mean to let you slip through our fingers again."

So saying, he bound his arms closely to his side with a rope, and then, with a shorter piece, fastened his ankles securely together.

"Now I will fetch the cart."

He had been gone but five minutes, when they heard a vehicle stop at the door. The others lifted the highwayman by his shoulders and feet, carried him out, and laid him in the cart. Tony closed the door quietly behind them, and then jumped up by the side of the driver, who at once started the horse at a brisk trot. They crossed Westminster Bridge, and, after another ten minutes' drive, stopped at a small house standing back from the road, in a garden of its own.

"We will carry him in, Tony," Charlie said, "if you will get the door open."

They carried him in through the door, at which a woman was standing, into a room, where they saw, to their satisfaction, a blazing fire. The prisoner was laid down on the ground. Leaving him to himself, Charlie and his friends sat down to the table, which was laid in readiness. Two cold chickens, and ham, and bread had been placed on it.

"Now, Tony, sit down. You must be as hungry as we are."

"Thank you, gentlemen. I am going to have my breakfast in the kitchen, with my wife."

As he spoke, the woman came in with two large tankards full of steaming liquid, whose odour at once proclaimed it to be spiced ale.

"Well, wife, we have done a good night's work," Tony said.

"A good night's work for all of us," Charlie put in. "Your husband has done us an immense service, Mrs. Peters, and, when our fathers come to their own again, they will not forget the service he has rendered us."

When they had made a hearty meal, Tony was called in again.

"Now, Tony, we will proceed to business. You have got pen and ink and paper, I suppose?"

"I have everything ready, sir. I will clear away this table, so as to have all in order."

When this was done, the highwayman was lifted up and placed in a chair, and the gag removed from his mouth.

"You don't remember us, I suppose, my man?" Charlie began. "The last time I saw you was when I brought my stick down on your head, when you were listening outside a window at Lynnwood."

An exclamation of surprise broke from the prisoner.

"Yes, I am Charlie Carstairs, and this gentleman is Harry Jervoise. By the way, I have made a mistake. I have seen you twice since then. The first time was in a wayside tavern, some twelve miles beyond Barnet, nine days ago. The second time was at another tavern in Barnet. You will remember that a mischievous boy threw a stone, and broke one of the lattice panes of the window, where you were sitting talking over this little affair of the North coach."

A deep execration broke from the lips of the highwayman.

"Now you see how we know all about it," Charlie went on. "Now, it entirely depends on yourself whether, in the course of another hour, we shall hand you over to a magistrate, as the leader of the gang who robbed the North coach, and took part in the robbery near Dorking--we have found some of the watches and other plunder in your bedroom--or whether you escape trial for these offences. You may be wanted for other, similar affairs."

"Yes, sir," Tony put in. "Now I see him, he answers exactly to the description of a man the officers have been in search of, for a long time. He goes by the name of Dick Cureton, and has been engaged in at least a dozen highway robberies, to my knowledge."

"You see," Charlie went on, "there is no doubt whatever what will happen, if we hand you over to the officers. You will be hung at Tyburn, to a moral certainty. There is no getting out of that.

"Now, on the other hand, you have the alternative of making a clean breast of your dealings with John Dormay, of how he put you at Lynnwood to act as a spy, how you hid those two letters he gave you in my father's cabinet, and how he taught you the lying story you afterwards told before the magistrates at Lancaster. After having this story written down, you will sign it in the presence of this officer and his wife, and you will also repeat that story before any tribunal before which you may be brought.

"I don't know whether this is a hanging matter, but, at any rate, I can promise that you shall not be hung for it. The Duke of Marlborough has taken the matter in hand, and will, I have no doubt, be able to obtain for you some lesser punishment, if you make a clean breast of it. I don't say that you will be let free. You are too dangerous a man for that. But, at any rate, your punishment will not be a heavy one--perhaps nothing worse than agreeing to serve in the army. You understand that, in that case, nothing whatever will be said as to your being Dick Cureton, or of your connection with these last coach robberies. You will appear before the court simply as Robert Nicholson, who, having met Captain Jervoise and myself, felt constrained to confess the grievous wrong he did to our fathers, and other gentlemen, at the bidding of, and for money received from, John Dormay."

"I do not need any time to make up my mind," the highwayman said. "I am certainly not going to be hung for the advantage of John Dormay, who has paid me poorly enough, considering that it was through me that he came into a fine estate. I take it that you give me your word of honour, that if I make a clean breast of it, and stick to my story afterwards, this other business shall not be brought up against me."

"Yes, we both promise that on our word of honour."

"Very well then; here goes."

The story he told was in precise accordance with the suspicions that his hearers had entertained. He had been tramping through the country, sometimes pilfering, sometimes taking money as a footpad. He had, one day, met John Dormay and demanded his money. He was armed only with a heavy cudgel, and thought Dormay was defenceless.

The latter, however, produced a pistol from his pocket, and compelled him to drop his stick; and then, taking him by the collar, made him walk to his house. He had asked him questions as to his previous life, and had then given him the choice of going to jail, or of acting under his instructions, in which case he would be well rewarded. Naturally, he had chosen the second alternative. And, having him completely under his thumb, John Dormay had made him sign a paper, acknowledging his attempt at highway robbery upon him.

The rest of the story was already known to his hearers. He had, several times, overheard the conversations in the dining room, but had gathered nothing beyond talk of what would be done, if the Pretender came over. John Dormay had taught him the story of the assassination plot, and had given him the letters to hide. He now swore that the whole story was false, and had been told entirely at the dictation of John Dormay, and from fear of the consequence to himself, if he refused to obey his orders.

When he had finished, Tony's wife was called in, and she made her mark, and her husband signed his name, as witnesses to the signature of Robert Nicholson.

"Now, I hope I may have something to eat," the man said, recklessly. "I am ready to tell my story to whomsoever you like, but am not ready to be starved."

"Give him food, Tony," Charlie said, "and keep a sharp lookout after him. We will go across, and show this paper to the duke."

"I will bring the matter, at once, before the council," the general said, when Charlie gave him the document, and briefly stated its contents. "There is a meeting at three o'clock today. I shall see the queen previously, and will get her to interest herself in the matter, and to urge that justice shall be done without any delay. I will arrange that the man shall be brought before the council, at the earliest date possible. If you will come here this evening, I may be able to tell you more. Come at eight. I shall be in then to dress, as I take supper at the palace, at nine."

"I have ventured to promise the man that he shall not be hung, my lord."

"You were safe in doing so. The rogue deserves the pillory or branding, but, as he was almost forced into it, and was the mere instrument in the hands of another, it is not a case for hanging him. He might be shipped off to the plantations as a rogue and a vagabond.

"What are you smiling at?"

"I was thinking, sir, that, as you said there were a good many of that class in the army, the man might have the option of enlisting given him."

"And so of getting shot in the Netherlands, instead of getting hung at Tyburn, eh? Well, I will see what I can do."

At eight o'clock, they again presented themselves. The duke looked at them critically.

"You will do," he said. "Put your cloaks on again, and come with me. Where do you suppose that you are going?"

"Before the council, sir," Harry suggested.

"Bless me, you don't suppose that your business is so pressing, that ministers have been summoned in haste to sit upon it. No, you are going to sup with the queen. I told her your story this afternoon. She was much interested in it, and when I informed her that, young as you both were, you had fought behind Charles of Sweden, in all his desperate battles, and that he had not only promoted you to the rank of captain, but that he had, under his own hand, given you a document expressing his satisfaction at your conduct and bravery, she said that I must bring you to supper at the palace. I told her that, being soldiers, you had brought with you no clothes fit for appearance at court; but, as at little gatherings there is no ceremony, she insisted that I should bring you as you are.

"My wife Sarah went on half an hour ago, in her chair. There will probably be two others, possibly Godolphin and Harley, but more likely some courtier and his wife.

"You do not feel nervous, I hope? After being accustomed to chat with Charles of Sweden, to say nothing of the Czar of Russia, Carstairs, you need not feel afraid of Queen Anne, who is good nature itself."

Nevertheless, both the young men felt nervous. After being conducted up some private stairs, the duke led them into an oak-panelled room, of comparatively small size, lighted by numerous tapers, which displayed the rich hangings and furniture. A lady was sitting by the fire. A tall, handsome woman, with a somewhat imperious face, stood on the rug before her, talking to her, while a pleasant-looking man, who by his appearance and manner might have been taken for a country squire, was sitting opposite, playing with the ears of a spaniel lying on his knee.

The tall lady moved aside, as they entered, and Charlie noticed a little glance of affectionate welcome pass between her and the duke--for the pair were devotedly attached to each other--then he bowed to the seated lady.

"Madam," he said, "allow me to present to you the two young officers, of whose bravery Charles of Sweden has written so strongly, and whose parents have, with other gentlemen, been driven from the land by villainy."

The young men bowed deeply. Anne held out her hand, and each in turn, bending on one knee, raised it to his lips.

"There," she said, "let that be the beginning and end of ceremony. This is not a court gathering, but a family meeting. I want to hear your stories, and I want you, for the time, to forget that I am Anne of England. I know that your fathers have always been faithful to our house, and I hope that their sons will, ere long, do as good service for me as they have done for a foreign prince.

"You have not seen these gentlemen yet, Sarah?"

"No, my husband has kept them to himself."

"I have had but little time to give them, Sarah, and wanted it all, to question them on the Swedish modes of warfare."

"And you thought I should be an interruption?"

"I am glad to meet you both, nevertheless. Since my husband likes you, I am sure to do so;" and she smiled pleasantly, as she gave a hand to each.

They were then introduced to the Prince Consort, George of Denmark.

At this moment, supper was announced. The queen and the duchess went in together, followed by the four gentlemen.

"Lord Godolphin and Mr. Harley were to have been of the party tonight," the queen said, as she took her seat at table, "but I put them off till tomorrow, as I wanted to hear these gentlemen's story."

During the meal, the conversation was gay. As soon as the last dish was removed, the party returned to the other room. Then the queen called upon the young men to tell their story.

Charlie began, and related up to the time when he had aided in the rescue of his father from the hands of his escort. Harry told the story of their military experiences, and then Charlie related his narrow escape at Warsaw, his adventure with the brigands, and the fight with the wolves.

"That is the most exciting of all," the queen said.

"I think that even you, general, would rather have gone through the battle of Narva, than have spent that night among the wolves."

"That would I, indeed, madam, and I doubt if I should have got as well through it as Captain Carstairs did. I am sure, madam, you will agree with me, that these young gentlemen ought to be fighting under our flag, rather than that of Sweden. There is no blame to them, for they were most unjustly driven from the country; but I hope that, by Monday at this time, I shall have the pleasure of presenting a document for your majesty's signature, stating that, in the opinion of the council, a very grave miscarriage of justice has taken place; and that the gentlemen, whose estates were four years ago confiscated, are proved to be innocent of the crime of which they were accused, and are true and faithful subjects of your majesty; and that the proceedings against them are hereby quashed, and their estates restored to them.

"I had the honour of relating to you, this afternoon, the manner in which these gentlemen have succeeded in bringing the truth to light."

Shortly afterwards, the party broke up, the queen speaking most graciously to each of the young men.

On Monday morning, they received a summons to appear before the council, at two o'clock in the afternoon, and to produce one Robert Nicholson, whose evidence was required in a matter of moment. They hired a carriage, and took the highwayman with them to Saint James's, and were conducted to the council chamber; where they found Lord Godolphin, the Marquis of Normanby, Mr. Harley, and the Duke of Marlborough, together with two judges, before whom the depositions, in the case of Sir Marmaduke Carstairs and his friends, had been laid.

Lord Normanby, as privy seal, took the chair, and briefly said that, having heard there had been a grievous miscarriage of justice, he had summoned them to hear important evidence which was produced by Captains Carstairs and Jervoise, officers in the service of the king of Sweden.

"What have you to say, Captain Carstairs?"

"I have, sir, only to testify that this man, who stands beside me, is Robert Nicholson, who was in my father's employment for two years, and was, I believe, the principal witness against him. Captain Jervoise can also testify to his identity. I now produce the confession, voluntarily made by this man, and signed in the presence of witnesses."

He handed in the confession, which was read aloud by a clerk standing at the lower end of the table. A murmur of indignation arose from the council, as he concluded.

"You have acted the part of a base villain," Lord Normanby said to Nicholson. "Hanging would be too good for such a caitiff. What induced you to make this confession?"

"I have long repented my conduct," the man said. "I was forced into acting as I did, by John Dormay, who might have had me hung for highway robbery. I would long ago have told the truth, had I known where to find the gentlemen I have injured; and, meeting them by chance the other day, I resolved upon making a clean breast of it, and to take what punishment your lordships may think proper; hoping, however, for your clemency, on account of the fact that I was driven to act in the way I did."

One of the judges, who had the former depositions before him, asked him several questions as to the manner in which he had put the papers into Sir Marmaduke's cabinet.

He replied that he found the key in a vase on the mantel, and after trying several locks with it, found that it fitted the cabinet.

"His statement agrees, my lords," the judge said, "with that made by Sir Marmaduke Carstairs in his examinations. He then said that he could not account for the papers being in his cabinet, for it was never unlocked, and that he kept the key in a vase on the mantel, where none would be likely to look for it."

In a short time, all present were requested to withdraw, but in less than five minutes they were again called in.

"Gentlemen," Lord Normanby said to the young officers, "I have pleasure in informing you, that the council are of opinion that the innocence of your fathers and friends, of the foul offence of which they were charged, is clearly proven; and that they have decided that the sentence passed against them, in their absence, shall be quashed. They will also recommend, to her majesty, that the sentence of confiscation against them all shall be reversed.

"As to you, sir, seeing that you have, however tardily, endeavoured to undo the evil you have caused, we are disposed to deal leniently, and, at the request of the Duke of Marlborough, we have agreed, if you are ready to leave the country and enlist at once, as a soldier in the army of Flanders, and there to expiate your fault by fighting in the service of your country, we will not recommend that any proceedings shall be taken against you. But if, at any time, you return hither, save as a soldier with a report of good conduct, this affair will be revived, and you will receive the full punishment you deserve.

"For the present you will be lodged in prison, as you will be needed to give evidence, when the matter of John Dormay comes up for hearing."

Nicholson was at once removed in custody. The two young officers retired, an usher bringing them a whispered message, from Marlborough, that they had better not wait to see him, as the council might sit for some time longer; but that, if they would call at his house at five o'clock, after his official reception, he would see them.

"This is more than we could have hoped for," Harry said, as they left Saint James's. "A fortnight ago, although I had no intention of giving up the search, I began to think that our chances of ever setting eyes on that rascal were of the slightest; and now everything has come right. The man has been found. He has been made to confess the whole matter. The case has been heard by the council. Our fathers are free to return to England, and their estates are restored to them; at least, the council recommends the queen, and we know the queen is ready to sign. So that it is as good as done."

"It seems too good to be true."

"It does, indeed, Charlie. They will be delighted across the water. I don't think my father counted, at all, upon our finding Nicholson, or of our getting him to confess; but I think he had hoped that the duke would interest himself to get an order, that no further proceedings should be taken in the matter of the alleged plot. That would have permitted them to return to England. He spoke to me, several times, of his knowledge of the duke when he was a young man; but Churchill, he said, was a time server, and has certainly changed his politics several times; and, if a man is fickle in politics, he may be so in his friendships. It was a great many years since they had met, and Marlborough might not have been inclined to acknowledge one charged with so serious a crime.

"But, as he said to me before I started, matters have changed since the death of William. Marlborough stands far higher, with Anne, than he did with William. His leanings have certainly been, all along, Jacobite, and, now that he and the Tories are in power, and the Whigs are out of favour, Marlborough could, if he chose, do very much for us. It is no longer a crime to be a Jacobite, and indeed, they say that the Tories are intending to upset the act of succession, and bring in a fresh one, making James Stuart the successor to Anne.

"Still, even if we had succeeded so far, by Marlborough's influence, that our fathers could have returned to England without fear of being tried for their lives, I do not think that either of them would have come, so long as the charge of having been concerned in an assassination plot was hanging over them.

"Now that they are cleared, and can come back with honour, it will be different, altogether. It will be glorious news for them. Of course, we shall start as soon as we get the official communication that the estates are restored. We shall only have to go back to them, for, as you know, yours is the only estate that has been granted to anyone else. The others were put up for sale, but no one would bid for them, as the title deeds would have been worth nothing if King James came over. So they have only been let to farmers, and we can walk straight in again, without dispossessing anyone."

"I don't know what to do about John Dormay," Charlie said. "There is no doubt that, from what the judge said, they will prosecute him."

"So they ought to," Harry broke in. "He has striven, by false swearing, to bring innocent men to the scaffold. Why, it is worse than murder."

"I quite agree with you, Harry, and, if I were in your place, I would say just as strongly as you do that he ought to be hung. But you see, I am differently situated. The man is a kinsman of ours by marriage. My cousin Celia has been always most kind to me, and is my nearest relative after my father. She has been like an aunt, and, indeed, did all she could to supply the place of a mother to me; and I am sure my little sweetheart Ciceley has been like a sister. This must have been a most terrible trial to them. It was a bad day for cousin Celia when she married that scoundrel, and I am sure that he has made her life a most unhappy one. Still, for their sake, I would not see his villainy punished as it deserves, nor indeed for our own, since the man is, to a certain extent, our kinsman.

"Besides, Harry, as you must remember well enough, Ciceley and I, in boy and girl fashion, used to say we should be some day husband and wife, and I have never since seen anyone whom I would so soon marry as my bonny little cousin; and if Ciceley is of the same mind, maybe some day or other she may come to Lynnwood as its mistress; but that could hardly be, if her father were hung for attempting to swear away the life of mine."

"No, indeed, Charlie. I know how fond you were of your cousin."

"Indeed, Harry, there was a talk between my father and cousin Celia, a few months before the troubles came, of a formal betrothal between us, and, had it not been for the coolness between our fathers, it would have taken place."

"Yes, I remember now your telling me about it, Charlie.

"Well, what is to be done? for I agree with you that, if possible, John Dormay must escape from the punishment he deserves. But how is it to be done?"

"Well, Harry, a week or two will make no difference to our fathers. They will have no expectation of hearing from us, for a long time to come. I should say it were best that I should go down and warn him, and I shall be glad if you will go with me."

"Of course I will go," Harry said. "Indeed, it were best that the warning came from me. The man is a villain, and a reckless one; and in his passion, when he hears that his rascality is known, the prize for which he schemed snatched from him, and his very life in danger, might even seek to vent his rage and spite upon you. Now it is clear, Charlie, that you could not very well kill a man, and afterwards marry his daughter. The thing would be scarce seemly. But the fellow is no kinsman of mine. He has grievously injured us, and I could kill him without the smallest compunction, and thereby rid the world of a scoundrel, and you of a prospective father-in-law of the most objectionable kind."

Charlie laughed.

"No, Harry; we will have no killing. We will go down and see him together. We will let him know that the orders are probably already on the road for his arrest, and that he had best lose not an hour, but at once cross the water. I should not think that he would wish to encumber himself with women, for I never thought he showed the least affection to either his wife or daughter. At any rate, we will see that he does not take them with him. I will tell him that, if he goes, and goes alone, I will do my best to hush up the matter; and that, so long as he remains abroad, the tale of his villainy shall never be told; but that, if he returns, the confession of Nicholson shall be published throughout the country, even if no prosecution is brought against him."

When they called upon the duke, he shook them warmly by the hand.

"This parchment is the royal assent to the decision of the council, that the estates of those inculpated in the alleged plot for the assassination of the late king should be forthwith restored to them, it having been clearly proved that they have been falsely accused of the said crime, and that her majesty is satisfied that these gentlemen are her true and loyal subjects.

"I think I may say," the duke continued with a smile, "that no affair of state has ever been so promptly conducted and carried through."

"We feel how deeply indebted we are, for our good fortune, to your kindness, your grace," Charlie said. "We know that, but for you, months might have elapsed, even years, before we could have obtained such a result, even after we had the confession of Nicholson in our hands."

"I am glad, in every way, to have been able to bring this about," the duke said. "In the first place, because I have been able to right a villainous piece of injustice; in the second, because those injured were loyal gentlemen, with no fault save their steadfast adherence to the cause of the Stuarts; and lastly, because one of these gentlemen was my own good friend, Mat Jervoise, of whose company I have so many pleasant recollections.

"I hope that, as soon as you have informed your fathers that their names are cleared, and their property restored, you will think of what I said, and will decide to quit the service of Sweden, and enter that of your queen.

"An officer fighting for a foreign monarch is, after all, but a soldier of fortune, however valiantly he fights. He is fighting for a cause that is not his own, and, though he may win rewards and honours, he has not the satisfaction that all must feel who have risked their lives, not for gold, but in the service of their country. But I do not want any answer from you on that head now. It is a matter for you to decide upon after due thought. I only say that I shall go out, early in the spring, to take command of the army; and that, if you present yourselves to me before I leave, I shall be glad to appoint you on my personal staff, with the same rank you now hold.

"You can now leave the country without any farther trouble. As to the affair of the man Dormay, a messenger has been sent off, this afternoon, with an order to the magistrates at Lancaster, to arrest him on the charge of suborning false evidence, by which the lives of some of her majesty's subjects were endangered; and of forging letters whereby such evil designs might be furthered. I do not suppose I shall see you again before you sail, for tomorrow we go down to our country place, and may remain there some weeks. I may say that it was the desire to get your affair finished, before we left town, that conduced somewhat to the speed with which it has been carried through."

After again thanking the duke most warmly for his kindness, and saying that they would lay his offer before their fathers, and that their own inclinations were altogether in favour of accepting it, the young men took their leave.

"It is unfortunate about Dormay."

"Most unfortunate," Harry said.

"I think, if we start tomorrow morning, Harry, we shall be in time. There is no reason why the messenger should travel at any extraordinary speed, and, as he may be detained at Lancaster, and some delay may arise before officers are sent up to Lynnwood to make the arrest, we may be in time.

"We must take a note of the date. It is one we shall remember all our lives. It is the 25th of November, and we will keep it up as a day of festivity and rejoicing, as long as we live."

"That will we," Harry agreed. "It shall be the occasion of an annual gathering of those who got into trouble from those suppers at Sir Marmaduke's. I fancy the others are all in France, but their friends will surely be able to let them know, as soon as they hear the good news.

"I think we shall have a stormy ride tomorrow. The sky looks very wild and threatening."

"It does, indeed; and the wind has got up very much, in the last hour."

"Yes, we are going to have a storm, beyond all doubt."

The wind got up hourly, and when, before going to bed, they went to pass an hour at a tavern, they had difficulty in making their way against it. Several times in the night they were awoke by the gusts, which shook the whole house, and they heard the crashing of falling chimney pots above the din of the gale.

They had arranged to start as soon as it was light, and had, the evening before, been to a posting inn, and engaged a carriage with four horses for the journey down to Lancashire.

"There is no starting today, gentlemen," the landlord said, as they went down to breakfast by candlelight. "I have looked out, and the street is strewn with chimney pots and tiles. Never do I remember such a gale, and hour by hour it seems to get worse. Why, it is dangerous to go across the street."

"Well, we must try," Charlie said, "whatever the weather. It is a matter of almost life and death."

"Well, gentlemen, you must please yourselves, but I am mistaken if any horse keeper will let his animals out, on such a day as this."

As soon as they had eaten their breakfasts, they wrapped themselves up in their cloaks, pressed their hats over their heads, and sallied out. It was not until they were in the streets that they realized how great was the force of the gale. Not only were the streets strewn with tiles and fragments of chimney pots, but there was light enough for them to see that many of the upper windows of the houses had been blown in by the force of the wind. Tiles flew about like leaves in autumn, and occasionally gutters and sheets of lead, stripped from the roofs, flew along with prodigious swiftness.

"This is as bad as a pitched battle, Charlie. I would as lief be struck by a cannonball as by one of those strips of lead."

"Well, we must risk it, Harry. We must make the attempt, anyhow."

It was with the greatest difficulty that they made their way along. Although powerful young fellows, they were frequently obliged to cling to the railings, to prevent themselves from being swept away by the gusts, and they had more than one narrow escape from falling chimneys. Although the distance they had to traverse was not more than a quarter of a mile, it took them half an hour to accomplish it.

The post master looked at them in surprise, as they entered his office flushed and disordered.

"Why, gentlemen, you are not thinking of going on such a day as this? It would be a sheer impossibility. Why, the carriage would be blown over, and if it wasn't, no horses would face this wind."

"We would be willing to pay anything you may like to ask," Charlie said.

"It ain't a question of money, sir. If you were to buy the four horses and the carriage, you would be no nearer, for no post boy would be mad enough to ride them; and, even supposing you got one stage, which you never would do, you would have to buy horses again, for no one would be fool enough to send his animals out. You could not do it, sir. Why, I hear there are half a dozen houses, within a dozen yards of this, that have been altogether unroofed, and it is getting worse instead of better. If it goes on like this, I doubt if there will be a steeple standing in London tomorrow.

"Listen to that!"

There was a tremendous crash, and, running out into the street, they saw a mass of beams and tiles lying in the roadway--a house two doors away had been completely unroofed. They felt that, in such a storm, it was really impossible to proceed, and accordingly returned to their lodgings, performing the distance in a fraction of the time it had before taken them.

For some hours the gale continued to increase in fury. Not a soul was to be seen in the streets. Occasional heavy crashes told of the damage that was being wrought, and, at times, the house shook so that it seemed as if it would fall.

Never was such a storm known in England. The damage done was enormous. The shores were strewn with wrecks. Twelve ships of the royal navy, with fifteen hundred men, were lost; and an enormous number of merchant vessels. Many steeples, houses, and buildings of all kinds were overthrown, and the damage, in London alone, was estimated at a million pounds.

There were few who went to bed that night. Many thought that the whole city would be destroyed. Towards morning, however, the fury of the gale somewhat abated, and by nightfall the danger had passed.

The next morning the two friends started, and posted down to Lancashire. The journey was a long one. In many places the road was completely blocked by fallen trees, and sometimes by the ruins of houses and barns. In the former case, long detours had often to be made through villainous roads, where the wheels sank almost to their axles, and, in spite of the most liberal bribes to post boys and post masters, the journey occupied four days longer than the usual time.

At last, they reached the lodge gate of Lynnwood. A man came out from the cottage. He was the same who had been there in Sir Marmaduke's time.

Charlie jumped out of the post chaise.

"Why, Norman, don't you know me?"

The man looked hard at him.

"No, sir, I can't say as I do."

"What, not Charlie Carstairs?"

"Bless me, it is the young master!" the man said. "To think of my not knowing you. But you have changed wonderful. Why, sir, I have been thinking of you often and often, and most of all the last three days, but I never thought of you like this."

"Why the last three days, Norman?"

"Haven't you heard the news, sir?"

"No, I have heard nothing. Captain Jervoise and I--my old friend, you know, Norman--have posted all the way from London, and should have been here six days ago, if it had not been for the storm."

"Well, sir, there is bad news; at least, I don't know whether you will consider it bad. Most of the folk about here looks at it the other way. But the man in there shot hisself, three days ago. A magistrate, with some men from Lancaster, came over here. They say it was to arrest him, but I don't know the rights of the case. Anyhow, it is said they read some paper over to him, and then he opened a drawer at the table where he was sitting, and pulled out a pistol, and shot hisself before anyone could stop him.

"There have been bad goings here of late, Mr. Charles, very bad, especially for the last year. He was not friends with his son, they say, but the news of his death drove him to drink, worse than before; and besides, there have been dicing, and all sorts of goings on, and I doubt not but that the ladies have had a terrible time of it. There were several men staying in the house, but they all took themselves off, as soon as it was over, and there are only the ladies there now. They will be glad enough to see you, I will be bound."

Charlie was shocked; but at the same time, he could not but feel that it was the best thing that could happen, and Harry freely expressed himself to that effect.

"We won't take the carriage up to the house," Charlie said, after a long pause. "Take the valises out, and bring them up to the house presently, Norman."

He paid the postilion who had brought them from Lancaster, and stood quiet until the carriage had driven off.

"I hope Sir Marmaduke is well, sir. We have missed him sorely here."

"He was quite well when I saw him, ten weeks ago. I hope he will be here before long. I am happy to say that his innocence of the charge brought against him has been proved, and his estates, and those of Mr. Jervoise and the other gentlemen, have been restored by the queen."

"That is good news, indeed, sir," the man exclaimed. "The best I have heard for many a long year. Everyone about here will go wild with joy."

"Then don't mention it at present, Norman. Any rejoicings would be unseemly, while John Dormay is lying dead there."

"Shall I go up with you, Charlie, or will you go alone?" Harry asked. "Of course, there are some horses here, and you could lend me one to drive over to our own place."

"You shall do that presently, Harry, and tell them the news. But come in now. You know my cousin and Ciceley. It will be all the better that you should go in with me."

His cousin received Charlie with a quiet pleasure. She was greatly changed since he had seen her last, and her face showed that she had suffered greatly. Ciceley had grown into a young woman, and met him with delight. Both were pleased to see Harry.

"We were talking of you but now, Charlie," Mrs. Dormay said. "Ciceley and I agreed that we would remove at once to our old place, and that this should be kept up for you, should you at any time be able to return. Now that Queen Anne is on the throne, and the Tories are in power, we hoped that you, at least, would ere long be permitted to return. How is your dear father?"

"He is well, cousin, and will, I trust, be here ere long. Our innocence of the charge has been proved, the proceedings against us quashed, and the Act of Confiscation against my father, Mr. Jervoise, and the others reversed."

"Thank God for that," Mrs. Dormay said earnestly, and Ciceley gave an exclamation of pleasure. "That accounts, then, for what has happened here.

"I do not want to talk about it, Charlie. You may imagine how Ciceley and I have suffered. But he was my husband, spare him for my sake."

"I will never allude to the subject again, cousin," Charlie said. "But I must tell you that Harry and I have posted down from London, in hopes of being in time to warn him, and enable him to escape. I need not say we did so because he was your husband, and Ciceley's father."

Harry then turned the subject, by a remark as to the effects of the storm. Then Ciceley asked questions as to their life abroad, and there was so much to tell, and to listen to, that even Mrs. Dormay's face brightened. Harry willingly allowed himself to be persuaded to remain for the night, and to ride over to his place in the morning.

The funeral took place two days later. Charlie went as sole mourner.

"He was my kinsman," he said to Harry, "and, though I can pretend no sorrow at his death, my attendance at the funeral will do something towards stopping talk, and will make it easier for my cousin."

The next day, Mrs. Dormay and Ciceley returned to Rockley, whose tenant had fortunately left a few weeks before. Charlie and Harry both went over with them, and stayed for three or four days, and they were glad to see that Mrs. Dormay seemed to be shaking off the weight of her trouble, and was looking more like her old self.

They then rode to Lancaster, and returned to London by coach. They crossed to Gottenburg by the first vessel that was sailing, and Sir Marmaduke was delighted to hear the success of their mission, and that he was at liberty to return at once, as master of Lynnwood.

"Luck favoured you somewhat, Charlie, in throwing that vagabond in your way, but for all else we have to thank you both, for the manner in which you have carried the affair out, and captured your fox. As for John Dormay, 'tis the best thing that could have happened. I have often thought it over, while you have been away, and have said to myself that the best settlement of the business would be that you, Harry, when you obtained proofs, should go down, confront him publicly, and charge him with his treachery, force him to draw, and then run him through the body. Charlie would, of course, have been the proper person, in my absence, so to settle the matter, but he could not well have killed my cousin's husband, and it would have added to the scandal.

"However, the way it has turned out is better altogether. It will be only a nine days' wonder. The man has been cut by all the gentry, and when it is known that he shot himself to escape arrest, many will say that it was a fit ending, and will trouble themselves no more concerning him.

"You are coming back with me, I hope, Charlie. I have seen but little of you for the last four years, and if you are, as you say, going with the Duke of Marlborough to the war in the spring, I don't want to lose sight of you again till then. You can surely resign your commission here without going back to the army, especially as you have leave of absence until the end of March."

Charlie hesitated.

"I think so, too," Harry said. "I know that the colonel told the king the whole story, when he asked for leave for me and obtained that paper. He told my father that the king was greatly interested, and said: 'I hope the young fellows will succeed, though I suppose, if they do, I shall lose two promising young officers.' So he will not be surprised when he hears that we have resigned.

"As for me, I shall, of course, go on at once. My father will, I am sure, be delighted to return home. The hardships have told upon him a good deal, and he has said several times, of late, how much he wished he could see his way to retiring. I think, too, he will gladly consent to my entering our own service, instead of that of Sweden. He would not have done so, I am sure, had William been still on the throne. Now it is altogether different."

"Well, Harry, if you do see the king, as it is possible you may do, or if you do not, you might speak to the colonel, and ask him, in my name, to express to Charles my regret at leaving his service, in which I have been so well treated, and say how much I feel the kindly interest that his majesty has been pleased to take in me. If there had been any chance of the war coming to an end shortly, I should have remained to see it out; but, now that the Polish business may be considered finished, it will be continued with Russia, and may go on for years, for the czar is just as obstinate and determined as Charles himself."

Accordingly, the next morning, Charlie sent in the formal resignation of his commission to the war minister at Stockholm, and Harry left by ship for Revel. Sir Marmaduke placed his business affairs in the hands of a Scotch merchant at Gottenburg, with instructions to call in the money he had lent on mortgage, and, two days later, took passage with Charlie for Hull, whence they posted across the country to Lancaster, and then drove to Lynnwood.

As soon as the news spread that Sir Marmaduke had returned, the church bells rang a joyous peal, bonfires were lighted, the tenants flocked in to greet him, and the gentry for miles round rode over to welcome and congratulate him.

The next morning he and Charlie rode over to Rockley.

"Oh, Marmaduke," cried Celia, "I am happy indeed to know that you are back again. I have never known a day's happiness since you went."

"Well, don't let us think any more about it, Celia," Sir Marmaduke said, as he kissed her tenderly. "Let us look on it all as an ugly dream. It has not been without its advantages, as far as we are concerned. It has taken me out of myself, and broadened my view of things. I have not had at all an unpleasant time of it in Sweden, and shall enjoy my home all the more, now that I have been away from it for a while. As to Charlie, it has made a man of him. He has gained a great deal of credit, and had opportunities of showing that he is made of good stuff; and now he enters upon life with every advantage, and has a start, indeed, such as very few young fellows can have. He enters our army as a captain, under the eye of Marlborough himself, with a reputation gained under that of the greatest soldier in Europe.

"So we have no reason to regret the past, cousin, and on that score you have no cause for grief. As to the future, I trust that it will be bright for both of us, and I think," he added meaningly, "our former plans for our children are likely to be some day realized."

Four years later, indeed, the union that both parents had at heart took place, during one of the pauses of the fierce struggle between the British forces under Marlborough, and the French. At Blenheim, Ramillies, and Oudenarde, and in several long and toilsome sieges, Charlie had distinguished himself greatly, and was regarded by Marlborough as one of the most energetic and trustworthy of his officers. He had been twice severely wounded, and had gained the rank of colonel.

Harry Jervoise--who had had a leg shot away, below the knee, by a cannonball at Ramillies, and had then left the army with the rank of major--was, on the same day as his friend, married to the daughter of one of the gentlemen who had been driven into exile with his father.

In the spring Charlie again joined the army, and commanded a brigade in the desperate struggle on the hill of Malplaquet, one of the hardest fought battles in the history of war. Peace was made shortly afterwards, and, at the reduction of the army that followed, he went on half pay, and settled down for life at Lynnwood, where Tony Peters and his wife had, at the death of the former occupant of the lodge, been established.

When Harry Jervoise returned to the Swedish headquarters, with the news that his father was cleared, he was the bearer of a very handsome present from Charlie to his faithful servant Stanislas, who had, on their return from Poland, been at once employed by Count Piper on other service.

When, years afterwards, the young Pretender marched south with the Highland clans, neither Charlie nor Harry were among the gentlemen who joined him. He had their good wishes, but, having served in the British army, they felt that they could not join the movement in arms against the British crown; and indeed, the strong Jacobite feelings of their youth had been greatly softened down by their contact with the world, and they had learned to doubt much whether the restoration of the Stuarts would tend, in any way, to the benefit or prosperity of Britain.

They felt all the more obliged to stand aloof from the struggle, inasmuch as both had sons, in the army, that had fought valiantly against the French at Dettingen and Fontenoy. The families always remained united in the closest friendship, and more than one marriage took place between the children of Charlie Carstairs and Harry Jervoise.

The Codes Of Hammurabi And Moses
W. W. Davies

QTY

The discovery of the Hammurabi Code is one of the greatest achievements of archaeology, and is of paramount interest, not only to the student of the Bible, but also to all those interested in ancient history...

Religion ISBN: *1-59462-338-4* **Pages:132**
MSRP $12.95

The Theory of Moral Sentiments
Adam Smith

QTY

This work from 1749. contains original theories of conscience amd moral judgment and it is the foundation for systemof morals.

Philosophy ISBN: *1-59462-777-0* **Pages:536**
MSRP $19.95

Jessica's First Prayer
Hesba Stretton

QTY

In a screened and secluded corner of one of the many railway-bridges which span the streets of London there could be seen a few years ago, from five o'clock every morning until half past eight, a tidily set-out coffee-stall, consisting of a trestle and board, upon which stood two large tin cans, with a small fire of charcoal burning under each so as to keep the coffee boiling during the early hours of the morning when the work-people were thronging into the city on their way to their daily toil...

Pages:84

Childrens ISBN: *1-59462-373-2* *MSRP $9.95*

My Life and Work
Henry Ford

QTY

Henry Ford revolutionized the world with his implementation of mass production for the Model T automobile. Gain valuable business insight into his life and work with his own auto-biography... "We have only started on our development of our country we have not as yet, with all our talk of wonderful progress, done more than scratch the surface. The progress has been wonderful enough but..."

Pages:300

Biographies/ ISBN: *1-59462-198-5* *MSRP $21.95*

The Art of Cross-Examination
Francis Wellman

QTY

I presume it is the experience of every author, after his first book is published upon an important subject, to be almost overwhelmed with a wealth of ideas and illustrations which could readily have been included in his book, and which to his own mind, at least, seem to make a second edition inevitable. Such certainly was the case with me; and when the first edition had reached its sixth impression in five months, I rejoiced to learn that it seemed to my publishers that the book had met with a sufficiently favorable reception to justify a second and considerably enlarged edition. ..

Reference   **ISBN:** *1-59462-647-2*

Pages:412
MSRP $19.95

On the Duty of Civil Disobedience
Henry David Thoreau

QTY

Thoreau wrote his famous essay, On the Duty of Civil Disobedience, as a protest against an unjust but popular war and the immoral but popular institution of slave-owning. He did more than write—he declined to pay his taxes, and was hauled off to gaol in consequence. Who can say how much this refusal of his hastened the end of the war and of slavery ?

Law   **ISBN:** *1-59462-747-9*

Pages:48
MSRP $7.45

Dream Psychology Psychoanalysis for Beginners
Sigmund Freud

QTY

Sigmund Freud, born Sigismund Schlomo Freud (May 6, 1856 - September 23, 1939), was a Jewish-Austrian neurologist and psychiatrist who co-founded the psychoanalytic school of psychology. Freud is best known for his theories of the unconscious mind, especially involving the mechanism of repression; his redefinition of sexual desire as mobile and directed towards a wide variety of objects; and his therapeutic techniques, especially his understanding of transference in the therapeutic relationship and the presumed value of dreams as sources of insight into unconscious desires.

Psychology   **ISBN:** *1-59462-905-6*

Pages:196
MSRP $15.45

The Miracle of Right Thought
Orison Swett Marden

QTY

Believe with all of your heart that you will do what you were made to do. When the mind has once formed the habit of holding cheerful, happy, prosperous pictures, it will not be easy to form the opposite habit. It does not matter how improbable or how far away this realization may see, or how dark the prospects may be, if we visualize them as best we can, as vividly as possible, hold tenaciously to them and vigorously struggle to attain them, they will gradually become actualized, realized in the life. But a desire, a longing without endeavor, a yearning abandoned or held indifferently will vanish without realization.

Self Help   **ISBN:** *1-59462-644-8*

Pages:360
MSRP $25.45

www.bookjungle.com *email: sales@bookjungle.com fax: 630-214-0564 mail: Book Jungle PO Box 2226 Champaign, IL 61825*

QTY

☐ **The Rosicrucian Cosmo-Conception Mystic Christianity** by *Max Heindel*　ISBN: *1-59462-188-8*　**$38.95**
The Rosicrucian Cosmo-conception is not dogmatic, neither does it appeal to any other authority than the reason of the student. It is not controversial, but is sent forth in the hope that it may help to clear...　New Age/Religion Pages 646

☐ **Abandonment To Divine Providence** by *Jean-Pierre de Caussade*　ISBN: *1-59462-228-0*　**$25.95**
"The Rev. Jean Pierre de Caussade was one of the most remarkable spiritual writers of the Society of Jesus in France in the 18th Century. His death took place at Toulouse in 1751. His works have gone through many editions and have been republished...　Inspirational/Religion Pages 400

☐ **Mental Chemistry** by *Charles Haanel*　ISBN: *1-59462-192-6*　**$23.95**
Mental Chemistry allows the change of material conditions by combining and appropriately utilizing the power of the mind. Much like applied chemistry creates something new and unique out of careful combinations of chemicals the mastery of mental chemistry...　New Age Pages 354

☐ **The Letters of Robert Browning and Elizabeth Barret Barrett 1845-1846 vol II**　ISBN: *1-59462-193-4*　**$35.95**
by *Robert Browning* and *Elizabeth Barrett*　Biographies Pages 596

☐ **Gleanings In Genesis (volume I)** by *Arthur W. Pink*　ISBN: *1-59462-130-6*　**$27.45**
Appropriately has Genesis been termed "the seed plot of the Bible" for in it we have, in germ form, almost all of the great doctrines which are afterwards fully developed in the books of Scripture which follow...　Religion/Inspirational Pages 420

☐ **The Master Key** by *L. W. de Laurence*　ISBN: *1-59462-001-6*　**$30.95**
In no branch of human knowledge has there been a more lively increase of the spirit of research during the past few years than in the study of Psychology, Concentration and Mental Discipline. The requests for authentic lessons in Thought Control, Mental Discipline and...　New Age/Business Pages 422

☐ **The Lesser Key Of Solomon Goetia** by *L. W. de Laurence*　ISBN: *1-59462-092-X*　**$9.95**
This translation of the first book of the "Lernegon" which is now for the first time made accessible to students of Talismanic Magic was done, after careful collation and edition, from numerous Ancient Manuscripts in Hebrew, Latin, and French...　New Age/Occult Pages 92

☐ **Rubaiyat Of Omar Khayyam** by *Edward Fitzgerald*　ISBN:*1-59462-332-5*　**$13.95**
Edward Fitzgerald, whom the world has already learned, in spite of his own efforts to remain within the shadow of anonymity, to look upon as one of the rarest poets of the century, was born at Bredfield, in Suffolk, on the 31st of March, 1809. He was the third son of John Purcell...　Music Pages 172

☐ **Ancient Law** by *Henry Maine*　ISBN: *1-59462-128-4*　**$29.95**
The chief object of the following pages is to indicate some of the earliest ideas of mankind, as they are reflected in Ancient Law, and to point out the relation of those ideas to modern thought.　Religion/History Pages 452

☐ **Far-Away Stories** by *William J. Locke*　ISBN: *1-59462-129-2*　**$19.45**
"Good wine needs no bush," but a collection of mixed vintages does. And this book is just such a collection. Some of the stories I do not want to remain buried for ever in the museum files of dead magazine-numbers an author's not unpardonable vanity..."　Fiction Pages 272

☐ **Life of David Crockett** by *David Crockett*　ISBN: *1-59462-250-7*　**$27.45**
"Colonel David Crockett was one of the most remarkable men of the times in which he lived. Born in humble life, but gifted with a strong will, an indomitable courage, and unremitting perseverance...　Biographies/New Age Pages 424

☐ **Lip-Reading** by *Edward Nitchie*　ISBN: *1-59462-206-X*　**$25.95**
Edward B. Nitchie, founder of the New York School for the Hard of Hearing, now the Nitchie School of Lip-Reading, Inc, wrote "LIP-READING Principles and Practice". The development and perfecting of this meritorious work on lip-reading was an undertaking...　How-to Pages 400

☐ **A Handbook of Suggestive Therapeutics, Applied Hypnotism, Psychic Science**　ISBN: *1-59462-214-0*　**$24.95**
by *Henry Munro*　Health/New Age/Health/Self-help Pages 376

☐ **A Doll's House: and Two Other Plays** by *Henrik Ibsen*　ISBN: *1-59462-112-8*　**$19.95**
Henrik Ibsen created this classic when in revolutionary 1848 Rome. Introducing some striking concepts in playwriting for the realist genre, this play has been studied the world over.　Fiction/Classics/Plays 308

☐ **The Light of Asia** by *sir Edwin Arnold*　ISBN: *1-59462-204-3*　**$13.95**
In this poetic masterpiece, Edwin Arnold describes the life and teachings of Buddha. The man who was to become known as Buddha to the world was born as Prince Gautama of India but he rejected the worldly riches and abandoned the reigns of power when...　Religion/History/Biographies Pages 170

☐ **The Complete Works of Guy de Maupassant** by *Guy de Maupassant*　ISBN: *1-59462-157-8*　**$16.95**
"For days and days, nights and nights, I had dreamed of that first kiss which was to consecrate our engagement, and I knew not on what spot I should put my lips..."　Fiction/Classics Pages 240

☐ **The Art of Cross-Examination** by *Francis L. Wellman*　ISBN: *1-59462-309-0*　**$26.95**
Written by a renowned trial lawyer, Wellman imparts his experience and uses case studies to explain how to use psychology to extract desired information through questioning.　How-to/Science/Reference Pages 408

☐ **Answered or Unanswered?** by *Louisa Vaughan*　ISBN: *1-59462-248-5*　**$10.95**
Miracles of Faith in China　Religion Pages 112

☐ **The Edinburgh Lectures on Mental Science (1909)** by *Thomas*　ISBN: *1-59462-008-3*　**$11.95**
This book contains the substance of a course of lectures recently given by the writer in the Queen Street Hall, Edinburgh. Its purpose is to indicate the Natural Principles governing the relation between Mental Action and Material Conditions...　New Age/Psychology Pages 148

☐ **Ayesha** by *H. Rider Haggard*　ISBN: *1-59462-301-5*　**$24.95**
Verily and indeed it is the unexpected that happens! Probably if there was one person upon the earth from whom the Editor of this, and of a certain previous history, did not expect to hear again...　Classics Pages 380

☐ **Ayala's Angel** by *Anthony Trollope*　ISBN: *1-59462-352-X*　**$29.95**
The two girls were both pretty, but Lucy who was twenty-one who supposed to be simple and comparatively unattractive, whereas Ayala was credited, as her Bombwhat romantic name might show, with poetic charm and a taste for romance. Ayala when her father died was nineteen...　Fiction Pages 484

☐ **The American Commonwealth** by *James Bryce*　ISBN: *1-59462-286-8*　**$34.45**
An interpretation of American democratic political theory. It examines political mechanics and society from the perspective of Scotsman James Bryce　Politics Pages 572

☐ **Stories of the Pilgrims** by *Margaret P. Pumphrey*　ISBN: *1-59462-116-0*　**$17.95**
This book explores pilgrims religious oppression in England as well as their escape to Holland and eventual crossing to America on the Mayflower, and their early days in New England...　History Pages 268

www.bookjungle.com *email: sales@bookjungle.com fax: 630-214-0564 mail: Book Jungle PO Box 2226 Champaign, IL 61825*

QTY

The Fasting Cure *by Sinclair Upton* ISBN: *1-59462-222-1* **$13.95**
In the Cosmopolitan Magazine for May, 1910, and in the Contemporary Review (London) for April, 1910, I published an article dealing with my experiences in fasting. I have written a great many magazine articles, but never one which attracted so much attention... New Age/Self Help/Health Pages 164

Hebrew Astrology *by Sepharial* ISBN: *1-59462-308-2* **$13.45**
In these days of advanced thinking it is a matter of common observation that we have left many of the old landmarks behind and that we are now pressing forward to greater heights and to a wider horizon than that which represented the mind-content of our progenitors... Astrology Pages 144

Thought Vibration or The Law of Attraction in the Thought World ISBN: *1-59462-127-6* **$12.95**
by William Walker Atkinson Psychology/Religion Pages 144

Optimism *by Helen Keller* ISBN: *1-59462-108-X* **$15.95**
Helen Keller was blind, deaf, and mute since 19 months old, yet famously learned how to overcome these handicaps, communicate with the world, and spread her lectures promoting optimism. An inspiring read for everyone... Biographies/Inspirational Pages 84

Sara Crewe *by Frances Burnett* ISBN: *1-59462-360-0* **$9.45**
In the first place, Miss Minchin lived in London. Her home was a large, dull, tall one, in a large, dull square, where all the houses were alike, and all the sparrows were alike, and where all the door-knockers made the same heavy sound... Childrens/Classic Pages 88

The Autobiography of Benjamin Franklin *by Benjamin Franklin* ISBN: *1-59462-135-7* **$24.95**
The Autobiography of Benjamin Franklin has probably been more extensively read than any other American historical work, and no other book of its kind has had such ups and downs of fortune. Franklin lived for many years in England, where he was agent... Biographies/History Pages 332

Name	
Email	
Telephone	
Address	
City, State ZIP	

☐ **Credit Card** ☐ **Check / Money Order**

Credit Card Number	
Expiration Date	
Signature	

Please Mail to: Book Jungle
PO Box 2226
Champaign, IL 61825
or Fax to: 630-214-0564

ORDERING INFORMATION
web*: www.bookjungle.com*
email*: sales@bookjungle.com*
fax*: 630-214-0564*
mail*: Book Jungle PO Box 2226 Champaign, IL 61825*
or PayPal *to sales@bookjungle.com*

Please contact us for bulk discounts

DIRECT-ORDER TERMS

**20% Discount if You Order
Two or More Books**
Free Domestic Shipping!
Accepted: Master Card, Visa,
Discover, American Express

www.ingramcontent.com/pod-product-compliance
Lightning Source LLC
Chambersburg PA
CBHW080725020726
47503CB00010B/2797